The Curiosity Killers

K.W. Taylor

DOG STAR
BOOKS

The Curiosity Killers © 2016
by K.W. Taylor

Published by Dog Star Books
Bowie, MD

First Edition

Cover Image: Bradley Sharp
Book Design: Jennifer Barnes

Printed in the United States of America

ISBN: 978-1-935738-81-7
Library of Congress Control Number: 2016937559

www.DogStarBooks.org

Acknowledgements

Thank you to my critique partners Jen Bigelow, Carrie Gessner, Crystal Kapataidakis, Anna LaVoie, Todd Moody, and Chris Wilk for asking the hard questions and pushing me to make this a better book. Special thanks to my perpetual workshop critique partner Alex Savage, whose own work I always love to read. The other students in the rest of my incoming cohort at Seton Hill University—Stephanie Brown, Charles Buechele, Amy Culey, Jenni Dillard, Traci Douglass, Sheri Flemming Becky Halsey, Lynn Hortel, Chase Moore, Annika Sundberg, Cathy Oswald, Shanna Sampson, and Eric Seidl—have also been instrumental in helping with this work and others, assisting with research questions, motivation, and general guidance and inspiration. My professors Michael Arnzen, Anne Harris, Scott Johnson, Nicole Peeler, and Albert Wendland provided the necessary tools to continue to improve my craft, as did workshops led by the above plus the fabulous Shelley Bates, Will Horner, and Randall Silvis. I also want to thank the members of my former writing group, "The League of Upsettingness," (otherwise known as Michael Burnside, Charles Long, Cynthia Marshall, and Steven Saus) for their help with early drafts of this and so many other pieces.

My deepest appreciation goes to Heidi Ruby Miller and Tim Waggoner. These two accomplished authors have been cheerleaders, idea cultivators, and true mentors to me in the fullest sense of the word. Not only are their talents apparent in their own work, but they are genuinely nurturing, kind, and patient human beings.

Thanks to the fine, friendly, and deeply weird (in all the best ways) authors and editors at Raw Dog Screaming Press and Dog Star Books, particularly Jennifer Barnes, a true delight to work with, and John Edward Lawson. I owe a lot to author J.L. Gribble for believing early on that this project was right for Dog Star and providing support, friendship, and enthusiasm.

Final thanks go to my husband Tom Kollman for listening to me prattle on about historical research, letting me drag him to an ugly metal statue of a cryptid in West Virginia, allowing a bunch of crazy fiction writers to inexplicably call him "Gatsby," for doing a critical continuity check of my work for any appearance of dangling paradoxes, and for always loving and believing in me.

Part I: The Enthusiast

It is possible to fly, but not without knowledge and skill.
—Wilbur Wright

Tuesday, June 7, 1910, Dayton, Ohio, USA

"My, what a musty basement."

The words were muffled, but Katharine Wright still heard them and dropped her pen, leaving a great dark smear across the paper. Lorin's letter would have to wait—there was an intruder downstairs.

As tentative footsteps mounted the stairs between the basement and the kitchen, Katharine scurried to the front parlor, where she'd secreted her small muff pistol, a double-barrel Remington .41 that Orville purchased for her with some reluctance. It was a tiny thing but packed quite the power when fired at close range. Katharine prayed she wouldn't have to discharge it.

She took *Crime and Punishment* down from the bookcase and withdrew the cigar box hidden behind it, within which the tiny gun rested, unloaded. There was a creak in the next room, and Katharine shoved the bullets in faster, with only a dim regard for proper loading. The metal became slick with her sweat.

She held the gun out, bracing her right hand with her left, and waited. A moment later a young woman inched from the now-open basement door to the breakfast table, which Katharine could see through the arch separating the kitchen and parlor.

The girl was younger than Katharine, and she had a headful of glossy blond curls. She wore a dress more suited for a cotillion than daily wear, all velvet and bustle and lace, and she was immaculate, despite traipsing through the brothers' messy laboratory.

Before Katharine had a chance to decide what to do, the stranger decided for her by spinning her way and letting out a shriek of surprise. Katharine, panicked, squeezed the trigger, and the other woman dropped to the floor. The shot went high, and an explosion of plaster rained down on the girl's head. Through a haze of smoke, Katharine could make out a deep gouge in the wall above the arch.

"Thank God I didn't get the molding," Katharine muttered. "Orville would've killed me." She put the gun down and rushed to the girl, who was still prone on the floor and gasping.

"I'm sorry," the girl cried. "Miss Wright, I'm a friend of your brother's. Please don't shoot."

"Well, then, don't go breaking into people's homes and I'll refrain," Katharine said. She took the girl's arm and eased her up to a sitting position. "Are you hurt?"

The girl shook her head.

"Who are you?"

"My name is Alison," she replied. "Alison Keller. I met your brother Wilbur in—" She stopped and cast her eyes across the parlor. "Wow, that's some beautiful furniture." She scrambled to her feet and examined the loveseat. "Oh, my gosh, this is all original. *It's all original.*"

"Heavens, Miss Keller, that piece isn't particularly special. A leftover from my father before we—"

"And your *books*. Oh, God, old books with all their pages. They smell new."

"Miss Keller, calm yourself," Katharine ordered as the girl flitted around the room, hands everywhere. "I'll thank you to watch your language while in my home."

The girl ceased her tour around the parlor, a look of childlike wonder on her face. "This is what Doctor Vere doesn't get, Miss Wright. Because he's a scientist, not a historian. He doesn't see the technology's true use—to get to be a part of this." She gestured at random items in the room. "You, this house, all of it...I feel like I'm in a movie."

"A...what?" Katharine narrowed her eyes and tightened the grip on her pistol. "Miss, I think—"

"Just call him. Call Wilbur. I know I sound like a crazy person, but he does know me, I swear."

Katharine shook her head. "If you mean I should telephone him, I can't. We don't have a line in the house."

Oh, dear. Perhaps it's better she think I can rouse the authorities at a moment's notice.

"Miss Wright, I promise you, I'm not insane, and I don't want to harm you." The young woman stepped closer, holding her hands up in supplication. "It's just...the circumstances under which I met your brother are a bit...what would you say? Fantastic."

No, it couldn't be.

Katharine recalled Wilbur's strange hints that morning, scraps of conversation between Wilbur and Orville about H.G. Wells and putting engineering to different use. This woman talked of history and seemed to simply appear...

"How did you get in?" Katharine asked at last. "Show me what he's got up to down there in the basement."

The girl spent the next half hour explaining rudimentary physics to Katharine, who felt quite faint at it all until the girl also produced the simplest of objects from her pocket.

"You see? Not only the name of the country, but—"

"The year." Katharine turned the penny over and over in her palm. Upon the shiny red surface was stamped the unmistakable truth. "How long ago was this minted? What year is it for you, where Wilbur walked into your school?"

"That's from this year," the girl replied. "Twenty seventy."

Upstairs, the front door opened and shut. "Kitty?"

A little smile flickered across the girl's face, a smile that caused Katharine to raise an eyebrow.

Well, it would be nice to see him happy, even if it's with a time traveler. One can't choose whom to love, after all.

Tuesday, March 8, 2060, Council Bluffs Riverfront Park, Iowa, disputed territory

The scout climbed down the ladder into the trench and looked around. "Vere!" the scout barked.

Vere poked a headful of chestnut curls out of the rear auxiliary unit. "J? That you?"

The scout pulled off her helmet and rubbed a hand through her short dreadlocks. "Yup. Where's Cap?"

"Supply run." Vere peered at her. "You don't look so good, Jasika. What—whoa."

As he spoke, Jasika blinked and stumbled against the ladder. Vere rushed to her side and caught her before she fell.

"Damn, I thought I heard shells…" Jasika pulled open her jacket. A circle of red bloomed on her abdomen. "Shit!"

"Hang on, it's probably not bad if you're walking around." Vere eased her to the ground. "I'll get the kit."

Jasika grit her teeth. "Shit, they don't tell you how much it burns, man." She clutched at Vere's sleeve and looked up at him with pleading eyes. "It *burns.*"

"You're all right, J." Vere took her fingers from his sleeve, not liking how cold her skin felt through the thin material. "Just gimme a sec and get the kit. I know right where it is." He jogged back to the AU, his eyes scanning the makeshift shelves backed in dirt. Canteens, canteens, why did they have so many damn canteens? Where was the goddamned medical kit? Beer…Jesus, why did Cap let them have *beer* out here, for God's sake? What was the—ah, there. White plastic, the size of a shoebox. Vere plucked it off the bottom shelf and rummaged through it.

Jasika screamed.

Vere quit rummaging and instead took the whole kit out to her. "I'm here, I'm here, I'm here."

"Ah, dammit! It didn't hurt this bad when I had my *kid*, Vere. Jesus."

Vere knelt down beside her. "You got a kid, J? Tell me about him." He pulled a syringe from the kit and, while trying to find a vein in her arm with one hand, gripped the cap in his teeth and spit it out. "I bet he's real proud of you, holding back the Raiders."

"Mmm...*gah*!" Jasika's whole body arched upward as Vere plunged the needle into her vein. After a second, she relaxed. "God, what *was* that? That hurt almost worse than the bullet."

"Epinephrine and cold-prep," Vere replied. "And I gotta give you a shot of Endiguer at the wound." He pointed at her abdomen. "Can I?"

Jasika nodded and unbuttoned her shirt to the waist. The bullet hole wasn't large, but blood flowed freely. Vere found a larger syringe, this one wider and full of thick, white plasma. "Tell me about your kid, J."

"He's gone, man," Jasika said. Her eyes lost focus. "The Raiders got him in '55 when they took Kentucky." She smiled, but the smile bothered Vere—it was dreamy, vague, resigned. "That's where we were from, all of us. Brent and his dad and my mom. Newport, pretty town on the river."

"You were close to Ohio, then." Vere pulled the cap off this syringe and searched for a spot clear of blood to inject her. "Coulda got safe."

"Yeah, but they had it all blocked. The bridges...it was no use."

Vere took Jasika's hand. "Don't tell me how it ended," he whispered. "Tell me how it started. Tell me about holding him when he was born."

Vere plunged the needle into her bullet wound, and Jasika screamed again. The grip of her hand almost broke Vere's own, but he held on.

"He was *beautiful*," she cried. "Eddy, Eddy, listen to me. Listen! The Raiders are here *now*, not in some memory, but *now*."

"Well, yeah, if they shot you, J. Kinda figured that."

"No, you gotta get Cap on the phone and get us *out of*—"

She stopped.

She stopped and her eyes got glassy and cold. Her hand slipped from Vere's.

"Shit, *no*, Jasika. *No!*" He slapped her face. Nothing. Head to her chest. Nothing.

Vere tilted Jasika's head back, shoved the remains of her shirt away, and started compressions. *Shit, what did they teach us? What? There's a song...something disco with a steady beat...shit, shit, shit*. The song eluded him, but he imagined himself playing an electric bass, a mirrorball spinning over his head. "Jasika!" He continued pumping in time to the bassline in his head.

In the sky over the trench, a grenade whizzed by, landing several yards to the east of where Vere ministered to Jasika. All too near, an explosion rattled the entire trench. The ladder knocked over to one side.

Vere pinched Jasika's nose shut, tilted her head back further, sealed his mouth on hers, and breathed.

This isn't how I pictured it...

He saw Jasika smiling in dress blues, clinking her champagne glass against his. The bassline timing out his CPR compressions was now part of the first dance at their wedding.

Push, push breathe…

Saw his arm holding hers on a dance floor, spinning her out and then pulling her back in close. Saw a toddler with her golden brown skin and his gray eyes jumping up at him, begging to be picked up.

Another grenade, and then Vere saw blackness, his body slumping over hers. When he came to later, it was with a corpse beneath him.

Monday, May 26, 2070, Flussville, South Carolina, Rénartian Alliance of America (RAA)

"Do you have the fertilizer?" Claudio asked.

"I don't remotely understand how that's going to help," his assistant replied.

Claudio pinched the bridge of his nose. Miss Rochelle was useful because she followed well, but she was nosy enough to be replete with questions along the way.

"I told you—it's for the explosives," Claudio explained. "Dear, I don't ask you how you cook or how you do those mountains of research you indulge in, do I? I simply take it on faith that you are the expert in those arenas and I let you do your best." He grit his teeth against his waning patience. "Let me do my best, won't you please?"

She nodded. "I just don't get why you can't tell me what—"

"*Miss Rochelle.*" The time for gentleness was past. "You work for me. End of discussion, unless you wish to cease your employment."

She scurried out. Claudio made a series of phone calls. As evening fell, the materials were either in his possession or on their way.

The university science laboratories should all be empty now.

Time for the men of Monsieur Rénart to take control. Not just of the Rénartian states but to advance into the New British Empire as well.

The entire continent would be reunified under his command, but it would be the RAA who triumphed. They would take Canada, too.

A fire starts from a single spark. After years of wary peace, tonight a new spark would ignite.

There was a knock at Claudio's office door. "For heaven's sake, Miss Rochelle, I—" But the words died in his throat as he opened it to reveal not the unreliable Tina Rochelle but instead an awkward young man in thick spectacles, his titian hair spilling every which way in a greasy mess around too-big ears.

11

"Mister Florence, good t' see ya, sir." The man spoke with a thick Cockney accent and, when he smiled, revealed a mouth filled with crooked yellow teeth.

Claudio stepped over to allow the young man to enter. "Ambrose, do you finally have some news?"

"No, sir," Ambrose said, "but we been gettin' some good video feed of the comin's and goin's, and I can safely say the doctor wot works outta this lab we're hittin' tonight is always out by seven, as of late."

"And no one else works past seven?" Claudio asked. "Not his assistants or anyone?"

"There was this bloke last week hangin' 'round," Ambrose said, "but 'e seems to 'ave moved on."

"Bloke? Was it the primary scientist, Doctor Vere?"

"No, no, we know Doctor Vere on sight right quick, we do," Ambrose replied. "No, this was another fellow. Taller, balding, dressed a bit funny. Saw 'im a few times with Vere's assistant, too."

"But when was the last time you saw him?" Claudio pressed.

"Not since Friday past," Ambrose confirmed. "'Less he's still in there or somefink, I'd say we're bloomin' good to 'ave a go tonight. An' even if we kill 'im, he's just one of them, yeah?"

"I will have you know," Claudio said, "I don't murder unless absolutely necessary." He straightened the lapels on his coat. "These hands have never been dipped in blood directly, and I aim to keep it that way."

"But a little sabotage gets the ol' heart pumpin', eh?"

"Something like that," Claudio said. "Let's be off, lad. If we take the concocopter, we'll be there in no time."

Tuesday, May 27, 2070, Avon University, Avon, Vermont, New British Empire (NBE)

Edward Vere was stoop-shouldered. It wasn't an actual disorder of the spine but more a disorder of attitude; Vere tended toward hunching his shoulders up around his ears even as a child. As an adult, he worked well into the night on his experiments, convinced that with the right particle acceleration, he could achieve actual, honest-to-God time travel.

The latest version of Vere's accelerator, which he called the Herbert Mach III in homage to H.G. Wells, was smaller and lighter than the Mach I and II, but it contained enough dangerous particles to qualify as a local health hazard, should the university get wind of what he was really doing.

The night involved heavy consumption of coffee, energy drinks, and more than a few illicitly obtained pharmaceutical-grade amphetamines that led Vere to his three a.m. epiphany. The equation he'd been using was a little bit off, and just a mere tweak was all it took to get the machine working with an entirely different timbre of sound, light, and color. Whenever he'd tried to make things work before, Vere would get high-pitched whines, flashes of white, and then the sound of gears grinding to a frustrating halt. Now there was a low, purring drone that wasn't subsiding, and the indicator bulbs all glowed a steady gold.

Wind whipped through the laboratory at an astonishing speed, sending papers flying from every surface. Vere pulled the lever that would turn the accelerator's status from low to high, and then—

Darkness.

Silence.

The winds died down, and the machine grew still.

Vere sighed the sigh of a man who'd grown far too accustomed to the rise and fall of his own disappointed breath. He scratched his head, his hair rising to wild corkscrews beneath the reading glasses perched there.

"I say, sir," a voice said behind Vere. "Can you give me a hand? I think I've…"

Vere's heart sped up, and he whirled around, even as the speaker continued.

"How the devil did I get out of my house?"

In the empty space between the accelerator's drive plates stood a man, tall and slim with a fringe of receding blond hair sweeping from a long expanse of smooth forehead. Atop a hawkish nose was a pair of goggles with smoked lenses. The man pulled the goggles off with a hand covered in a heavy leather glove. In the other hand was a blowtorch, but something about the torch seemed off, antique somehow but also a bit artificial, as if it were individually crafted rather than mass-produced.

Vere gaped. "How the hell did you get in here?" he asked. "Who are you? Maintenance?" He shook his head. "Goddammit, I told maintenance this was a classified area."

"I-I…no, no, I'm not from 'maintenance,' whatever you mean by that," the man said. He looked around, frowning. "Not a minute ago, I was in my cellar, and then there was a great cacophony, and then—" A slow smile spread across his face. "It worked," he murmured. "Oh, my stars, it worked."

"What worked?" Vere narrowed his eyes. "What were you working on, buddy? If it was the same thing I was working on…" Vere mused, letting his voice trail off. "This'll sound like a helluva thing to ask, but back in your cellar, as you say." Vere leaned in. "What year was it when you were slingin' that blowtorch, huh?"

"Precisely the question to ask, sir," the man said. "Precisely. Because I'd wager it is decidedly not nineteen hundred and ten here, is it?"

Wilbur Wright stepped forward, lowered his blowtorch, and took in his surroundings.

"I was trying to create a vacuum," Wilbur said, staring off into space and sounding distracted. The windows of the room were caked in layers of soot. The man before him wore trousers that were far too blousy, too feminine, and too short at the ankle. Unkempt and untidy, this other man looked to be a few years younger than Wilbur, yet seemed more world-weary, more woebegone and confused.

"A vacuum? When? Where?" The other man withdrew a pocket watch and held it out to Wilbur. "How long ago? Because that was exactly what I was trying to do here."

"To what end?" Wilbur asked.

The other man drew back. "I don't know who you are, and I don't like telling strangers my classified experiments."

"Because I was trying to travel in time," Wilbur continued, "and if we were both attempting something of the sort in different eras…"

The other man blinked. "…Then one of us could have been thrust forward or backward to the other's accelerator," he said. "My God. And you said it was 1910?"

Wilbur nodded. "End of May, yes, precisely."

The other man stroked his chin. "End of May?"

"The twenty-seventh, I believe."

A shaking hand pointed at a wall, where a page-a-day calendar hung displaying the number "27."

Wilbur withdrew his own pocket watch. "I've got a quarter to midnight. Show me your time again, sir, if you don't mind."

"Of course." The minute hand of the man's watch was pointing at a Roman numeral nine.

"Dear me," Wilbur said. He looked about him and realized he was still standing upon a metal plate. "Do you think…do you think if I remove myself from your apparatus that anything dire will occur?"

"I shouldn't think," the man said. He held out his right hand. "By the by, I'm Doctor Vere. Eddy, if you'd like. And you are?"

"Wilbur." Wilbur grasped the other man's hand and shook it. "Wilbur Wright."

Vere dropped Wilbur's hand and drew back a step. "My God." He chuckled. "Well, I wonder if this'll make the history books, Mr. Wright. In addition to flight, you've just assisted in the invention of time travel."

Wilbur grinned. "I rather like the sound of that."

He stepped off the plate and vanished.

Vere stared at the empty plate, keeping his eyes open so long they felt like rocks carving out the insides of their sockets. He blinked at last, delicious moisture washing away the dry remnants of his disbelief, and collapsed into his desk chair.

It isn't real. It's exhaustion and too many cans of some amphetamine-yellow caffeine swill. I'm simply high on vitamin B and sleep-deprived hallucinations.

But as Vere shook his head and let out a short, rueful chuckle, a skittering danced across the plate's surface once more. Vere raised his head, shoved his glasses back on, and shot to his feet.

Like a flashlight, battery low, flickering with its last gasp of power, the image of Wilbur Wright came trembling back into view. The man looked somewhat dazed, holding his arms at an angle a few inches from his body as if trying to stabilize himself on a shaky surface. At last, the picture stopped being a picture and became the man himself, stable and solid looking.

Vere reached out a tentative hand to Wilbur. "You back, then?" he asked. He realized now that Wilbur was no longer holding his blowtorch.

"Made some calculation readjustments," Wilbur replied. "Did you? Here, on your end?"

Vere shook his head. "Not a bit."

"Must've been my…" He trailed off but then looked down at his hands. "Dare I wonder if it was the iron in my lamp?"

It took Vere a moment to understand Wilbur meant the blowtorch, and upon some consideration of the problem he nodded. "Iron, yes. I think that could very well be. This here," he said, tapping the surface of the machine's acceleration plate, "is made of a material you wouldn't have seen in your time, an artificial alloy called goddardium, which when the acceleration process is activated becomes charged differently than common iron. Just as a lodestone *attracts* iron, goddardium is essentially a metal-infused antilodestone. If this connection is already unstable between our two time streams, even the smallest change in particle neutrality could compromise it." He felt a flutter in his stomach. "We're actually fortunate you weren't destroyed, man. The instability could have done a lot worse than send you back home."

"I've accomplished so much already," Wilbur said. "Do you know how many times my brother and I almost died?" He waved a hand through the air. "Piffle. The risk of it all, it's why I don't have a wife and half a dozen children running about. Too unfair to them when I'm not likely to see fifty, all the things we get up to."

Vere blanched. He couldn't quite recall his history, but if he wasn't mistaken, Wilbur wasn't too far off and would, indeed, die decades before his famous sibling. This wasn't the sort of thing to say, however; who knew what the information could do?

"Paradox," Vere muttered.

"Beg pardon?"

"Nothing, nothing." Vere shook his head. "Well, sir, if you're not too concerned with your own welfare, do you want to give it another go? Carefully, of course."

Wilbur shrugged. "If I fly into bits, I suppose no one will know what became of me, will they? Quite the mystery, that."

A thought far more fantastical than Vere usually entertained entered his imagination. "I wonder. You hear of people disappearing from time to time, even in your day, don't you?"

"Of course," Wilbur replied. "Various folks of all stripes sometimes vanish without a trace. I wager many of them have met with misadventure. Things of that sort occur where the remains are too-well concealed, I suspect."

Vere nodded. "But this, us here…doesn't it make you wonder if perhaps some of those going missing haven't met with not so much misadventure as—"

"*Adventure*," Wilbur cut in. "Oh, sir, now I *have* to do this, danger be damned."

Wilbur Wright stepped off the plate again, but this time his feet touched down on Vere's floor. The percussive sound of his thin leather boots on the hard concrete was like the first strains of someone bursting into applause.

Someone knocked at the door. Vere bristled. "Oh, hang it all, what time is it?"

"I'm very much the wrong man to ask, my friend."

"Quite right." Vere glanced up at the wall. Dawn was breaking, and though Alison was early it wasn't unprecedented for her to come in before the rest of the labs. "My graduate assistant is in. Pretend you're an old friend. Don't tell her your surname, for God's sake, and don't tell her what we've been up to."

Wilbur raised an eyebrow. "Will she think me odd-looking, do you suspect? Shall I appear out of place?" He gestured down at himself.

Vere whisked a worn lab coat from the back of an empty desk chair. "Here, toss this on." The knocking became more insistent.

"Doctor?" The voice on the other side of the door was gentle. There was a rattling of keys. "I can't believe I beat you in for a change. I thought you lived here."

"No, I'm in, Miss Keller." Vere jogged across the room and opened the door.

As the young woman entered, Vere heard Wilbur's sharp intake of breath.

"Thanks, doctor." Alison hung up her coat and hat. "Hi, are you helping today?" she asked Wilbur. "I'm Alison Keller, Doctor Vere's assistant this semester."

"Much to my chagrin," Vere said, though his tone was kind.

"Sorry, sir, my scholarship is general rather than department-specific. I think it's helpful for you to have an outsider's perspective. You're so insulated with your physics students all the time."

"Ah, so you're not of the doctor's discipline?" Wilbur asked. "What are you studying, then?"

"History," Alison replied.

Wilbur looked pained. Behind Alison, Vere made a motion as if locking his lips and tossing away an invisible key. At this pantomime, Wilbur's expression softened into a smile. "What sort of history?" he pressed.

Vere flailed his arms, urging Wilbur to quiet. Wilbur ignored him.

"I'm sorry, how rude of me," he said, holding out his hand to Alison. "Wilbur Koerner, at your service."

Alison laughed. "Oh, that's amusing. Almost my own name, isn't it?"

"My mother was German," Wilbur said.

"Your mother?" Alison asked. "Or your father?"

Wilbur gave a non-committal shrug and sat down on a stool behind a table strewn with small pieces of metal.

"But to answer your question," Alison went on, "I study American...well, Empiricist and Rénartian history, I suppose, but pre-war, too, all the way back to the first Civil War."

Wilbur blanched. "I beg your..." He paused and cleared his throat. "Fascinating."

"It really is." Alison joined him at the table. "Doctor Vere is thoroughly uninterested in the past. All he cares about is particle acceleration."

Wilbur glanced at Vere. "Is that so?"

"She exaggerates," Vere said. "And is inaccurate. I do care about the past, Miss Keller. And the future as well. But science for science's sake, that's far more relevant than history itself, wouldn't you agree, Wilbur?"

Wilbur canted his head from side to side. "One could look at it that way, I suppose," he allowed. "But I think what's most interesting is the intersection of history and science. Using science to *make* history and using history to inform science."

Alison beamed at Wilbur. "Precisely so," she said. "So how do you and Doctor Vere know one another?"

"We have shared interests," Vere replied.

Wilbur didn't take his eyes from Alison. "Some, I suspect, more than others."

Vere frowned. This couldn't be good, this obvious interest Wilbur was taking in the young woman. If this were allowed to continue, would history be unmade? Would there be a paradox?

"Wilbur, I think we ought to..." Vere said. "That is, I have a lot of work for Miss Keller, and you and I need to do some work of our own."

"Sorry, doctor," Alison said. "I was cataloguing your tools yesterday. Should I finish that?"

"Please," Vere replied. He motioned toward a smaller chamber within the lab, and Alison scurried off.

"You're no fun, are you? Just like my brother," Wilbur said once Alison was out of earshot.

"I'm quite sorry I ruined your breaking of the space-time continuum," Vere snapped.

Wilbur nodded. "No, you're quite right. That...ahem. Yes." He rose. "But what's this about a *first* Civil War?"

"There's been a second," Vere said. "But I think the less you know about that the better." He shook his head. "I'm really not so very interested in this *thing* we've managed to do for the sake of its research properties. Rather, I want to get down to the core of how we did it, don't you?"

Wilbur shrugged. "Loch...something."

"What was that?"

"Eh, this fellow I correspond with, a German graduate student I met when my family and I were abroad. He and I stayed in touch and he began working on this 'hole' concept." Wilbur's brow furrowed. "What the devil did he call it? 'Spange' or 'Spaniel' or something 'loch.'"

Vere racked his brain for his middle school German. He tapped his tablet to life and typed a bit on the screen. "*Schlangeloch?*" he suggested. His blood ran cold.

"Yes, that's it. It's a kind of bridge between space and time, and I've been working on accelerating matter in between various—"

"Hang on." A depressing thought nagged at Vere. "Do you mean—you discovered—no, no, that can't be, because I had the calculations, I had the device ready to go, and if you'd done this on your own, wouldn't we have known? Historically, wouldn't we have known you disappeared?"

"I know you're living decades ahead of me, my good man," Wilbur said, "but could you slow it down a bit for a poor fellow forced to walk while you sprint? What did I discover?"

"A wormhole," Vere replied. "You discovered a wormhole. A functioning one, one capable of allowing time travel."

"Fascinating," Wilbur said. "Wouldn't that be *we* discovered it? You were working on it, too."

Vere shook his head. "I wasn't even approaching the problem that way at all," he said. "You did it. I merely provided you a spot to land."

"But what you were nattering on about, there. You were right. If I really *had* done that, wouldn't I have disappeared from history? I presume I had to have expired at some point. How did I?"

"Not from disappearing, not from any experiment gone wrong, and not with a Nobel Prize in Physics under your belt, that's for sure." Vere cast his eyes to the ceiling. "What happened? What made this attempt different? Surely you tried this in the original history as well."

"Well, but that was before you were even born," Wilbur said. He paced, growing more animated as he talked. "I believe my pen pal Mister Weyl suggested that this hole needed two ends, yes? If you were, unbeknownst to your own genius, creating one end and I created the other, yours would not have existed until this morning, would it?"

"I suppose," Vere allowed.

"And yet I opened mine once before, as far as you're concerned, but you say it didn't make the history books." Wilbur paced over to a white board mounted on the wall. "What on earth…where's your chalk?"

Vere chuckled and uncapped a pen for Wilbur, who promptly sneezed.

"What in the blazes? These *chemicals*. How can this be healthy?" Wilbur demanded.

"It's not," Vere said. "Neither are a great many things. That war for one. Probably everything we've done today." He waved at the board. "Go on. Explain to the feeble minded how this works, then."

Wilbur gave Vere a sidelong glance. "Do you really think this," he said, gesturing to the accelerator plate, "is unhealthy?" He wandered a step toward it. "I mean, paradoxes and physics and the like, the explosive danger, but…"

Vere's eyes followed Wilbur's. He said nothing but returned to his still-open tablet, brought up the on-screen keyboard and tapped at it.

Typhoid fever.

That was Wilbur's fate, a simple death in a simple time just two years from the time Wilbur left. Not some horrible, lingering brain cancer or radiation sickness, and definitely not an explosion. Still, those sorts of things weren't as exact back then, were they?

Vere tapped the screen again.

Delirium, hemorrhage, coma…who was to say whether that was caused in the gut or the brain?

He looked at Wilbur, who was now drawn and ashen.

"It's already got me, hasn't it?" He threw the marker across the room. "Confound it, you told me I didn't disappear."

"You didn't!" Vere shouted. "But…"

Soft footsteps approached. "Did Doctor Vere give you some horrible disease with his time travel experiments?"

Both men whirled around to spy Alison.

"Of course I recognized you, Mr. Wright," Alison said, a sad smile playing across her face. "I'll be top in my class in scientific history, thanks to this job. And you, doctor, what have you done? I always knew you were trying to do something secret, something dangerous, but time travel?"

Vere sighed. "Well, if she knows, we might as well just *let* her know, hadn't we?"

"I think there's a lot of things we all need to be caught up to speed on," Alison agreed. "He's worried he's hastened your death, I think."

"My God, what is this? You think this thing has given me some sort of fever?"

"Not really, no," Vere replied. "I think this thing may have given you some sort of cancer, and back in your own time it'll wind up mimicking the symptoms of typhoid to the point where they won't know how to treat you and you'll die."

Wilbur's chest rose and fell slowly. "When?"

"Nineteen twelve," Alison replied.

"Then I've got some time after all," Wilbur said. "Not endless amounts, but enough, I suppose." He clapped his hands and rubbed them together. "Show me everything this time has to offer. I'm a dying man, after all."

"Doctor," Alison said, "do you think this is an opportunity to prevent the schism? Because without the interference of the Rénartians, wouldn't your funding have been better? Wouldn't you be able to do your research more openly?"

"What's this?" Wilbur asked. "Who are these Martians?" He paused. "Dear me, things *are* different. Things out of meteors have invaded us. Heavens, Wells was right." He sighed and fell back against the nearest wall. "Does this happen in my lifetime? No, don't tell me. It's too frightening."

"The war," Vere said. "It's not Martians, it's Rénartians—a political group, not an extraterrestrial one."

"Thank heavens." Wilbur smiled. "Well, that sounds more reasonable to hear about. What happened?"

Vere and Alison looked at each other. "Oh, screw it. Fine," Vere said. "We've already damaged history, what's a little more?" He retrieved something flat and leather-covered from his desk and then placed it into Wilbur's hands.

At first, Wilbur thought it was a book, but the edges did not reveal pages that could be turned. Vere touched the middle of the surface and a moving scene appeared. Wilbur gasped at the swirling colors. "Is it a window? To another world?" he marveled.

"Something like that." Vere told Wilbur to slide his finger along the bottom of the scene, and Wilbur obliged, causing the scene to shift and reveal several smaller moving pictures floating atop the larger one. "Press that one labeled 'documentary,'" Vere instructed.

As he did so, Wilbur was greeted with a full-color film taking over the object's surface, complete with sound that Wilbur could feel vibrating against his hands. "It's an entire cinema, right here," Wilbur said. "I'm holding a veritable nickelodeon."

Vere sat beside Wilbur. "Yes, you are," Vere agreed. "But if you want to know about what happened to the country, ignore the technology for a bit and just watch."

Over the next hour, Wilbur learned of the ideological split in the country, much like the Civil War that raged only a few years before his own birth. This one, however, seemed less concerned with mostly one issue but rather several, complex changes in society that came to a head when some states could no longer agree with each other. As states took sides and stances, the war began when one man—a gaunt-looking fellow called Claudio Florence—took power as governor of Nebraska and insisted on creating a new political party: the Rénartians, named after Reynard College, the governor's alma mater. For having so much influence, Florence was seldom seen after he took the governorship and used others as the primary public face of the party. He called himself a governor rather than a president due to his dedication to decentralization. After several years in hiding, Florence appointed a Lieutenant Governor, a hyper-masculine, almost cartoonish man named Garrett Spaulding. Spaulding had been the public face of the RAA ever since, though few believed he held legitimate power.

The documentary droned on to reveal a brightly colored map showing the division of the country. In green were states that joined a new union with Canada and Great Britain as the New British Empire, and the remaining areas were now known as the Rénartian Alliance of America, taking up the center of the former country.

Abruptly, the surface of the object Wilbur held darkened and then reverted back to the swirling windows. Vere took it from his hands.

"That's quite a bit of history summarized very quickly," Wilbur said. "I can't say I'm terribly shocked, given what I know of the first war, but it's still an unfortunate turn of events."

"It wouldn't have been so bad," Alison said, "if it weren't for what the Rénartians began doing later."

"Alison claims we could have lived in peace as two separate nations," Vere said. "I couldn't quite be bothered to care, except after they began sabotaging our universities and sending our technology backward to nearly Victorian-era antiquity." He paused a moment. "I suppose that's not quite antiquity where you're from."

"I've done enough research and development to know how limited my resources of time, money, and scientific advancement were," Wilbur said. "To stymie progress and intellect…oh, dear." Wilbur leaned forward to prop his chin on one shaky palm. "Is there no preventing it? What if the seeds of this dangerous proclivity of theirs could be subverted long before they're sown?"

"You want to go back to your own time and prevent an ideological shift that won't even really begin to get groundswell until about fifty years after your death?" Alison asked.

"You say that, and yet I have to know…is that ever quite how things happen?" Wilbur asked. "The war waged about slavery…that system existed for a century before people realized it was clearly intolerable and mounted a war. When you talk about when the groundswell for these new movements began…hadn't those ideas been swirling about long before that?"

Alison considered the question. "You may have something there," she allowed.

"This is all very dangerous," Vere said. "I find it difficult to imagine you could really make much difference." He gave Wilbur a sad smile. "I was a soldier for a time before I went to college. The war, when it stopped being a cold one and actually went into the trenches, was terrible. I…" His voice trailed off. "Never you mind, son. You do what you'd like, ask what you like. We've already told you too much. What's a little more?"

Wilbur paced for a moment. "What about my family?" he asked. "Even if I'm on my last legs here, does my family survive me by much?"

"Yes," Alison replied, "but honestly, Mister Wright, do you think they'd believe you, let alone be willing to become activists all of a sudden? Activists for things you can't even imagine at your point in history?"

"You say they began sabotaging educational systems," Wilbur said. "I think I could get them invested that way, at the very least."

Friday, June 6, 2070, Avon, Vermont, NBE

The grounds were dark. Claudio and Ambrose both wore black, head to toe, but Ambrose refused the ski cap Claudio suggested. This wasn't as much of a problem under the moonless sky, but once they entered the building it left Ambrose's light hair uncovered and reflecting back the red emergency exit lights.

"Idiot boy," Claudio said while they prepared. He pulled on his own skip cap. "If you get us caught, I'll do worse than fire you."

"It makes me all itchy-like," Ambrose whined, scratching his greasy head. "I don't like it. We'll be right as rain, sir. In out, spit spot." He'd unrolled the building's blueprints on Claudio's desk. "We put it in the doctor's lab, we barely even need to be in there. Load-bearing walls here, here, and here," he'd said, tapping various points on the drawing. "My maths are perfect."

"If you say so," Claudio muttered.

But it was almost too late—they were moving along at a good clip, and Ambrose was stopping in front of Edward Vere's lab space before Claudio even expected. "This is it?" Claudio asked. He handed Ambrose the lock pick kit and crouched beside him.

"Yeah, just gimme half a mo'…there." The door swung open and both men hurried inside.

Claudio busied himself with the explosives, using the clay adhesive to stick them to the beam Ambrose's blueprints indicated, but a low whistle from across the room distracted him.

"Lord almighty, but this is a thing o' beauty, Mister Florence, sir."

Claudio turned to see Ambrose standing in awe, staring at a contraption that seemed to Claudio nothing more than a meaningless set of connected bars, metal plates, and satellite dishes. "Boy, get *over* here. Help me set the timer," Claudio stage-whispered. "Quit gawking at things you don't understand and do something productive."

"Oh, but I do understand it, sir." Ambrose whirled around, a shit-eating grin plastered across his rubbery cheeks. "Do you know what this fellow's done?"

Claudio's eyes fluttered shut. "Do I care?"

"You ought to. And *we* oughtn't explode this place 'fore he finishes." Ambrose turned back to the contraption and withdrew his mobile phone. He snapped pictures of the thing. "Since it's dead easy breakin' in 'ere, we could come back, steal all his research, and use the tech ourselves." Ambrose paused between photographs to pull a crumpled sheet of paper from his pocket, on which he scribbled hasty notes.

Claudio strode over to the young man. "Why would we care about doing that? This technology is tainted. It's *theirs*. They don't invent important things. They don't let us use what they design, just as we don't let them use what *we* design."

Ambrose looked at Claudio. "We design things?"

Claudio felt his face grow hot. "We hire people who can. And even though we don't *now*, we could." He stamped his foot. "We hamper the NBE's ability to use existing technology. We stop their trade routes. We intercept their packages. We—"

"We need to pay attention to this one," Ambrose interrupted. He narrowed his eyes, and his upper lip quivered. "Sir, I'm sorry, but God's honest truth, this bloke is on the verge o' sussin' out one of the most impenetrable mysteries o' science, and I don't feature you stoppin' me from studyin' it."

Claudio blinked, feeling as if he'd been slapped.

"Don't care if I work for you," Ambrose went on, his voice rising in his excitement. "I'm a bloody physicist, not your errand boy, and I'll thank you to start listenin' to things I tell you."

Friday, July 4, 2070, Flussville, South Carolina, Rénartian Alliance of America (RAA)

To Ambrose Richards, the machine—stolen though its conception may have been—was his crowning glory, proof of all his years of studying physics. Claudio may have thought him a simple man with simple tastes and affectations, but that was mostly due to his intense focus on those things that mattered to him: the space-time continuum and creating political anarchy. If he could use one to help the other, well then, that was a bright-blessed thing, wasn't it?

He spent weeks breaking into the lab at night, studying the changes Vere brought to the machine, poring over his notes, and replicating the clockworks and steam valves back at his own lab on the Rénartian border. The travel was a grind, the places he had to secret himself in between jaunts were filthy backwaters and roach-infested flops, but Ambrose presented his achievement to Claudio at last, his dingy teeth flashing in a giddy grin.

"But why the hell should I even bother?" Claudio droned as he walked around the machine in lazy half-circles. "I care about now. I care about the future."

"Right you are, sir, but just imagine for half a mo'. What if you could fix up the present *into* the future by futzing about with the *past*?" Ambrose asked.

Claudio pursed his lips and tapped a scrawny index finger against them. "Get what I want now by…" He waved his free hand in the air in the vague manner of a magician aiming at misdirection. "Accelerating some attitudes, as it were?"

Ambrose nodded.

"I want to get rid of the universities, that's for certain. This side can't be able to begin their own manufacturing infrastructure again, and inventions culled from research is the surest way for them to get back on their feet," Claudio said. "The problem there is that would negate Doctor Vere's laboratory, the very spot you figured out your little gearbox here."

"What if his were the only one?" Ambrose asked. "Or perhaps time self-corrects and the doctor still invents the thing, still leaves it out plain as day for me to cadge, but he's got a…oh, I don't know, mayhap 'e's workin' for you in private industry or some such. That's possible, innit?" Ambrose raised his eyebrows, waiting for Claudio to reply. When he didn't, Ambrose grew agitated. "See, mate, my theory's 'at a paradox, what you describe there, that ain't possible, not as such." He made a sphere with his hands. "World won't let it, ya see. So no danger o' me not bein' able to make this, 'cause it's already been done. Yeah?"

Claudio shook his head. "No, no, no, not *yeah*, you simpleton. If I'm unmaking and changing all sorts of things back there, God only knows what might self-correct."

"No, I s'pect only the time travel itself would self-correct," Ambrose replied. "Not things unrelated-like."

"You're giving me a migraine."

Ambrose felt a pang of concern. "You want some menthol drops, guv? They do wonders for the ol' noggin, they do. That what me gran always used to give me."

"And clearly it did wonders for your intellect," Claudio said. "Shut up and get the thing ready for testing."

"You want we should find a recruit to—"

"On me," Claudio cut in. "We're testing it on me."

Ambrose drew back, his eyes wide as he stared at his boss. It was then he realized common menthol drops were insufficient to repair what maladies resided in Claudio Florence's brain.

Thursday, August 30, 1888, London, England

Claudio's eyes were shut, but his nose was already assaulted. Sharp, sooty stenches assailed him—not mere smells, no, these assaults to his senses were *stenches*, hot and bestial—and he knew before opening his eyes that the process worked. It was coal and it was manure and nothing in the clean and tidy gardens of his southern compound just inland from Myrtle Beach. There it was salty sea air, singed car exhaust, and exotic flowers he imported from South America. Here…horses. Lots and lots of horses, and their hoof beats increased in volume from all directions, along with…no, he was still back in Ambrose's laboratory, because that was his voice, wasn't it?

"Good clean fish*es*!" the voice rang out, always emphasizing the last syllable of its throaty cry. "Good hot *breads*! Good clean fish*es*!"

Why was Ambrose telling him about bread and—oh. It wasn't Ambrose. The tone was lighter, younger, though the accent was the same. Beneath him, Claudio could feel wetness seeping into his clothes, and there was a hard lump on the back of his head. He hoped it was something under him on the ground and not that he'd been injured and was now in the midst of developing a firm knot of swelling there.

He let his eyes float open at last, and above him was sky, gray and unforgiving and on the verge of rain. Framing this desolate air were buildings coated in black from the visible smokestacks belching inky smoke. Claudio coughed. There was tightness in his lungs from the mere idea of inhaling that foul darkness.

He sat up and spotted the food vendor.

"Good clean fish*es*!" The boy was very young and very dirty, his clothing all colors identical to the sky and the smoke. Around him were other salespeople—sales*children*, in point of fact—holding out wilted flowers or dirty rolls. Claudio imagined trying to wrap his teeth around one of them and losing a crown in the process.

"*Soup* only a pence! *Soup* only a pence!"

Claudio's head rang. The lump came with him from the street, causing Claudio to groan in pain. He stood on wobbly legs. His vision swam, leaving black streaks across his eyes for an instant, and he had a sudden urge to vomit. He looked around at a small alley adjacent to a wider thoroughfare—on market day, it appeared—and nearby was a rain barrel sitting beneath the sagging eaves of a pub. The nausea intensified, and Claudio heaved *bœuf bourguignon* and half a bottle of *Spätburguner.* Claudio thought through his sick, dizzy haze that the animal slaughtered for his meal wouldn't be born for hundreds of years.

The barrel reeked of red grape and hot, noxious sick, but as soon as Claudio raised his head, he smelled only the grime and horseshit. He suspected some of the latter resided on the sole of his right shoe, as there was a suspicious softness there with every other step.

"You feelin' a bit under the weather, luv? I got just the thing."

Claudio looked up to see a woman grinning at him.

"Name's Polly." She batted her eyes and sidled up closer. "I got a bit o' medicine back at me flat, if you'd like. It's not far 'tall."

Claudio considered the offer. He had nothing in the way of appropriate money, but perhaps he could offer something in trade.

The woman was snub-nosed, with her auburn hair in a messy topknot. Her clothes stank of drink and sweat, but there was a kind of devil-may-care appeal to her smile—yellowed teeth notwithstanding—that made Claudio think she could be an amusing companion for a few hours.

Polly giggled when Claudio nodded and indicated that she should lead the way back to her place. "Won't regret it, sir. I'm well taught in how to please a gent, if I do say so me self. Got some whiskey, too, if you'd like a nip."

"Sounds divine, fair Dulcinea. Do let's make haste."

"Dulci-whatnow?" Polly asked. They walked together. "Oh, gov, you lookin' for another girl? Said it was Polly, though me mum called me Mary. Never cared for that. Ah, 'ere we are." She nodded up at one of the soot-colored buildings. A sign designating the place as an inn without a name hung half off its hinges above the door. "Not technically me own flat, but I'm paid up for a time."

They swept through the downstairs, part lobby and part pub. The bar area was still playing host to a few men muttering into pints of ale, and Polly led Claudio past them to a sparsely furnished room on the second floor. "Not much, but then I s'pect we don't need much," she remarked, indicating the thin mattress.

Claudio chuckled and took Polly into his arms. The evening began with a hint of promise, but as the first pink streaks of dawn blossomed through the holes in the curtain, he was listening to her snore and holding his head in his hands.

Goddammit, man, you started a revolution. So why can't you manage this one simple act?

He looked down at himself, at his thin form and unresponsive organ, and felt the first stirrings of rage. It was her fault, this disgusting whore, and he would make her pay. Never mind that this wasn't the first time he'd been impotent, never mind that, indeed, he had authority and money and now powerful science behind him.

You're no man. You're worthless.

Claudio looked down at Polly and put one hesitant hand on her throat. For a moment, her breathing stopped, her face growing at first a jaunty pink to match the dawn, but then redder and darker. Claudio's arm trembled. He tightened his grip and watched as the veins in the back of his hand stood out in angry lines like writhing snakes undulating just beneath his skin's surface.

A little more pressure. One last squeeze…

Before Claudio could clamp his fingers down tighter, Polly emitted an emphatic snore and wriggled away from him. She snorted and fell back into her drink-induced slumber.

I could do it again, though. No one would miss her. She's of no import to history. The way she bends her elbow, the cirrhosis will take her soon enough. My way would be merciful.

Claudio reached for Polly's throat again, this time pressing with both hands. A knot in his left hand throbbed, and he gasped as the tiny room spun away from him. He felt himself falling, and then came a rush of wind and a feeling of being punched in the gut. He groaned and doubled over.

Friday, July 4, 2070, Flussville, South Carolina, RAA

When Claudio straightened back up, Ambrose's concerned face floated above his.

"You all right?" the younger man asked. "Hang about, don't try to move, got to check you—oh, sir, you might…here." Ambrose looked around his lab, grabbed a sheet from the exam gurney across the room, and tossed it to his boss. "Seem to have lost your clothes in the transfer. Did that happen when you arrived, too?"

Claudio shook his head, but then thought better of that response. Ambrose didn't need to know that he'd been nude on purpose. "I…it's a bit fuzzy," he mumbled. He looked at Ambrose. "I didn't mean to come back when I did. What happened?"

"Well, there's a retrieval protocol in Vere's notes," Ambrose replied. "It's linked with the subject's left hand, but I didn't think it would work without installing the chip under your skin. Perhaps it's a biological connection that's made, even without that. The chip could make the retrieval more precise, though."

"More precise would be preferable," Claudio snapped. He wrapped the sheet around his waist and stood up. "Get me something real to wear, and get to work on this chip. Tell me when you've got something."

Ambrose tapped a pencil against a notepad. "Sir, when we do have something, where do you want to go? Where did you wind up, and it would be more helpful if we sent you—"

"Yes, yes, send me to something around the war, but…" A thought occurred to Claudio. "Keep this time handy, if that's even possible. I may wish to go back there again regardless."

"It takes a lot of power for each trip," Ambrose said. "Just how relevant d'you think o' that time and place?"

Claudio imagined slitting Polly's throat, and a shiver of delight coursed through him. It wasn't anything he'd ever thought of doing before, but the mere idea now stirred arousal in him. None of Polly's ministrations worked, and yet thinking of killing her seemed to be doing the trick.

"It's very relevant, Ambrose. Very relevant indeed." He hurried from the room.

Monday, July 7, 2070, Flussville, South Carolina, RAA

Ambrose pored over the notes he'd transcribed from Edward Vere's materials. The retrieval mechanism was still more theoretical than actual, and it involved binding a chip to the drive plate's electronic signature and then implanting it in the subject's skin. The left palm was recommended, the notes stated, because the biological retrieval was bound to a vein direct to the cardiovascular center. The heart, Vere posited, was the source of the subject's own electrical functioning; therefore, the mechanism required a jolt not unlike jump-starting a vehicle.

As Ambrose sketched a design before commencing to solder wires and metal together, he fretted.

Too many jolts to the heart could be catastrophic over time. Should I insist the governor get a checkup? What if he's got an arrhythmia? Poor blighter could drop dead centuries ago, and I'd never know what happened to him. Or would I just summon back a corpse? No, the electricity's the thing. He'd simply become a mystery. I got to make sure he's fit for this.

Knowing his employer, however, Ambrose suspected Claudio would resist a medical evaluation.

When Ambrose had a workable design functioning, he read further in Vere's notes, which cited a projection jump spot that the retrieval device could pinpoint—a safety zone, where within a certain radius the chip could detect if there were native humans or animals present that could get sucked up into the subject's area. When the chip was activated, the subject needed to find the safety zone and be retrieved there, so as to ensure no one else would come back to the present. Though Vere had an annotation that indicated even he was unclear on that point. In someone else's handwriting was the cryptic note "Intent—they have to want to go with you," which left Ambrose more confused than ever.

Ambrose worked through the rest of the evening and into the next day, interrupted every so often by his impatient boss urging him to work faster.

"You want to get stuck centuries in the past?" Ambrose demanded at one point, feeling exhaustion and hunger overtake him. "Then, sure, bloody well let's shove this thing right into your hand and just hope everything sorts itself out. I'm sure your citizens will be comforted knowing you died needlessly from your own fucking hubris."

Claudio stalked off, muttering about Ambrose's retirement plan getting smaller by the hour.

Saturday, June 7, 2070, Avon, Vermont, NBE

Several days after he'd first arrived, it was time for Wilbur to return home, leaving Vere and Alison to work out ideas in the present.

"Now, now, none of that."

Alison turned around to face Wilbur, who stood with one foot on the plate. She readied the retrieval mechanism, a flat square of metal fitted into the palm of a fingerless leather glove. "I don't know what you mean," she said. She gestured to Wilbur's left hand. "Let's see if this fits."

"I see the shimmer in your eyes," Wilbur said. He held his hand out.

Alison had assumed he would take the glove from her and put it on himself, but this seemed to indicate otherwise. She took his hand in hers. His skin was rough, with callouses along each fingertip. As she tugged the glove onto his hand, her thumb brushed one of the hardened spots. "Does that hurt?" she asked. "Is it from controlling the plane? I imagine that's not easy, keeping everything level and steady without electronics."

Wilbur looked at his hand. "There? No." He laughed softly. "That's from the winding key on my Kodak. I do have other interests, you know."

Alison felt her face grow warm.

Wilbur cleared his throat. "I have to go. It'll be fine, Miss Keller. Not to worry." He finished pulling on the glove and gave her a salute. "If I'm able to influence my present, perhaps your future will be brighter."

~

"How long before we can tell if it's worked?"

Vere looked around his still-shabby laboratory. "It didn't," he said. "It's been hours, but for him it's been a lifetime. If it had worked, my equipment wouldn't have to be cobbled together like so much driftwood after a hurricane, and I wouldn't have shrapnel in my leg or memories of young people being blown to pieces around me. We would have funding, and I wouldn't have only you here to assist me."

Alison tapped at one of Vere's data pads. "His encyclopedia entry hasn't changed," she noted. "Still dies the same date, the same way."

"And, honestly, it may have nothing to do with the machines that hastened his demise," Vere said. "Disease and contagion aren't uncommon back then."

"But my shots are all up to date," Alison said. "If Wilbur wasn't able to do anything on his own, what if I gave him some help?"

Friday, July 11, 2070, Flussville, South Carolina, RAA

A full week after Claudio's return, Ambrose knocked on his door, a small box in his hand.

"Got it," he said. "But Mister Florence, before I do the install, I think…" He hesitated, running his hands together and staring at the floor.

"Spit it out, boy."

"I'll say again, sir. We ought to run you through some medical tests." Ambrose flinched as he spat out the words.

Claudio saw himself running a scalpel along Polly's abdomen, pictured feet of blood-slicked intestines spilling from the incision, and almost cried. More stupidity delaying him from his release, getting to feel so much warm, coppery blood slipping between his fingers? No. He wouldn't allow it.

"Medical tests?" He stood, pounding a fist on his desk. "What the hell for?" There was no way some stupid, arbitrary thing was going to delay his power, his revenge, his *feelings* any longer. When he dreamed of murdering the London prostitute, Claudio felt alive, real, and in control. Having that control taken away now was not acceptable. He wanted to smell her fear, see her eyes cloud over and the light behind them flicker out like a candle.

Ambrose gave his boss the rundown of cardiovascular considerations. When he finished, Claudio was still determined to avoid the test.

"You're going to believe some fucking Empiricist scum over *me*? I'm *fine*, you idiot. Get that in me and send me back. *Now*."

"But, sir, if you die—"

"If I die, then God intended it, and our citizens will understand. They already look to Spaulding, and I'm sure my team could advise him."

"If you die, Mister Florence," Ambrose said, his tone a little more forceful than usual, "forgive me, but Mister Spaulding is an idiot. Who d'you *really* feature takin' over for your real duties, hmm? *Me*? I'd wager not. If you don't want a medical test, then at least finally appoint a lieutenant."

Claudio studied the young man. He was educated—despite his woeful lack of street smarts—capable with his science, and his values were right. But he was a foreigner, born in the NBE, and despite his defection and apparent allegiance, one could never be quite sure of someone's lingering feelings about his homeland.

It occurred to Claudio that he himself was trying to get back to England—an England of centuries ago, but still the country of Ambrose's birth. Still the seat of power of the NBE in present day.

But I'm going back to kill one of them. An inconsequential one, but a citizen of that future nation nonetheless. I'm doing my work back there. I'm getting rid of a whole Empiricst bloodline, perhaps.

He took a deep breath, urged himself to calm down for appearance's sake. Claudio walked around his desk and clasped a hand on Ambrose's shoulder. "Son, you know I value your contributions, no matter how much I point out your shortcomings."

"With great frequency, sir," Ambrose said, narrowing his eyes and standing up straighter.

"I'm just trying to *challenge* you," Claudio said. "You have great potential."

Ambrose relaxed and smiled. "Thank you, Mister Florence."

"However, I can't make you my successor. And you're right about Spaulding. I appointed him because he's malleable. You're not. But you're also not native born."

Ambrose shrugged. "Didn't think it would be me, sir, but still. Fellow has to ask, right?"

"Of course."

"But you have to appoint somebody," Ambrose continued. "Won't do it otherwise, unless you want to consent to the physical."

You aren't immortal, but what if you could bring someone forward in time, someone who could really lead Rénertia to greatness? That should be your successor, someone bold who understands keeping this young country great, pure, and strong.

"You're right, boy," Claudio said. "Go ahead and check my ticker. I'm sure you'll see it's in tiptop shape. I'll draw up some paperwork about any necessary change in power."

Ambrose nodded and led his boss to the medical suite.

Friday, August 31, 1888, London, England

Polly Nichols wandered out of the inn when her rent was used up. "Oy, I got me a nice new bonnet, and it's bound to earn me enough for tonight's bed!" she shouted at the owner as she left.

"We'll see, girl. Now out with ya."

Polly adjusted her bonnet and headed for the pub across the street, but when she spotted the scrawny man who'd left her the night before she turned to head the other direction.

"Miss Polly, please, dear, don't rush off so."

She turned with some reluctance. "You got a lot of nerve, gov. Didn't pay me nothin', 'spite me doin' me best, and didn't even buy me breakfast."

The man withdrew a small leather purse from the inside of his coat. He smiled as he shook it, coins inside jingling together like bells. In one hand he carried a smart bag, cornered like a doctor's.

"Blimey, you got a bit of a windfall there, eh?" Polly imagined how much was inside and what it might do for her—a bed for a week, perhaps? Food? *Drink?* Oh, glorious drink. Polly could enter that beautiful oblivion that took away memories of her father's yelling, her husband's other women, her children…oh, God, her beautiful children whom William never let her see since he turned her out. Henry would be almost ten now, yet the last time she laid eyes on him he hadn't even been walking yet. When she drank, Polly forgot her womb had ever been full, forgot the rough men and unforgiving women who'd made her resort to this life.

"Polly, we're going to have to send you off." Anna Cowdry, her last employer for her last respectable position, had held out a satchel to her. "We can't have you drinking. This is a dry house, girl, and my husband—"

"Your husband's been givin' me eyes like he wants to wet his whistle," Polly spat out. "Fine. You lot put on your airs and your do-goodings and whatnot, but I know why I bother the both o' ya, and it's got less to do with the cooking sherry 'n' more to do with my unlocked bedroom door."

The satchel held a week's worth of funds and a list of addresses of inns in the city. Polly spent the shillings on alcohol; it had lasted her two days.

Was this man, this *gentle*man, going to fund her better? Going to give her some respectability? Fellows just wanting a night with her didn't flash their money like this one did. If he was the sort to have trouble with the act itself, maybe he just wanted companionship, someone to keep house. And if he let her have her whiskey, Polly wagered she'd be right chuffed to sweep the man's floors. Doctors needed housekeepers, 'specially poor bachelor doctors who also might need a bit of company without the hassle of a wife.

"It *is* quite the windfall, Polly." The man's grin widened. He held out an arm to her and escorted her into the alley.

~

An hour later, a horse-drawn carriage stopped short near Buck's Row. The driver got out to unlock the stable doors and nearly tripped on Polly's corpse as he did so.

Across the street, a man drew the brim of his hat down over his eyes, pressed the center of his palm, and walked ten feet to his right to the alley from which he'd dragged the woman's body. He never exited the other side.

Saturday, July 12, 2070, Flussville, South Carolina, RAA

"You do what you wanted to back there, sir?"

Claudio felt a rush of information enter his mind—articles, books, documentaries, comic books, all of it soaked in blood and shadowy sketches that resembled his own slender frame clad in Victorian garb.

The press-bestowed nickname hung in his mind like a slap in the face, like a cruel playground taunt.

"Jack the Ripper."

"Sir?" Ambrose gasped. "Oh, hell, sir, I don't know why I didn't warn you about that first time you…you didn't *see* him, did you? Were you near the scene of one of the murders?"

"Ambrose," Claudio said, "do you remember the first time you heard about Jack the Ripper?"

Ambrose looked puzzled. "What? I don't know. Back home, it's somethin' you 'ear 'bout soon as you're old enough to get told not to run off by yourself at night." He took another step back. "Why d'you ask?"

"Just curious, son."

"With all due respect, sir," Ambrose said, "you can be right barmy, y'know that?" He placed a blood pressure cuff on Claudio's left arm. "Did you decide who you'd like to bring back as your successor?"

"Virginia Dare."

"Don't think I'm familiar. Surprised you'd want a woman."

"I don't want a woman," Claudio explained. "I want a child."

Part II: The Scholar

I've built walls, a fortress deep and mighty, that none may penetrate.
–Paul Simon

Benoy Jonson took the trolley back to his home, a large brick affair built in the late 1800s that survived through two civil wars and countless natural disasters. Throughout his stalled academic career, Ben spent nearly half of every interest check from his trust fund restoring the house to its original Queen Anne glory, installing embroidered furniture, doilies, and marble-topped tables in every room. The trend toward Victorian rebirth slowly migrated into the former New England states from the end of the war in 2082, when Ben was still working on his undergraduate degree. Now it was less fashion and more necessity, as the neighboring country labored to prevent the importation of silicon-based technology this far north.

Today's return home was a joyless one. Ben didn't understand being told "no." He knew there were people in the world—people on the same continent, in fact, and people who weren't his indulgent parents or teachers—who might not love him on sight. But he'd also always thought that was for stupid reasons, bigoted reasons that spoke to the unreachable minds of the less educated. He never thought it was because he was actually not lovable, not brilliant. Of course, his family suffered for being Indian in a nation settled by Europeans, but only intermittently, and their brilliant careers mitigated much.

And yet today, he was being rejected for the very thing he prized the most— his innate need to understand the world's deepest mysteries. It was Ben's *mind* that was being rejected, not the color of his skin or his personality quirks or even prejudice against his family money. It was what made Ben *Ben*, and it stung like a slap in the face.

"I don't have the sense that you feel your work," his advisor told him. "You understand history cognitively, but there's no passion, no sense of its rich, living qualities."

Ben shook his head. "No, no, I can assure you. These issues matter to me. They haunt me, even."

"That explains your fascination with the more macabre eras." Professor Summit rested a fleshy jowl on the palm of her hand. "I mean, really. Unsolved serial killings?"

"Doesn't it bother you," Ben said, "knowing these mysteries have never been solved?"

"Not particularly." She closed Ben's file and handed it back to him. "I'm sorry, Ben, but I just don't see this edit as being any more promising than the last three. The chair is going to ask that you reconsider your ability to defend by December. I don't honestly see any way to it unless you have a breakthrough and vow to abstain from sleep."

A stone seemed to drop into the pit of Ben's stomach.

Last chance. This was my last chance, and I blew it.

Professor Summit rose. "I worry that the department accepted you in the first place because of your family's accomplishments." She smoothed the sleeves of her jacket and kept her eyes from Ben's. "Perhaps I shouldn't speak so frankly, but having the last son of a legacy of esteemed scientists choose to study a humanities discipline was a coup." She gave Ben a sad smile. "Did you go this route just to rebel?"

He thought of his father's long, painful death, tethered to oxygen in a quarantine tent. Their goodbye was through clear plastic with layers of latex and paper masks between them. That was what the great Biren Esh Jonson's bravery led him to—dying of the diseases he traveled the world curing. A man of action and science could not pursue his noble ventures long and would cough up blood in a sterile hospital ward at fifty-six, already a widower, not yet a grandfather.

"I never rebelled from anything my father taught me and wanted for me," Ben said, "except that I would wish for a longer life."

As he collected his things and left the professor's office, he considered this more. His parents saw the world, but they both died for it in one way or another. His uncle, too, killed in a hate crime committed by Rénartians. By studying the past, Ben always hoped to save the future. And by studying it from a distance, the distance afforded by books and databases and words, he could save himself. Now that dream was gone.

Ben entered his front parlor to find his personal assistant, Kris, attending to his mail. "Heya, boss. Am I gonna get to come with you to the college when you start teaching?"

"There won't be any teaching," Ben replied.

The young woman's elfin features melted from happiness to shock. "Wait, what? Is it because they want to give a job to someone..." Kris looked around the room. "Eh...someone who like *needs* to work? Because the way the funding for schools has been going, I know they can't really afford to have a big faculty."

"That's not it." Ben sighed and sank down in the chair on the other side of the desk. "It's not that they wouldn't hire me. I can't even finish my doctorate at all. My project's died on the vine, and my time's run out. If I tried again, I'd have to do a new set of courses, and probably at another school entirely."

"Oh, man." Kris scurried to Ben's side and patted his shoulder. "You could do that, though, if you wanted? I mean, not to be crude about it, but your folks left you pretty flush."

"By the time I picked a school, moved, got my coursework done...I'd be pushing fifty, if I were lucky." Ben shook his head. "No, I need to change course. Pick a new career." He gave Kris a weak smile. "You can go home for the day. I need a good wallow. See you tomorrow."

Kris nodded and collected her things from the coatrack. "Oh, almost forgot. I put a guy on your calendar during your foundation hours tomorrow. Notes are in your book. Kind of rude, wouldn't take no for an answer. Wants funding help with some science-y thing. I told him that wasn't normally your specialty, but he wants to pitch to you anyway."

Ben shrugged. "I could use the distraction. Hell, maybe I'll just be a layabout philanthropist instead of a professor. I'll pay other people to be amazing if I can't be amazing myself."

Kris tried to give Ben a pep talk, but he wouldn't hear it. After she left, Ben consulted her notes in his appointment book. "Doctor Edward Vere, physicist, Avon University." The meeting was set for just after lunchtime at a nearby teahouse.

Of course he'd been from AU. The school that won't give me my degree? Why should I help one of their faculty?

Still, physics was worlds away from history, and this man had nothing to do with his proposal failure. Hearing him out wouldn't cost him but an afternoon at most.

That's all I have now. Nothing but time to kill and money to burn.

Wednesday, July 7, 2100, Dayton, Ohio, NBE

"This isn't Doctor Vere's laboratory," Wilbur said. He stared at a garishly painted building with blinking lights festooning every visible surface. Small vehicles that he'd seen on his first trip to the future—Vere called them "hovercars"—sailed beneath an awning and pilots exited.

"What are they doing?" Wilbur pointed to a pilot pulling a long string from the rear of his vehicle.

"Refueling," Alison replied. She elbowed him and pointed to a building in the opposite direction. "I think we're in the right time, but not the right place. Doesn't that look familiar?"

It did indeed—a few yards away was a large stone church from Wilbur's neighborhood, only now instead of cheery row houses flanking it, it was bordered by something called a Video Station on one side and Milton's Fine Clothier on the other.

"What the devil happened to my house?" Wilbur demanded.

"Never mind," Alison said. "Keep your voice down." She threaded her arm through Wilbur's and nudged him toward the refueling station. "We can rent a car here and get back to Vermont in about four hours."

"Four hours?" Wilbur was astonished. "It takes six times that long to get to New England. Why, when we flew from New York to—"

"Look." Alison stopped walking, hands on hips, and glared at Wilbur. "I am gonna find this story super interesting when we're safely on our way to the university, but I don't think it's so helpful right now. Just don't stand out too much, follow my lead, and nobody'll look at you funny."

"Miss Keller, why are you so upset? I do apologize for finding the future still so wondrous, but you seem unduly angered by our location." Wilbur took her hand in his and gazed at it, surprised at his own boldness. "You promised Kitty you'd protect me, but I dare say I bear the responsibility of some protecting as well."

Alison smiled, but there was sadness in her eyes. "Look, Mister Wright, you're sweet. Seriously. There's something more off than just where we are." She looked around. "I don't think this is the right year."

"I'm afraid I can't help there." Wilbur shrugged. "It all might as well be Jupiter as far as I'm concerned."

"See, that's just it," Alison said. "Some things look like that to me, too."

"Do you think perhaps we changed something, when you followed me to my own time?"

Alison looked around again. "Maybe that's it."

"You're skeptical of that theory."

"I'm a skeptical sort of gal."

Wilbur ran his thumb across the back of Alison's hand. "The best way to test your theory is to find some evidence, hmm? Do they still publish newspapers?"

"Some, in the NBE but not the RAA. They have only TV, but we don't have TV anymore. We only have internet and print."

"Rephrase without speaking another language, please."

At this, Alison laughed aloud. "Come on, old timer. We'll find one of them fancy bits of writin' for ya."

The station's shop opened its doors for them as soon as they were a foot from the entrance. From within came the forlorn sounds of a man singing about how a rock feels no pain and an island never cries. There was a news rack just inside, and Alison's temporary joviality disappeared as soon as she saw it. She tapped the page and handed it to Wilbur.

"When was it we were last with your employer?" Wilbur asked.

"Thirty years ago," Alison replied, keeping her voice low. "I was aiming for 2070 in Vermont, but instead we stayed in Dayton and it's thirty years later than I intended." Her face was turning crimson. "Shit. What're we gonna find when we get back home? Oh, my God. What if Doctor Vere's *dead*?"

"Would your retrieval system have worked if he were?"

Alison put the paper back on the rack. "I have no idea." She shut her eyes and rubbed at the closed lids. "We gotta get to the university."

"Well, you said it only took a few hours." Wilbur gestured at the counter, where a bored-looking clerk punched keys on a screen.

Alison pulled a wallet from her pocket. "I don't know if my credits will work. Hell, it could cost three times as much as it did to rent a car."

"We won't know until we try."

Alison made her request to the young man without making eye contact. He quoted back a price that gave her pause, but she nodded and handed over a small flat object.

"This is expired," the clerk said after sliding the object through a slot in the screen in front of him. He squinted at the display. "Oh, but it says this account is linked to another one." He nodded. "Yeah, you're good. Your dad paid your bill or something. Here." He handed Alison a tiny black box. "Can you drive hydrogen-fueled?"

"Oh, thank God, they still use hydrogen transmissions."

The clerk blinked. "Still? Why wouldn't we?"

"Nothing, never mind." She took the box. "Thank you."

"It's the green Tesla Twelve in space Z2."

Wilbur followed Alison out to the car. "What did he mean about your father paying the bill?"

Alison spun around and grinned. "I saw what his system said. Doctor Vere is *alive*, Wilbur. At some point, he had all my bank records put into his name by claiming to be my father." She paused. "Kinda presumptuous, actually, but hell, I'll yell at him about it later. The point is he's *alive*."

Wilbur smiled as he climbed into the vehicle beside her.

Tuesday, June 17, 1890, Rio, Wyoming, USA

This wasn't a trip with purpose. This was Claudio trying to stay calm, focused, to pursue interests outside of blood and lust and pain. The prairie was quiet, the weather warm and windy. He closed his eyes and took a deep breath, savoring the sweet scent of cactus flowers.

When he opened his eyes again, he was face to face with a winged creature, its head canted to one side, studying him. He shrieked and took a step back, stumbling in his haste and landing hard on his seat.

The creature was on two legs, wings twice as long as its body, and its head was an amalgam of man and bird, the eyes laser-red and piercing into him. Claudio couldn't move. His heart battered out a frighteningly fast rhythm in his chest. "What are you?" he whispered.

The bird-thing screeched and took flight. When it reached a point in the sky a few feet above Claudio's head, it disappeared, but not in an instant, more as if an invisible window hovered there and the thing slid through it, head to foot, each part of it becoming invisible down its body.

Claudio racked his brain. Something about the beast was familiar. Was it alien? Myth? He activated his return device; there was no way to research from here, unless he wanted to speak to someone from the reservation. He sniffed.

As if that would happen.

The lab was empty and dark when he returned. He rushed to his office, where he conducted fast searches on his tablet.

Mothman.

He thought of the way the creature slid through to invisibility, as if passing through a doorway. Could that be the source of the things? If time travel existed, was it so very far-fetched to imagine portals, or even a wormhole such as what Ambrose used for his machine, but one that went elsewhere than into the past?

It could be another planet, even.

And where there was another planet with an advanced civilization, there was the potential to have an advantage against the NBE, to potentially even wipe it out. If he could ingratiate himself with the other plane, or perhaps harness or exploit its resources…

I have to get someone there.

Wednesday, April 12, 1587, Roanoke Island, British colony

Two young men stood sentry at the gate. As the woman staggered into their field of vision, they each gave a start and trained their muskets on her.

"What witchery is this?" one demanded.

"Ye are not of the colony," the other accused. "Who goes there?"

The woman opened her mouth but then immediately closed it. She held her hands up in surrender. "I…I mean you no harm!" she called. She attempted a smile. "I am, ah, Goody Fallon, of…Newfoundland. Yes, just a ways up the coast to the north, with Sir Humphrey Gilbert's collective. I was shipwrecked upon your shore and seek asylum, kind sirs."

The guards exchanged a glance. The one to the left of the gate, a broad-shouldered blond youth, lowered his musket. "Aye, come in peace, mistress. We can offer you aid."

The guard on the right seemed taken aback. He was slightly older and sported an auburn beard. "Goodman Cage, we are not permitted to—"

"Goodman Warner, this woman is our elder and in clear distress," the first guard interrupted. "We will do as our conscience dictates. The governor will understand." He smiled at Fallon. "You are our neighbor, after all, and we presume a fellow former English subject?"

Warner gave Cage a dubious look but stood aside and lowered his own weapon. Together, the two men tugged the gate open and bowed low, entreating that Fallon enter. "Welcome, mistress," Cage said. "Welcome to our humble party."

Fallon bowed her head and passed through the open portal. They failed to see the slight upturn of one corner of her mouth as her skirts swished the ground between them. Once inside, the gate swung shut behind her. She looked up and gasped.

Cottages, light, and even the faint sound of music…it was civilization indeed, or at least as close an approximation as could be found on the island. Laughter spilled out of a makeshift public house. Torches glowed, and upon every available spot, there grew small, cordoned-off gardens filled with the start of green sprouts and vines.

A huge, ancient apple tree sprung forth in the quadrangle of several large buildings. Its fruit was still yet unripe, but Fallon gazed at it.

At her left stood Cage. "Ye shall be wanting a place to pass the night," he told her. "I must rouse the governor, if he is not already about."

Her eyes grew wide. "Oh, dear, I don't want to trouble him."

"'Tis but a moment's inconvenience, mistress. Do not fret."

Before she could protest again, Cage was already scurrying off, slipping inside the largest of the buildings near the apple tree.

Fallon leaned against the wall's interior, taking an overly casual posture as she stared after the guard.

"Jesus, this is a helluva lot weirder than I thought," she muttered. "Trippy. As. Fuck." She shook her head, smirking.

~

The council members' voices fell to a hush. The strange woman stared at White as if he were a veritable angel, winged and haloed and lit about the edges in gold and silver. She was an odd thing, shorthaired and wearing finery gone to tatters.

In the colonies, however, White wasn't ill used to seeing the effects of weather-borne destruction. Still, he was unaccustomed to celebratory treatment, as if he possessed any shred of fame beyond his own people.

"Governor, it is in an honor." The woman bowed low, sweeping a hand beneath her bosom in a most bizarre manner.

The governor felt this gesture seemed improper, especially performed by a woman of her age. He frowned.

"Do get up, mistress," he implored. "I am neither king nor countryman." He raised one ginger eyebrow at her. "You are from the Scottish settlements?"

The woman looked confused and somewhat chagrined. "I, um, is…yes?" She coughed and looked down at the hem of her dress.

White stepped forward and narrowed his eyes. "Are you sick in the head, madam? Do you know the year, Goodwife Fallon? Who is the Queen? And what is your Christian name?"

Cage gaped at the governor. "Sir, this lady is in clear distress," he protested. "Is it kind or fair to imply she is of unsound mind?"

"We have faced dangers before," the governor said. "I will not be contradicted." He looked back at Fallon. "Now, if you would be so charitable as to indulge an old man's suspicious nature…"

The woman laughed and touched her forehead. She paced and stared out each window of the meeting room. "It's so beautiful here," she said. "So unspoiled…"

"Madam." White banged a fist on the table. "It is the dead of night. Please. Just give me your name. Your origin. And tell me, how on earth did you come to be here?"

"Sinéad," Fallon replied. "And…" She sighed, her shoulders sagging. "Ah, hell, I don't remember what I told you guys." She laughed again, this time her face splitting into a mad grin, and then bolted for the door.

White stared after the retreating figure. "Guards!" he called. He gestured at her, and the two younger men were soon in pursuit. "That woman is a spy."

~

Fallon ran on and on until she reached almost all the way to the shoreline. Behind her, the colonists added to their numbers and were now wielding honest-to-God pitchforks and torches. "I'm not you people's Dracula," she muttered. "Goddammit, I thought this kind of thing was a cliché."

She didn't figure they'd go after her as a spy. That was the funny thing. Depending on how she'd been found, the worst the agency warned her against was accusations of witchcraft. Hide, they instructed her. As soon as you realize you've made it, you've got to hide until you can collect yourself.

She'd have to tell them they got the clothes wrong. Way too fancy and impractical. As she ran, her breath growing ragged and labored, Fallon wished she could rip the moldering skirts off, escape from the confines of her petticoats, and run in just her linen knee-length drawers. When she caught the cry of men shouting "Whore!" behind her, Fallon knew this idea would add fuel to that fire. "Damnable whore! Spy!"

So much for solving a mystery. Shit, what a disappointment.

At the shoreline, she scanned the roiling waves for… "Fuck, where is it?" she grunted in frustration. She crouched low, picking her way down the precarious rockface, making sure to keep the beach in sight. If she wasn't precise in her aim…But no, she dropped down and knew as soon as she felt the ground give a little more under her weight that she'd made it.

This wasn't the retrieval spot, though. Fallon raced toward the tree line, the colonists at her heels.

They've made me. They know there's something not right with me. I'm not from here. I'm not from now. And they all know it.

It wouldn't do to already go out to Croatan if that wasn't where the colonists wound up. No, she would need to go to the groups of Chowanoke or Iroquois in and around the settlement. Fallon scuttled along the beach until she reached the far side of the island, the side uninhabited by the colonists. She shut her eyes, trying to call up the image of the period map she'd almost-but-not-completely memorized. At least one of the tribes shouldn't be far.

When she wound her way through the trees to the clearing, she was startled. She expected nudity, savagery, ritual, drums. Instead, there were silent tents and huts, a few men sitting around a fire laughing together and murmuring in what was clearly English. One of them wore deerskins, but another wore a shabby scarlet jacket, a hand-me-down from a British soldier. She found it all incongruous and offensive, these natives wearing the clothes of the colonists. Were they so civilized? How on earth did Roanoke put up with their presence, let alone teach them their language, give them their clothes? Yes, the theories were that White's group intermarried with them, but Fallon could not fathom such a thing—they were kidnapped, in her opinion. What respectable English people would take up with savages? Once she was back to her own time, she would take up with the RAA, full stop. The Empiricists understood nothing about racial purity.

She'd been musing too long, and soon she knew they'd sensed her.

"Come out," one of the men said, not unkindly. "Governor? Is that you?"

Shit. "Um, no, no, it's not the governor." Fallon walked forward into the clearing. Too late, she realized she hadn't reasoned this out enough to craft an understandable story for them. "I am from the north, and I was shipwrecked," she tried, simplifying the tale she'd told the colonists. "May I have shelter?"

They exchanged looks and quiet words in a tongue she didn't understand. A young woman came forward from between two groups of men. "Roanoke?" the woman asked.

Fallon shook her head. They couldn't find her here, not if she wanted to be safe. "No, I haven't located Roanoke," she tried. "I was from the Canadian colonies." Shit, did they call it Canada yet? Her mainlining of seventeenth century North American history meant to prepare her for this all went out the window under the intense pressure of the situation. Her heart pounded, louder and louder, the blood rushing against her eardrums. Fallon felt her face flush hot, red. She laughed, too tired to protest anymore. "I don't know what I'm doing here," she admitted.

The young woman frowned. "Come, you are tired," she said. She put her arm around Fallon's shoulders and steered her into one of the huts.

Inside, much to Fallon's shock, was a white man, but his clothes weren't those of the colonists. Instead they looked centuries newer, though perhaps not as new as the twenty-second century. If Fallon hadn't worried she was half-crazy with fear and hunger by this point, she'd have thought the tall, slender man was a subject of Queen Victoria, with his dark wool suit and wire-rimmed spectacles.

"Well, you weren't one of *mine*," he said, looking Fallon up and down. His accent was Midwestern, which was impossible, given the Midwest didn't precisely exist yet.

The man smirked, revealing near-lupine teeth and making his thin face look more skeletal in the firelight. "Vere must've sent you. Do you work for him?"

Vere. The man from the travel agency, the physicist. It could be another tourist, Fallon supposed, but she wasn't sure how to respond.

"The fact that you chose to come here speaks volumes, miss." He chuckled. "I'll have to find you later. Yes, indeed." He withdrew a pen from his pocket, held it in front of himself, and squeezed it. Fallon thought she saw a small flash of light.

"Did you—was that—"

"Your imagination," the man said. He drifted off to speak to one of the natives, and soon a young woman brought her a bowl of hot liquid. The Victorian man exited the hut.

Not Victorian. American. Rénartian, in point of fact, if he is from the Midwest.

Jonson and Vere had led Fallon to believe only the New British Empire had time travel, that their agency was secret to keep the tech out of RAA hands.

The young native woman was expecting Fallon to drink, and so she pulled herself out of her reverie and did. It was a broth, and she was grateful at the heat and sustenance. "I didn't even know I was so cold," Fallon told the woman.

More women appeared beside the first one. "This will return you," the first woman said. "That man, he says this will work for your kind, those who dance on the stars. Soon you will be called home and disappear. He says you will sleep now and awake in your own time."

Wait, what? No, I can't leave. And how can they make me? How—

She felt pressure on her left palm.

Darkness. And then a rushing like a train, like a thunderstorm, water echoing in a seashell.

The sea, I have to stay close to the sea...

Thursday, August 19, 2100, Avon, Vermont, NBE

"Oh, shit, Ben, the client's back, but she's unconscious." It was a young woman's voice. Fallon couldn't peel her eyes open.

Footsteps. Someone patted her face. "Kris, go get Eddy." It was a man, the younger one, Fallon knew.

"He's no medical doctor," the girl protested.

"Go."

When Fallon opened her eyes, the young man's face was above hers. He smiled, his thick black eyebrows relaxing in relief to see her awake. "Welcome back to the twenty-second century, Ms. Fallon."

It was gone. Her one and only chance, and Fallon blew it. She wept.

~

Whispers behind closed doors. A first-aid exam by the older of the two men in charge of the agency. Finally, Fallon was given cups of tea and bland, stale little circular things halfway between crackers and cookies to nibble on. A gray and white tabby cat stared silently at Fallon from a bookshelf. Fallon could only muster weak smiles for the young woman called Kris who continued to dote on her and ask if she was all right. Kris returned from some secret corner of the building to ask if Fallon felt like debriefing the staff.

"You don't have to," Kris assured Fallon. "Doctor Vere at least would like to speak with you if you're not up to a formal interview."

Fallon nodded. "I'll talk with him a bit."

Doctor Vere looked to be in his early sixties. His hair was tightly curled, his complexion tan but his features Caucasian. Fallon herself might have thought him handsome in a shabby way under different circumstances—that is, if she could be sure he was white, which was hard to tell—but his gruff demeanor was tough to get past. He spoke in the affected tone of a Mid-Atlantic accent, despite its having gone back out of favor at least twenty years earlier.

"Did you go to one of those 'new etiquette' schools?" Fallon asked after he'd seated himself.

Vere smirked. "You're not nearly as backward as you seem, Ms. Fallon. Very perceptive of you."

Fallon gaped. "Backward? What do you—"

"Let's cut through these miles of bullshit," Vere interrupted. "Look, I've met others like you before, Empire citizens wishing they lived in the RAA, who use history as an excuse to proliferate racism." He glared at her. "I'll not have good people like Miss Moto and Mr. Jonson exposed to your twisted ideologies." Vere leaned forward. "They're naïve, you see. But I'm not. It may not exist anymore as an organization, but people who want to see Virginia Dare, the first white person born in this fractured country, just because she symbolizes some horrible racial purity ideal to you…my God, woman, you make me sick.

"And so," Vere went on, sitting up straighter, "when we finish procedures today, you'll not pursue this line any further lest you get an unwelcome visit from me that perhaps involves something metal placed in an uncomfortable spot in your person." He raised an eyebrow at her. "Are we clear?"

"You don't want me trying this again," Fallon clarified, "because you dislike my politics? Or are you just embarrassed I made it through your screening?"

Vere pounded the table. "It's not politics if it's sheer hate, madam, and we are within our rights to refuse service to anyone." He pointed to the closed kitchen door. "That young man out there, our Mr. Jonson…he didn't start this agency in order to help people destroy others. Do you understand?"

This was all getting a trifle overdramatic for Fallon's tastes. "Look, I've been through a lot today," she said. "Do you want to hear about what happened or not?"

Vere folded his arms in front of his chest. "Sinéad Fallon, did you discover what became of the lost colony of Roanoke? Or were you somehow stymied in these efforts?"

Fallon was startled at the way the question was phrased. "Stymied," she blurted out. Shit. "I…I mean…oh, hell, fine. Yes, yes, I was stymied. I couldn't get where I needed to go in time, and they thought I was a witch or something."

Vere nodded. "It's funny. Some research Mister Jonson hadn't found a few days ago sprang up just this morning." He pulled a folded sheet of paper from an inside pocket of his jacket.

Fallon stared at it, a feeling of dread settling over her. "What is that?"

Vere unfolded the paper with agonizing slowness and passed it to her. Fallon scanned the blurry photocopy, feeling the first stirrings of panic.

Before the trip, before contracts were even signed, Jonson and Vere went over everything with grave seriousness. "Client shall in no way impact historical events," the stipulation went. The younger one, Ben, read that one and smiled at her. "But that's super unlikely," he'd assured her. "You'd have to really screw up to do that."

And yet here was a page out of a history book showing a woodcut of a woman with short hair who looked all too familiar.

"Is that me?" she murmured. Her stomach felt heavy and yet empty at the same time, as if she'd been filled with air. "Oh, my God, that's supposed to be me."

Vere snatched the paper away. "It isn't you, Ms. Fallon. Of course it isn't you." He cleared his throat and drew a pair of half-moon spectacles from his shirtfront pocket. "It seems there's an old legend amongst the Iroquois of a sorceress who served as a kind of portent of the Roanoke disappearance." He lowered the paper. "And of course, that would have been centuries ago. So it couldn't be you."

Fallon's eyes darted to the corners of the room.

Exit, exit, where the hell is the exit?

Just as she spotted the door, a hand clamped down on her wrist. She shrieked. "Let go of me!"

"I think not."

Fallon struggled, but then a piece of hard plastic pressed to her temple.

"What is that thing?" Fallon asked.

Vere turned his hand over and studied the device now resting in his weathered palm. "This?" He scanned the dark plastic and small white buttons. "This is for our memory erasure, which you're already aware of as a stipulation of our services." He turned his hand around so that Fallon could see the buttons. "Can you read that?"

Fallon squinted. One of the buttons said "Restore." Another said "Revert." In a row beneath the other buttons, a third said "Delete All."

"This is what I use to erase the memory of your adventure. You know we do this with all our clients, though perhaps in a slightly nicer manner. Because it's the gaining of the knowledge that's important, isn't it? Not so much the keeping? The keeping, well…that's too dangerous. That's what our whole business model is run on. Knowledge gain for its own sake, the retention of which is immaterial."

"I wanted to know what happened," Fallon said, "and I knew I wouldn't get to keep the memory, but…*delete all?*"

A wicked grin split Vere's face, and he let his thumb move to the "Delete All" button. "Yes. Activating this command…"

"Deletes *all?*" Fallon whimpered.

"As in every memory, not only your trip, but everything." He stared at her. "The sentimental falling of leaves on your first day of kindergarten, your first kiss, your graduation, your parents' funerals." He leaned even farther over the table, his face inches from Fallon's, so close she could feel the heat of his breath. It held a whiff of peppermint tea, stale enough to be unpleasant at this distance. "I mean the

memory of how to walk, talk, read…dare I say function. You would be a baby in an old woman's body."

Tears fell from Fallon's eyes. "Please, no."

Vere squinted hard. His eyebrows knit into a long, steel-gray caterpillar. "You won't try this again." It was as much a statement of fact as a command.

~

The woman who left Jonson's Exotic Travel that evening seemed serene. In a freshly pressed pair of jodhpurs and a gauzy white blouse that buttoned down the front, she looked pristine and put together, if a bit confused.

Fallon could swear she'd been on her way to the library, but this building… this wasn't it, was it? She glanced back up at the unmarked townhouse, gave a shrug, and sauntered down the sidewalk.

The front windows, they'd looked like eyes in a way, and Fallon felt them boring into the back of her neck.

A slender man approached her. "Ms. Fallon, I'm sure you don't remember me," he said, "but we met once, long ago."

Fallon stopped walking and studied him. He wore a dark gray suit, Victorian in style though not like the retro fashions that were popular today. No, these clothes looked vintage, looked dusty and worn and battle-scarred.

"I suspect we share similar political leanings," the man went on. "May I buy you a drink?"

Thursday, August 5, 2100, Avon, Vermont, NBE

The lobby looked like a nineteenth-century drawing room, though this was not a private residence. A stack of parchment-printed brochures sat on a table near the entry. "Jonson's Exotic Travel," the front of the brochure proclaimed. "Services available by referral only." The room was silent and smelled of eucalyptus, a sweet, heady scent that made it seem as if the dwelling were always on the cusp of Christmas.

Deeper inside the building, a clerical assistant filed pieces of mail into slotted trays while her employer—the very Mister Jonson of the agency's title—dabbed a spot of spilt tea from his shirtsleeve. The pyramidal ebony nameplate twelve inches in front of him revealed his given name to be Benoy. A cat slept on a crimson cushion in front of the unlit fireplace. Downstairs, an older gentleman in a white laboratory coat fussed with beakers and wires and keyboards, muttering to himself about quantum theory and transistors.

All in all, a normal afternoon. That was, until young Mister Jonson sat up straighter in his chair and got a faraway look in his eye. "Shit," he said, rubbing his bushy eyebrows. "Kris, we got trouble."

"We do?"

"It's Tuesday afternoon," Ben informed her. "Look at the appointment book."

The girl's heart-shaped face grew ashen. "Damn," she exhaled, her smile melting into a frown. Her bob of shiny black hair fluttered as she turned to look at the wall clock. "It's way past time."

Ben and Kris stared at each other, eyes wide. The unthinkable had happened—Brimley Wheaton failed to appear for his retrieval.

Ben felt an uncomfortable moistness that he knew from experience would overwhelm his carefully applied cologne. When Ben was experiencing the very heights of panicky stress, which was more frequent than he cared to admit, he had the embarrassing tendency to sweat through all his layers of cotton, silk, and velvet.

Since giving up his dissertation, Ben's stresses were minor, to do with getting the paychecks out on time and being impeccable in his customer service or attempting—and usually failing—to chat up an attractive lady at the local tearoom. It was years since he had broken things off with Lily, and there was no one serious since.

At the agency, problems had arisen before, but not this specific one. Doctor Vere was reticent on the matter, but several weeks earlier, a client had some difficulty returning from Roanoke. Vere had still been able to retrieve her, but the debriefing session was cancelled. Kris, in particular, voiced her disappointment.

"Trust me, Miss Moto," Vere had instructed, "what our client was endeavoring to do was unpleasant. She has no more information about the mystery than we do even at present."

But that was the only hiccup in several years of providing services. To have another—perhaps more serious—glitch was dire. If this one involved a botched retrieval, anything could have happened to the missing Mister Wheaton.

Ben's mind raced with the possibilities. Death? Death in an era without medicine, when leeches were cutting edge, when people drank from the same rivers they let their cattle excrete in? *This* was the kind of danger they'd subjected an innocent civilian to.

What the hell am I doing with my life? What right do I have to endanger these people?

~

For the next twenty-four hours, there was a flurry of panic and yelling and sleeplessness. No one went home. No one ate. It was all full of stress and bloodshot eyes and half-finished cups of coffee. Telephone receivers were lifted and put down without numbers being dialed. There was no precedent for this level of disaster, nothing in the company manual. What to tell the next of kin? Ben dreaded the conversation that might follow. A new flash of sweat beaded up on the back of his slim neck. He fished out a handkerchief from a trouser pocket and mopped under his collar.

"You've got to get him back," Vere said. "Son, there's nothing else for it."

Ben was just beginning to make the preparations for installing himself in the machine, much to his reluctance, when a whooshing sound came from the direction of his office.

At first, it was a great relief to Ben when his client appeared in a puff of soot and cinder. What surprised the agency's director were the man's location—the top of Ben's desk—and his state of dress, which was something resembling either a very short monk's robe or a very long potato sack. Wheaton's feet were bare and dirty, and Ben cringed at the thought of twelfth-century detritus being smeared across his fresh ink blotter. Ben's cat looked from Wheaton to Ben and then gave a disgruntled hiss.

"Well, that's a weight off." Ben said. He tisked the hissing cat. "Hush, Bodhi." He urged the feline away from the desk, strode to the older man, and held his hand out to him. "We'd given you up for dead." Ben hoped the client read his coldness as casual, even as a strangling panic seized his body. What could have happened to delay Wheaton?

Wheaton's eyes darted, rabbit-scared, around the room. "Where am I?" His gaze fell on Ben. "Oh, Mister Jonson, thank goodness." He took Ben's hand and let himself be helped down from the desk. Once on the floor, Wheaton bounced from spot to spot, his gait springy despite his size. He beamed at the younger man. "My, but that was a heart-stopping turn." Wheaton was filthy, covered in muck and dust and God knew what else, and for a moment Ben felt pristine by comparison in his sweat-soaked business finery. Wheaton grinned at Ben. "It was exhilarating, that's what it was."

Ben looked at his client. "You know in a bit I'll have to suppress the memory," he reminded him. "We can discuss the events at length, and we'll replace it—"

"I recall the sales pitch," Wheaton interrupted. "I'll think I had a restful spa weekend or some such." He nodded. "I know, but blimey, the things I saw." He elbowed Ben in the ribs. "The *ladies*. I know I wasn't there for the ladies, but what a lovely surprise."

Ben's face grew hot. At a loss for words, he gestured to the outer room. "Let's have a chat, then."

After a short rest, Wheaton was much more appropriately attired in a loose white dress shirt and mock equestrian breeches. He lounged by the enormous fieldstone hearth for his debriefing. The rest of the staff of Jonson's Exotic Travel was there as well. Doctor Vere joined Ben on the settee opposite, cups of tea placed into their waiting hands by their assistant. After serving, Kris proceeded to splay her lithe form out on the rug, half-reclined into something resembling a modified *supta baddha konasana* position, legs tucked to her sides. Bodhi nestled beside her and began to purr.

Ben marveled at Kris's impossibly bendy young form, but then quickly shoved the thought away. Not only was she his employee, the young ladies who occasionally squired her away to mid-afternoon tea made it clear to Ben that he was decidedly not her type. Still, he loved the beauty of how her hair shone blue-black in the firelight.

"So did you find out whether the kids were aliens or not?" Kris asked Wheaton.

Vere allowed his foot to swing into her arm.

"Ow! I was just asking what we were all thinking."

"Young lady, that was impertinent," Vere said.

"Miss Moto doesn't care about being impertinent," Ben pointed out to his colleague. That was what they all loved about her, after all, even Vere, despite his gruffness toward the young woman. "Mister Wheaton, please," Ben continued. "In your own time."

Wheaton sat up straighter, squaring his shoulders and putting his teacup down. "As you know, I grew up near Woolpit. I lived with the legends of the green children my whole life, and when I came into my inheritance, I wanted nothing more than to find out the definitive answer, once and for all."

"But you went out on the town with a bunch of old-timey chicks instead?" Kris asked. She slid out of Vere's reach when it looked as if she would be kicked again. "I swear, man, you're gonna lose a limb," she warned.

Vere waved a hand at Kris. "My dear, I could earn a Nobel Prize in Physics without the use of a single finger."

"I'll give you a single finger," Kris muttered.

"Sir, please continue," Ben said to Wheaton. "If you don't, I'll have to listen to more of this and worse."

Wheaton chuckled and went on. "Right, well. I found out what I wanted about the mystery." He grinned, flashing a mouthful of tea-yellowed teeth. "And here I am, back safely to the twenty-second century, inquisitiveness fully sated." He picked up his tea and took a long sip. "You're welcome to do your bit erasing this knowledge, as I know is your process." He sighed, gazing off at the ceiling as if examining constellations. "For it's not the end *result*, you know, so much as the *hunt* for the *knowing*." Another sip. "And now I do know, much to my immense satisfaction."

Wheaton looked proud and inhaled the scent of his tea. "Ah, very good, Miss Moto. What *do* you put in this? Very fragrant."

Ben cleared his throat. "It's customary before we begin the process to at least, well—"

"Tell us," Kris interrupted. "All the clients, they get mindwiped so it doesn't get out into the world, all the conspiracy theories, cryptids, cults…but *we* get to know, usually." She looked at Ben. "I mean, I guess it's not a *rule* that we get to know, but I just always thought…"

"No one hasn't wanted to tell us before," Ben said.

Vere tapped the side of his head. "Our minds are steel vaults, young man. We're master secret keepers." Vere didn't meet Ben's eyes but continued to look at Wheaton instead. "Rest assured we don't divulge anything." He leaned back in his chair. "Personally, I only care about the physics of time travel, so whatever unsolved mystery you unraveled is of no consequence to me."

"Regardless," Wheaton said, "it's not a matter of trust. It just seems a bit unfair, you getting to keep the memory while I don't. I mean, do I *have* to tell you?"

"Of course not, sir," Ben immediately assured him. He rose. "If you're ready, then, we'll get on with the erasure."

Wheaton put his teacup down and got to his feet. He sighed and got a faraway look in his eyes. "The legend said the green children came out of the wood and startled the village with their strange appearance, odd manner of speech, and gifts of precognition. Over time, theories changed from angels to aliens to visitors from another dimension."

There was a sudden change in his movements, a shifting and turning and then a terrible clicking accompanied by a flash of metal. "They were *green*, after all."

Wheaton trained the gun on all three of the agency's employees in turn.

"I'm going to leave here with everything intact," he said. His voice was even and his face relaxed, but there was a hint of hardness in his eyes. "And none of you will stop me."

It was true. None of them did stop him as Wheaton sprinted out, still in full possession of the key to a piece of unresolved—if unremarkable—history.

Probably unremarkable. Hopefully. Yes, most likely totally insignificant. Still…

"That gun…did anybody else think that looked a little weird?" Kris asked.

"Kind of," Ben agreed. "Well, yeah, weird. Not like any kind of thing we see these days."

"I search everyone's belongings upon check-in and -out," Vere confirmed. "I can't imagine where he was hiding it."

Kris shuddered. "The green children gave it to him."

"From their home planet?" Ben asked. "Kris, that's just a legend. Research indicates those children were Flemish, not Martian. The citizens of Woolpit didn't recognize their features or dialect so the kids only *seemed* alien."

"Lots of nutritional deficiencies could give one a green pallor," Vere added. "I'm sure it was all perfectly natural."

"That was no Colt forty-five is all I'm sayin'," Kris said. "You want to put words in my mouth and say I'm calling it an alien ray gun, I'm cool with that." She held her hands up and gave her boss a little shrug. "So what we got for this afternoon, huh?"

Ben wandered to the window, lifted the lacy, sheer curtain, and gazed out. Somewhere, a man roamed the city streets with dangerous knowledge. "An FBI agent wants to know what happened to D.B. Cooper," he murmured, sounding distracted.

"Do you think that's for the best, Benoy?" Vere asked.

Ben let his hand drift off the lace edge of the curtain. "Probably not, Eddy." He gave the doctor a weak smile. "Probably not."

Friday, August 6, 2100, Avon, Vermont, NBE

Violet Lessep smoothed her skirt before ringing the bell. The building was unassuming and quaint, and that comforted her. She was already outlaying a lot of cash for this trip; to also be visiting some creepy underground lair or big shiny evil-looking glass-enclosed corporation would have just made her more self-conscious than she already was.

When she'd secured the last few hundred she'd needed for the down payment, her father was skeptical. "Kiddo, you already run around the world for the sake of truth, justice, and the Empiricist way. Can't you be happy with your FBI work? Why you gotta have adventures in your personal life, too, huh?"

"Oh, Pop, you're too damn practical." Violet kissed his bald head and scampered out in a manner undignified for her age. But Violet never felt her age, and even with a fancy, important job with a fancy, important government agency, she was prone to whimsy and ebullience. And even if her down-to-earth dad disagreed with the expense of her vacation, he still loaned her the last bit of cash.

Such a softie.

A girl much Violet's same height and build, though a decade younger, swung the door open. Eyes the color of Violet's name greeted her, big ones fringed with thick black lashes and eyeliner that gave them a cat-like look. "Hey, you must be Agent Lessep," the girl said. She took a step backward and held the door wider. "I'm Kris. Mister Jonson is expecting you."

"Thank you."

On her quick spin through the front parlor into a back conference room, Violet saw only a blur of knick-knacks and polished wood and brass. This area was more traditionally appointed in a business motif, all laminate plastic tables and uncomfortable, institutional chairs. The walls were a bland shade of off-white and there was the subtlest scent of ozone in the air, as if it were pumped in artificially.

Kris plopped down in a chair opposite Violet and put a thick binder on the table. "So, you want to find out what happened to D.B. Cooper," Kris said. She paged through the first few sections of the binder. A scratching sounded at the door behind Kris. She sighed and rose to admit a cat, who proceeded to leap up on the conference table.

"Ignore him," Kris said. "You're not allergic, are you?"

"Hmm? No, no," Violet replied.

"You were saying, about Cooper, you wanted to know what happened to him?" Kris asked.

"Well, no, not precisely," Violet said. "It's not so much the *what* as *who*."

Kris nodded. "That'll make a difference when we send you," she said.

"Not where?" Violet asked.

"Did you not..." Kris's voice trailed off and she laughed. "Oh, wait, wait. What...we thought you'd gotten a referral here."

Violet squared her shoulders. "I did. One of my supervisors used your service."

"Oh, but if they've already *been* here, no wonder you don't know exactly..." Kris whistled. "Hoo-boy, you're in for some interesting news, lady." She flipped the binder shut and patted it. "You'll want to start reading this, cover to cover. There's more training after you've read that. We leave clients with an urge to refer inquisitive friends here, so you must know someone who had a great trip he can't remember."

"But wait, training? For a conference on profiling?"

Kris shook her head. "No," she replied. "Training for time traveling."

Kris rose and exited the room. Violet heard the door snap shut and then lock from the outside.

What the hell *was* this? Violet's boss, Jason, came back from what he claimed was a profiling conference with all kinds of new inspiration for cracking cold cases. "And it was all thanks to these guys," he'd said, handing Violet a card. "It costs a pretty penny, but it's worth it."

Violet thought of Jason, of their hands touching as the business card passed from his palm to hers, of his sandy hair and sad, soulful eyes. If this was real, if this place was what it said it was and Jason had sent her here...where did he go? For how long? She tried to remember if he'd had more laugh lines when he returned than when he left.

Maybe. Just a hint. And was there a streak of silver in his hair that wasn't before?

Violet scrabbled around in her purse now for the card. "Jonson's Exotic Travel," same as the sign outside. "For the adventure of a lifetime."

That's when Violet noticed that the final four letters of the last word were in a slightly heavier font.

Time. Adventure. Exotic. Oh, jeez, this can't be real.

She swung the binder over to the expanse of tabletop in front of her. There was nothing on the cover, nothing pronouncing the mystery within, and yet the first page laid it all out.

"By now you're probably thinking we're con artists," it read, "but we're excited to announce that it's true. Time travel is real. It's possible. And you will be in another month, day, and year in the past before sunset. You may spend hours or weeks there, but when you return, you'll resume your old life as if nothing ever happened.

"But you will, actually, be changed.

"Because at Jonson's Exotic Travel, we specialize in the knowledge-hunter, the thrill-seeker, the person with a nagging desire to know the unknowable.

"We help you solve a mystery."

Violet exhaled, not even realizing she'd been holding her breath as she read. My God, was it true? Everything in her training told her no, this was a con, this was a scientific impossibility. Didn't some people with a particle accelerator prove decades ago that nothing could move faster than the speed of light? And didn't you have to go faster than the speed of light to travel in time?

"You'd think so."

Violet jumped. A young man stood in the now-open doorway, studying her. He was of South-Asian descent and had wild dark hair and thick eyebrows. His velvet blazer looked soft to the touch but also somewhat frayed around the hems. His voice was deep, deeper than Violet imagined someone with his boyish looks would have.

Violet blinked. "Was I thinking out loud?" she asked the man as she stood up.

He smiled and nodded. "You wonder how we actually do the time travel thing, hmm?" He strode across the room and stretched a hand out to her. "I'm Jonson, Ben Jonson."

Violet shook his hand. "You own this?" she asked.

"I own the building and the business," he replied. "But my partner owns the tech."

"Tech," Violet said. "So…"

"Yes. It's true. My partner owns and operates a time machine."

"You think so, but I'm a rational person, Mister Jonson. I have a really hard time believing that."

"It's easier to think I'm crazy?" Ben asked. "Go ahead. Sometimes I think I am, but I know too much."

"You've time traveled yourself, then?"

"Ironically, no," he said. "But I still have proof." He tapped the binder. "Keep reading, agent. And don't worry about the locked doors. It's just for security. We'll let you leave whenever you want. *If* you want." He shrugged. "It's all up to you. Until you sign on the dotted line, this is all theoretical."

Violet moved a hand closer to the holster resting under her skirt, strapped to her right leg. "I should warn you, sir, I'm a federal agent of the New British Empire. I'm armed and will take offensive action if threatened."

Ben held up his hands. "No need for that, ma'am. I've seen too many guns today. Just hang out here for a while. Let's talk after you've read the manual." He wandered out.

The door locked behind him.

~

After he was sure the agent wasn't going to make a break for it, Ben took a winding metal staircase down to the sub-basement that Vere used as his lab. "Eddy, you got a fix on him yet?" he called.

Vere gnawed on a messy-looking sandwich. He looked up from under veils of wrinkled eyelids and nodded to Ben. With a sideways nod, the doctor gestured to one of his computer stations, an ancient cobbling-together of huge, monochrome CRT monitors connected to sleek, steel-encased servers. The entire mess was controlled by the disembodied keyboards of pre-war manual typewriters and mid-century adding machines jury-rigged with coiled landline telephone wires.

Vere tore the sandwich from his mouth. "He thought he was being clever, going down to the sewers," he mumbled with his mouth full. "Poor lad didn't know our LoJacks are a bit more sophisticated than most."

Ben cringed and rubbed at the bridge of his nose. "I take it you've already done it without checking with me, called in for a removal?" His voice quavered on the last word.

Vere finished chewing his bit of sandwich and shuffled forward. "Boy, you've got no head for this part of the business," he said, laying a hand on Ben's shoulder.

"It's a stupid folk tale," Ben said. "We can't let a guy go who just wants to keep that memory? He wanted to *know*, Eddy. He said when he hired us that he's a historian. I can relate. Why else do you think I like hearing their stories when they come back? I like knowing. I get why he did this."

Vere bowed his head. "It's not just the green children he knows about. It's you and me and Miss Moto, our work here, our location, everything." He swept a hand around the room. "He's been in the lab, Benoy. Not just the upper room, not just the public things we use for recruitment and advertising, the innocent things. I can't have the tech getting out. The consequences of unregulated use of time travel? Do you understand how dangerous that is? What would happen to it?" Vere grew impatient. He slammed a fist down on a nearby counter. "My God, man, what do you think the Rénartians would do with this?"

Ben felt a chill course through him.

"Do you think that's what he is?" Ben asked, his voice low and hollow.

Vere glared at Ben. "That woman, that awful woman who had us believing her intentions were pure...she might not have been one of them geographically, but she was one of them spiritually. Emotionally. They exist among us, spies to that infernal cause of hate-mongering and such."

"But what would Rénertia care about a Welsh legend from the eleven hundreds?"

"If those children weren't Flemish, as you say, if they were from another world where technology is stronger and things like that man's little weapon are the norm, it may not be anything more than firepower," Vere replied. "Any advantage, no matter how small, is still an advantage. Or perhaps they just want this," Vere continued, sweeping a hand through the lab to indicate its entire contents. "Perhaps they want to travel backward or forward in time and further strengthen their cause with money or power or...God, it could be anything. Do you want their success on your conscience?"

Do I?

Ben's gaze fell upon some of Vere's books, tattered covers on both physics and history, texts the two of them pored over time and again. He stepped toward a stack with one volume on top, a book he knew well because it was from his own teenage library.

Civil War II, the title proclaimed, followed by *The Second War Between the States* in a smaller font.

Vere's voice called Ben out of his reverie. "We can't let that man stay on the loose with that knowledge," Vere said. "You have to agree, Benoy, honestly. There's no other choice."

A nod. The signing of a form with Ben's sweaty, nervous hand. And then Ben walked back upstairs with a much heavier heart.

Kris was at his office door waiting for him. "Agent Lessep is done with her reading," she told Ben. "And, man, she's cute. You gonna do anything about that?"

Ben sighed. "I can't date a client. None of us can. You know that."

"Is that, like, in writing somewhere?" Kris asked. "Because you might want to—"

"I thought it was a pretty obvious thing, but if you want to add it to the minutes of the next freaking staff meeting, we can get it in the employee manual, okay? That's hardly the biggest thing we have to deal with today, Kris. Jesus." Ben sighed. "Sorry. That was harsh. Yes, she's very cute. I'm sorry. I'm just..."

"It's cool," Kris said. "I'm sorry I was trying to be all lighthearted me when we got a situation going. I get it. It's less-than-awesome that guy got out."

"Understatement."

"Yeah." She tidied up the remains of the tea. Cups and saucers clinked together.

Such normal noises, Ben marveled. Dishes and liquid and people with plans and people thinking about dates and silly things when…

When I have to decide to murder someone before the day is over. Murder. Steal someone else's actual ability to live, the one thing we each have that's ours, that makes us special, human, real…I decided to murder this man.

"You want me to set her up in the inner office?" Kris asked.

When he didn't respond, Kris moved closer to Ben. "Dude, you're looking a little more haunted than usual. Actually, a lot paler. Like you-are-in-the-middle-of-seeing-actual-ghosts-right-this-minute haunted."

Ben could no longer feel his body. He was numb from head to toe, knees locked rigidly to keep him upright.

"Tell me about the gun again, Kris." The sound of Ben's own voice sounded faraway and unreal. His eyes stayed averted from hers. "I need to believe it wasn't normal technology. Tell me it was an alien gun, a gun from another planet, another time…anything. Please." He looked at her, moisture stinging in the corner of one eye. "Tell me we're doing the right thing."

There was a client not ten feet from him, sequestered behind wood and metal, learning about what they were going to do to her, and yet the last person who trusted them with his life was about to lose it.

He wasn't going to pull the trigger himself, but that didn't matter; it was still his orders.

"Wow," Kris said, "I thought you and Eddy were always kidding about that stuff." She lowered her voice. "You *weren't* going to let him go? It really is… you're gonna off him?"

Ben flopped down in his chair. He looked at the desk and could still see Wheaton's footprint on the blotter. He didn't answer, but instead just stared at the dusty outline.

Monday, August 9, 2100, Avon, Vermont, NBE

Rupert Cob didn't realize he'd read this manual six times already.

Every few months, Cob learned—through the Jonson's Exotic Travel training process—that he'd been mindwiped before, and then he'd recall his weekend in a small cabin in the mountains and chuckle to himself at how unreal such a bland vacation seemed in retrospect.

Hell of a thing. What did I really do while I was away? Did I learn whether Patty Hearst was in on her kidnapping? Did I thwart some murder plot to assassinate a king in the 1500s? Or do I know where a centuries-dead pirate buried his treasure? The mind reels.

Cob would feel a scratching at the inside of his brain, like insects seeking exit from a glass jar. Then he'd spend a few hours in meditative pondering before offering up a mild shrug and continuing on his day.

Now he read the manual a seventh time, receiving coffee from the efficient and beautiful Miss Moto and warnings from the sad-eyed Mister Jonson at regular intervals. Jonson himself was a bit of a downer, with his dark eyes cast to the floor and muttered warnings of things. At last the physicist, Doctor Vere, entered and led Cob downstairs.

"You must forgive me if I seem too casual in my instructions for you," Vere rumbled in a deep voice. "It's just that, as you now know, you've been our client for so long…from *our* perspective, we feel as if this should all be old hat for you, lad." Vere chuckled. It was a rusty enough sound that Cob suspected it was rare to hear the scientist express mirth.

"Indulge me," Cob told Vere. They'd reached the bottom of the spiral staircase and stood in a crowded laboratory. "They tell me I have a bit of a memory problem." He barked out a boisterous laugh that in all other company never failed to be infectious, but Vere did not join him. Cob quieted and looked around.

Buzzkill.

"So…do I need some new threads? Things that won't make me stick out? I don't know the drill, but I'm sure you're about to tell me you've run me through it before."

"That's step one, yes," Vere replied. "Let me see, let me see. Nineteen… when is it again you're going? Ah, yes." He rummaged through a sheaf of papers and nodded. "Off to wardrobe with us." Vere canted his head toward a darkened hallway to the left of the main room and shuffled off. "Benoy left instructions on the style. He's quite the thorough researcher. You'll want to be completely inconspicuous, so we've got to outfit you with things that will work for multiple occupations. *Blend in.* This is not the time to express yourself, as you apparently do in your daily life." Vere nodded with a raised eyebrow at Cob's garish attire.

Cob shrugged, confident in his personal sartorial choices. Spats and velvet were always appropriate these days. The velvet in particular was important, because it tended to make ladies want to touch him.

"Location matters, too, I expect," Cob remarked. The two men were now in a wider hallway with racks of garments on either side. The elbows of Cob's jacket brushed against something dusty that made him stifle a sneeze. "What's formal in Jersey might not be so formal in Paris, y'know?"

"Indeed, indeed." Vere produced a bag from one of the racks. "You've actually used this same suit before for a similar time period, so I hope you haven't drastically changed sizes since then."

Cob took the bag. Black plastic covered the contents, but through the zippered hole in the top he could make out dark wool. "Feels heavy. This stuff gonna slow me down if I have to make a run for it? Is it liable to be too hot?"

"It will be late in the year, when we send you," Vere said. "Nearly wintertime, and decades before the seasonal designations ceased to mean much. You should be quite comfortable."

"Right, the first sighting…well, the bridge collapsed at Christmastime," Cob muttered, more to himself than to Vere. "But it's the south…"

"It's only too warm for that sort of clothing in the *deep* south. You aren't going into Alliance states, after all," Vere said. "Now, get changed and return to the main room. Be quick about it."

Vere returned to his lab, leaving Cob alone.

Christmastime. The folks who had premonitions of the disaster reported having dreams about presents bobbing up and down in the water.

He shut his eyes. That was the part of this trip, this mystery, he didn't like thinking about. It wasn't so much the bridge failure that concerned him, it was what else appeared that strange late autumn and early winter of 1966. Monster hunting was glamorous; a disaster that killed almost fifty people, not so much.

Cob took the dark plastic off the hanger and whistled when he saw the outfit. He imagined this was where some of the myths come from. How many of these dudes in black suits were time travelers?

He stepped out of his crimson trousers and purple jacket, keeping on his plain white dress shirt, and pulled on the replacement clothing. There was a full-length mirror in an attached dressing area, and Cob sauntered over to it as he tightened his necktie. He brushed dust out of his straight dark hair and stroked the three-day growth of scruff that filled the hollows of his cheeks.

Might want to shave. They'll give a lotta side-eye to someone who's not all boring and clean-cut.

In the pocket of the black blazer was a pair of vintage Ray Bans with perfectly opaque lenses. Cob set them on the bridge of his nose and took in the effect.

Man in black. I am an honest-to-goodness man in black. God, this is about as far from inconspicuous as you can get.

He exhaled a short laugh and put the shades back in the jacket pocket.

In the lab, Vere turned dials and tapped the screens of level meters. "You ready, Mister Cob?" he asked.

"Think I need a shave," Cob replied.

Vere cast a quick glance over his shoulder. "Upstairs. Benoy keeps a kit in the smaller lavatory. Miss Moto will show you."

Cob jogged up the winding metal staircase and almost collided with another figure. A feminine voice let out a squeak, and Cob took a step backward.

"I'm so sorry."

"No, my fault, my fault."

Cob blinked, expecting to see that he'd nearly run into Miss Moto, she of the sleek dark hair and excellent hot drink service, but it was someone else. This woman was older than the secretary, though only by a few years, and had shoulder-length platinum hair. She wore some sort of nondescript overalls, liberally streaked with oil or grease along the front, and had a rolled-up blue bandana holding her bangs away from her forehead.

"Damn, my office clearly needs a new IT department if I can hire folks who look like you," Cob remarked before thinking the words through.

"Excuse me?" The woman's pale skin turned rosy.

He shook his head. "Sorry, sorry, I just…you, ah, you work here? I'm looking for the head. The…ah, that sounded gross. The restroom. You an employee?"

"No, I'm a…oh! Are *you* a client?" The woman laughed. "We probably shouldn't be talking. It was in the manual, wasn't it? Or…do you…"

"Right, yes, no. We probably shouldn't be talking," Cob agreed. They both laughed again, and the woman disappeared into the conference room.

I never literally bump into chicks that hot. Wonder where she went.

He found the bathroom on his own and shut the door. On a small shelf mounted above the sink, he spotted a mug of soap and shaving brush. A few more moments' searching revealed a half-empty bag of disposable razors in the medicine cabinet behind the mirror.

Cob wet the brush and placed it in the mug of soap, swirling it around until lather formed. Where would a girl like that need to wear a pair of overalls? And, damn, did she fill 'em out nice. What did she do where she would get all greasy? Based on how she was dressed, maybe she'd been polishing the landing gear of the Spruce Goose. Cob wondered if he'd ever satisfied his curiosity about Amelia Earhart, given all the jaunts he couldn't remember. Were there times he was told a trip wasn't a good choice? They were letting him go to West Virginia, so he must not have learned about this particular mystery already.

Cob imagined red eyes glowing in the dark. He slid the protective plastic off the razor and shaved. Even as he watched the dusting of whiskers disappear from his face, he still imagined those eyes, the wingspan reports cited, a hulking thing stepping out in front of a car…

I have to know.

He rinsed off the razor and thumbed one cheek's worth of hair onto the white porcelain below. How could someone hear a mystery without needing to know the truth, even if the truth is a bunch of bored kids putting on crazy outfits and walking around scaring people in the woods? Puzzles existed to be solved just like mountains existed to be climbed.

Unclimbed mountains like Cob's sudden, desperate need to know whether the woman wore a wedding ring or not…

Or, hell, maybe a ring doesn't matter. Maybe I gotta try anyway…

Cob let the razor clatter into the sink and took a step toward the bathroom door. He imagined the conversation if he caught up to her. "Miss, I know this is crazy, but if you'd like to join me on a little adventure…I'd be happy to pay your way, and then you could get two memory erasures at once. What do you say?"

No. Not a good idea. Not after Elizabeth.

Wait. Elizabeth? Who?

Everything slipped sideways and Rupert Cob crumpled to the floor.

Tuesday, January 14, 1947, Los Angeles, California, USA

A scream. Deafening claps of thunder. A flash of lightning—but no, not lightning, because it kept going, and it was too yellow and it was swinging. Swinging and spinning. It was a light bulb, and it wasn't outside, it was here, in the bathroom, and the bulb was even yellower than a normal bulb because—

Thunk!

Metal into meat. A wet sound, of something being pulled from a sopping pile of rags. That was when the light bulb went yellow, that was when the blood splattered across the wall, the sink, the tiles, the light.

Swinging and spinning, swirling light all around the room…no, not just a room, an apartment. Dirty as hell. Crazy patterns on the walls from the swinging light, light arcing all over the walls making Cob feel like he was on a roller coaster. The screams weren't from joy or thrilling at the lurch of popcorn-filled stomachs leaping over hills and rushing through tunnels. The screams had been from the thing that arced through the air, glinting and dripping. And it was the one person doing the screaming.

Elizabeth.

The man emerged from the bathroom, a smallish half-bath not unlike this one, and he wore a smile smeared with gore, a dazzled and keen glint in his eye. "I got

another bag," he grunted at Cob. "I got another bag, and I can put you in it, too."
A loud banging came from somewhere, maybe in the hall. Was it the police?

Monday, August 9, 2100, Avon, Vermont, NBE

Cob's feet scrabbled at the floor, remembering the need to flee back then but feeling unable to, feeling glued to the dusty floor of the empty apartment, gazing into the eyes of Elizabeth's killer. He'd known, somewhere in the back of his mind, that he must push a button and get to the site where he could disappear back to safety, back to something…what? Where? He couldn't remember. He only knew his palms sweated against the floor, the sawdust gritty and hard beneath his skin.

The hardness was what brought him to something like sanity again. The floor was something solid, something to hold onto, and it was real. The banging in the hall continued. Cob sat up, his breath rapid and catching in his throat, leaving him choking and sputtering. He blinked hard. Tears streamed down his face, and he felt a squeezing, gripping tightness in his chest. The banging still kept on; that was real, that was now, he understood through the terror of the memory.

"Mister Cob? Mister Cob, are you quite all right?"

No. No, I'm not quite all right, because I can remember parts of my last trip. I shouldn't be able to remember. That wasn't part of the contract.

BANG BANG BANG.

"Mister Cob! Kris, get the tool kit. Mister Cob, I'm afraid I'm going to have to take the door off if you can't reply. Sir, are you ill? Did you—oh, thank you. No, it looks like…oh, blast it, how do we get to the hinges with these covers on?"

A feminine voice, farther off, said something too muffled for Cob to understand.

"Okay, yes, sounds good. You know everything, Kris. Bring over that chair."

Cob struggled to calm his breathing and heart. He swallowed and scrambled to his feet. A glance in the mirror revealed that his face was still only half-shaven.

"Whoa, hold it still, please. Hand me the screwdriver. No, the flat head."

At the sound of metal against metal, Cob shook his head hard and squared his shoulders. He shoved aside the image of the long, pale arm resting in a pool of blood.

Focus, man. Act like a person. Pull it together. You're Rupert fucking Cob, you have a crap ton of money, and you are the bravest bastard you know. Act like it.

Cob knocked on the inside of the door. "Hey, it's okay, I'm okay!" he called.

On the other side of the door, he heard shuffling and a sliding like heavy furniture being moved. Cob depressed the locking mechanism beside the doorknob and turned it.

"Sorry, sorry," he said, trying to smile at the concerned faces of Mister Jonson and Miss Moto. "I, uh, had something for lunch that…" Cob let his voice trail off and widened his eyes in mock terror and puffed out his cheeks. He made a vague gesture at his abdomen. "Just workin' through it, if you catch my drift. I'll just be a sec." He shut the door again and leaned over the sink.

Bad lunch indeed.

The pool of blood once again invaded his memory. His hand trembling, Cob picked up the abandoned razor and finished shaving.

~

"Benoy, should we discuss Mister Cob's condition upon his last return?"

Ben cupped his head in one hand, his eyes scanning his ledgers. This was always comforting, this examining of the ever-increasing income. Don't worry about morals, don't worry about whether various people were alive or dead, just worry about the money.

"No." Ben kept looking at the ledgers, turning page after page of neatly inked black columns. "Besides, what condition do you mean? Emotional?"

Vere sat across from Ben. "He was in good spirits after the memory erasure. He didn't bring anything dangerous back with him. He behaved well upon intake today. But that was a close call, if you'll remember, and he was veritably covered in blood—"

"He wanted to know what happened," Ben interrupted. "He told us. He just got too…" Ben looked up at Vere. "I don't know, too *near*. It's one thing to say you want to know who killed somebody. You can do that a little more sneakily. What Cob did still got him the answers he wanted but, yeah, it was risky."

"I'm surprised you wanted to take him on again," Vere said, "given that risk-taking nature of his. And after we had to send a team after Brimley Wheat—"

"We're not talking about Wheaton," Ben said. "He's dead, isn't he?"

Vere nodded.

It was one thing to imagine it, Ben realized, but it was quite another to have confirmation. "Wait, wait, wait." Ben lowered his voice and leaned forward. "You *know* he's dead?"

Vere raised one silver-streaked eyebrow. "That was what we decided upon," he replied, his voice cold. He rose. "There's much to do with both Mister Cob and Miss Lessep. I suggest you tear yourself away from your precious bank accounts and join us for the latter's debriefing." Vere half turned away. "That is, if you still care about your precious historical knowledge after all."

Ben bowed his head. "That's *all* I care about," he said. "You know me better than to suggest that I don't—"

But as Ben looked back up, Vere was already gone.

On Cob's way back to the lab, he passed a sitting room whose doors were open before but were now firmly shut. They were pocket doors, well worn from centuries of sliding in and out of the walls. Though they were latched together at their center point, a sliver of light fell across the hallway floorboards. Every few seconds, laughter erupted through that thin gap.

Cob held his breath and tiptoed forward to peek.

There was the woman, now out of her mechanic's uniform, sitting in front of a roaring fire telling the others a story. A cat was silhouetted sitting near her on the carpet, looking up at her as if paying attention to her words. The woman's eyes flashed with eagerness and excitement, and her gestures were grand and demonstrative. When she stood to act out a part of her tale, Cob could see that she now wore a smart, practical pantsuit, not unlike the men-in-black attire he himself sported. An ID badge swung from her left lapel, but with her back to the fire, the light behind her, Cob couldn't make out what it said.

"And then he was gone, parachute and everything," the woman said. Her audience erupted in wild applause.

"I can't believe it," Miss Moto said. Cob now saw that she was reclining on the floor in what appeared to be a very uncomfortably complicated posture. "Seriously, that is the last person I would have suspected."

"I know," the other woman agreed.

Someone was shuffling toward the pocket doors, and Cob scooted out of sight and down the corridor toward the kitchen. He didn't look back but instead hurried straight down to the lab as he was originally supposed to.

He was gone...parachute...last person they would have suspected...

The woman's ID badge was blue ink on a white field.

Cob had no further time to ponder these clues before Doctor Vere trundled down the stairs. "Ready to go find the Mothman, Mister Cob?"

"Ready as I'll ever be, doc."

"Have a seat there." Vere nodded toward a round metal stool. He picked up a flat clear object with a pair of tweezers. "Hold out your left palm."

Cob obliged. "Is this the retrieval device?"

"Yes," Vere replied. "This might hurt a bit." He set the object on Cob's palm, and as soon as the material touched his skin it sank into it. A sharp, liquid feeling shot through Cob's veins, followed by a twinge and cramping in his hand. He gasped and made a fist against the pain, but Vere grabbed his hand and held it open.

"It'll just be a second, son. You can get through it. If you close your hand around it, the button might migrate too deep into your tissue. That makes it hard to activate in an emergency." Vere held Cob's fingers together and placed his other hand on Cob's shoulder. "It's all right. I know it's quite unpleasant."

The pain sharpened. "Gah!" Cob clamped his mouth shut, fearing he'd cry if he let himself. "Hoo, man. That is…wow." Unbidden, little tears trickled out from the corners of both eyes. "Damn, doc, that sucks a *lot*." The pain lessened, and Cob could see his skin was smooth and unbroken. No one would have guessed that something just slid through it. A moment later, Cob felt fine once again.

"Flex it a bit," Vere instructed.

Cob obliged. The hand moved freely, but he could feel a knot under his skin, as if he'd suffered a minor sprain.

"Is it numb?" Vere asked.

"A little."

"That will subside even more over the next few hours," Vere said. "Now, I need you to press the center of your palm…"

Cob did so, and a small device on Vere's table vibrated.

"Very good, son," Vere said, picking up the device. He pressed a button on it. "Look at your hand, then."

On Cob's palm, there was now a faint red X.

"When you see that, you want to search for the same marking in your surroundings," Vere instructed. "It will be roughly the same spot where you arrived, though it may be slightly off if there is something blocking the original spot, or if the climate is too damp to allow the necessary electricity to flow. The system will locate the nearest usable location. If you wind up off a bit, you'll return—" Vere gestured around the room. "Well, you might not return right on the drive plate, but rather somewhere else within the building."

Cob chuckled. "Anybody ever land on the roof?"

Vere gave Cob a stern look. "We expect you within the time frame we discussed," Vere said. "So. Any other questions?"

"I can't interfere, right?"

"No. So this is not the time to think about preventing the Silver Bridge from collapsing, Mister Cob. Unfortunately, those poor souls are gone, and there's nothing to be done without causing tremendous paradoxes."

Cob shrugged. "I mean, it sucks, I'm not saying I love that that happened or anything, but that's not what I'm going back there for."

"You want to know what the creature was, the cryptid that seemed to portend the accident," Vere said.

"Yup," Cob said. "It could be an alien, it could be a kid playing a prank…"

"You realize the going theory is a barn owl or a sand hill crane, do you not?"

"No matter what, I just gotta know."

"You are one of our most frequent clients," Vere said, "so yes, I am well acquainted with your insatiable need to know various things." Vere snapped his fingers and scurried to a desk across the room. "Almost forgot." He withdrew a small cloth bag from a drawer, scrabbled around inside for a moment, and then produced a money clip with a small clutch of cash in it. "Era-appropriate currency," Vere said. "Try not to spend it if you can help it. Emergencies only. It's antique. We're starting to run out." Vere handed the money to Cob, who shoved it into his right front trouser pocket.

Vere pointed to a low metal platform in the corner of the lab. "On you go."

Cob wondered again. The murder flickering in his memory…what were these other things he'd come here to learn?

"Doc, is there any way I could ever…uh…"

"Mister Cob, we're on a very tight schedule here." Vere was glaring at him. "Get on the plate, sir. I won't ask again."

Cob nodded.

Later. I can figure it out later. Maybe offer 'em lots of coin when I get back if they'd let me keep one memory. Just one. If this ends up being a good one, I'd rather keep this than the blood and terror and pain and stuff.

The murderer had worn pinstripe trousers held up with suspenders, underneath which he'd had just a blood-smeared tank top that had once been white. He had slicked-back hair and crazy eyes…the apartment was abandoned; it hadn't been hers, Cob knew somehow. No, Elizabeth lived—

There was that name again. Elizabeth. *Who was Elizabeth?*

Elizabeth lived with…friends? In—

"I'm rooming near the Florentine Gardens." The voice was musical, low and husky with a kind of lilting quality to it. Cigarette smoke swirled around her black hair. *"Do you know it? The owner…he's kind of a creep, but he lets me stay at his joint for practically nothing."*

Cob dragged his attention back to the present.

Focus. You can worry about that later. If the memories come back, you got plenty of time to worry about them then. You got other stuff to do now.

"Bon voyage, Mister Cob," Vere said. "See you soon."

Cob gave Vere a little salute. His hand exploded in pain again, and he doubled over. His vision swam. One second he was staring at the scratched metal of the time machine's drive plate, and the next everything went black.

Sunday, November 27, 1966, Point Pleasant, West Virginia, USA

"Mister? You all right?" Someone shook Cob.

He coughed and blinked up into the brown eyes of a small boy. The boy relaxed and let go of Cob.

"Thank God," the boy said. He wasn't quite a teenager and had the scrawny, underfed look of a kid on the brink of a growth spurt. He wore a tee shirt with contrasting piping along the collar and sleeves and a ball cap with a cartoon of a knight's silver helmet on it. "You need me to call the doctor? I think he's havin' his lunch just in the coffee shop there." The boy pointed across the intersection at a cheery brick building. In the window, carefully painted red letters spelled out JOHN'S DINER.

"Nah, I'm okay." Cob flexed his hand; the cramping and pain were gone. He took a long, deep breath.

The air smelled oily, hot, and full of sharp tar.

EPA doesn't exist yet. Car emissions not so good. People are probably smoking everywhere.

The crumpled butts on the sidewalks confirmed part of that. His eyes watered, and the sun shone bright, right overhead. He pulled the Ray Bans out of his pocket. "Thanks, kid. I owe ya." He got to his feet and fished around in his pocket. Vere hadn't given him any coins, so a dollar would have to do. "Here, buy yourself a… malted? Is that what you guys like these days?"

The boy regarded the dollar with awe. "Wow, sir, I could get about three of 'em with this. Thanks." He snatched the bill from Cob's hand and hurried off to a bicycle lying on the corner.

Cars flanked both sides of the street, all late 1950s and early 1960s models of various mid- and low-priced varieties. No imports, nothing brand new.

Cob mused over the kid's hat for a moment until he spotted a sign in one of the storefront windows. He walked closer. The hardware store was closed, which meant it must be Sunday based on the hours listed on the door. A blue and white mimeographed flyer proclaimed that AT DUNMORE'S HARDWARE, WE'RE CHEERING ON THE KNIGHTS AND YOU SHOULD TOO! There was the same cartoon knight helmet, beneath which were the dates of the regional football playoffs in nearby Ravenswood. WATCH THE KNIGHTS FLATTEN THE DEVILS!

Cob grinned. Sports used to be important in little towns like this. This was a time Cob only knew from history books and the ramblings of his great-grandmother Annie; she'd recorded a vlog in her youth that he'd watched growing up. Annie's high school days weren't much earlier than this.

"Time was people didn't talk politics."

Cob remembered from one of her videos; he remembered that she'd had his same dark hair, cherub face, and blue eyes.

"I never cared what others thought, so long as they were kind about it."

He walked a little farther and found almost no businesses open but similar signs advertising the football game. He passed a record store, a pet shop with eager puppies bouncing in a pen in the front window—Cob entertained a dark thought that all the dogs were now long dead—and a shoe repair shop, the counter piled high with ladies' pumps. Every person he passed tipped his hat or nodded at him, and Cob again remembered Grandma Annie's stories of the mid-twentieth century.

"It only got worse later, the divisiveness. That's the thing this war and its aftermath have managed to get right, since Empiricists are so much nicer to each other at least."

Cob wound his way back to the corner he'd first awoken on, the corner near the coffee shop. Good a place to start as any.

You're not here for nostalgia.

Cob crossed the street to John's Diner.

You're here to find a monster.

~

The interior of the diner was dingier than Cob imagined. Inside, he found a checkerboard floor, smoky air, and Paul Simon on the jukebox plaintively insisting that a rock feels no pain.

Three men sat at the counter—two were heavyset, and all had a cigarette in one hand and a cup of coffee in the other. Pie slices in various states of consumption sat on white plates in front of each of them. A willowy waitress—no uniform, just a plaid shirt with fringed pockets and a nametag reading "Peggy"—looked up when the bell on the door jingled.

"Anywhere you like." Her voice was husky and her smile gentle. Her dark blond hair fell in soft curls down past her shoulders. On a black-and-white TV behind her, cardboard UFOs sailed in front of a painted sky.

Cob smiled. He wanted to do more than smile, because Peggy's big light eyes and full mouth reminded him of the woman he'd grown infatuated with at the travel agency.

Oh, hell, who was he kidding? She was a *woman*, and women piqued his interest, period. She was a woman in a roomful of men who likely also saw something appealing in her gently world-weary look and tall, slim figure, so Cob figured he was just another poor sap being pulled into her fan club.

Besides, he reminded himself, getting up to funny business back in the past was the best way to fuck things up.

Don't accidentally become your own grandpa and all that jazz.

Cob plunked himself down at the counter, a few stools away from the other men. Close enough to hear their conversations, but far enough to go unnoticed.

"Think they'll take it?" one man—white-haired and bearded—asked another.

"Hell, no—'scuse me, Miss Peggy—but the team ain't been worth a lick since Shad Williams graduated."

The first man chuckled. "The Williams boy graduated back in sixty-four."

"And that's the last time they were any good," the second man replied. He was younger, perhaps in his forties, with short curly hair and a beakish nose. Something about him looked familiar to Cob.

Was he one of the guys who saw it? Did I see his picture in one of the books I read for research?

A man to the left of Beak Nose took a long drag on his cigarette. "You passin' through town?" he asked, eyes narrowed on Cob. He was younger than the first man, older than the second, with steel-gray hair and horn-rimmed spectacles. "Don't think I seen you 'round here 'fore."

"Oh, leave a man in peace, Clement," Peggy said. She came over to Cob's side of the counter. "What can I get ya? Got some nice fruit pie these boys are too unrefined to try. Coffee's fresh, too."

"Pie sounds fine, ma'am," Cob replied, trying to affect the hint of Southern accent he heard in the other men's voices. "And I'll take some of that coffee, too."

Peggy slid a black plastic ashtray and a set of silverware wrapped in a paper napkin at him. "Back in a jiff." She disappeared through the batwing doors separating the kitchen from the counter.

"Clement, you know what they say 'bout curiosity and cats," Beak Nose said. He turned to Cob. "Gotta apologize for him, sir. My older brother's a rude one. You'd think we was raised in a barn."

"You was, Bob," Clement muttered. "He ain't my brother. He's my *step-*brother, and that step's a steep one."

The white-haired man laughed. "Will you two cease? Heaven's sake, this boy will think everybody in Point Pleasant's got a terrible sense of humor."

Cob couldn't help but join in the white-haired man's laughter. "Nah, I suspect that isn't so," he replied.

"So you don't *know*," Clement said, chuckling. "Ain't from here. You a salesman?"

This was what he'd been dreading. The cover story seemed flimsy. He didn't want to use it, but it was in the instructions: *Do not deviate from historical accuracy. Stick to the plan. Don't make the details too hard to remember, but don't divulge details about your own life, the future, or the agency.*

72

The last few bits were easier. It didn't seem difficult to not tell people about the future, the agency, or time travel. Remembering everything he'd devised in consultation with Ben Jonson and also not deviating from historical accuracy... that would all be much more difficult, if for no other reason than the fallibility of the human mind. He couldn't know and remember every little thing, could he?

Have I before? I must have. And if it had gone horribly awry on an earlier trip, they wouldn't have let me go again.

Cob saw the light bulb swinging on its chain, covered in blood. *That* couldn't have been according to plan...

"Henry Condell," Cob said. He plastered on a grin. "Not in sales, in reporting. Work for a rag over in Raleigh. We're just starting, don't even have a masthead yet."

Was that right? Or was it "mastfront"? What did that even mean? Crap, I'm not fooling them.

Cob's mind raced, but he maintained his composure. "I, uh, heard there was some local color this way."

Peggy was back now, carrying a plate of something red and crumbly. "First one's free," she said in that honeyed voice. "Especially for those just passin'."

"Naw, he's not just on his way somewhere more interesting, Peg. He's out for the kinda ink that smells of blood." The white-haired man chortled. "You hear about our celebrity here, Mister Condell?" He jerked a thumb at Bob, whose face turned crimson. "Go on, son. He must be the last man in six counties ain't heard tell of it."

"It's nothing, John," Bob said, suddenly very interested in ashing his cigarette. "Skip it."

"My brother's a goddamn psychic now," Clement announced.

"Got nothing to do with being psychic," John said. "It's like our own personal Sasquatch. You don't gotta be special to see one of them hairy apes, do ya, Clem?"

"Oh, so I'm not even special now?" Bob's tone was almost lighthearted, but Cob could see embarrassment in his eyes, and that beak nose was still tinged with the blush of shame. It couldn't be easy seeing a monster in these parts and having to live it down.

"I do human interest stories. Don't have one in particular I'm chasing," Cob lied. "But, sir, you saw a creature, did you?"

Bob shook his head. "Naw. And I don't wanna be in papers neither. Sorry, man, but I'm just sick of talking."

"Maybe Lyla don't feel similar, brother," Clement said.

Bob shot him a hard glare before turning back to Cob. "Don't go talking to my wife without me, Mister Condell." He studied each man in turn. The air grew heavy. Bob took a long sip of coffee.

"If you keep my name and hers outta things," Bob finally said, "we'll give you the scoop."

~

"I wanna go out there," Cob said.

"To TNT? Man, *no*," Bob said with a shake of his head. "Nobody's been going out there, not after what we saw."

"It's too dangerous," Lyla agreed. She was a slight woman with a long nose not unlike her husband's.

Even the people out here look like birds. Maybe I'm chasing a giant owl that inbreeds with the population.

"Look, I know you folks don't know me from Adam, but this is a story and I gotta chase it," Cob insisted. "I'm a journalist, after all." His mouth felt awkward around the cover story lies. "Now, if you won't drive me, can you tell me where to rent a car?"

Bob agreed to drop him at a place nearby renting moving vans by the hour, and it would have to do. "Sunday and all," Bob explained. "Sundays, a feller can't get so much as a glass of beer or a decent steak or nothin', let alone a car."

"That'll be fine, sir."

Cob walked the remaining few feet, studying the hastily sketched map of what Bob Scornbury called "The TNT area."

"Used to make bombs for the war," Bob explained.

Cob wanted to tell him such details were unnecessary. He'd studied up on the former site of the West Virginia Ordinance Works, as it was there most sightings of the Mothman originated. One theory he kept stumbling across in his research postulated the creature resulted from old chemical leakage, causing mutation in local fauna. Decades after the sightings ceased, environmental protection entities found contaminants in the water supply seeping from the area, and they went into containment and cleanup mode soon after.

Probably exposing myself to ten types of carcinogens.

Cob approached the storefront. The stenciled letters in the window read ZANE'S MOVING AND STORAGE and confirmed beneath that "we rent vans."

The man behind the counter—presumably Zane—looked up as Cob entered. "Help ya?" He looked enough like John, the diner denizen, that Cob wondered if they were brothers.

"Need a van," Cob replied. "Got cash."

"How long?" The man eyed Cob up and down.

Cob itched to get to the site before dark and no longer felt like talking. He dropped cash on the counter, hoping his money did the explaining for him.

"Pleasure doin' business with ya, sir." Worn green bills made Zane warm up to a man. He slid a set of keys across the counter. "White vee-dub in space thirteen out back. Bring it back full by ten."

Cob smiled and touched his right index finger to his hairline in a little salute.

The "white vee-dub" turned out to be a split-front microbus, the first import Cob saw all day, and he whistled when he saw it. It was dirty, sure, but it was a classic, bringing to mind ancient episodes of whimsical 1970s-era family sitcoms. If he didn't have to return the thing, Cob would've liked nothing more than to clean it up and paint giant red daisies all over it.

Cob climbed in behind the wheel, noting the rear seats were gone to allow renters to haul furniture. A rusty dolly covered with a pale blue felt blanket sat near the back door. He turned the ignition, disappointed to see that the horizon had grown dark and the first hint of the moon shone.

The roads to the TNT area didn't have much in the way of streetlights, and the few Cob did see flickered, their glow sodium-pink and weak. Fortunately the van's headlights were bright enough that between them and the moonlight, Cob managed fine.

He glanced down at the map for an instant, knowing he was coming up on the area, only to shriek when he looked back up. Right in the middle of the road was a furry shape and two pinpoints of red several feet above it.

Cob slammed on his brakes and threw the van into park. His breath was gone, and he felt a surge of panic rise up in his chest.

The shape was dark, taller than the top of the van, and the pinpoints of red light were roughly where the creature—if it *was*, indeed, a creature—would have had its eyes. Cob opened the van door, careful not to scare the thing, and as he did he heard a wet flap and rustle, as of a heavy mop moving from bucket to floor. A pair of huge wings, membranous to the point of being almost transparent was silhouetted in the van's high beams. It was like looking through the ear of a housecat and seeing tiny veins here and there, only these veins were gray instead of reddish, which led Cob to wonder what sort of blood coursed through this being.

If any.

The face was indistinct, just a dark mass with the red, red eyes. So red... *too* red, Cob noticed, as if they were tiny laser pointers. And it wasn't, as some of his research suggested, that they were being reflected in his headlights and casting back a reddish tint, the sort of eyes seen on opossums or even raccoons or albino squirrels. No, these eyes were actually *producing* light, little beams cutting through and leaving dots of red bouncing back on the VW's windshield.

Dammit. Why don't I have a camera?

75

Because that was evidence. Because this wasn't about evidence but the experience. Experience gone unrecorded even by his own brain. Cob felt a mixture of sorrow and panic, a fluttery pain rushing through his chest.

There was a rumbling off behind the creature, like another vehicle approaching from the direction of the abandoned Works site. Cob glanced beyond the thing and, even though he thought he was keeping it in his peripheral vision, when he refocused his attention back on it, it was gone.

The mop sound came again, farther away, and Cob imagined the flap of huge batwings. Nearby, an animal shrieked, a bloodcurdling sound unlike any animal in pain Cob ever heard. Something about it sounded almost as if a child were being tortured.

With an exhale, Cob fell back against the driver's side headlight of the van. He sank down a little so his butt hugged the edge of the front bumper, and he felt a distinct urge to weep.

No, come back. Let me see you again.

He scanned the skies, searching for any sign of the thing.

Nothing.

And so, after willing his breathing to calm, Cob trundled back into the van and pulled it deeper into the TNT area. He came to a spot off the road and turned the headlights off.

The distant vehicle noise sounded again, and Cob got out of the van. No car, no truck, nothing.

Nothing? It's fall, but it's not winter. There's nothing nothing, not just no Mothman or other car. Where's the breeze? Where's the crickets or birds or even a dog in the distance?

There were several low granite tunnel entrances across a field littered with rusting equipment parts, and from one of the tunnel entrances there came a groaning sound, like ancient metal being moved on seldom-used hinges. The groaning turned to a squeak and then a squeal, and then a different figure emerged into the moonlight. It wasn't the Mothman; it was smaller, though still taller than Cob himself.

Cob blinked, and somehow the van's headlights were back on, the figure now standing right in front of him instead of being several feet away.

His skin was fish pale, and he wore round spectacles with dark lenses. His nose reminded Cob of Bob Scornbury, but it was longer, thinner, even more beaklike and hawkish. And he was thinner all over, cadaverously so, in fact. Still, the combination of height, slenderness, and pallor was striking, as was the fact that the man wore a suit identical to Cob's own.

"You scared me," Cob said, hoping the man was at best a Point Pleasant resident out monster-hunting and at worst was another of Ben Jonson's clients, perhaps from earlier than Cob or later, but it would explain the generic attire.

No, it's not all generic. Those glasses aren't something you'd see now or even in the twenty-second century, not really, and why would someone wear them at night?

"Did I?"

Cob heard the man's words, but didn't see his mouth move. He drew back, pressing himself closer against the van. "Who are you, mister? Whatcha doin' out here?"

"Whatcha doin' out here?"

It was Cob's voice coming back to his ears, and again the man's mouth wasn't moving.

The mop sound. Cob felt woozy. He slumped down to the ground, where he clutched the grass and vomited.

When he lifted his head, the slender man was gone.

Of course. That's how this works. Nausea. Men in black—not all of whom are me, apparently—and this fucking place. All bunkers and dangerous chemicals and...

And the Mothman. He'd seen it. *He had seen it.* Even if he never saw it again, never got to figure out what it was, Rupert Cob got to see the actual Mothman live and in person, a cryptid whose last recorded sighting was a century before his own birth.

This really happened. And no amount of mindwiping, failure to get to the heart of the matter, or creepy intimidating people could take that away from him.

Cob wondered how many times he'd thought similar things, how many times he'd seen—

—*"I can put you in the bag, but I gotta chop ya up a little first, you understand, don'tcha, boy?"*—

How many times he'd seen something, understood something, experienced something and felt similarly, felt excitement and a soaring sense of pride at being able to witness it, even if sometimes he was too late to—

—*"What did you do with her? With Elizabeth?"*—

He planted his hands on the van's bumper and struggled to his feet.

Without thinking, Cob walked toward the tunnel from which the man had emerged. The moon hid behind a cloud, and shadows clung to that part of the TNT area. Even the van's headlights didn't quite cut through the gloom this far. Cob stayed quiet, as quiet as he could in dress shoes and loose-fitting trousers that brushed with a swishing sound against every area of taller grass. He felt his tractionless shoes slide out from underneath him as he stepped on a patch of earth that was more mud than dirt, but by tightening his abdomen and holding his arms out like airplane wings, Cob was able to steady himself once more.

He stood at the mouth of the tunnel. It was taller than he'd thought, seeing it from a distance, a black circle cut into concrete that gaped a good fourteen feet from top to bottom. From deep within the tunnel, Cob could almost make out the faint sound of water running.

These don't go to any kind of river. I've seen the maps of these things. They're supposed to be just bunkers where the explosions were tested. How is there water back there?

Cob stepped toward the middle of the entrance and tried to peer into the blackness. Nothing. Not even the faintest hint of light. It was as if light itself crawled into this tunnel and died—

No, not just died. This place murders light.

— *"Is that her name? She's happier now. She was a bad girl, that one."*—

Light doesn't want to die here. It doesn't come here when it feels the end is nigh. It's dragged here, kicking and screaming and begging for its life. And someone—

— *"I'm rooming near the Florentine Gardens. The owner is kind of a creep."*—

Someone drags the light here and beats and tortures and kills it.

Cob's shoe brushed against something yielding and noxious, something that wouldn't let go of the black patent leather once it held it. He looked down.

His foot was embedded in the stomach of a dead dog. The clouds parted, moonlight streamed down into the muck and fog to reveal the canine's face frozen in a rictus scream of terror.

Cob's own scream—this one audible and real—rose to a high-pitched keening on the night wind.

Tuesday, January 14, 1947, Los Angeles, California, USA

"He's kind of a creep, but he lets me stay at his joint for practically nothing."

Elizabeth took a drag of her cigarette. It was Turkish, the paper brown with a gold filter at one end, the cherry glowing darker than a bland old American cigarette would, and the smoke that wafted toward Cob was less a smoke and more a perfume, the smell of incense soap, the combination beautifully apt, given Elizabeth's exquisite beauty and bearing. She was a princess, Snow White and Rose Red writ large and real and fleshy, and princesses deserved beautiful, exotic things from every corner of the globe. Cob wanted to bury his face in that perfumed glossy hair, to kiss those full lips that he imagined tasted of clove and wine.

Something nagged at his brain, however, even as they sat and laughed and flirted. Something dark and foreboding and...

That creep. The club owner. Elizabeth shouldn't be renting a room from him. No good would come of it. But why was that? Cob knew it had something to do with who she was, why he knew her even before he knew her, why her name and voice and hair...

"Flower for the lady?" A young man sauntered up to their barstools with a basket of flowers, all sorts, the stems cut short. "She'd look lovely, all that dark hair, with a flower."

"Oh, please, baby? I'd love that." Elizabeth crushed out her cigarette and smiled at Cob. Off on the stage, the band laid into a new number, hotter than the last, and the kids got up for a try at the Lindy hop. Skirts swirled, shoes seemed to touch the very sky. Girls squealed as their partners tossed them over broad shoulders and between legs spread wide.

Sunday, November 27, 1966, Point Pleasant, West Virginia, USA

Cob woke up with a start. Already rattled, he screamed again when his eyes settled on the dead dog. Scooting away, he looked around, still feeling and seeing the old nightclub.

But this wasn't 1947 Los Angeles. This was 1966 Point Pleasant. And there were monsters afoot.

How did I know where and when that was? Cob shook his head, clearing cobwebs. *I thought of her before, back...Elizabeth...*

No. It didn't matter now. Now what mattered was—

There was something above him, something in the tree. Cob looked up and saw red pinpoints of light fixed on him. There was a screeching as of multiple owls, all crying in different tones at once.

"There you are," Cob told the creature.

The wings spread once more and this time he saw it take flight, saw it scrunch up its enormous body like a spring coiling, then stretch out, arms forward.

It soared, glided, slid and cut across the air like it was nothing, like it wasn't taller than the tallest man and heavier, certainly. It was an effortless thing, like swimming, floating. Just a few flaps of the wings were all it took to keep itself aloft.

"Christ, what a sight," Cob muttered.

It didn't jerk about like a moth, despite its nickname; it soared with beautiful effortlessness. He continued to stare until the thing got too close to the edge of the clearing. Not wanting to lose sight of it, he made chase, keeping his eyes pinned not on the land ahead but on the sky.

Even as he stared at the dark shape passing the face of the moon, the nightclub came back, a fuzzy overlay to the stars and the creature. He saw himself paying the flower man a nickel, saw the man then give Elizabeth her flower. It was pink with a cheery yellow center.

The flower floated over the moon, a pink orb over a silver one.

The Mothman dipped behind a copse of trees and was gone again. Cob cursed and looked around for the VW. "Shit shit shit." It was too far back in the TNT area, which now almost seemed miles away. Cob was pretty quick for an amateur, but he couldn't run two miles in less than ten minutes.

He looked back to the sky. The Mothman was gone, but the pink flower still hung there, as if projected onto a screen.

Elizabeth pressed the flower to her nose. "Dahlia," she said, taking in its scent. "My favorite."

Cob jogged again, shoving away the half-dreamed memories, pressing onward in the direction he thought the Mothman must've flown. But just as he thought he should be nearing a wooded area, the ground ahead was clear of trees and shrubbery, and the light was different, paler.

It was no longer late at night. It was dusk. And this was an open field.

He spun around, expecting to see the TNT area behind him, but instead it was more field.

Field, everywhere. Empty and open and green. Tidy. A few flowers sprinkled throughout. No trees. No shrubs.

But, overhead, a dozen Mothmen sailed through the air.

Tuesday, August 10, 2100, Avon, Vermont, NBE

Ben flung his jacket at a startled Kris as he ran to the spiral stairs leading to the lab. "Get the medical kit!" he shouted. "Get water and a blanket!"

Vere's call from the basement level came less than a minute earlier. The client was back, and he was in bad shape. The retrieval wasn't due for another few hours. This was the second time Rupert Cob returned from a trip a little worse for wear, and now Ben was convinced Cob would be the first entry on the company's "no more trips" list.

They'd always had an idea such a thing might be necessary. Injury was the usual thing they worried about, injury of body or mind or both, and of course a stunt like what Brimley Wheaton pulled would get you on a different sort of list you'd never get off of.

He was still rolling up his sleeves when he reached the bottom step. Vere stood there in his shabby lab coat and reading glasses doing something Ben never saw him do—comforting another human being.

"It's all right, son. There, there. You're perfectly intact. Do you want me to ask Miss Moto for some tea?" Vere's low voice soothed like a midnight radio newscast from the continent.

Beside him, perched on the edge of a metal stool, was Cob. The client was still wearing the clothes they'd sent him off in, but they were disheveled and dirty. His necktie was gone, as was one shoe.

"Mister Cob, thank God." Ben was at the client's side, Kris flying down the stairs after him.

"Here." Kris put down the first aid kit and wrapped Cob in a gray wool blanket. "Mister Cob, I'm just going to take some vitals, okay?" Kris took a few small instruments from the first aid kit, and a moment later she'd placed a thermometer beneath Cob's tongue.

"What happened, son? What made you activate your return chip early?" Vere asked.

Cob shook his head. "They were everywhere. I...I don't..." The young man blinked and frowned. "It's all gone now," he murmured. "I remembered...I remembered *everything*, but now it's all gone. They...who? Someone made me come back." He shook his head. "I'm sorry, doc, I have no idea what happened."

"You had to have pressed the chip," Vere said. "You got to the retrieval site. You *wanted* to come back. No one could have made you come back."

Ben looked at Vere until the older man returned his gaze. "We should let Kris tend to him, check his blood pressure and stuff," Ben said, canting his head toward the stairs. "Help me get him some tea."

Vere patted Cob on the shoulder. "Let Miss Moto know what you need, Mister Cob." He followed Ben upstairs to the kitchen.

To Ben's surprise, Vere filled up the teakettle once they were upstairs. "I didn't think we were going to actually make him tea," Ben remarked.

"Two birds," Vere replied. "Besides, you promise a man a cup of tea and you return without one? Terrible and suspicious, don't you think, Benoy?"

Ben opened a cupboard and took out a silver tea ball, a canister of loose-leaf chamomile, and a small cup. "How long after he escaped did the...the *cleaners* get to Wheaton?" he asked. He sifted a teaspoonful of tea into the bell and placed the bell in the cup.

"Not long," Vere replied. He ignited the flame on one of the burners of the stove and set the kettle atop it. "Why? What are you thinking?"

"I'm not sure," Ben said.

Vere adjusted the flame beneath the teakettle. It flared and whooshed, licking the edges of the silver metal.

Sunday, November 27, 1966, Point Pleasant, West Virginia, USA

The slender man emerged from the tunnel and quietly observed Rupert Cob chase the Mothman. Once the transfer to the Beta universe occurred, he got into the rented van and drove it to the motel.

A middle-aged woman met him at the front desk. "Did he go?" she asked.

The man nodded.

"Where is he now?"

"He's still there." When he spoke to the woman, he did so normally, no longer employing the time shift tricks he did to Cob to make it seem as if he were communicating telepathically. "I'll send him back to his present in a bit, after I've had some dinner."

The woman smiled. "The foods of this time are nuts, man. I could get you a Salisbury steak in a half an hour."

"Oh, Miss Fallon," the man said, "you are far too easily impressed. I have a bit of something upstairs."

She nodded to the man, and he proceeded down the hall to the elevator.

Once inside his room, the man withdrew a microcassette recorder and spoke into it as he made a sandwich. "The interdimensional crossings work best with someone who's time traveled before," he said. "Subject W, whom I intercepted from Jonson's set of *vacationers*—" At this word, the man paused in his food preparations. "This Subject RC proved to be the ideal candidate. It took almost nothing to send him to Beta." He chuckled as he spread a thick line of jam on a slice of white bread. "I can only hope the creatures don't decide he looks tasty."

The man studied his knife. It was covered in crimson liquid. Claudio shivered as he licked it clean.

Part III: The Cleaners

We count our joys not by what we have, but by what kept us from that perfect thing.
–Paul Laurence Dunbar

Tuesday, August 10, 2100, Avon, Vermont, NBE

The signal reached Alison's ear as she washed a dish. It was such a foreign sound, something she'd only trained for, that at first she didn't remember what it was and feared she was having a stroke. As it went on, however, her preparations kicked in and she dropped the bowl and dishcloth into the sink and dashed across the room to her husband.

"Did you get it, too?"

He nodded and patted his jacket pocket.

"Is it loaded?" Alison pressed.

Her husband sighed and withdrew the pistol, checking its chamber. "Yes. Check in with Vere, and let's go."

Alison opened the left cupboard of the dining room buffet and took out a telephone. It was partly ancient, partly not, and powered up by turning a crank at the rear of the unit. She lifted the handset and pressed her thumb to a glossy panel where a rotary dial might have been a century and a half earlier.

"Doctor? We got the signal." She listened for a moment. "Send his picture." The glossy panel on the phone shifted to show a portly man with dark hair. Beneath the image was the name "Brimley Wheaton." Alison placed her thumb over the man's face, and a three-inch square piece of paper slid out of the bottom of the phone with the photograph printed on its surface. "Last seen?"

In the room behind her, Alison's husband scurried about sliding switchblades into hidden recesses of his clothing. He then proceeded to withdraw Alison's gun from its hiding place in the right cupboard of the buffet. As Alison listened to Doctor Vere's instructions, she idly wondered when the last time she'd shot the thing was.

Back in Ohio. So long ago, yet not quite so long as it ought to have been.

The gun was an antique, not like her husband's model, which was smuggled like new from Rénertia when Vere hired them to do this nasty bit of work. No, hers was far older, the dainty sidearm favored by a young woman long dead.

"Here, it's a loan," she'd told Alison as she looked at the two of them with tears welling up behind her spectacles. "Bring him back safely, miss."

But she hadn't. She'd brought him back unstuck in time, a ghost and now a hired killer.

"Did you get the target?" her husband asked.

Alison nodded and handed the photograph to Wilbur. "Let's go."

Alison took Katharine Wright's gun from her and slipped it into the pocket of the clothes that felt like a strange costume to her. "We won't be long," she promised. "He'll be home for dinner." Hand in hand, Alison and Wilbur walked to the backyard of the Wrights' house, the spot that seemed to glow as they neared it.

Alison felt her palm tingle. "Here," she told Wilbur.

And then her insides roiled with nausea, pain racked her head, and then Alison and Wilbur were elsewhere, though not the elsewhere she'd hoped.

~

Brimley Wheaton wasn't hard to find. He stood waiting in line at Hawthorne's, a known RAA hangout, and the way he craned his neck around made Alison think he wasn't sure who he was supposed to be meeting. She took advantage of his ignorance and sidled up to him, emitting a ladylike cough as she approached.

"You a friend of Monsieur Rénart?" she asked, invoking the underground RAA greeting. She peered up at him through her eyelashes and hoped the effect was charming, despite her discomfort at uttering the words.

Wheaton studied her. "I…what? Who are you?" He leaned over her. "Who sent you?"

It wasn't working. Alison went straight for her backup plan and pressed the nose of her gun into his ribcage. "Who I am doesn't matter." She nodded behind her, where Wilbur waited at the car. He wore sunglasses, and the brim of his top hat was pulled down. "You'll be joining my colleague over there."

Wheaton moved, but Alison pushed the gun deeper into his side. He grunted. "You won't be going for that crazy-ass weapon you got, man. Don't even. Let's not alarm these nice wannabe Rénartians by having me blast your guts all over their little coffee joint here, huh? There are kids present. I don't like killing people around kids, even if those kids are assholes."

I don't like killing people at all. Vere's never made me actually have to go through with it.

She felt nausea stronger than she'd felt in months, not since the last time she'd time traveled. If what they had to do didn't work…would she—or Wilbur—have to actually kill this guy?

As Alison steered Wheaton outside, Wilbur opened the backseat of the hovercar and rustled him in. He slid next to Wheaton, and Alison took the driver's seat. Behind her came the sound of small gears and then a metallic snap.

Wheaton let out a little whimper. "Those a bit tight?" Wilbur asked, his voice gruff. "It's for your own protection."

"How do you figure that?" Wheaton asked.

"If you fight back, we'll have to kill you," Alison snapped.

"Aren't you going to kill me regardless?"

"Not necessarily," Wilbur replied. "If you cooperate…" His voice trailed off.

Alison steered the car through light traffic, remembering another such flight when they'd first arrived in this year—this *wrong* year, where her old university mentor was much older and had a new protégée, a year where the RAA was practically a cult instead of just a separate country.

A year without family.

Alison stared at the words etched in marble. A name, a pair of dates, "Beloved wife and mother."

She and Wilbur were in 2100 for only a week when she asked to find her mother's grave. As she'd stared at the placard behind which rested an urn, Wilbur patted her shoulder.

"They're all gone now, my whole family."

"Mine, too," Wilbur said. He drew close, breath warm against her ear. "We'll have to be family for each other now."

This same tender man now held a gun on a stranger in the backseat of a vehicle invented over a century after his death. Alison felt a brief, inappropriate urge to begin giggling, not out of joy but from sheer madness.

She set the hovercar down in an alley beside an abandoned factory. Her hands shook when she took them off the controls.

~

Wilbur pulled the man from the hovercar and led him into the warehouse after Alison. "I promise you, sir, you have only yourself as an enemy here. If you'll settle down, we'll explain our purpose."

"Go to hell," Wheaton said.

Wilbur wanted to tell him he was already there, but that wasn't true. So long as Alison was near, it wasn't ever *all* hell, despite the abject chaos of this time.

The room they entered was dark, the dust so thick it assaulted the nose before the eyes. Alison pulled an electric lantern down from a metal shelf and snapped it on. One six-foot circle of the space was now illuminated in eerie blue-white light. Once the lantern was on, she set it on the floor and walked behind Wilbur to shut the door behind them.

Wilbur led Wheaton to the shelf and unlocked one wrist from its handcuff, securing the free end to one of the shelf's supports. "I'm going to have to search you for the weapon now, sir. You'd save both of us a lot of time and embarrassment if you simply produced it."

Wheaton sighed. "Left front jacket, inside," he replied. "But you'll never figure out how to work it."

Wilbur reached inside Wheaton's jacket. "I don't much care about working it," he said. "Mostly I just want to know what it is."

"You gonna torture it out of me if I don't tell you?"

"No, not me," Wilbur replied. He looked at his wife. "That's her job."

It shouldn't be, though. I should be willing, if it's what's needed, but it shouldn't be needed.

Alison went to another set of shelves and pulled something heavy to the floor. It clattered against the concrete. She knelt, and there came the sound of metal working metal. In a moment, she was back within the circle of the lantern's light with a scalpel in her hand.

"I didn't take anatomy," she said, "so I'm probably gonna be really bad at this."

Wheaton fell apart. "God, no. Stop. I got it for this British guy. I don't know his name, but it was for the RAA. They were gonna pay me because I could get over to Beta and they couldn't do it alone. Please, for fuck's sake, *not the face.* Anywhere but the face!"

Wilbur gaped at Alison, who'd already dropped the scalpel. All their nervousness, all their worries…

"My dear, I believe that's what they call 'too easy,'" Wilbur said.

"I'll say," Alison agreed. She turned to Wheaton. "Let's get you more comfortable, Mister Wheaton. I think we can do business."

Wheaton canted his head forward, gazing at the weapon in Wilbur's hand. "Be careful. I have no idea what the thing does."

"What did your contact say it does?" Wilbur asked.

"He didn't say anything about a gun at all, just that they needed tech."

Wilbur looked to Alison.

"Technology," she explained.

"Is this nation so starved?" Wilbur asked. "You have flying motorcars, time travel…I dare say this is utopia."

"Not all of it," Alison said. "And ixnay on that stuff in front of *him*," she said, gesturing to Wheaton. She tugged at Wilbur's elbow, pulling him a few feet from the man. "Don't get all ooh-isn't-the-future-amazing in front of some guy we might have to…to…"

Wilbur put a hand against Alison's cheek. "It's all right, my dear," he whispered. "I forget myself." He approached Wheaton. "Sir, we have two options, and I don't feature having to exercise one of them. I'm certain you would be in agreement."

Wheaton's face grew stern. "If it's putting a bullet in my head, then yeah, I'm in agreement that sounds not so hot."

"Our other option is for you to tell us how you came upon the device, and then my lovely wife is going to administer something to assist you with your memory," Wilbur continued.

"Assist me?" Wheaton laughed. "You mean assist it *out* of me? That's what they were going to do back at the agency in the first place."

"This one is a little different." Alison withdrew a hypodermic needle from her pocket and took the cap off its end. A bilious yellow liquid resided inside. "It goes back a little further than what the agency would have given you."

"How *much* further?" Wheaton asked.

"It's this or I have to dispose of your body," Alison said, "which is *so* not what I went to school for."

Wheaton squirmed. "How *much further?*" he repeated. He tried to force his chair to jump away from her approach. "Are we talking vegetable or are we talking last week?"

Alison tilted her head from side to side. "Eh, somewhere in between, I'd guess. I don't really know. I'm not the scientist."

Wheaton, now panic-stricken, looked at Wilbur.

"Different sort of scientist," Wilbur said. "But I put a keen amount of trust in those who are better at these things than I." He stepped aside, allowing Alison better access to Wheaton. "Go on, my dear."

The scream Wheaton emitted as Alison hit the needle's plunger was deafening. Wilbur wished for a rag to put in the poor man's mouth. When it was over, Alison took the weapon, and Wilbur removed the bonds from Wheaton's limbs.

"Are we going to the circus?" Wheaton mumbled against Wilbur's shoulder.

Oh, dear.

"I suppose, sir." Wilbur glanced up at Alison. "I can't leave him here like this."

"Put him in a taxi," she said. "Give the driver his home address. I have things to take to the agency."

Agreeing to reconvene at their own home after both errands, Wilbur deposited a kiss on the back of his wife's hand and hoisted Wheaton up, wrapping the heavier man's arm around his own shoulders.

"Where's my mommy?" Wheaton asked.

"You'll be all right, sir."

But Wilbur knew this client was likely never going to be quite all right ever again.

Wednesday, August 11, 2100, Avon, Vermont, NBE

Kris liked old jazz records. She liked pianos and hi-hat cymbals and saxophones, all things she'd only seen in films, never in person, and she liked to listen to the lot of it on old records, great crates of them found in dusty shops. The technology to run things off plastic discs and streamed from the ether was gone, the power in the agency house all diverted to the time travel mechanisms, but the Victrola replica only needed a few watts of power. With just a near-invisible needle, a few inches of black vinyl engraved with subtle grooves via a technology so old, so lost it might as well have been magic, and Kris was awash in the tenderness of fingers pressing ivory, lips blowing across brass and wood, dead fingers and mouths working instruments that were now long destroyed, burned in battles or buried deep in landfills.

These dead men—and, dammit, Kris knew most of the instrumentalists were indeed men, but that was apparently something they were good for, coaxing these things into scales and climaxes—inspired nostalgia in her for things she'd never experienced, things she never would, unless she let Ben and Vere slip a bit of microchip into her hand and send her molecules splattering across the centuries.

No, that wasn't her. Kris lived for the stories, lived for the flickers of images on a sputtering tablet screen or sepia-toned photographs in a well-read book. She lived for the way the clients recounted their journeys, and she lived for these haunting, tinny sounds from the point of the needle. These men's names were like mantras to her, these moments alone with the Victrola were her church, her meditation, her everything.

Dave Brubeck. Miles Davis. George Winston. John Coltrane. Chet Baker. Django Reinhardt.

But today it was Harry Connick, Jr., though none of his schmaltzy vocals for her. She'd returned all those to the shop with a sigh of disappointment. "No singing," she'd told the owner. He'd promptly given her vinyl dubs of his earlier work, piano solos or spare arrangements where the New Orleans prodigy accompanied just a bass and drums. This was where Kris's heart swelled today, lying on the floor of the agency's front room with her eyes shut, listening to a dead man's nimble fingers running across the keys of a tune called "I Mean You." Ben's cat Bodhi was nestled next to her, and his rumbling purr was like an extra bass line beneath the music. Kris reveled in the song even as a stack of mail sat unopened, even as she knew things were bad and Ben and Eddy were fretting about important, scary matters. Somewhere deep in her soul she felt a pang of knowledge that it was too long since fingers had touched her the way Connick's caressed the piano keys...

Somewhere there was a girl with dark, sad eyes, brows shaved back to effect a strange, haunted look, glossy hair in a shaggy blue Mohawk. This girl had hands almost as magical as these musicians' elegant hands, but their very absence from Kris's lithe body had gone on longer than their relationship had lasted.

Maura...

The track changed, and this one was more strings heavy, the bass line thrumming out the melodic motif of Simon and Garfunkel's "I Am a Rock." Kris preferred the piano to dominate instead and wasn't a big fan of the tune. She sighed, stretched, and peeled herself from the rug. Bodhi stretched and sauntered off to the kitchen. One of Kris's feet protested, pins-and-needles numb. She shook it, favored it, half-limping over to the record player.

"You getting back to work?"

It was Ben, tired and irritable. Kris took the needle off the record and filled the room with the sound of the fire licking quietly at the inside of the hearth.

"Just takin' a break, boss," she said. "Mail's in." She went to her desk and sorted through the stack of letters. "Everything okay?" One pile for Ben, one pile for Vere, one pile for the agency generally—her pile, by default—and one pile of obvious junk—her other pile by default, but that one went easier and mostly wound up as kindling. She took one letter from the pile, hand addressed in calligraphy to Ben. "You might want this one first."

Ben opened it. "An invoice," he read.

Kris held out her hand. "That gets done with accounts," she told him. "I do those on Tuesdays."

"Not this one." Ben tucked it away inside his vest pocket.

"No offense, man, but that's *my* job," Kris said. "Like I said. Tuesdays. If you need it to go out faster, I can do a batch this afternoon instead. It's gotta go in the ledger."

Ben's shoulders sagged. "Kris, no. Not this one." He stepped toward her and gave her a gentle pat on the arm. "It's nothing. Just…I need to do this one." His eyes got a faraway look in them. "Actually, Eddy does this one, to be precise." He passed Kris and headed downstairs.

Invoice. Maybe for the cleanup of Mister Wheaton? *Oh, geez.* Kris knew it was the contractors she'd never met, the contractors who'd apparently succeeded in doing whatever it is they did that resulted in there being something she wasn't supposed to see locked up in the cabinet at the top of the stairs leading to the third floor.

Kris crept to the laboratory door and listened for a moment. They were both down there, Ben and Vere, and the conversation was hushed and calm. How long would they be?

Screw it. If they find me, I'll just be honest. But if they don't find me…

Kris took a poker from the fireplace before slipping up to the staircase at the center of the building, running up the treads two by two, until she reached the cabinet on the landing before the attic.

It was polished cherry wood, dark and oil-scented, one of the pieces Ben still had from his family before converting the home into the business. Though Ben locked it once he put the object inside, he didn't know the lock wasn't as secure as it seemed or that Kris had another way in.

She knelt on the carpet in front of the cabinet, turned her wrists a bit to limber them up, and then wriggled her hands, palms up, between the floor and the cabinet's bottom panel. With some small effort, Kris was able to push the panel through a thin slot at the unit's rear just enough until there was a soft "thunk" sound, indicating the panel hit the wall. She slid the fireplace poker into the gap, up inside the front of the cabinet, and jimmied the lock from the inside.

The door swung open, revealing mostly things that would only be treasures to the Jonson family. Kris had only ever broken into the cabinet in the first place out of boredom, not larceny, and the lack of anything much beyond old travelogues and family photographs kept her disinterested. But she'd seen Vere hand off a package to Ben, who then squirreled it away in here.

And there it was, no longer in its wrappings but just sitting on a shelf as if it were a curio instead of a weapon.

It was silver and larger than her palm, with an oblong barrel that started out somewhat bulbous toward the grip and then slimmed as it reached the muzzle. Where there should be a hole for a bullet to eject at the muzzle instead was only more smooth metal, making Kris wonder if this was, indeed, a weapon after all. Just because it resembled a gun didn't mean that's what it was. She cradled it in her right hand.

The grip seemed to shift and undulate beneath her skin, molding itself to the exact size and shape of her palm and fingers. The movement tickled and then stopped once the grip customized itself for her.

No, this is a gun. What else but a weapon would actually be designed to do that?

And yet there was no visible trigger, no buttons or latches or levers visible anywhere. She examined the base of the grip, the underside of the barrel…nothing. Kris raised her arm and pretended to aim at the vase on a small table at the end of the hallway. She lined up the slight rise at the end of the barrel with the very center of the vase, squeezed one eye shut to get better aim, and then—

Dust.

There was no sound, no explosion, no flying pieces of vase anywhere, but one second there was a smooth white vase with jaunty blue flowers dancing across its surface, and the next second the vase was gone, replaced by a small pyramid of dust just a few inches tall.

Kris stared at the gun, wanting but afraid to drop it. She placed it back on its shelf in the cabinet and shut it back up.

Scrambling to the table, she stared, wide-eyed, at the dust. Some was white, some was blue, and it was all the remains of the vase. The valuable, antique vase that survived God-knew-how-many wars and political upheavals and moves from place to place. Kris imagined an older woman with Ben's features lovingly packing it in newspaper and straw in a cardboard box labeled "VERMONT." And that same woman, not quite as old, smiling at the vase in a store window. A young man with a paintbrush as thin as horsehair painstakingly adding blue swirls to the vase's surface before firing.

How many hands had this porcelain gone through before winding up on this table in this hallway? How many bouquets of flowers had been lovingly displayed in it, only to have the thing be relegated to nothing in the blink of an eye, and at her own hand?

Kris thought of her record collection, the hands that played her favorite trills and melodies now rotted to bone, shoved into boxes underground all across the world. She'd meditated to those records, dreamed to those records, loved to them. What if they were cruelly ripped from her life? Was this vase a gift from mother to daughter, from daughter to son? Did it celebrate births and weddings and—

A door shut somewhere far downstairs. Kris wiped at moisture at the corners of her eyes and dashed across the hall to a water closet. She grabbed a towel from the rack and swept the vase's remains into it, which she then bundled up into a tiny, makeshift bag. She picked up the fireplace poker and raced back to her desk.

But Ben was already standing there, and his caterpillar brows angled downward to point at his nose. "What were you doing upstairs?" He gestured to the poker. "What's going on?"

"I heard a noise," she managed, breathless. "I, uh, thought somebody was breaking in."

"*Upstairs?*" Ben nodded to the staircase. "How could—"

"I don't know," Kris interrupted. She put the poker back in its stand next to the hearth and hoped he wouldn't notice the towel still clutched in her left hand. "Crazy shit's goin' down lately. I didn't know what to think."

"If something like that happens again, just call for me, okay?"

"You're so busy. I didn't want to worry you."

"I worry. It's what I do," Ben said. "It's why I can't…Nevermind."

Something about the way his shoulders sagged pulled at Kris. Ben was never a happy man, but he'd grown more content in his business venture, relishing the stories the clients brought back. "You've been nothing but kind to me, you and your family," Kris said. She opened the towel and held out its contents to him. "I'm sorry. I have to explain something."

After Kris related the story of the gun, Ben's mood changed. "I guess that thing isn't so secure after all," he said.

Kris flinched. "I don't…that's not a habit or anything. I guess I wanted to know what it was."

"I get that," Ben said. "Trust me, I get that. Hoo, boy. Okay. If it's not scaring you too much, you wanna show me what that gun can do?" Ben headed for the stairs.

"So long as I don't aim it at any more priceless heirlooms, I guess we're good," Kris replied, following him.

"Nah, I picked that thing up at a garage sale. Fifty cents. And it was fake."

"You're not just saying that?"

Ben paused in his ascent to the next story. "Of course not."

Thursday, November 8, 1888, London, England

I can't do this anymore. I can't waste my trips on this side project. I have to get to the child.

And yet here Claudio was, long past midnight, watching a young woman in a pub. He was seated several tables away, barely touching his own drink, but the woman downed ale after ale and sang, loudly and off key, in a thick accent. Irish? Welsh? It was hard to place, but it wasn't the Cockney lilt of the men vying for her attentions.

"Aw, c'mon, then, Ginger, let's give us a go tonight, eh?"

"No, no, not 'im, Mary. I got a bottle of rum at me house, and the misses is out."

"Please, Miss Jeanette. Give us a go."

"Gents, I can't tonight," the young woman replied, answering to so many different nicknames that Claudio had no idea what her parents called her. "My Joe is comin' home and there'll be a row. He's tossed out our flatmate, and I've got to help 'er sort things 'forehand." She took one last swig from her tankard and scrambled off the top of the table where she'd perched amongst her suitors. "Ta, loves. I'll be 'round in a few days or so."

She wobbled out, her pale bosom heaving with the effort, but it seemed she wasn't so drunk as she'd let on. Claudio slipped out after her and once in the street, the woman smoothed her strawberry blond hair back into a neat bun. She whistled and strolled toward a row of flats near an alley.

Claudio balled his hands into fists. This would be the last, he decided. He'd slaughtered several now, and each one made him feel more alive, more powerful, and more *real*.

It's training. Training for wiping out the whole lot of them, the Empiricist scum, the race traitors, the women who wrong me.

But still he wanted the girl—Virginia—so he could protect her and bring her up to take his place when he died. Virginia was female, and he would raise her as his daughter. So if women were half the problem, how could Claudio curtail his rage so it wouldn't explode against the baby when he finally got her? Virginia was the most racially pure human on the continent, and yet she would still grow up to be one of those foul women, inferior to men. He would have to learn not to hurt her.

Channel it into the grown women. Channel it, and then make sure to raise Virginia right so she won't grow up a bitch, so she'll know her place and treat her men with proper respect.

This woman, this Mary or Jeanette or Ginger…she was too forward in her sexuality, too brazen and delighted with herself, too full in the corset and too wide-hipped and replete with fertility. It was disgusting, the flagrant way she took up space in the alley. It was disgusting and provocative, and Claudio wanted to possess her, wanted to tear and rend and then look inside to see how everything worked. Maybe then he would understand.

Virginia. I'm doing this for Virginia so she won't grow up in a world with people who don't acknowledge their superiority, people who mix and mingle and think permissive thoughts.

The woman spun on her heel and turned to face him. Claudio stepped back.

She grinned. "You was followin' me, yeah?" She batted her eyelashes at him. "I was goin' to take the night off, but if you got somethin' for me, maybe I'd be coaxed to have somethin' for you." Her smile widened, and Claudio was shocked to see that her teeth were barely yellow.

She's very young. The rest were older, but this one can't be much out of her teens.

"What's your name?" he asked.

"Mary Jane," she replied. "But if that don't suit ya, it could be whatever ya want." She stepped closer and slid a finger along his lapel. "What d'ya fancy I call you, hmm? 'Cause you look like a right devil, you do, all that dark hair and bein' just a slip of a man—"

"A *slip*?" Claudio swatted her hand away.

Mary Jane pouted, displaying the fullness of her crimson mouth. "I just meant you're passin' elegant, sir. You's the sort what can eat like a horse 'n' not gain an ounce. I like it. It suits your face." She examined his face now, growing serious. "Got a haunted look 'bout ya like ya lost a lover."

Claudio thought of blood and screams quickly silenced by the tools in his bag. "Several, actually," he said.

Polly. Siffey. Liz. Kate. A slash to the throat in a grimy alley, a slash to the stomach in a deserted backyard. Garroting in a stable, face pummeled in behind a warehouse. That last was quite satisfying and made Claudio wonder what this Mary Jane would look like without a face.

"Oh, sir, that's a right shame, 'tis." Now Mary Jane brightened again, finger back at his lapel, sliding it up and down the tweed and sneaking a fleshy lip between her teeth. "I don't got much but I got a stove. Bit chilly this time o' year, innit?"

He threaded her arm through his and allowed her to steer them to her flat. "Don't you fear the murders nearby?" he asked.

Mary Jane laughed. "What's it they call 'im? The Leather Apron?" She looked Claudio up and down. "Don't see you wearin' such nonsense."

"I think he prefers other monikers, according to the papers."

"This is me place." Mary Jane unwound her arm from Claudio's in front of a tiny, whitewashed affair with a broken front window. She took a handkerchief from her pocket and covered her hand with it, then slid her hand through the shattered panes of glass and wriggled around near the lock on the front door. "Lost me key months ago. Joe's a bloomin' cheap bugger 'n' won't spring for a new 'un." She frowned in concentration as she worked the lock on the opposite side. "Ah, there we 'ave it." The door popped open, and Mary Jane drew her hand from the window. She stopped Claudio before he entered. "You got a sovereign?"

Claudio grinned. A single pound was going to do? If she only knew how little that was to him in his time. He handed over the coin, followed her into the room, and exited two hours later, bathed in her blood.

Thursday, August 12, 2100, Flussville, South Carolina, RAA

As Claudio sailed through time, returning to Ambrose and power and responsibility, he tried to think of his larger mission. Goals, procedures, plans… *that* was what was important. *That* demanded his focus.

Plan, plan, plan. Rest up and go to Roanoke.

He'd been on a mission for years now and made little progress because of his increasing distraction.

Focus on your legacy.

And yet instead he saw knives and the glittering gore of Mary Jane's intestines slipping through his fingers. When he opened his eyes on Ambrose's laboratory table, all he could see was the mess he'd made of those pretty lips and young white teeth, all he could hear was the "snick" and "thunk" of his knives as they'd slashed and torn through skin and muscle. When he was done, her body was in so many pieces he'd had to pile some up on her kitchen table to clear space for his exit.

"Sir, you gonna be going back there much more?" Ambrose asked. "I worry if I'm not precise about the date, you might find you're running into yourself or some such. 'Sides, I got some updates on Wheaton. He got the weapon taken away from him and is a babbling mess. Think you need to try Cob again."

Claudio didn't even hear him. Instead he was thinking about going somewhere else, some*when* else, to continue this hobby but not cause temporal problems. Could he? Should he?

"Not now," Claudio replied. "Not for now, not for a while, anyway. I've got to work on another matter."

"Worried about your plan for Virginia Dare, too," Ambrose said. "Roanoke's such a finite period, and this would be your third time back there as well. Same problems. Got to be careful."

"My research there is done," Claudio said. He hopped off the table and headed for his office, where he kept multiple sets of clothing. He gestured to Ambrose to follow him. "Next trip to Roanoke, I'm getting Virginia first thing and bringing her back with me."

"What about the second bit of all that? Sending her to yourself a few years back so you can raise her?"

Claudio opened the closet in his office and surveyed his clothing options. There were several sixteenth century items, but he found each trip they were still off enough that the locals noticed him. The nineteenth century clothes sometimes stood out less, so perhaps he shouldn't bother, should just go in his blood-stained Victorian get-up...

Shit. There's blood everywhere.

He looked down at himself and noticed he'd been less fastidious in his cleanup than on previous trips to London. He'd kept the blood off his coat, but not the shirt beneath it and not his trousers, and by now Ambrose had to have seen.

He turned and faced the younger man, not waiting to find out if Ambrose noticed yet. "I've been working back there," he said. Something deep inside Claudio felt like it was shutting down, a light switch flipping from on to off. His voice sounded robotic to his own ears. "I had work to do, getting rid of them."

Ambrose drew his head back. "What're you on about, sir?"

Ambrose must be lying. He'd noticed. How could he not? Claudio, his clothes for Roanoke forgotten, grabbed Ambrose by the front of his shirt and shook him. Ambrose struggled to get away, but Claudio was faster, his hands strong and trained these past few months on throat slashings and strangulations and the fastidious art of leaving bloody faces to molder atop limp and dirty pillows.

"There are five fewer of your countrywomen back there, you idiot." Claudio let go of Ambrose, tossing him hard enough as he did so to cause Ambrose to hit the opposite wall.

He cried out, a mewling sound that set Claudio's teeth on edge. "You *child.* You weak *child.*" He felt the rage stir and boil in him and leapt upon his employee, taking the younger man's neck in his hands and squeezing.

But it wasn't the same satisfaction, and Ambrose struggled far more than a disease-weakened whore half out of her wits with drink. Ambrose gagged beneath Claudio's grip and pulled hard at his arms.

Claudio envisioned Ambrose's dead body, saw rooms of technological devices he couldn't operate, and he saw a future without the daughter he wanted to acquire.

Sinéad burst in. Simple as she was, she was still possessed of ears to hear the skirmish. She stormed through the door at the sound of the screams, screams not coming from Claudio's victim but Claudio himself, screams that grew to a keening whine that was no longer human but sounded more and more like a desperate animal caught in a trap.

Sinéad shouted at Claudio, but Claudio couldn't understand her. He dragged himself off Ambrose and huddled in the corner as Sinéad knelt by Ambrose and began first aid.

"What the hell is wrong with you?" she demanded. "Get out of here."

Claudio couldn't move. Ambrose and Sinéad were just a blur to him, just a nebulous pile of colors all swirled together, meaningless.

"Get *out*," Sinéad repeated.

This time Claudio crawled. He scuttled along on bony hands and knobby knees, getting carpet burns on his palms and beneath his trousers, until he made his way back to the lab. With a groan, he pulled himself up to standing. The machinery was before him, whirring and glowing. In a silver surface he caught sight of his cadaverous and sunken face, his pupils blown out so wide there was no iris visible, only blackness.

"Let me go," he whispered. "Release me."

He pushed a button on the machine at random and let the sweet smell of ozone remove him from the century.

Thursday, August 12, 2100, Avon, Vermont, NBE

Ben poked his head around the archway between the parlor and the kitchen, where Vere was consumed with calling the toaster names. "Blast you, incompetent thing."

"You have to activate the battery," Ben said. He took up the duct-taped pack of nine volts from the table and handed it to Vere.

"You're saying I forgot to plug it in," Vere said.

"Essentially."

Vere wagged a finger at Ben. "Watch it, young man. I remember when we could get small things to still run from alternating current coursing through the walls." He busied himself with plugging the toaster into the battery and turning it on. "If you're interested in seeing that sort of thing firsthand—"

"I don't think anyone, least of all me, should be going anywhere just now," Ben interrupted. "I had a little conversation with Kris. She tested the gun for us."

Vere raised the arm of the toaster, re-secured his bread, and depressed it again. "Ah-*ha*! There you go, you rogue sourdough." He pointed to the now-glowing coils. "If we had AC over here, we'd see a much brighter, faster toasting, Benoy. Now what's this about Miss Moto?" Bodhi jumped up onto the counter, and Vere shooed him away from the toaster.

"She went a little rogue herself and got the gun. The one from Woolpit. And…" Ben rubbed his hand along the back of his neck. "She, uh, engaged in a little target practice with it."

Vere leaned against the cabinet and shoved his hands in the pockets of his trousers. "I see. I'm assuming, since I know the young lady in question, that the results were disastrous."

"Nothing damaged of any value," Ben said, "but we're lucky there was no organic matter in the room." He described the gun's effects.

"Yes," Vere said. "It would indeed be a boon for nefarious forces to gain such an implement."

Vere looked across the room, but the less focused his eyes grew, the more Ben could tell the older man wasn't seeing wallpaper and dark-stained wood—he was seeing into the past.

"Back in the war, that goddamned little punk Florence would have given his scrawny left arm for something like that gun," Vere remarked. "He could've wiped us all off the fields at Smith County with that thing." He looked at Ben. "How much power does it have? How many shots did she get off before it ran out?"

Ben didn't answer at once. Vere was right—it wasn't tested. "I have no idea," Ben finally said.

"Testing!" Vere laughed. "Testing must be done, my boy." Behind him, his toast sprang up. "But first, sustenance."

Tuesday, January 14, 1947, Los Angeles, California, USA

Claudio came to his senses in a hospital bed, but it was simple enough to leave when the nurse was out of the room. His clothes were still bloodstained, and when he caught sight of the date on a newspaper masthead he marveled at how many decades back and forth poor trusting Mary Jane Kelly's bits of dried DNA had traveled.

Two hundred twelve years forward, one hundred fifty-three years backward. And yet I was elbow-deep in her intestines less than twenty-four hours ago, by my mind's clock...

He knew he looked a wreck as he stepped out into the California sunshine, but all his money was in coins, old and suspect. And yet it wasn't as if he were somewhere respectable. This was a hedonistic place at a hedonistic time, full of celluloid and immorality. No one would question a rusty shirtfront or a coin collection too much, not if threats and bribery were involved.

Sure enough, by evening Claudio's pockets were full of crisp, era-appropriate cash. A dapper wool suit with wide lapels and a slim necktie hung from his slender frame. His hair was too long, and it was causing people to gape, but the addition of his dark-lensed spectacles made him—if not less conspicuous—less apt to notice the stares. As evening faded to pink dusk, Claudio ducked into a nightclub.

At the bar, a woman with a cloud of coal-black hair and skin glowing moon-white sat knee-to-knee with a familiar man. Claudio gaped at Rupert Cob, the man looking every inch the same as he did in the wild grasslands of the West Virginia field, some thirty years ago from his own perspective but perhaps not even part of Cob's past yet. Why travel here? What was special about this place, this woman, this—

Kill her.

A waitress hovered over Claudio's table. "Cigar? Cigarettes? Cocktail? What's your poison, mister?" Her lips were painted cherry red, and a tiny smear of it marred one yellowed front tooth as she smiled. "Maybe all three, huh? What'll it be?"

The voice inside Claudio's head, the one that sang with joy and revelry when he hacked and slashed, spoke again, a guttural growl similar to his own voice but oh, so much darker, feral, *needful.*

Kill her!

The waitress? The expectant woman in the pillbox cap and fishnet stockings?

"Uh, cognac. And a packet of..." Claudio gestured at a tobacco ad on the wall. "Those will do. Matches, please."

Not the waitress, you idiot, Cob's girl.

Young, slender, clean, nothing at all like the women on the soot-covered streets of London. This girl—and that was the other difference, her age, so young!—

wasn't out whoring herself, wasn't rheumy-eyed and sore-riddled, wasn't half-full of gin on the inside. She was laughing and talking and had tidily painted fingernails, carefully curled hair.

Cob paid the club's flower-peddler a few cents for a dark blossom, which he helped the girl tuck up into her hair. Then they danced and twirled across the room to the brassy rhythms of the house band, returning to their stools sweaty and hysterical. Cob steered her out after another drink, and Claudio stared at them all the while.

He dropped too much cash on the table and snuck after them. The girl was too tipsy to navigate well in her stilettoes, but Cob kept a firm arm tucked around her waist. Their heads tipped toward each other several times in giddy, first-date conversation, and the sight sickened Claudio.

No woman has ever... his thoughts swirled, but the animal voice, the cruel and deadly voice, cut in.

Kill her! it chanted. *Kill her! Kill her!* The words came more and more rapidly until they blended together.

Kill her kill her kill her killher killher killher!

Killer!

KILLER!

By the time Cob and the woman reached her boarding house, the voice screamed so loudly Claudio clapped his hands over his ears and retreated to a nearby alley. He couldn't think, couldn't see, and couldn't hear.

STOP!

At once, his murderous mind retreated, leaving Claudio alone with his saner thoughts. For the first time in hours, he felt clear-headed and in control, and yet he was grateful for the moment of peace so he could better concentrate on carrying out his intended crime.

For he would kill her, all right. Before going back to his own time and place, he would indeed calm himself by slicing up this young woman's body. And then, after he was steady and free and once again himself, he could work on saving Virginia.

The life of one girl for the life of another. It was simple and fair.

Cob gave the girl a tender kiss and walked across the street. Once the other man was out of sight, Claudio went to work.

But wait, who was that? Claudio squinted at a shape moving behind the shrubbery next to the building. A heavyset man with a bag. He took off his hat and licked his lips.

This wouldn't do. Claudio emerged from the alley only a few inches, just far enough to catch the man's attention.

"Hey, buddy," he whispered. "There's a cop across the street."

The heavy man turned his head and peered into the shadows. "What's that?"

Claudio's knife was already out. It slid easily into the man's gut. Only a little effort was required to drag him into the alley, just far enough to stay out of sight.

No glory for you, old chum. This one's all mine.

~

Cob didn't leave Elizabeth on her doorstep alone. He circled around the other side of the park so he could watch. He knew tonight was the night and wanted to spend it with her, to prevent it, but that wasn't allowed.

"You can't change history," Jonson said in the training session, "only observe it. You can know it, but you can't stop it."

But Elizabeth Short wound up being so much more than a snapshot in an old newspaper when he met her. History can make things seem flat and inhuman, unrelatable in their staleness. Facts and figures, dead people doing dead things that were no longer fresh and new and alive. Sure, he'd craved the knowing and the mystery solving, but she was still just The Black Dahlia to him, a nickname, a victim. All her photographs were of an unsmiling, pale woman with a dated hairstyle and cold eyes.

That wasn't the woman he took to the club, however. The woman he danced with and kissed and petted in the coatroom. This woman, this real flesh and blood creature, laughed and glided and spoke in a throaty, hearty voice full of smoke and joy. She wanted to be an actress, wanted to be a model, wanted to have a better relationship with her father, wanted to find the perfect sweater to wear for auditions. But most of all she wanted to move to her own place and fall in love, in that order.

"I can't let you in, Bobby." She'd given him a pouty little smile that spoke of promises and things she wanted but didn't dare ask for. "Not when I'm a little in the glass and we only just met."

"Promise me you won't let that creep touch you." The club owner. The boardinghouse owner. The man Cob figured would probably cut her in two tonight.

"You can't change history," Ben warned. "You can see what happened, but you can't stop it from happening."

"Promise me, Lizzie," Cob repeated. "Please."

Her eyes were so big, so blue, a deep blue that matched her scarf and looked stark and beautiful in the moonlight against her pitch-black hair. She smiled wider, the big eyes crinkling up in merriment. "You're worried about me."

Cob didn't remember what his training told him about slang, not in the cool moonlight next to a beautiful woman, so he just went with what he felt. "I want you, if you'd have me."

She looked away, just a little, but kept smiling.

"And I'd protect you from him," he continued.

She giggled and patted his shoulder; standing on the stoop, she was up higher than Cob, gazing down at him like a statue, like a Madonna blessing a child.

"Take me out tomorrow night, Bobby." She waved and was gone.

And now Cob would wait, would sit on the park bench and stare up at her windows until the gold light behind the shades winked out.

That was when the shadow from the alley moved. At first it looked as if there were two shadows, but then Cob blinked and it was only one. There was a grunting sound, and then a man emerged, a slender man in a too-big suit. He didn't enter the building as if he belonged there.

That's because he doesn't.

Even with Jonson's admonishing voice in his head, Cob couldn't let it happen. The news reports he'd studied before leaving were clear: Elizabeth Short's body was found dismembered, so mangled and ripped apart that it took some investigation to determine her remains were even human. The thought of that lovely face, the pert nose and full lips being slashed, that perfect lithe figured he'd slid between his legs as they swing danced...he couldn't bear the idea of this shadow man being allowed to hack that all to pieces, drain her limbs of their blood.

Cob's stomach felt heavy, as if a stone rested inside. A sharp burning sensation rose in his throat.

The man was inside the building now.

Cob's feet felt bolted to the sidewalk.

Move.

And yet he worried. What if he *did* stop this, but the man murdered him instead? What would that do? What would his sister think happened to him, the agency men, his friends?

Get a grip, man.

Cob walked across the street, first casually but then faster and faster until he was running, feet pounding up the front steps, searching for Elizabeth's name on one of the pencil-scrawled tags on the mailbox fronts.

Fuck it. Knock on 'em all.

Ah, but no need, there was a muffled scream from the third floor. Cob took to the stairs, clinging to the railing for dear life as he ran.

There was a heavy thud, then silence.

The apartment door was open a crack, just enough that Cob could see a figure in a dirty shirt staring down at a giant slab of pork round, one side butchered to separate the loin from the leg. The man held a knife and raised it at the pork round again, only, no...

Cob knew it wasn't a pig on the floor, and yet he couldn't see it as anything but. He blinked. He knew it was Elizabeth's body there, knew it was her blood pooling between the cracks in the hardwood, and knew this murderer dissected her torso, but no matter how hard he rubbed his eyes, all he saw were cuts of hog meat, as if hanging behind the deli counter at a supermarket.

Thank God for a little mental breakdown.

Mourning and reality would come later. But right now...at least he would get what he came for. He stared at his hands until they stopped shaking, and then Cob pushed the door open wide enough to step inside the apartment.

"Who are you?" he asked the man.

The man turned toward him. He was silhouetted from behind by a bare bulb, the golden glow coated in blood turning the light orange, like buzzing sodium parking lot lights. It left the man in shadow, but Cob could tell he was tall and thin.

Still backlit and shadow-faced, the man walked behind Cob and shut the apartment door, bolting it. "If you don't stay quiet—"

"Who are you?" Cob demanded. "Who was she to you? Why'd you do it?"

The man walked from the near-empty living room to the bathroom, where he paused a moment, looking around.

Cob's heart raced. He felt his ears grow hot.

Don't look down at her. Don't look, because maybe this time she'll be a girl, not a pig.

He felt a wetness seep into the cracks in his shoes and knew it was her still-warm blood, tacky and metallic.

"Here we are," the man said from the bathroom. He withdrew an empty garbage bag from beneath the cupboard under the sink. As he rose to his full height, Cob caught sight of his cadaverous face in the mirror.

Streaked with blood, the man was hawk-nosed and skeletal with too-long, stringy black hair. He turned and stared at Cob.

"I got another bag," he said. "I got another bag, and I can put you in it, too." He took a step forward. "Would you like that, Mister Cob?"

Cob felt a sharp sting in his chest and for an instant he thought he'd been shot.

The man grinned. Even his teeth were smeared with Elizabeth's blood. "That's right. I know you. Or rather...I suppose I *will* know you. I haven't quite figured when this is."

All thought drained from Cob's mind, leaving him a hollow shell, a robot turned off and left out to rust in the rain. But then his body dragged him along on autopilot and he first scrambled away from the man, then pressed his return switch and—

Blackness.

~

Claudio stepped clear of the return zone just in time. The lightshow resulting from Cob's departure was quite a dazzling sight to behold, making Claudio wonder what it looked like whenever he'd made a hasty getaway from the body of a murdered whore.

Speaking of…

He looked down at the decimated corpse and felt nothing but peace and the bored necessity of cleaning. He chucked the remains of Elizabeth Short into the trash bag, rinsed himself of her congealing blood, and left to find a nice field somewhere.

Thursday, August 12, 2100, Flussville, South Carolina, RAA

Ambrose looked up from Claudio's notebook, carefully avoiding the edges of the pages covered with something resembling rust. He nodded to the younger version of himself standing before him. "He's on his way back now."

"Right," the other Ambrose said. This one—still sandy-haired and optimistic—held an infant in his arms. He tucked the baby's blanket around her. "God, I don't want to send 'er back to 'im, not with what you've told me." His eyebrows drew up into a triangle. "Why'd you have to tell me? You're probably feelin' the flood of all this now, too."

"I feel the memory of being you now," Ambrose said. "It's all crashin' down. I remember how it really happened, though, how I didn't know there was somethin' amiss with 'im until today, didn't know about his…" Ambrose swallowed hard, trying to keep down a slick thread of bile. "His research trips…an' what 'e was really doin'."

"So I got 'er, like you told me to," the younger Ambrose said. "From thirty years ago, I went back and got 'er, and now I'm s'posed to go back to me own time and let Mister Florence raise her? Knowin' he's Jack the bleedin' Ripper?"

"I don't know," Ambrose said. He dropped Claudio's journal on the desk and leaned over it. He noted that his hands looked older than they'd appeared just a day ago.

Maybe the weight of all this wore on me more over the years.

Ambrose wondered if he should look in a mirror but thought better of it. He'd already grown leaner, grayer-haired, and angry-looking about the mouth in the last three decades. He didn't want to know if working for a serial killer made it worse.

"Did you avoid him back there, back in Roanoke?" Ambrose asked.

His younger self nodded. "Yeah. But Sinéad almost spotted me."

"God, makes you wonder if anybody at Roanoke was ever really there." Ambrose exhaled something resembling a laugh. "All of us runnin' about." He gestured to the child. "She's the only one, eh?"

105

"Hell, it ain't all paradoxes and ridiculous theories, mate," his younger self said. "There were a right number o' colonists and whatnot." The baby fussed. "It's all right, little Ginny." He looked back at Ambrose. "No, but I think the natives are gettin' more 'n a bit suspicious. Seem to know what we're all up to by now. One woman, she offered me soup..."

Ambrose looked up at the younger man. "Soup?"

The younger Ambrose half-shrugged the shoulder less encumbered by the baby. "I wonder if they don't have some biological way to send people about space and time."

Ambrose was struck by the memory of Claudio telling him about his trip to Point Pleasant, the sight of the creatures beyond the veil separating the known Earth from the parallel one, a version of the planet Claudio dubbed "Beta."

"Maybe not through space and time, but perhaps to the other side..." He told younger Ambrose about the Mothmen and the technology stolen from Beta. "Claudio means to exploit the resources there, use 'em to triumph in the war."

"Then what's *she* for, eh?"

Ambrose studied the child. "She's his heir. Pure, he says. The first white person born in America."

"I don't like this cause anymore," the younger Ambrose said. "And I don't think this little girl should suffer because I've been a stupid git what hitched my wagon to the wrong star."

"You and me both, mate."

The younger Ambrose stopped and looked at his older self. "I'll take her back, but I won't take her back to him," he said. "Tell him it was a failure."

"What do I say happened to 'er?" Ambrose asked.

"She died?" the younger man suggested.

Ambrose blanched. "And it was my fault? He'll flay me alive. And he'll *enjoy* it."

The younger Ambrose considered this. "Well, we got a lot o' sins to make up for."

"No, I'm leavin' 'ima note and gettin' the fuck out."

"You'll remember soon what I did with 'er," the younger Ambrose said. "She'll be safe." He stepped back from Ambrose, pressed his palm, and vanished.

Papers swirled around the room in disarray. When they settled back in the wake of the brief wind, Ambrose Richards felt a flood of memories swell in him, a series of flashes and words and phrases that poured into his mind and body like water into a balloon, his mind filling and expanding until he felt full, resigned, and at peace.

I have to get to her.

Thursday, August 21, 2070, 1 mile east of Cattle River, Kentucky, RAA/NBE border

Ambrose returned to his own time and place but then immediately left, infant in tow.

The last town Mister Florence would go to on 'is own. That's where I got to take 'er.

And so he was renting a hovercar at quarter to midnight, getting falsified papers in as much order as he could to make it look like Virginia was his daughter, and he was off to the border.

The walls weren't monitored as much going from the RAA into the NBE. It was the other way that things were dicey, but Ambrose knew he'd be less conspicuous on the way back. No baby. Virginia wouldn't be returning to Rénartia.

Still, he sweated as he initiated the landing process and felt the car touch down on the pavement outside the guard station. His palms left dark wet streaks on the steering panel controls. Behind him, Virginia let out a soft coo of contentment.

"You stay quiet, little one," Ambrose warned her. "Don't draw attention an' we'll be right as rain."

She let out an inquisitive little mewl.

Wish I could keep you. But no, you need to be as far from me an' my people as you can bloody well get.

He inched his car forward until it was right in front of the wooden arm that raised and lowered to let cars through after the patrol check. The night held a soft-focus glow of fog, turning the headlights and guard station lights into surreal pinpoint stars with four tips, Christmas tree lights as seen by a myopic sans spectacles. The smell of ozone seeped through the hovercar's ventilation system from the other vehicles' vapor exhausts. Usually Ambrose found this scent pleasant, but tonight it seemed cloying and plastic, with a hint of something not dissimilar from the stench of burning hair.

A man exited the guard station cubicle. He wore a jaunty blue and white hound's-tooth suit with a white silk shirt and a crimson cravat.

Bloody dandies.

And yet he felt a stirring of sympathy, as their European-inspired dress and art were all they had, really.

We're takin' their tech away, bit by bit, leavin' 'em crumbs. They got these centuries-old things to keep 'em comforted an' that's it. Who'm I to call 'em out on it?

The man's clothes struck him as absurd, however, in their vintage knock-off style. Here Ambrose was, trying to smuggle an infant born almost five hundred years earlier into a country now two hundred years behind the times with their technology. Ambrose wanted to shriek with hysterical, mad laughter.

Keep it together, mate. We're almost there.

"Hallo, there," the guard chirped. He sounded like he'd grown up across what used to be the Canadian border. "And how're we doin' this nice night, fella?"

"Oh, grand, sir," Ambrose replied. He enunciated with care, trying to polish his rough Cockney into the posh, Received Pronunciation he knew would go over well in this state. "Just picking up my daughter from my ex's place." He jerked a thumb at the backseat and dropped his voice. "She's sleeping, so…" He pressed an index finger to his lips.

The guard nodded and smiled. "Got an eighteen-month-old myself," he remarked in a stage whisper. He peeked at the bundle of blankets in the car seat and then looked back at Ambrose with a grave expression. "Her mother joined up over there, did she?" He let out a series of "tsks." "Such a pity. I lost more than a few good friends from university that way. You never can tell."

"It was always a mixed marriage," Ambrose said. "That is, ideologically," he added.

"The things we do for love," the guard said. "Don't blame ya none. Sorry you gotta take the little angel over to that place just to see her ma. Darn shame, that is."

"Indeed."

The guard asked to see Ambrose and Virginia's papers, and Ambrose produced them with a shaky hand. The baby stirred and whimpered, distracting both Ambrose and the guard.

"Forgive me, sir, I've got to get her home and fed."

"'Course, 'course. We'll have you both outta here before you know it." The guard made only a quick glance of the papers, too quick to notice the forged seals. "Have a lovely time with your little girl there, Mister, ah…" The guard looked at the paper one last time. "Mister Lessep."

Long ago, that might've been my name.

The guard's words played over in his head.

I lost more than a few good friends from university that way.

"Surely will do, sir." Ambrose took the documents back and gave the guard a little wave.

Virginia settled back to sleep as the hovercar took to the skies once more.

As Ambrose drove, he remembered a young man, head bowed over knobby knees, dreadlocks trembling as he sobbed.

"Please don't be angry," Ambrose said.

"I'm not angry," the other man said, raising his head and wiping his face. *"I feel sorry for you."*

~

Michael Lessep almost shut the door when he saw who stood on his front porch. "Oh, for Christ's sake," he muttered. Then, more loudly so the person outside would hear, "No, you bastard. Not letting you in, not after last time."

"Mike! God, mate, you gotta help me."

"Not your mate, Ambrose."

Not anymore.

"It's freezin' out 'ere and I got a fucking *baby.*"

Michael opened the door. Sure enough, Ambrose stood there with something the size of a loaf of bread in his arms. The blankets surrounding it stirred, revealing a milky-white arm and tiny mitten-clad fist.

Michael looked from the baby to Ambrose and back again. "What'd you do?" he demanded. "You left me and got some fucking stupid woman knocked up and now the both of you've gone on some bender or other and want me to watch it?"

Ambrose drew back. "God, no."

"Then what?"

Ambrose seemed to be trying to smile, but it was all hesitant and sideways. "Can I come in? Thirty minutes tops, love."

"*Don't you dare,*" Michael growled.

"Mate. Mike. M-M-Michael, sorry. Michael. Mister Lessep. Sir."

Michael stepped aside and opened the door wide enough for Ambrose to enter. "I'm not your father, Ambrose. Jesus. Just don't call me 'love.' You lost that right when you decided you were a fucking heterosexual." Once Ambrose was inside, Michael slammed the door shut. "You have thirty minutes. I'm timing you."

"Right. So. This is the first white baby born on American soil and I time traveled to steal it from Jack the Ripper—who is my boss and a bloody racist who wants to exploit her for his cause—and now I want to see if you'd adopt her and hide her for…oh, until she grows up at least? Probably longer? Probably until my boss dies, at any rate."

Ambrose sat down, still holding the infant, and cuddled her close to his chest. "I can…go into more detail, but yeah. That's…yeah." He looked up at Michael. "It sounded more complicated in my head. I thought it would take longer."

Michael blinked. "That's the *un*complicated, short version?" He glanced at the clock on his mantle. "All right, I'll give you *forty* minutes."

Friday, August 13, 2100, Avon, Vermont, NBE

"Kiddo, you already run around the world for the sake of truth, justice, and the Empiricist way. Can't you just be happy with your FBI work? Why you gotta have adventures in your personal life, too, huh?" Adventure to Michael meant risk. Risk of getting caught, risk of getting found out, risk of someone discovering something, or—God forbid—Violet herself discovering something.

"Oh, Pop, you're too damn practical." Violet kissed his bald head and scampered out with the credits he'd loaned her, off on some vacation or business trip that made Michael's jaw tense up.

She'll be okay. She joined the FBI, after all, and you let her do that. If she were gonna find something out, she would have by now.

Oh, but that was a weird way to think of it. "Let her." There was no "letting" Violet do anything, and besides she was an adult now. She could take care of herself. The heat was off.

When she returned from her vacation, she was listless and preoccupied, even less relaxed and at ease than she'd been when she left. She took him to lunch at his favorite restaurant to give him back some of the cash she'd borrowed, and her eyes seldom left her water glass.

"I thought the whole point of a vacation was to reboot yourself," Michael said. "Honey, you seem more on edge than you were before you went away."

"I don't know why," Violet admitted. She smiled and smoothed the napkin on her lap. "Why do you like this place, Dad? The service is terrible."

"Where'd you go, anyhow?"

"A spa," she replied, but her eyes seemed to lose focus and her voice came out robotic, almost an echo. "A spa in Maine. In the woods. There was a hiking path. I had a nutritional profile done."

"Yeah?" Michael studied her. "You think I should do that?" He patted his ample waistline. "Been thinking I should shed a few pounds. I don't seem to be getting as many dates as I used to."

Violet brightened. "That's because I came along." She giggled. "The kind of guys you said you used to date before you adopted me probably weren't into instant parenthood."

Yeah, the guy I used to date is who dropped you off on my doorstep. What was that old song about irony?

"I've been wondering something, Pop." Violet swept her long blond hair around to cover one shoulder and then twisted it into a coil, a nervous habit she'd been doing ever since childhood.

"Yeah?" Michael took a sip of his water. The waiter dropped off an endive salad in front of Violet and a plate of sausage and potatoes in front of Michael.

"See, told you I could use that nutritional—"

"I want to find my birth parents," Violet interrupted. She closed her eyes and sat back, exhaling. "Hoo, boy, I thought I was going to die waiting to say those words." She fanned herself with one hand. "Okay, we survived it. It's out there and nobody exploded."

"Nobody's gonna explode, baby, but...what brought this on?" Michael gripped his knife so hard he felt his fingernails dig into his palm.

Violet tugged at her hair again. "I don't know. I got back from my vacation feeling kind of like...there were things...I don't know." She shrugged. "I don't know," she repeated.

She's not acting right.

He relaxed his grip on his knife and let go of it, reaching across the table for her hand. "Do you feel okay?"

Violet let go of her hair and gave Michael's hand a squeeze. "I'm okay, Poppy. It's my job, you know, digging for information. But I've just never dug into the most personal information of all, and I guess now it's time." She let go of Michael and picked up her fork. "But I want your blessing. If you don't want me to, I won't. You *know* you're my dad. You'll *always* be my dad. You're the only parent I've ever known, and that won't change. But it's important to me. I want to know... more *roots*, you know?"

Oh, you don't know the half of it.

"I don't know that you'll find much," Michael said.

Ambrose. I'll find Ambrose and see if it's safe to tell her or not.

"Why not?" She stopped her fork in midair. "You always told me you didn't know. But you *do* know, don't you?"

He looked at her delicate features, her small frame looking vulnerable and young, even in her crisp, professional suit.

But she's not a little girl. Under that jacket, she's got a gun. I can't lie anymore. I can't keep protecting her.

He felt a vibration beneath his jacket. Just five words showed up on the screen, caller unknown, but he raised his head and looked around the restaurant.

"We have to go," Michael said. He nodded to a door across the room. "We have to go, and we have to go with that man over there. Right now."

Violet dropped her fork, her right hand fluttering over the left side of her jacket where Michael now noticed a subtle bulge. "Why? What's going on?"

Michael stood up and took her arm. "You wanna find out where you come from?" he asked. "You're about to find out."

Violet stood and followed Michael to where a man with silver hair stood.

"What's happened?" Michael asked.

"Told you this day might come," the man replied. "We gotta get 'er into hidin' an' fast."

"Where?"

"I know a place," the man answered. He looked at Violet. "You won't remember it, love, but you've been there before. An' not too long ago, in fact."

"Who are you? I'm not going anywhere with you," Violet said. She took a phone from her pocket. "Pop, I'm calling this in. This man is trying to kidnap us."

"No, I *know* him, baby."

"Then I need answers or this place'll be swarming with agents."

"Miss Lessep," the man said, "please accompany your father an' me to a lovely little shop not a five minute walk from 'ere. As I said, I think you know the place. Jonson's Exotic Travel."

At the mention of the name, Michael saw Violet's face harden even as her eyes brightened with an instant of recognition.

"That's...what? Why there?"

"That's where the answers are," the man replied.

Violet quieted and allowed herself to be led outside to the sidewalk. Michael patted her on the shoulder once they were under the midday sun.

"Pop," she whispered to him, "who is this guy?"

"I don't know what's safe to tell you yet," Michael replied.

"'S all right, Mike," the man said. "I'm on the run now m'self. Name's Ambrose. Your dear old dad here's not your first guardian. I've known 'em all."

"*All?*" Violet asked. "Wait, so my parents didn't give me up for adoption and then..."

"You weren't half wrong about me kidnapping you," Ambrose continued, "only it didn't happen just now. It happened thirty years ago."

~

Violet recognized the house. "This is my travel agency," she said. "Why are you taking me here? Are we going on a kinda-boring vacation together?"

Ambrose shook his head and laughed. "God, those bloody stupid false memories. I have no idea what good they think they're doin', but one wrong twist o' the dial and you're o' block of Swiss cheese." He climbed the front stoop and turned the antique key that activated the doorbell inside.

"False memories?" Violet climbed to the top of the stoop. "Wait, what are you talking about?" She looked from him to her father. "What the hell? Is *anything* I think real?"

Ambrose nodded at the building. "What do you remember about this place?"

Violent glared at him. "I remember a guy at work recommending it. I remember coming here to consult with the owner about a vacation package. I'd be going to…" She paused. "The owner. I know I met him, but it's…" She shook her head. "I don't know. It must not have been important."

"You borrowed money from me," Michael said. "Just how expensive was this trip? You said you went to Maine? To a spa?"

Ambrose turned back to Violet. "How much did it run you? All told?"

Violet rattled off a figure.

"Oh, baby, no," Michael said. "God, no, no. You only borrowed half that."

Violet could feel herself blush. "I only needed half. It really was that much, Pop."

The door opened, and a young woman with glossy dark hair stood in the entryway. "I'm sorry, we're not open to new clients on Friday afternoons," she said. "Can I help—oh. Oh! Agent Lessep. Did you have a special appointment?"

"How much is a *real* trip to Maine, Miss Moto?" Ambrose asked. He swept past her, despite the young woman's protests, and made his way deeper into the house. "Vere, get out 'ere, and bring young moneybags, too."

"I'm so sorry," Violet said to the receptionist, scrambling inside after Ambrose. "Mister Richards, what did you mean a real trip to Maine?"

"I meant," Ambrose said, "that you were never in Maine. You were never at a spa. You were somewhere else entirely. And this young lady an' 'er employers did some…" He gestured at his head. "They scrambled up your brains right good to make you forget what you learned on your trip."

"Oh, my God." Miss Moto scurried past the group to her desk and dialed the telephone. "Ben, you gotta get up here yesterday. There's this guy here and this other guy, and Agent Lessep, and I have no idea but—yes…" She listened and nodded and then hung up. "You people can't just barge in here, and—"

A door opened and shut from somewhere deeper in the house. Ambrose took a step back closer to the foyer.

The man who entered was only a little older than Ambrose and Michael, but his air was far graver, far more intimidating. "Did you call Benoy, Kris?" His voice was all gravel and smoke.

"Yes, he's coming."

"Good." He turned to Ambrose. "So why were you calling my name? Should I know you?"

"You know my employer," Ambrose replied. "You know of me by reputation, I suppose. Least a little." His shoulders sagged. "But I'm done with 'im, doctor. I threw in with the wrong sort, and I can't get out of it." He sank into the nearest chair and pointed at Violet. "You have to protect her. From *him*."

Doctor Vere looked from Violet to Michael. "I have to protect a client from…I don't even know this gentleman." He peered down at Ambrose. "And I don't know you, no matter that you think I ought to."

113

Ambrose looked up at Vere through tears. "You helped someone else look for her once." He took a wrinkled sheet of paper from his jacket pocket and held it out. "Recognize that?"

Vere took the paper. "Woodcut. Native Americans at Roanoke."

"But you know that woman."

Vere raised a bushy gray eyebrow. "That isn't Agent Lessep," he said.

"No, it's one of my associates."

Vere was quiet for a moment. "You work for Florence," he finally said.

His tone was so cold that Violet felt her heart quicken.

"Florence?" she asked. "Not *Governor* Florence, from the RAA?"

Another man entered the room. "Miss Lessep, it's good to—"

"Benoy," Vere interrupted. "I know we've met with Agent Lessep before, when she booked a trip with us, but have you ever noticed her appearance?"

Ben rubbed the back of his neck. "Um, what now? Eddy, I don't..." He exhaled a nervous laugh.

Vere tossed the woodcut back to Ambrose. "Oh, no one cares if you have a crush on the poor girl, you idiot. Just *literally* her appearance. Anything interesting about it."

Ben stammered again.

"Beyond its obvious appeal. Stop, boy, and just *think* for me for a moment," Vere said. "You're the historian. Tell me what you see."

Violet felt as if she might sink into a hole in the floor as the younger man scrutinized her. "Stop it! I'm a person," she said. "What the hell is going *on* here?"

"I'm sorry, Miss Lessep," Ben said. "I'm not trying to make you feel awkward here..." He looked back at Vere. "I see a lot of people, Eddy," he admitted. "I'm not really getting it."

"I think she's been pulled out of time," Vere said. He pointed across the room at Ambrose. "Isn't that so? Your employer's been behind the appropriation of one of our clients, hasn't he? He's gotten some of my designs."

Ambrose shrugged. "I swiped 'em for 'im. Back when you were developin' the whole thing."

"Security was too lax in those days," Vere said.

"Yeah, well, I was right good at lockpickin' in me youth, and—"

"I'm still not seeing who she's supposed to look—"

"*Hey!*"

Violet's shriek made all the men's chatter stop. She climbed on top of the coffee table in the center of the room and pulled her sidearm from its holster. The room quieted.

"My name is Agent Violet Lessep of the North American branch of the New British Empire Federal Bureau of Investigations. I am *not* coming down until someone tells me what the *fuck* is going on." She held her gun in the air, pointed at the ceiling. "First person who says something that doesn't give me an answer is getting…" She realized now that everyone looked wide-eyed and terrified.

Defuse. Get a grip.

"Is, ah, getting plaster in their hair," she finished. She took a deep breath. "But *start talking*." She clicked the safety off her gun.

It was Michael who finally spoke. "Baby, I never lied to you," he said. "But I never told you how you came into my life, either." He held out his hands. "Please come down."

Violet put the safety back on the gun and lowered her arm to her side. "I'll put this away, but, Pop, for God's sake, I'm a foot off the floor."

"It's my fault, Violet," Ambrose said.

"Eleanor Dare."

"What?" Violet turned to Ben, who was now running across the room to a bookshelf. He pulled a volume down and paged through it.

"Eddy, we had that client a while back who—here we are." He found the page he sought and held it up to Violet's face. "You look like Eleanor White Dare, daughter of the governor of the lost colony at Roanoke." He turned to Vere. "You know, we never did find out what happened to the colony, since that woman left before she—"

"She's not Eleanor Dare," Ambrose called out. "She's not. Don't make any sense, that, unless I'd arranged to 'ave 'er whole life's worth o' memories wiped." He looked up at Violet. "You remember your childhood growin' up with old Mike 'ere and all?"

"Of course."

"Does it seem fake, the way your little Maine holiday does?"

"My Maine holiday doesn't…" Except, no, it *did* seem fake. She remembered some basic things, but it was fuzzy, dreamlike, and bland.

"Where was she really then, doctor?" Ambrose asked Vere.

Vere looked at Ben. "We should restore her," he said.

"What? No. Remember what happened…" Ben shook his head. "*No.*"

"Not even for the patron saint of the Rénartians, Virginia Dare?" Ambrose asked.

Violet tucked her gun back into its holster when the words registered. "Wait, who, *me*?" she asked. She laughed. "How does *that* work? I look really good for being, what, five hundred?"

"You were just a baby when I took you," Ambrose said. "Florence wanted you, but I found out what he really was doing, so I went instead and kidnapped you, brought you to Michael."

"What was he really doing?" Vere asked.

"Claudio Florence is…" Ambrose paused and closed his eyes. "He's a murderer. I'm done working for 'im. Got to tell you lot what 'e's up to. He's been time traveling for thirty years, all based on your tech."

Violet climbed down from the coffee table. "Time travel is real?"

"You should know," Vere said. "You've done it apparently on multiple occasions." He turned to Ben. "I'm reversing it, Benoy. At least temporarily. She ought to know everything."

"But—"

"She didn't *do* anything, boy. For God's sake, the woman can't accept all this unless we give her proof!" Vere shouted. "It isn't as if she went back to witness the birth of Christ. She solved a relatively minor theft case."

"It doesn't matter," Ben countered. "We don't let them keep the memory. Even if she's not a risk, it's how we've always operated."

"Sometimes one has to adjust to new methods," Vere said. He moved toward Violet. "This is unrelated to your identity issue, Miss Lessep, but it'll prove to you that all this is even possible." He took a small box from his pocket and aimed it at her like a remote control.

"Wait, what're you—"

Vere pushed a button.

Violet sank to the carpet as a swell of memories flooded her. She gripped the patterned fibers of the rug between her fingers and clung to it as the waves swelled and crashed. Nausea threatened, but she swallowed hard, and soon the feeling passed.

Violet saw herself in the same room but on the other side of Kris's desk. She was wearing overalls with grease smeared down the front, and there was a man, Ben's age but not Ben, gaping at her. He was wearing a dark suit, and a hint of a beard peppered his cheeks.

"Damn, my office clearly needs a new IT department if I can hire folks who look like you," the man said.

"Excuse me?" Violet's perspective shifted, and now she was in her own body, but her body from several weeks earlier. She took in the man's smile, his faint scent of soap and something oaky. Whiskey?

The man shook his head. "Sorry, sorry, I just…you, ah, you work here? I'm looking for the head. The…ah, that sounded gross. The restroom. You an employee?"

Violet laughed. He was cute. Not her usual type, which was, truth be told, more like the agency's owner, more trim and mature but perhaps equally nervous. "No, I'm a…oh! Are you a client?" She laughed again and remarked that they probably shouldn't be talking to each other. "It was in the manual, wasn't it?"

The man agreed that it was against protocol. Violet scurried to the conference room, where her own clothes were waiting for her. Kris held out a cup of tea. "Get changed and come out to the lobby," she told Violet. "Almost time for debriefing."

Debriefing. Yes. Of her trip. The false memories of the time spent at the spa shifted and fell away, thin as gossamer and half as substantial. How could she have ever thought that was real? How could she have been fooled, when she was trained to observe and investigate?

"I was on a plane," she said. "I followed a man onto a plane and watched him jump." The enormity of what her real trip involved sunk in. "Oh, my God, I was in 1971." She scanned the faces in the room. "You!" She leapt at Vere. "You sent me back to 1971. And you." She whirled around to Ben and Kris. "You heard my story. You had me tell you what I did there but…" Tears rolled down her cheeks, but she didn't weep, her voice didn't crack. "I had the most amazing experience of my life and solved a century-old mystery and *you took it from me.*"

"We had to," Ben said, bowing his head. "Security. It's dangerous."

"Then *why do it at all*?" Violet demanded. "Why send people back in time if they don't get to remember?" She was shaking now.

"That's what you're bloody vexed 'bout?" Ambrose asked. "You find out I kidnapped you, that you're a relic of another age, and what you care about is a bleedin' crime you solved?"

"Because that's who I am." Violet pounded her chest. "I solve crimes." She picked up the book with the woodcut of her mother in it. "I wanted to know what I came from, but that's…that's a long-term issue. That's not who I am today. *You people took away who I am today.*" She looked around the room. "I didn't understand the magnitude of agreeing to that part."

"What was it?"

Violet looked at her father. "What?"

"What was the crime you solved?" Michael grinned. "Hey, I don't think you got your mystery-loving skills from some dead white lady. You got that from me, from watching old crime shows on the internet with your old man."

Violet relaxed slightly and moved toward Michael. "D.B. Cooper," she said. "I wanted to find out who he was."

Michael looked impressed. "No shit? Nice. Who was he?"

Violet turned to Ben and noted the pleading look on his face.

"Can't, Pop," she finally said, still keeping her eyes locked on Ben. "It's classified."

Ben leaned against the corner of the desk to steady himself.

"But apparently my real identity isn't, not anymore," she continued. "So I need the full scoop." She took a step back to Ambrose. "Finish talking, Mister Richards."

In the kitchen, Violet helped Ben bring in empty teacups and plates with the remains of cookie crumbs skittering across their surfaces. "Thank you," he told her.

"For what?"

"For not telling your dad what you learned." He filled the sink with water. "Why didn't you tell him? It's a good story, even if it's not like the co-pilot was famous or anything. It was a good scheme, and if Mike's a crime buff, he would've loved hearing about how the guy pulled it off."

Why didn't I tell? Was it because it would've spoiled Pop's own theorizing over the events himself? It wasn't like it was his favorite unsolved mystery or anything. So what harm would it have done to tell him?

"Maybe I still will, someday," Violet said. She spotted a bottle of dishwashing soap on the counter and squeezed a dollop into the filling sink. "But not today."

Part IV: The Ripper

There have been tyrants and murderers, and for a time, they can seem invincible, but in the end, they always fall. –Mahatma Gandhi

Ambrose told the others the last time he saw Wheaton. "I was still warily aligned with Florence. We needed to send a frequent time traveler to this other place, acquire some of their technology," he said.

"I met him at a tearoom. He was on his way here." Ambrose relayed the events of a few weeks prior.

"Just remember: we can't promise your extraction at all. You may need to rely on being able to return to the agency via their extraction means." Ambrose *scribbled a note on a napkin and slid it across the table to Wheaton. "When you return, meet me at this address and we'll arrange the transfer of funds. But we need something tangible, usable, or at least detailed information. We won't pay for nothing. This isn't one of your usual vacation excursions with them."*

Wheaton shook his head. "My usual vacation excursion with them is to a spa in Maine."

"First of many lies they've told you, mate. You've been time traveling every couple of months or so for several years."

Wheaton drew back. "I...no. Wouldn't I...no." He shook his head. "Last time I was at the spa, I have a distinct memory of..."

Ambrose grinned. "That's just it, innit? You don't have a distinct memory of those trips at all, do you?"

Wheaton groaned. "I've been paying them to do this to me. Mucking up my brain? Exposing me to these atomic whatsits you're talking about?"

Ambrose nodded. "Given all that, what's a little sleeping with the enemy if you can get some remuneration for your pain? All the ways you've been deceived?"

"And this trip? The memory?"

"You'll keep," Ambrose said. "So choose your mystery wisely, 'cause I'm afraid it'll be the last one you'll get to solve."

"That was it," Ambrose said. "I don't know where he decided to go after that, and then everything started falling apart with Florence." He shook his head. "I'm done with him, done with it all. I would hope Wheaton's done with it all as well."

Ben and Vere exchanged a look.

"Is he?" Ambrose asked. "Done with it, I mean?"

Silence.

"Well, if you can't tell me that, what mystery did he want solved?"

"A rather mundane one, if you ask me," Ben replied. "And only Mister Wheaton ever knew whether or not he was truly successful in solving it."

Saturday, September 12, 1136, Woolpit, Suffolk, England

He heard the wolves before he found the pits.

Wheaton materialized in a forest, birds twittering overhead and the smell of damp moss heavy in the humid air. There came a low howling and he started, forgetting for a moment that the town's original name—from even earlier than this medieval time—was "Wolf Pit," that the citizens made their trade from trapping the most pervasive of species.

Wolves.

For their meat, skins, teeth, fur, and sometimes as companions, Woolpit made good trade with other towns and smaller villages throughout this part of Suffolk. Wheaton remembered it all in a flurry of sinking back into his senses from the trauma of the trip—the feeling of free fall, the sense that his very structure was being torn apart and reassembled, all of which he now imagined was more than a little like transforming from human to werewolf, if such a thing weren't the stuff of fairytales.

I'm here for a fairytale, in fact.

From his research, he knew the children should be sequestered at the home of the local doctor, or what passed for doctor, barber, dentist and veterinarian in these primitive times. He set off toward the sound of the wolves, knowing the town would be just beyond.

I hope my clothes are right enough they won't think me one of the fae as well.

The pits were impossible to miss, with wide-spaced posts and crude signs fencing them off such that humans were warned but unwary beasts might still wander in under the slender starlight. The howling subsided as Wheaton passed. He dared a quick glance down in the dark depths of one and spotted a creature small enough to be mistaken for a husky pup. For a brief instant, he felt a pang of longing to rescue the thing, but he shook off the impulse and proceeded.

With the money the Rénartians are giving me, I can rescue twenty dogs back in my own time.

The town was now in sight, larger and more bustling than he'd imagined. Men and women in rough-sewn cloth rode carts drawn by horses. Children rode ponies. And everywhere were the scents of sweat and open sewer, though no one save Wheaton seemed to take note of the mingled stench. He coughed once, urging down a slick ribbon of bile. If he couldn't even stomach the air, this whole endeavor would be nigh impossible, he knew. He tightened his abdominal muscles and forced himself forward.

Wheaton ambled up to a vegetable cart staffed by a young man, wan and shabbily dressed. "By your pardon, lad. Is the physician near?"

The boy gestured to his throat and shook his head, then to one ear and nodded. He then pointed across the straw-lined path to a stone cottage with a square of wood on the door. Though the lettering was too far to read, Wheaton suspected it announced the services of the dweller within. "Many thanks," he said. He thought of buying a carrot from the boy but knew he needed to conserve his coins as best he could.

As he approached the door, the lettering came into focus; there was a name next to a crude drawing of a snake coiled around a staff. Wheaton rapped on the weathered door. A ruddy-faced woman in a flat white cap opened it.

"Aye?"

"God's blessings." Wheaton took off his own cap and bowed low. "Pray, is the physician within?"

She squinted at him. "Surely you heard of the young travelers what got in this morning," she said, "and knew Doctor Terric took them in to examine."

Wheaton's heart sped up. It couldn't be this easy—today was an estimate of when the children were supposed to appear. When Jonson assisted with his research, they hadn't been able to determine much beyond a season (late summer, just before harvest) and location. But to think they'd appeared *this morning*?

The woman was still staring at Wheaton. He shook his head. "Aye, that is the cause of my visit," he said. "I heard them described and thought they resembled my kin, a niece and nephew who fell into a well in Bury Saint Edmunds on holiday. My sister thought her children lost forever."

Wheaton stepped upon the cottage's threshold stone, but the woman held her hand out, not quite pressing against his chest. "I'll ask kindly that ye step back, sire." She set her own foot beside Wheaton's. She was stout, though shorter than Wheaton, with powerful arms well muscled from tending to all the duties a twelfth-century home required. "These children are no innocent babes. Did ye not hear of their faces, their hands? Did ye not know they weren't speaking nothing resembling a language the likes of anything in Suffolk? These cannot be your kin." She looked around at the passers-by walking behind Wheaton, then leaned forward and pitched her voice low. "Methinks they're like to be from the devil himself."

"The wee things don't speak as we do," Wheaton said, "most because their father is a Fleming, and they have heard a good four different languages since birth." He laughed. "The two are so small, they're not clear on whether to speak Dutch or—"

"It isn't Dutch," came a deep voice behind the woman. She turned and looked backward into the darkened anteroom, opening the door wider as she did so. Wheaton took the opportunity to step across the threshold stone.

"It isn't?" Wheaton asked.

Doctor Terric came into view, a spare man of middle age in a coarse chambray shirt with a tie winding around a slender throat. He wore a leather apron, upon which he now rubbed his hands before holding one out to Wheaton. "May we be acquainted, sire?"

Wheaton shook the doctor's hands. "Braiden Welty," he said. "As I told your woman, I am visiting from Bury Saint Edmunds to see the children your town discovered. I believe myself to be their uncle."

"News travels quickly," the doctor said. He nudged the woman. "Eveline, let him in. He shall see soon enough they belong to no man or woman of earth."

"Doctor, we know this man not and have no one to vouch for him."

Terric took Eveline by the shoulders and steered her out of the way of the door. "Madame, if it gets these creatures out of our sight, I would endeavor to find them a home with anyone. Please." He opened the door wider to permit Wheaton entry.

The doorway was cut small, and only upon needing to duck did Wheaton realize how much shorter the doctor and his housekeeper were than his own six-foot frame. He wasn't freakish by comparison—no kids would have accused him of being a giant—but were he to be a native of the time, he would have still been remarkable.

I have all my teeth, too, Wheaton noted to himself, spying Eveline's jack o'lantern mouth. *Would have been quite the catch back here.*

As he followed Terric into an inner room of the cottage, he reminded himself he was only partly here to solve this mystery; he still needed to find the portal for the Rénartians.

But I have to see them. Just once. Even if I can't figure out for myself what they are, who they are, I have to see them…

They were smaller than he'd imagined, huddled up together on a rosewood bench. They were indeed not what modern explanations gave them to be—foreign, malnourished, or con artists. They weren't Flemings at all, nor were they from the next village over. While he doubted Eveline's assessment that they were devils or demons or some other nebulous evil, he knew they weren't of this earth or this time.

For these children were hairless, not shorn to stubble but smooth about the head, sans eyebrows and lashes. The famous green pallor Wheaton imagined from all the stories was in fact not a tinge due to poor diet but bright, fluorescent green, the green of neon and cars and acrylic paint; a vivid, artificial, far-flung future green impossible to create from the resources of medieval England.

Their clothing, too, was impossible. These weren't the tattered but recognizable vestments from Eastern Europe or Wales. These were silver lamé jumpsuits, so ridiculously 1950s B-grade science fiction movie that Wheaton almost let out a high-pitched giggle. These kids were only missing bobble-round clear helmets to complete the look of cliché aliens.

Except that aliens weren't cliché here and now, of course, and so they were fairies or demons or worse.

Ambrose told Wheaton that the Beta universe he sought was full of things Earth took to be cryptids. Why couldn't it also be home to what Earth thought were little green men from Mars?

I may have just killed two birds with one stone. These kids might be able to lead me to the portal.

"There you are," Wheaton sang out. He took one child by each hand, expecting them to flinch and being relieved when they didn't. "Your mum is going to be right chuffed." He turned to Terric. "These are my kin, indeed."

"Then you're kin to the devil," Eveline cried. She tugged at Terric's sleeve. "Have them all put in the pillory."

Terric shook his head. "We do not well know the ways of other counties, let alone other nations," he replied. "Let them be." He nodded toward the still-open door. "Off with you lot, though. I beg you to pardon our superstitious ways here, but Woolpit will be glad to be gone with you."

"Ni volas iri hejmen."

Wheaton felt the children's hands clutch his tight, and his body went rigid. He looked down at them. One—he took it to be the girl, as her face was narrower, her eyes larger and somehow more feminine—was looking up at him, glints of moisture in the corners of her eyes. "Hejmo," she said. "Bonvolu. *Hejmo.*"

"You see? A devil tongue," Eveline said. She tutted. "They haven't graced us with much speech since their arrival, but when they have, it has been that."

"Our scholars couldn't parse it," Terric said.

Wheaton pondered the cadence. "Hej...mo?" he tried.

The girl relaxed and nodded. "Vi prenas al ni hejme?"

"It's their Flemish dialect of Dutch," Wheaton said. "My distant relatives come from even farther afield, and as such odd words have entered our familial lexicon."

Eveline and Terric exchanged a look.

I have to get them out of here before I'm burned at a stake as well.

"Many thanks for their good care," Wheaton said, steering the children to the door. "God be with you both."

The three of them were barely through the threshold when the heavy wood slammed shut behind them. From inside, there were muffled tones that Wheaton took to be Eveline's great relief at being rid of the children.

"Right," Wheaton said, tugging the boy and girl along toward the forest. "I can't speak it, but I recognize what you're doing there. Esperanto."

The boy struggled a bit against Wheaton's hand and managed to pull away. "Esperanto!" he cried. He hopped up and down. "Komprenas?"

"Komprenas?" the girl echoed. She, too, wriggled away and looked up at Wheaton with an open-mouthed, hopeful smile.

"I don't *comprende* very well," Wheaton said, shaking his head, "but your language wasn't invented back in this time, in this place." Esperanto was close enough to the bits of various Romance languages Wheaton knew in passing to help him identify it, but its influences were vast and its cognates limited. Perhaps if the children were from an alternate world, similar to this one but not quite, this language developed there on its own as the dominant one in lieu of others with Latin bases. "Eh...I know you two aren't demons, aren't fairies, not really. But I need you to take me to your home. Is there a doorway? Door?"

The children both frowned.

Wheaton racked his brain. "*Puerta*? *Porte*? Um...*porta*?"

The boy, the taller of the two, clapped his hands. "Pordo?" he asked, his eyes lighting up.

Wheaton shrugged. "I guess, sure, pordo." He mimicked opening a door and walking through it. "To your home?" He looked at the girl, thinking back to what she'd said in the doctor's house. If strangers to a strange land wanted to get away, wouldn't they ask to go home? What had she said? "Hej—"

"Hejmo," the girl said. "Pordo a la hejmo."

"Yes. Pordo a la hejmo. Where is it?" Wheaton pointed around the edges of the town, pointed to the forest, then held out his hands and shrugged. "Where?" He put his hand at his brow line and mimed shielding his eyes from the sun to look around.

"Kie." The boy tugged at the girl's sleeve and pointed to a spot deep within the forest. "Ni eliris el la arbaro."

"Arbaro?" Wheaton pointed to the forest. "Arbor. Tree. Trees? Woods?"

"Arbaro," the boy repeated, flapping both arms toward the forest. "Arbaro. Ni eliris el la arbaro hieraŭ."

"Pordo to hejmo in arbaro?" Wheaton tried.

The girl giggled and mimed a mouth with her hand, turning it into a makeshift puppet. "Vi parolas malbone." She shook her head and mimed the mouth again before pointing to Wheaton.

"Yes, yes, well, this is my first lesson," Wheaton said, getting the gist of her criticism of his speaking skills. "Come on, take me to this pordo." He strode toward the place the boy indicated and beckoned to them to follow, then pointed ahead. "Go on, show me where you arrived." He placed his index and middle finger on his palm and mimed the fingers walking, then pointed ahead once again, then to the children.

The boy and girl looked at one another. The boy nodded, and scampered ahead of his sister, who then took Wheaton's hand and led him into the woods.

Several feet under the darkened canopy of leaves and branches, Wheaton noticed a shimmering quality to the air and a vaguely electric feeling, as if a thunderstorm were imminent. He took a deep breath and smelled the subtle, vacuum-like whiff of ozone. It reminded him of plastic, metal, dehumidifiers, and chemicals, products of centuries far in the future.

The boy grew excited as he approached one tree in particular. He turned and danced back to Wheaton and the girl. "Patrino!" he called. He stopped and stood still. The girl opened her mouth to speak, but her brother shushed her. "Aŭskulti," he whispered, shaking his head. He clamped a hand on his mouth and then tugged on his ear. "Aŭskulti," he whispered again.

The girl now stood at attention, her tiny body straining forward toward the tree. After a moment, her eyes widened. "Patrino," she whispered. She pulled Wheaton forward. "Nia patrino estas tie." She pointed to her ear. "Aŭskulti. Vi povas aŭdi la flugilojn."

Wheaton only recognized the vaguest of stems and verbs and gestures between the children, but he gathered enough to understand that they heard something beyond the tree. With the shimmer and the ozone, he also gathered that the portal was very near. He looked at the tree and then shut his eyes, trying to hear what the children did.

Thwip, thwip, thwip.

It was faint, but Wheaton heard something. He thought of tongues darting from the mouths of reptiles, ceiling fans with palm-frond blades whirring in lazy summer air, the soles of sandals slapping between bare feet and sidewalk pavement.

Thwip...snap...thwip...

Flags furling and unfurling on a blustery early-spring day.

The scent of ozone grew stronger. Wheaton flashed back to childhood, imagined himself drawing with markers and pausing to sniff the sharp scent of the ink, giving himself a dizzy, swimmy feeling.

Thwip...snap...snap...thwip...flap...

Now he saw a bird, sailing and coasting along a crystal-blue sky, feathered wings spanning twice the length of its massive body.

Flap, flap, flap.

The sky in Wheaton's mind darkened, the bird now stark against the light of a full, silvery moon. It passed behind a branch and emerged on the other side, glowing and featherless now, a gray thing with leathery skin and red eyes—

The image startled Wheaton, and he jumped backward, opening his own eyes as he did so.

The pinpoints of red bored into him, not his imagination but so vibrant, so strong were these beams of light that he'd seen them behind his eyelids.

The children grabbed the creature's hands and scampered around it, caressing its massive bat wings and snuggling against the smooth, short fur that grew along its torso and flanks.

"Patrino!"

The creature cooed like a dove and drew the children closer to it.

"Bebojn," it said. Its voice was ethereal, unreal, part echoing growl, part purr. Wheaton marveled at all the different species it reminded him of—cat, owl, bird, bat…but most terribly, most upsettingly of all…

Human.

The thing raised its head and stared again at Wheaton. Its expression changed, though Wheaton couldn't tell how he knew, as its mouth didn't move, its eyes didn't cease or change their glow. Still, he sensed it felt warmth toward him. It clutched the children closer and nodded.

Wheaton smiled, in spite of himself. *It knows I protected them. It's thanking me.*

The children looked up at Wheaton. The boy wriggled away from the creature and took his hand again. "Pordo," he said. He guided him past the creature, past the tree, and the shimmer in the air became a glow, a blur, and then—

Wheaton stood in an open field. The trees were gone. He spun around, and behind him was more field, no forest. The shimmer was still there, however, and from within it emerged the creature and the children.

"Welcome," the little girl said. "Thank you for helping us remember how to get home."

Wheaton gaped at her. "I can understand you."

"We don't belong there," the boy said. "We shouldn't have been able to cross, because we're too little."

"We don't have our wings yet," the girl added.

The creature nudged the children from its side and spread its wings out wide. "Once they can fly, they can travel through the doors more easily," it said.

"This is our mother," the girl said. "I am Agnes."

"I am Richard."

"And I am Gael, but all of these words are simply how you can best understand them," the mother said. "They are different in our languages."

Wheaton could now see the more human features in the grown creature, could see the gentle curve of breasts beneath its fur. "What are you?" he murmured.

Gael looked down at her children. "They do not yet resemble it, for they are still young, but on your side of the door you have called our kind the Mothmen."

Wheaton remembered this bit of modern myth, a cryptid discounted as a mutant or a crane spotted in a region now belonging to the RAA-controlled states. "There are more of you?"

The tip of one of Gael's wings fluttered, and Wheaton looked over his shoulder. Other creatures who resembled Gael sailed in the sky, while some at a clearly intermediate stage of development between the green children and their gray, winged mother strolled along grassy hills. The ones in a sort of adolescent state were a paler green than the children, with fur cascading down smooth cheeks and firm torsos. Some still wore silvery trousers, while others did not. A few had tiny wings—fluffy and white—sprouting from exposed shoulder blades. Still others exhibited what looked like painful knobs, as of broken bones ill-repaired or even goiters or tumors, poking pink and raw from their backs. These knobs didn't seem to be painful, however, as all the youths talked and walked without apparent discomfort.

Gael cooed and took flight, and as she passed overhead the others watched her. Children clapped and laughed, and older creatures returned her cooing cry. Wheaton left Agnes and Richard to their own devices and walked, keeping his eyes pinned on Gael and following her flight path.

Once over the hill, Wheaton saw a low circular building. The top was brown, earthen, and thatched with sun-bleached straw. At its middle was a thin strip of black material, below which square metal panels were installed at regular intervals every few feet. Gael flew a few feet beyond Wheaton then slowed, hovered vertically for a moment, and landed on her feet.

"I should take you back to your world," she said.

Wheaton gave a slow nod. "I suppose. But I mean you no harm and am merely interested in this place."

Gael cooed. "You would like what your people call a tour."

It struck Wheaton that she was laughing, though he heard no such noise and her mouth stayed small, unsmiling. He couldn't help his own grin.

"I suppose," he said. "I may never manage another trip like this one. This is quite possibly the strangest place I've ever been."

That I remember. I'm on a mission, not a holiday. She has to let me into that building. If I can take anything back with me, it'll be in there.

~

Hours later, back in the forest, Wheaton withdrew the gun from the pocket of his waistcoat. Silver, smooth, the grip oddly comfortable in his hand. When he'd swept it off the table in the hut Gael called her laboratory, he didn't think it would discharge, but it did. A pop, spark, and then Gael's red eyes had locked on his.

For the first time all day, her face registered expression. Just for an instant, but it was seared into Wheaton's brain.

Horror. Shock. Sorrow.

She'd looked at him, mouth open as if to scream, and then she was gone.

He scurried over to where she'd stood and stared at the empty space. No ash on the floor, no scorch marks. No trace that Gael had ever existed.

He scrambled away, past the other creatures still talking and playing, and swept past Agnes and Richard.

"Is Mother with you?"

He paused just a second, but didn't turn around, couldn't look at them. "She's working," he said. "She said I have to leave soon, so I don't get trapped on this side of the door."

"Good travels." Agnes bounded over to him, clasping him around the middle and giving him a squeeze. "Thank you for helping us."

"We could never have stayed over there," Richard said. "If you had not helped us—"

"They wanted to kill us, I think," Agnes said.

Or at least render you into dull humans.

In the legends, the children stayed in and around Woolpit, the boy growing ill and dying, the girl working as a servant. As she grew up, she'd lost her green tint and gained a reputation for being listless, frustrated, and eccentric.

Of course you were. You didn't grow up in the right place. You didn't grow your wings.

An adolescent creature whose wings were almost full-size swooped down in front of Wheaton. "Children, your mother is missing."

Wheaton hadn't thought before withdrawing the gun. As soon as the creature disappeared, he ran.

They were fast, but he wasn't far from the door, and now he was through it, but still unsafe.

They can still find me.

It wasn't time for retrieval, not yet, but he had to get away from the forest. Running through the clawing branches, he emerged at a different angle than the one he'd arrived in.

Along this side of the town, the pits were not as well marked.

Wheaton spent an anxious night pressed against a dirt wall, cowering in the presence of a sleeping wolf. When it was late enough that the sounds of activity in the town ceased, he withdrew the gun and turned the wolf into a patch of scorched grass.

Saturday, August 14, 2100, Avon, Vermont, NBE

Claudio hated Vermont, hated coming here because of incompetence. Days earlier, Claudio had poured tea from a pot into two small mugs and asked after Wheaton. He felt more like his old self than usual today, more in control, less interested in blood and death and murder. All thanks to wondering with glee what this mysterious weapon could do, which of course led back around to murder, but it was more abstract, this wondering. Could he go back to a pivotal battle of the war, perhaps allowing his side to take back a segment of the more northern states? Or, more personal yet, could he wipe Edward Vere straight out of history, perhaps have Ambrose connect with young Jonson and steal the agency concept from the get go?

Ambrose had remained quiet. Claudio put the teapot down and held out a mug to him. "We've run out of sugar, I'm afraid."

"Wheaton's gone missing," Ambrose had said. "Never met back up at the café. His message described this gun in perfect detail." He shook his head. "Bastard must've been compromised."

"By *them*?" A chill ran through Claudio. He thrust the mug into Ambrose's hands and stalked into the outer room. "I'll find him myself. Never send an amateur to do a professional's job." He pulled his overcoat off its peg in the hall with such force a great chunk of plaster and wallpaper came off with it.

Now in Vermont, the streets were lined with eager college-aged youths, and Claudio seethed at their laughter and easygoing pace.

He ran, shoving a long arm between people moving slowly, squeezing himself between them to pass. Wheaton didn't live far, but Claudio hailed a pedicab and ordered the rider to the address.

"And I'm in a hurry," he barked.

"Mister, you might wanna take the subway if you need to get somewhere faster," the cyclist told him as he pushed off from the curb. "I'm good, but I ain't got an engine, you know."

"Oh, for God's sake. You're worthless." Claudio threw bills at the man and leapt from the seat. He sped up to a sprint the closer he got to Wheaton's street.

"Mommy?"

And there, huddled in an alley, was Brimley Wheaton. Only Ambrose had met with him in person, but Claudio saw digital video of him. The Brimley Wheaton he'd seen was a large man, robust and boisterous. Both the life of the party and from a prominent family, Prince Hal and Falstaff in one. Wheaton seemed the sort to wear the finest waistcoats, though they might be stained with the evening's food and drink.

This was not that Brimley Wheaton.

And yet the man's round face and floppy dark hair were unmistakable. He was crouched in a ragged black overcoat, bits of fluff in his stubble, garbage stink all around him. Claudio caught a whiff and recoiled.

"Mister Wheaton, is that you?"

"The man said we could go to the circus." There was a wistful mirth in Wheaton's voice, but his expression remained blank, stupefied.

"Mister Wheaton, you are a human being, not a sewer rat." Claudio held his breath and tugged on Wheaton's arm. "Get out of the gutter. I'm going to take you home."

"I was home," Wheaton said, allowing himself to be stood up. He leaned against a garbage bin. "The man and the lady took me, but I wanted chicken." He giggled. "They throw away old chicken here, from the store. Mommy used to say not to eat it, but I'm fine."

"Would you recognize the people who took you home if you saw them?" Claudio asked.

"Pro'ly."

Claudio pulled out a miniature data pad from his coat pocket. He whisked his finger along the pad's surface until he found a folder full of intel on Jonson and his associates. "This one? This one? This one?"

Wheaton kept shaking his head until Claudio got to a sepia-toned portrait of Wilbur Wright.

What's that doing there? Vere sent him back to his own time.

"Him!" Wheaton clapped his hands. "That was the man. He was nicer to me than the lady."

"Did you see her in these pictures?" Claudio asked.

"Huh uh." Wheaton pouted, an almost grotesque expression on a grown man. "I want Mommy."

"Of course, of course." Claudio wondered how useful Wheaton was in his current state. The clients from Jonson and Vere's agency were mindwiped about their trips, but this regression was different, more complete. Someone got to him. Could it have been Wilbur Wright? Or was Wheaton's brain so scrambled he imagined things?

"Are we going home now?"

"It depends how you define *home*." Slowly, Claudio drew a switchblade from his pocket. "Let's take the shortcut. Just walk a bit deeper into this alley here, right this way…I always did do my best work in alleys."

"What do you mean?"

But Wheaton never got the answer. The first slash caught him in the right kidney, and the second whisked across his throat, cutting off his scream to a gurgle.

Saturday, August 28, 2100, Avon, Vermont, NBE

Two weeks later, Claudio was making do without Ambrose, who was gone from both the Vermont and South Carolina offices and laboratories for days at a time. For the surveillance of the agency house today, he resorted to a false moustache and an ancient pair of mirrored sunglasses.

Still, it paid off. The connection was now clear.

Young Jonson's assistant left on errands one afternoon. She was a slender girl with close-cropped dark hair. Claudio didn't know her name, but he'd come to think of her as Elizabeth, the girl from so long ago, the girl with the flower in her hair whom he'd stolen from that other worthless sort, Rupert Cob. Elizabeth Short, all Snow White features and crimson blood. He thought it so beautiful the poetic nickname they gave her in the press after he'd done his work.

Too beautiful, more poetry than these girls deserve, all of them whores...

Claudio watched this one walk six blocks to a modest neighborhood, shabby houses and ill-tended gardens, children fixing bicycles right in the middle of the street. Skeletal cats slipped between untrimmed hedges, running away as he followed the girl.

She stopped at an orange house with purple shutters and a yard full of withering phlox on the wrong side of its season. He tucked himself behind a parked hovercar across the street. At her knock, the door opened, and Claudio could hear murmured voices. The room beyond the foyer was too dark, however, and he couldn't make out who let the girl inside.

He walked up and down the street a few times, always keeping his gaze pinned on the house. At last, the girl left, skipping down the front stoop. Claudio ignored her. She was of no particular consequence now that she'd led him here.

Claudio strode down to the corner and around to the rear of the house. An alley-facing garage was painted the same shade of purple as the house's shutters. Beside the garage was a gate, locked from the inside of the yard, but short enough to be scalable. Claudio made a furtive check for observers, but only the scrawny neighborhood felines watched. A dingy tabby plopped down on the gravel next to the garage and stared at Claudio, pinning vertical black slits of pupils on him as it licked a dusty paw.

"Keep a lookout, won't you?" Claudio said. He planted his hands on the top of the gate and groaned as he pulled himself over.

The backyard was all brick, a few weeds poking through the grout, with a small circular fire pit in the middle. At the back of the house were uncovered windows, but Claudio fretted about peering in where he could be seen. He crept along the right side of the house, past the side closest to its front door, and crouched at every windowsill before peeking up enough to catch a glimpse of movement.

He saw him in the dining room.

There, plain as day, sitting at a long, polished wood table, a chess set laid out in front of him, was a hollow-cheeked man in his early forties, a fringe of ashy blond hair circling a smooth, high forehead. He had a long nose and creases about his mouth, and he lifted the white rook with slender, elegant fingers before moving it to another space on the chessboard. He smiled and mouthed words to his unseen opponent.

That's him. Wilbur Wright.

And if Wright still worked for Vere, if he'd been the one to wipe Wheaton's memories, then Claudio knew where to find the missing weapon.

~

"And you're sure you're all right, Miss Lessep?"

"It's been quite a while since you restored my memories. I'm fine." Violet hopped off the examination table. "Honestly, Doctor Vere, you worry more than my father."

Vere packed away his retinoscope in a small black bag. "Unlike your father, I have to determine if you're suffering ill effects of changes to your neurological system. Changes I created." He slid the bag into a cabinet over his desk and closed the door. "I don't expect Mister Lessep has to worry about having given you permanent brain damage."

"No, just emotional damage."

"Oh, now, now."

"No, you're right, it's not Michael's fault. It's Ambrose's. Or Claudio Florence's. Or, God, who knows anymore, right?" Violet gestured to the spiral staircase leading to the agency's main floor. "We all need to discuss the next stage, don't we? I'll find Ben."

"I'll be after you in a moment." Vere nodded at Violet and heard her quick footsteps on the stairs.

So it's Ben now, is it?

Vere thought of the slim volume of photographs he kept in the cabinet next to his medical equipment. He thought of the photograph of himself and Alison Keller, all smiles—even him—at his induction into the NBE Physicists' Union. He thought of another photograph, one much more recently taken, giving Alison away at her small wedding. Alison looked the same in both pictures, but Vere went from black hair to gray, deep shadows visible under his eyes in the second photograph. A hardness crept into his mouth, jaw, and eyes in his intervening years.

I've become my father.

He didn't need to look at the photographs to know what they proved—he'd let decades of his life go by, and though others around him found love in the most unlikely places, Vere himself was alone.

Like anyone would put up with me. Stop being a foolish old man, Eddy.

He clicked the lights off in the lab and followed Violet upstairs.

~

"Wait, you're the history expert." Violet looked up from the map. "Why do you think I should go?"

"You're, um…" Ben shoved his hands in his pockets. "You know, the FBI thing. You investigate for a living. You should get investigative." He nodded at the map. "Don't think of this as going back in time. Think of this as catching a serial killer. Isn't that an FBI deal?"

"Yeah, but usually there's a team," Violet replied. "There's not usually a lone agent tracking some dangerous criminal without backup."

"Benoy, why are you trying to have her go without backup?" Vere was now behind Ben, a steaming cup of coffee in hand.

Ben turned around. "Hey, d'you bring one for me?" Ben asked. He pointed to Vere's cup.

Vere gave Ben a withering look. "Are you still pretending I'm thoughtful, son?"

Violet whistled. "Wow, you act protective of my brain cells, but that's how you treat your business partner?"

"I've learned to expect nothing less from Eddy," Ben said.

"You're a client, dear," Vere said. "I'm more polite to you because you help me earn money. Though I don't let that stop me if a client is breaking rules."

"He can get damn scary when he needs to," Ben said. "Trust me."

"Am I still a client, though? Really?" Violet looked around the conference room. "Hell, is this still going to be open to the public at all? Or, well, you know, the *referred* public. The carefully trained public." She walked around the room. "I mean, if we're going to get on board this crazy train and try to *do* something with your technology rather than just you two using it for financial gain, then isn't that the first step shutting down your commercial operation?"

Ben shrugged. "Yeah, I guess. I mean, I've already had Kris put off any potential clients, even the repeat ones."

"I, ah, that is…" Vere coughed. "Not all of us are as well-off as Mister Jonson here, so perhaps a cessation of commercial operations isn't yet warranted."

"Eddy, your salary's not going anywhere," Ben said.

"On the other hand," Vere continued, not missing a beat, "commercial operations are highly overrated."

"So who's coming with me, if I go try to stop this guy?" Violet asked. "Come on, I'm not going alone, and I can't exactly tell the rest of the bureau the truth, right? Talk about *definitely* ceasing commercial operations. As in forever."

"Some sort of treason, I suppose," Vere said. He shook his head at Ben. "Not wise, Benoy. That's why we've employed the Wrights, after all." He walked from the conference room. "I have an idea of who you should bring, Miss Lessep," he called.

"Wait, no, Eddy, nobody's going with her." Ben scrambled after him. "Unless you mean that Richards guy or, hell, even her dad or something."

"I am *not* bringing my father on an investigation." Violet followed the others to the lobby. "I'm a perfectly capable adult with several years' experience in law enforcement. I don't need my parent along on the field trip."

"It's not your parent, Miss Lessep." Vere sat down at the desk and rummaged through the top drawer. "Where does Miss Moto keep her—ah ha!" He withdrew a flat container covered in a plastic film stamped with faux chatoyant amber. Along the side of the container was a tiny triangle of metal. He moved the triangle down the side of the container, pressed a recessed button on its side, and activated a spring. Now the device opened to reveal address cards. Vere fussed about with the pages before pulling one free and handing it to Ben. "There you are. Give this one a call."

Ben studied the card. "I don't know," he said. "His last trip didn't go well at all."

Violet looked over Ben's shoulder. "Rupert Cob?"

"A client," Ben said.

"An *adventurous* client," Vere amended. "Mister Cob has gone through the Bermuda Triangle, spent the night in not one but two haunted houses, tracked several serial killers, and knows who killed Kennedy."

"John?" Violet asked.

"*All* of them," Vere said, "and Marilyn Monroe as well."

"He's a thrill seeker, sure," Ben said, "if you, um, like that sort of thing…" His voice trailed off to an inaudible mumble.

He glanced at Violet. There was a wild look in her eyes.

"Wow, who killed Marilyn Monroe?" she asked.

"You'd be shocked," Ben replied. "It all started when Peter—"

"Children, focus," Vere interrupted. "Mister Cob would be ideal for this. Shall we consult him?"

Ben dropped the address card. "Eddy, Rupert Cob was decidedly not okay when we brought him back from West Virginia. He had memory loss even before the usual procedure, and he couldn't report what he found out about the Mothman."

"Whoa, the Mothman?" Violet picked the address card up. "I think I'd like to meet this Cob guy."

Of course you would.

"Fine, but Eddy, you have to give him a full physical and make sure he's okay. He takes risks. He's going to be on board when we tell him everything, he's going to want to go, and I don't want him hurt."

Vere raised an eyebrow. "I didn't think you cared much for Mister Cob."

"I...no, no, he's a good client," Ben said, "but no matter what I think of him personally, I don't want to see the guy dead. He's told us a lot of good tales, after all."

"Florence has left enough dead bodies throughout history, huh? Don't need one more, no matter who it is?" Violet patted Ben on the shoulder. "Yeah, there was this agent going through Quantico North with me. Brody. She annoyed me to no end, but then when we were shadowing a senior agent in the field, this guy pulled a Taser on her. I pushed Brody out of the way and took the hit." She shuddered. "It was the fourth model, too, jacked up and powerful as hell. I could've been paralyzed if the perp got me just a few inches up, but I didn't even hesitate. I'd do it again, too." She quieted briefly. "Now that I think about it, Brody later slept with this researcher I liked, so maybe in hindsight I made the wrong decision."

"Is that the problem, Benoy?" Vere closed the desk drawer and stood up. "Did Mister Cob—"

"Let's go." Ben took the address card and held out his arm toward the front door. "Why don't you join me on an errand, Miss Lessep?"

"I think fieldwork earns you a first name basis, don't you?"

"Of course." Ben smiled, hoping it didn't look too eager. "Violet. Sure." He followed her through the front door and out onto the sidewalk.

"Why does your partner always call you Benoy?" she asked. "Does anybody else?"

Ben looked up and down the street for a hovercab. "I don't think he realizes he's doing it," he said, "but I think he enjoys making me feel like a kid, the whole full name thing." A stamper slowed down as it neared Ben.

"Oh, jeez, no. These things are so slow," Violet said. She eyed the vehicle. The main body was the same size and shape as a hovercar, but it rode higher, not on the magnetic lines but via four clockwork legs, horse-like, that whirred and bucked and propelled the vehicle along at an average speed of only thirty miles an hour.

"Yeah, but they're cheaper than hovercabs and faster than pedis," Ben pointed out. He withdrew a flat cap from his jacket and waved it at the stamper driver before setting it on his head. "Cob doesn't live too far, just too far to walk. This keeps us out of the weather."

The stamper slowed down, and the front legs swerved in to meet up with the sidewalk. The driver was now close enough for Ben to see his movements on the control panel. He was young, too young for a hovercar license, and he danced around the cockpit moving wheels and pulling levers at a frantic pace. After a few tugs of an overhead fob on a chain, the vehicle came to a wheezing halt. The gears on the legs groaned as they telescoped down, bringing the passenger area to street level.

The driver wound a crank on his dashboard, and the right hand porthole opened up on a hinge in response. "Last run of the day," he called. "If you're goin' south, I can take you, so long as it's not beyond mid-town. My garage is by the cemetery off Route 24, and I don't want to backtrack."

"No, we're just going to Avon Heights," Ben said.

"That'll do well, then." The driver wound another crank, and the vehicle's back door sprang up. A rectangle of metal slid from the vehicle floor to the sidewalk. "Mind the escalator, folks. It's runnin' a mite slow, but if you step on before it's done, it'll take your feet off. Wait for the green light."

The rectangle whirred and panels opened up on each side. Four steps now connected the passenger area to the sidewalk.

Ben climbed each step instead of waiting for the escalator to pull him along. Behind him, Violet stepped on, but she waited for him to get settled before ascending.

"Avon Heights, huh?" she asked. "This guy must be loaded." Violet pulled on her harness. "But then, that's what Vere…well…" She shook her head. "Never mind, it's rude."

The door slid down and the stamper rose back up on its legs. Ben felt his stomach flip flop at the movement. He cringed, wishing for a mint to ease the faint nausea.

"Oof, see, that's the other reason I hate these things." Beside him, Violet leaned over and held her head against her knees. Beneath her long skirt, one leg was bouncing with nervous energy.

Ben reached a hand out toward her, his fingers pausing in the air above her back. He'd been about to pat her, comfort her against the jerky motion of the stamper, but that was too familiar.

Don't be creepy.

He withdrew his hand just in time; Violet soon sat back up and gave him a weak smile.

"What, ah, what's rude?" he asked. He watched the scenery move as the stamper made its slow way from downtown Avon to its southern suburb.

"Well, you pay Vere's salary, but he treats you like a kid." She blanched. "I don't even know why I'm curious."

"You're a curious person," Ben said. He'd neglected to pull on his own harness and he now busied himself with remedying that. "If you weren't, you wouldn't be an FBI agent, you wouldn't have ever wanted to go find out about D.B. Cooper, even."

"I guess."

"But to answer your question…" Ben laughed. "I'm not sure what your question is, really, unless you just want to know if I have money."

"Oh, God, that's so not what I was trying to ask," Violet protested.

"It's okay," Ben said. "I do. And that's why Eddy sought me out in the first place, to fund his tech. I ran a foundation. I could afford to fund him. It was my idea to partner together, to start the agency and bring in clients and stuff."

"So he gets to use his machine, to keep going with his science," Violet said. "And you make that possible. But other than client money—which you probably don't really need—what do *you* get out of it?"

The stamper lurched at a four-way stop. A traffic cop was holding out a flat hand to their driver while a funeral procession of pedicabs and a carriage hearse meandered through the intersection. Ben looked over at Violet. Her big blue eyes were wide. She smelled like coffee and strawberries. Ben's stomach grew fluttery again, but not from the motion of the stamper this time. This time it was because he imagined pulling her to him, tasting her lips and smelling her scent even closer.

"Ben?"

"Sorry. Yeah. What do I get out of it?" He exhaled and looked back at the funeral procession. "You see that?"

Violet followed his gaze. "Yeah."

"I see something like that, I start wanting to know—no, *needing* to know—who that funeral is for. That's not just a corpse being carried along there, not to me. To me that's a whole life, and I have to know everything about it."

In the cockpit the driver, growing bored as he waited for the cop to let him through, pulled out his data pad and activated a radio station. The stamper was now filled with soft music, a classical score of piano and strings.

"So when you send your clients back to solve a mystery…"

"I couldn't care less about the money part," Ben said. "My payment is hearing their story." His desire for Violet fell away as he remembered her return from 1971. She'd been grinning ear to ear, her mechanic's disguise covered in airplane grease, eager to share her findings about Cooper.

The funeral procession ended with a horse-mounted police officer bringing up the rear. The traffic cop made a beckoning gesture at the stamper, and their driver eased them forward once more.

"But when I told you what I found," Violet said, "you didn't act that interested. Now that my memories are back, I know how you listened. You were almost detached."

Ben's breathing grew shallow. "I'm not exactly the most emotional person," he said. "I might not have seemed like it, but I can assure you I was very interested."

Sunlight streamed in through the stamper's portholes, turning Violet's face golden-pink.

The doorbell seemed louder than usual. Cob groaned. "Donald!" he yelled. "Donald, door!"

On the marble-topped table beside Cob's bed, an ancient intercom crackled to life. "Of course, sir," a crisp British-accented voice said amidst hisses and pops. There were footsteps and indistinct voices, and then the intercom came to life again. "Sir, there's a Mister Jonson and Miss Lessep here to see you." There was a pause. "She says she's with the FBI, sir."

Cob pulled the blanket from over his head. "What does the FBI want with me?"

"I shouldn't know, sir."

"I'll be right down." His bare feet shuffled against empty beer bottles as Cob tugged on his robe. He blinked at the sunlight streaming through the half-open blinds. "Fuck, what time is it?"

"You asked that I dispense with the wake-up call today, sir."

"Hush, you." Cob raked his hands through his sleep-mussed hair. "Offer our guests some tea or something. I gotta take a piss."

"Shall I tell them—"

"Jesus, *no*," Cob snapped. "God, you're so literal."

A few minutes later, Cob was more presentable, though still in his pajamas. In the living room sat a man in his mid-thirties, dark hair and bushy eyebrows, but it was the woman across from him who caught Cob's attention. She was blond and slender and wore a snug black jacket and matching ankle-length skirt. Something about her eager smile was ingratiating…and familiar.

We were both on trips, but we couldn't talk about it.

The memory was dim, as if it were a long-buried encounter from decades earlier, and yet he could swear the way this woman looked now was how he remembered her.

Impossible, if it was so long ago…

"Ah, Mister Cob." The man rose. "You won't remember, but you and I are quite well acquainted. I'm Ben Jonson, and this is Violet Lessep."

The woman stood as well. "*Agent* Lessep," she amended. "We met once before, too, though very briefly."

"We did," Cob said. He meant it to be a question, but it wasn't. "I know. I don't know how I know, but I do."

Blood and light bulbs and strange creatures sailing through a cloudless sky…

God, I'm hungover.

Cob rubbed his temples. "Forgive me, folks, I had a few too many tugs at the bottle last night." He swept a hand down his robe. "Even I'm usually dressed by

140

this hour." Cob sank down on a loveseat, and the others sat as well. "You wanna remind me where we all know each other?"

The man cleared his throat. "Mister Cob, we need your help to stop a killer."

Cob looked at both of them. "Um, you…what? I'm not really in the business of…" He laughed. "Well, I'm not really in the business of much of anything except spending my trust fund on trips to Maine."

Why do *I go to Maine so much?*

"But Mister Jonson here speaks very highly of your bravery," the woman said.

Cob laughed again. "My *bravery*?"

"We should've brought some sort of proof," Jonson said to the agent. "Mister Cob, are you familiar with the Zodiac killer?"

Cob frowned. "Yeah, sure, the unsolved serial murders in the twentieth century. To tell the truth, I've always been fascinated by that case. I'm kind of a history buff."

"You were fascinated by the case, yes. And you solved it."

Both Cob and the agent stared at Jonson.

"I did?" Cob asked. He realized a second later that the woman asked the same question at the same instant. They exchanged a glance, and she blushed and looked away.

"I did?" he asked again. "Why don't I remember it?"

Cob pictured a dark city street, a man walking up to a parked car and aiming a pistol through the passenger window.

Am I imagining that? Or remembering it?

Jonson leaned forward and clasped his hands together. "So what I'm about to tell you is going to seem impossible."

"I can assure you it's not, though," Agent Lessep said.

"We need you to go back in time," Jonson said. "Which you've actually done on more than one occasion."

"I have." Once again, Cob meant to voice his words as a question and once again, they came out as a statement.

You have *time traveled before. You've done it tons of times, and you've hired this guy to make it happen.*

"Let's say I believe you," Cob said. "What do you need me to do, exactly?"

Agent Lessep gave Cob a pleading look. "We need you to catch Jack the Ripper."

Not just Jack the Ripper. This guy killed Elizabeth Short, too. And wow, how did I know that?

He wasn't going to tell them that, not just yet. But Cob believed them already, even as something nagged at him not to let on.

"I'm gonna need a better sales pitch, folks." Cob sat back and rested one hand on the telephone next to the loveseat. "And I can have the cops here in a hot minute if this is all an elaborate con."

Headlights shone on a creature with eyes like bright red lasers. And a man, emaciated and terrifying…he'd seen him before.

"Mister Cob, are you familiar with the governor of the RAA?" Jonson asked.

The governor sauntered toward him with a cleaver, Elizabeth's body bleeding out onto dusty floorboards.

Oh, my God…

Cob choked back a sob and buried his face in his hands. "I'm remembering things," he blurted. "God help me, but I'm remembering things."

~

"*J'arrive, j'arrive…*"

Nothing existed but pain. No identity, no memory, no purpose or drive. Just pain, white and bright and screaming. It was ceaseless, not a dull throb or localized to one area of the body, but everywhere, through every cell and atom. Primal, peeling, shredding, and endless. There was some sense of music, but it was garbled, warped, and wrong.

And just when Cob thought he would be trapped in the pain forever, it stopped. Not a slowdown or a gradual ending, but a snuffing out, as of a candle flame being pinched by saliva-moistened fingers. One second all he knew was searing and pressure and agony, then the next it was gone, with the only residual effect being a kind of exhaustion, as if Cob collapsed at the finish line of a marathon.

"Mister Cob? Is everything a bit less fragmented?"

Cob opened his eyes. An older man hovered over him, his eyes made freakish and multi-sized by the lenses of his bifocals. At first, Cob couldn't place him, but then he recalled trips to a costume wardrobe with him, trips to this very laboratory, and a remote control being aimed at him. Somewhere, very quietly, a phonograph played a piece of French chanson, and he caught snatches of lyrics.

"*J'arrive, j'arrive…*"

"Doctor Vere." Cob struggled to sit up. He looked around, and yes, he was in the lab of the travel agency. "Ben. Miss Moto." He struggled again before giving up and falling back against a flat, uncomfortable pillow.

Violins swelled.

"*Mais pourquoi moi, pourquoi maintenant…*"

"You're very weak. Don't try to move," Vere instructed. "I'm a bit alarmed by your state, as Miss Lessep didn't experience such things upon her memories being restored."

"I went on a lot of trips, doc," Cob said.

An accordion.

"*Pourquoi déjà et où aller...*"

"Of course. That could be it, but I'd still like to run some further tests." Vere moved toward a cabinet.

"Can I have a drink of water?"

"Certainly." Vere knelt out of sight, and there was the sound of rustling. He rose holding a bright purple bottle of House Stream. "I'm afraid it's not very cold. Most of the electric down here is routed to my more pressing equipment." He nodded at the staircase. "I can have Miss Moto bring you something else in a moment."

Cob shook his head and took the bottle. "This is fine," he said, his voice coming out raspy. He downed the water. The song was winding down. Cob spotted the phonograph in the corner of the lab, an early model with a giant horn through which the record played its last seconds. The singer became more plaintive.

"*J'arrive bien sûr, j'arrive. N'ai-je jamais rien fait d'autre qu'arriver....*"

Cob translated, albeit imprecisely, tapping into things he remembered studying in Paris in college.

I come, of course, I come, but have I ever done anything but?

Now other memories were flooding him. The Black Dahlia. The slender man who'd killed her. The Mothman. The brief moments he'd laid eyes on Violet Lessep before today. The record continued on to another song, this one he recognized as "The Port of Amsterdam." As Jacques Brel's anguished voice cried out, Cob saw the face of the man he'd met in the TNT area in Point Pleasant.

The slender man...that man, he's—

"Claudio Florence killed the Black Dahlia!" he shouted. Cob sat up, sore arms and legs screaming in protest. His head swam, and he saw a rainbow of dim colors blur in his field of vision.

"Steady there, son, you'll be dizzy, I suspect," Vere warned.

"The RAA governor, I *saw him*. In the forties. And—oh God, in the sixties, too. Has he been following me?"

"Slow down, let's get you straightened out, then you can tell us what you know." Vere pressed the back of his hand to Cob's forehead. "Your temperature is all out of whack. You're sweating." He swiped a small cylinder from his desk and snapped off the top to reveal an oral thermometer. "Open up."

Cob allowed the thermometer to be placed under his tongue. "My harfda tall Bun an Mish Lashop abot da—"

Vere looked up from his pocket watch and glared at Cob. "One minute. Silence."

Cob sighed but quieted and tried not to fidget. The phonograph stopped playing, and Vere turned it off when the speaker filled with needle hiss. He checked his pocket watch again as he walked back to Cob. After another few seconds, Vere plucked the thermometer from Cob's mouth.

"I have to tell Ben and Miss Lessep about this guy," Cob tried again. "They think he's Jack the Ripper, but that's not all. He's killed others. I've seen him, and I think he's stalked me."

There was a flicker of something in Vere's expression as he examined the thermometer. "Son, there'll be time for that, but I'm concerned about you for entirely different reasons." He put the thermometer down. "I need to bring a consultant in. Or, rather, bring you out to one."

"Huh?"

Vere took his glasses off and chewed on the end of the earpiece. "I'm not a medical doctor," he said. "Oh, I muddle through well enough, but if Benoy and Miss Lessep are going to send you off into the past again, God knows where or when, I shouldn't feel good about that until I've had you examined properly."

Cob felt a pinch of pain nag at his head. "You think there's something really wrong with me?"

"You were having memories bleed through the erasures, even before today," Vere said. "Most of that was an aberration, but your reaction to the restoration just now was dramatic, painful, far more than I expected." He pointed to the water bottle still clutched in Cob's hand. "Finish that off, get cleaned up and whatnot. I'll tell Benoy...well, I'll tell him something. Let's not alarm him yet."

Cob exhaled a bitter laugh. "No, let's just alarm *me*."

Monday, August 30, 2100, Avon, Vermont, NBE

Kris arranged the plate and cup on a wicker tray before setting out for the lobby. Cob and Vere were halfway to the front door. "Food. Should I have food?" Cob asked Vere.

"Later," Vere said.

Kris put the tray on the coffee table. "Somebody else can eat this stuff, then, if you're going," she said.

Ben wandered over and picked up a triangle of buttered toast. "Eddy, you sure he's okay?"

"It's a precaution," Vere replied. "Fitzhugh is an old colleague and needn't know any of our other activities beyond the simple tests I want done on Mister Cob here."

"Remember what I said." Cob called before being ushered out the door.

"What'd he say?" Kris asked. She plopped down on the floor and wound her legs into a half-lotus position.

Ben and Violet exchanged a look.

"Oh, come *on*," Kris said. She picked up the other piece of toast. "I'll find out anyway. I already know things are badness with a capital B."

"Cob thinks Claudio Florence isn't just Jack the Ripper but also murdered the Black Dahlia," Ben said.

"We should just generally start looking at unsolved serial killings," Violet said. She sat down next to Kris, a heavy book in her hands. "You said he found the Zodiac?"

"On one of his trips last year, yeah," Ben said. "But that wasn't Florence. That was a guy who'd been stalking one of the first victims. A normal psychopath, not a psychopath time traveler."

"Still, it's like he has a keen eye for that stuff," Kris said. "Might even kinda attract it, in a weird way." She took a bite of the toast.

Ben pointed to the teacup. "Anybody care if I take this?"

Both women shook their heads.

"You might have a point," Violet said to Kris. "I mean, not in any mysterious way, just that if he's the thrill seeker you all describe him as, solving unsolved serial killings is about as thrill-seeking as it gets."

"There a lot of folks in the bureau like that?" Kris asked.

Violet shrugged. "I guess I have a little streak of that in me, even. Not as much as some of my colleagues."

Kris noticed Ben studying his tea a little too carefully. Thrill seeker was not a term that came to mind when she thought of Ben Jonson. "Repressed," "nerdy," "awkward," plus all the normal boss terms like "inflexible" and "not willing to see my creative potential." But Ben knew these things about himself—Kris was willing to tell him, in fact, when he was being geekier than usual or indulging in his sad sack propensities. So why should the idea that Cob and Violet shared a common seeking-of-thrills bother him?

She glanced from Violet to Ben and back again. *Oh!*

A giggle escaped Kris, and she quickly clamped her lips together and worked to stifle it.

"What's so funny?" Ben asked.

Kris shook her head and waved a hand at him. "Nope. Nothin'. Carry on."

~

Fitzhugh shut the door of his office before crossing the room to greet Vere and Cob. "Gentlemen, I'm afraid the news isn't great," he said. He withdrew several sheets of X-ray film from a file folder and pinned them to the light box on the wall behind his desk. He switched the light on and rubbed at his beard as he pointed to a spot on the first image. "This is the place in Mister Cob's brain that troubles me."

145

"What is that?" Vere asked.

"Well, it's not supposed to be there, for one thing," Fitzhugh replied. "Are either of you familiar with the Charcot-Bouchard-Rillsman scale?"

The patient's face was blank, but Vere frowned. "It's been a long time since I took neuroscience, Allen."

Fitzhugh nodded. "Of course. It's a measure of the severity of a type of cerebral aneurysm. Vogel Rillsman discovered the minute sub-subtypes of traumatic brain events back in 2050, and—"

"*Allen.*" Vere looked impatient. "Can we dispense with the history and more complicated science?"

Fitzhugh gave his old friend a sad smile. "I always was a bit more of a researcher than a practitioner, I'm afraid, Eddy."

"I'm sorry," Cob said, "but we gotta cut to the chase if I'm about to die. Am I?"

Fitzhugh pointed to the spot again. "Someday, of course, Mister Cob. But discovering your aneurysm's place on the scale is important in telling me when. If it's a certain grade, we can halt its progress with drugs, even shrink it down to nothing. If it's a different grade, we may be talking surgery, and if it's still another..." He sighed.

"If it's another, I'm dead," Cob finished.

"Son, it may not be—"

Cob held up a hand to Vere. "No, it's cool, doc. I get it." He smiled up at Fitzhugh. "You wanna do more tests, I bet."

"As soon as possible," Fitzhugh confirmed.

"We'll let you know." He stood and shook Fitzhugh's hand. "C'mon, doc, let's you and me have a talk." Cob headed for the door.

~

Violet handed Ben the legal pad she'd been using. "That last one is what I'm curious about," she said.

Ben canted his head to one side. "Hmm. That doesn't ring a bell." He held out a hand. "Do they talk about it in that book, or one of the ones we left in the conference room?"

Violet picked up the book she'd been looking at. "No, it's in here." She flipped through several pages, not finding the section. "It's in here. It's not a long article, though I don't know why. The case was gruesome enough to be interesting, if you're into that sort of thing." Frustrated, she checked the index and found the passage. "Here you go." She tapped the page and handed the book over. "Left side, halfway down."

Ben read for a few moments. "Okay, this is *sort* of sounding familiar. I've probably read this before." He put the book down and stood up, letting out a soft groan. "God, how long have we been at this?"

"Few hours."

"I'm getting old." He stretched, bending over at the waist and pulling on his arms. There was a percussive popping sound, and Ben let out a brief moan. "There we go."

Violet giggled. "You should do some yoga, like your assistant. You're not very flexible."

"I am *very* flexible, thank you very much, I just can't be sitting on the floor all day. Let's sit on real people chairs. I think I have another book that might talk about this, or we can see if the 'net's not being suppressed right now."

Very flexible, huh?

Violet grinned as she stood up. "I could use some coffee." She headed toward the kitchen. "You want anything?"

"No, let me." Ben followed her. "So what caught your eye about this case, the Cleveland Torso Killer? Man, what a terrible name."

"Similar M.O. as the Black Dahlia, which itself is kind of—not identical, of course, but still—kind of similar to the Ripper." Violet snapped on the kitchen lights. "Where do you guys keep stuff?"

"You know, this has been kind of a terrible day." Ben opened the fridge and pulled out two bottles of beer. "Is it really coffee time?"

"It doesn't have to be." Violet spotted a bottle opener magnet on the side of the refrigerator and took it down.

They clinked bottles. The front door opened. "Who's got two thumbs and is ready to time travel?" Cob called. A second later he poked his head in the kitchen and pointed his thumbs at his head. "This guy."

Violet laughed. Behind Cob, she caught sight of Vere, who was frowning and pacing.

"So, clean bill of health?" Ben asked.

Cob stepped into the kitchen and took Ben's beer from him. "I am ready for some grand-fucking-adventure," Cob said. He took a long swallow of the beer. "When do we leave?"

Vere opened his mouth but then shut it and wandered away. A moment later, Violet heard the clatter of footsteps on the spiral staircase to the lab.

"Where's Eddy going?" Ben asked. He walked out to the lobby.

"Is everything really all right?" Violet asked Cob.

Cob took another swig of the beer. "Hey, I'm just happy to be backing you up, agent. It'll be great." He followed Ben out of the kitchen.

He never answered us.

Violet left her beer on the counter, untouched.

Tuesday, August 31, 2100, Avon, Vermont, NBE

Ben finished reading the passage aloud and closed the book with a flourish, causing the pages to thunk together audibly. A tiny puff of dust rose from between the leaves. He studied Vere, noting the other man's deep frown.

"You have to admit it's similar, both to the original Ripper and to the Black Dahlia," Ben said. He sat down in the chair to the left of the loveseat and leaned forward, watching Vere for any change in expression. Bodhi nudged his whiskers against Ben's hand, and Ben absently scratched the cat behind the ears. "If we can capture him there, somewhere he's not expecting us to be, I think we've got a pretty good shot of getting to him."

Vere nodded. "It's also a violent time we're discussing," he said. "Cleveland in the 1930s, full of mobsters and whatnot. Big city, lots of strife." He raised an eyebrow. "We could take care of him and leave him back there."

"Whoa, wait." This wasn't something Ben envisioned. Murder? Of a public figure? "Are you saying—"

"The man has committed genocide, in essence. Economically if not in actuality," Vere said. "And we now know he's also committing serial murders throughout all of history."

"Let's make sure I'm right first, okay?"

"How do you propose that, Benoy?"

"Send one of us back there, just to investigate."

Ben held up a hand for Vere to stay quiet. "*Investigate.* That's all. Stick to the shadows, stay out of Claudio's sight."

"But he's met us all by now at one time or another," Vere pointed out. "Or knows us all by reputation."

"Reputation, yes. Sight, no." Ben fussed with his necktie. It felt like it was strangling him. "I may be the funding around here, but that's all. I've been stuck in my books for decades, not exactly living the life of a bachelor benefactor at social functions."

Vere stared at Ben. "Son, are you saying *you* want to go?" His expression softened, and he laughed. "Oh, good heavens, I…no, no, Benoy, that isn't your strong suit." He patted Ben's arm. "Stick to the research. We can figure out a way to disguise Mister Cob and get him sent off, if you think this is really important."

Cob chatted with Kris and Violet in the foyer, regaling them with stories he now remembered from his adventures. Kris was unimpressed, Ben could tell, for more reasons than that she'd heard these stories before. But Violet…Violet lived adventures of her own in her daily life. This would all be far more impressive to her than his research, however vital to their cause. He thought of her gentle smile and her courage in the face of all she'd learned in the past few days. He wanted to save the future for her. He wanted her by his side during the fight. *His* side, not Cob's.

I could die, though. Something could go wrong, and I could die in the past and none of them would even know. I spent my whole life protected from danger, reading about other people's lives and never living my own…

"It's me," Ben said, his voice low and gravelly. "It has to be me. I'm doing it, Eddy." He sounded older to himself, brusque and practical, like his father. He stood up. "I'm going to get supplies and wardrobe. Meet me in the lab."

"Wait, *now*?" Vere rose. "Benoy, you have to tell the others, see if anyone else has an idea here. This is *rash*, what you're doing."

Ben shook his head. "I've spent over three decades never doing anything rash. Maybe it's time I did."

"I don't like this one bit." Vere wasn't meeting Ben's eyes now. "There are complications that…well, I'm not pleased about."

Ben frowned. "Complications?"

Laughter floated from the foyer. Ben took a few steps out of the parlor to get a better view of the group congregated there. Cob looked every inch the silent film hero, all wavy hair and bright white teeth. Beside him, Violet was tucking a strand of golden hair behind her ear.

Ben turned back to Vere. "What do you mean complications?"

"It isn't Miss Lessep," Vere said.

"Cob?"

"It could be nothing."

Ben sat back down. "But it could be something."

"Perhaps."

"So the clean bill of health?" Ben asked.

Vere shook his head. "I think once we've solved this current conundrum, we should indeed shut down as we've discussed. Temporarily, until I can work out studying side effects."

"But Alison and Wil, all our other clients," Ben said. "We haven't had any trouble before."

Vere's gaze slid away from Ben. "Mister Cob's got more stamps in his passport than the average traveler," Vere said. "And it could be simply his constitution." He placed a hand on Ben's shoulder. "I give you a bit of a tough time, son, but I…" Vere's voice trailed off. There was a hint of a shimmer in his eyes.

"I know," Ben said. "Thank you."

"So you'll rethink this?"

"No," Ben replied. "If I've been endangering my clients all along, I can't let any of them go anymore." He rose. "No, this is my trip to take."

Saturday, September 21, 1935, Cleveland, Ohio, USA

The sensation of falling over a century into the past was eerily like a roller coaster ride. One moment Ben was sitting on Vere's table in the lab and the next he was falling, his stomach seeming to leave his body like the lurch of the first drop of a coaster. But this ride did more than just plummet his body down a drop—it also plunged him into darkness, a darkness so total it made Ben worry he'd died. The only thing keeping him grounded was pain, a nebulous, numb, fleeting ache. It was over quickly; Ben soon felt his body slam back to something resembling normalcy before he dropped into a crumpled, rag doll heap.

He blinked and regarded his surroundings. Boarded-up windows in a brick warehouse, rusty railroad tracks, and shallow, mud-gray water running under a short bridge. It was neither warm nor freezing but a chilly in-between. The shrubbery surrounding the tracks was lush and full, but it held the cold, depressed look of greenery after a rain. Ben looked up at a late-afternoon sky full of dark clouds. The ground beneath his knees and palms was wet. He suspected the rain was leaving rather than arriving, but that made the weather no less miserable.

He scrambled to his feet and pulled his tweed sport coat closer around his chest. It was too big—purchased, most likely, for Cob, who was more muscular around the shoulders—and the whole suit taken together gave Ben the rumpled look of a teenager borrowing his father's clothes for a job interview.

As he looked across the water at the opposite side of the stream bank, Ben spotted a collection of dirty white rags clinging to the side of a bush.

No, not rags.

He flashed back to the history books he'd been reading just before leaving, the sepia-toned photographs showing crime scenes and blanket-covered corpses.

That bush is familiar. Those aren't rags.

Oh, God.

Ben looked around, trying to spot a simple way across the stream. The railroad trestle had no pedestrian ladder. The stream ran as far as the eye could see in both directions. With a heavy sigh, he rolled up the legs of his trousers and splashed across. Midway, he sank deeper into unpleasant muck to his waist. He felt a biting cold all the way to his bones and hastened his journey across, now desperate to be free of the dirty water.

Once on the other side of the bank, Ben hoisted himself up on the muddy grass and crawled free of the stream. The bush was farther away than it appeared on the other side, and he jogged the few yards toward it, leaving deep footprints in the muck.

After just a few moments, he was certain—this was indeed no pile of rags. It was a body, death-pale and twisted into a grotesque position that would be impossible to contort someone into without breaking bones. One leg was coiled around the bush's trunk, while the other was sticking straight out. The arms were folded in on each other as if the body were embracing itself, yet the position of the thumbs was backward, further convincing Ben of the work the killer did to the victim's bones. There were gashes along the front of the torso—male, which was indeed different from Claudio's work as Jack the Ripper—and a gaping maw where the head and neck should've been. The sight got Ben's stomach roiling again—the empty, dark-reddened cavity where once everything that made the man have a sense of his identity existed—face, brain, all of it just gone with the whisk of an axe or cleaver. A bright spot of white poked through amidst the bloody meat. At the realization that it was a vertebra, Ben turned from the mangled corpse, bent double, and vomited onto the grass. As the contents of the day's meals left his body, Ben coughed, sweat dripping from his brows. When it seemed he was done, he still stayed hunched over, his eyes shut, and listened to a faint humming coursing through the brush.

Flies. Flies finding that thing that used to be a person. Jesus. Pull yourself together, man. You're here to find the killer.

He straightened up and looked around. The body lay undiscovered. Though Vere's calculations should have placed him here the day the first victim was found, it could still be off by a few hours or even a few days. Ben was a mess; he needed to find out what time and day it was and wait.

The killer always returns to the scene of the crime. Claudio might come back when the cops do.

He spotted a guardrail a few feet up and to the left, and Ben headed for it, hoping a road led to a hotel. As he climbed the slope to the road, Ben thought he saw a dark bundle of clothing out of the corner of his eye, but when he turned toward it, it shimmered and disappeared.

Phantom corpses?

He shook his head and continued climbing.

Suddenly the air in front of Ben warped and swirled, as if the sky were turning to liquid. It darkened and a wind howled from within a growing oval opening.

"Ben!"

A hand reached out and yanked Ben into darkness.

Ben yelped but his voice was quickly torn away by the void, and in another instant he was crashing back down to a hard surface, his limbs sore and his head pounding.

Tuesday, August 31, 2100, Avon, Vermont, NBE

"What the hell, man?"

Cob couldn't answer, not just yet. His whole body roared, blood pounding loudly and painfully everywhere, rushing, waves crashing, hurtling him against rocks and washing him up on a shore where the sand burned and the sun burned and everything burned, skin and eyes and hair and mouth, all boiling away and leaving bleached bones behind, an empty skull grinning up into nothing.

"Stop, no," Cob whimpered. He pressed the heels of his hands against his closed eyes and willed the rushing to cease so he could talk.

"*What the hell?*" Ben demanded again. He yanked Cob to his feet. "I'd barely gotten there. I didn't even find him yet."

"No, but he was going…uh, I don't know, I can't think."

Something cold and hard pressed against Cob's cheek. "Here, careful, take this." It was Vere, wrapping Cob's fingers around a smooth, wide cylinder. Footsteps shuffled against the floor near where Cob sat. He downed the glass of water. Above him, Ben and Vere hovered, but they both remained blurry, indistinct. The smaller of the two blurs—Ben—waved his arms and gestured.

"What's going *on?*"

"We had to go back," Cob said, voice hoarse. "The book, your book…it changed. There was a newspaper—" A fit of coughing cut off his words. Vere sank back down next to him again and pounded him on the back.

"Steady yourself, Mister Cob, I'll tell him," Vere said. "Son, the research you were doing on that case, it started changing as soon as we sent you back there." A rustle of paper. "There, look at that."

Ben gasped. "What the—oh, my God! Wait!"

Cob looked up and could finally see men instead of blurs. He reached up to the table and dragged himself to his feet. "What happened?"

"The clipping disappeared," Vere said. "I knew it would, not long after you brought him back. Benoy, apparently Claudio made you his next victim the very day after the police found the first body. You would have been Joe Doe Two if I hadn't sent Mister Cob back to rescue you."

Now that Cob's vision was clear, he could see the unmistakable clenching of Ben's jaw. "Thank you," the other man managed, his tone anything but grateful.

Cob frowned. "Buddy, I think I saved your life. What's with the attitude? I'm kind of a mess here, and it's all for *you*." He coughed again and drank more water.

Ben didn't address Cob, but instead glared at Vere. "Why couldn't *you* have come?"

"I have to stay here and provide retrieval."

"Kris? Violet?"

"Shit, Ben, this guy tends to prey mostly on women. Are you *serious*?" Cob asked. "No, I had to go."

Ben sighed. "But I know, man. I know you shouldn't be doing this anymore."

Cob looked at the doctor. "Seriously? You told him?"

Vere shrugged and nodded. "I had to, Mister Cob. But then, as you said, we couldn't risk sending one of the ladies back for him. If you're already unwell—"

"What's one more trip, huh?" Cob laughed. "Look, fine, whatever. I'm feeling better. It's okay. Let's just risk me again. Hell, let *me* off this bastard. I'm expendable. I'll be a suicide bomber or some shit. Sound good to you two?"

"No, not at all," Vere said.

"What about you, huh?" Cob asked Ben. "You'd miss my money, but you wouldn't miss me, would you? Why is that?"

"Let's not," Ben replied.

"No, I think we should." Cob put down his water glass and strode toward Ben. "You would've been less annoyed if someone else rescued you. Admit it."

"Fine. I admit it."

"So why is that?" Cob asked. "And don't tell me you're concerned about my health. Yeah, maybe you are in that generic we-don't-love-seeing-other-human-beings-die kind of way. But *really*, Jonson, why the hell is it such a big bloody deal if it was *me* who rescued you instead of, say…" *Oh. Oh, that's why*, Cob realized, midsentence. He let his voice trail off. "Never mind," he said. He gave a vague gesture and hopped up onto the examination table. "Forget it. I'm sorry. It's been a tough century, and I'm exhausted." He stretched out on the table but still caught the confused look Ben and Vere exchanged.

"You rest, Mister Cob," Vere said. "I'll bring Benoy up to speed on the new plan."

"The *new* plan?" Ben asked. "What was wrong with investigating and then maybe bringing him back from Cleveland?"

"What's wrong is that it's gotten worse, all of it," Vere explained.

Cob closed his eyes and heard the other two men's footsteps on the metal stairs. He dreamed of putting flowers between the dark shiny locks of Elizabeth's hair.

~

"Damn, boss, what happened to you?" Kris stood and held out a hand. "Gimme that coat, and get your shoes off the rug."

Ben looked down at his mud-streaked clothes. "In all the excitement..." he murmured. He tugged off his jacket and handed it to Kris. "I should probably clean up."

"But you're okay," Violet said. She rose from her seat beside the one Kris vacated. "I mean, we figured, when we heard voices—"

"This article just appeared?" Ben asked.

Kris snapped her fingers at him. "Shoes. God, you're a mess. We're gonna have to shampoo the whole rug now."

"I was apparently almost murdered," Ben said. "I think the rug can wait." He tugged his shoes free and handed them to her with brisk motions.

Kris backed up a step and dropped the coat and shoes, held up her hands, and stalked out to the kitchen.

"You didn't have to be so harsh with her," Violet said. "Or anyone else, for that matter."

"You heard an argument." Ben wanted to sit, but knew he needed to change first.

"Cob had to get you back," Violet said. "I don't know why there was anything to fight about." She frowned. "I didn't think you were the fighting type."

"This isn't a normal situation," Ben said. "Look, I should..." He pointed at the stairs leading to the second floor. "We can pick this up once I'm not such a wreck, okay?"

Violet nodded. "We were all worried, you know. Nobody was going to leave you back there to get killed."

"I know." Ben crossed the room. As he passed by the sofa, Violet stood and stalled his arm with her hand.

"Do you?" Violet asked. "Seriously, do you know that the moment that article materialized, the moment your book changed..." Violet looked away and stared out the front window. Her bottom lip quivered, and she covered her mouth with her hand. "It was terrifying, Ben. Truly." She turned back to him. "I would have gone, you know. They didn't think it was a good idea."

Would you have gone for him, too? Or just me?

He tried to speak, tried to thank her, to reassure her, but no words came.

Cob emerged from the lab and leaned on the staircase railing.

"God, you *both* look awful." Violet was suddenly all laughter and lightheartedness. She went to Cob and held out a hand to him. "You okay?"

Ben drifted to the other staircase, but Cob's voice stopped him. "Did she tell you what we decided?"

"No." Ben returned, trying to keep his footprints on top of each other to avoid causing more mess than necessary. "What was decided? What do you mean?"

"I didn't get a chance," Violet said.

Cob batted her away. "I got this, it's cool." He hoisted himself up the last few steps and let out a groan. "I'm okay, just hungry."

"Is that really all it is?" Violet asked.

No, but that doesn't matter now. "What was decided?" Ben repeated.

Cob and Violet exchanged a look. "They…instead of capturing Florence, they just want to…*eliminate* him."

"Who is they?"

"Everybody," Cob replied. "Doc was making phone calls, getting opinions on Florence. You know all the bullshit he's put the whole continent through for decades, even before he started time traveling."

"He was going to kidnap me, Ben," Violet added. "Let's not forget that. I should've lived and died centuries ago, but I didn't, all because it would've been too dangerous for him to…to *use* me as some kind of sick poster child for racial purity." She shuddered. "God, when I think of that, I just feel sick."

Days ago, he authorized Alison and Wilbur to find Wheaton and, if necessary, murder him. Claudio Florence was a public figure, in a way, but he was also a killer and a psychopath. Ben leaned against the back of his desk chair and rested his forehead on his hands.

"We have time," Cob pointed out. "We got a whole machine that ensures we have time. But I don't think Doc's gonna let anybody do this thing if you don't give it the go ahead."

"What's the immediate threat?" Ben asked.

Violet gasped. "Ben, we *had* one," she said. "You were *dead* back there. Probably given just a little bit of time, your whole life could have been unmade."

Ben straightened up. "What? No. *No.* That's ridiculous."

Cob approached the desk. "No, dude, it's not. Think about it." He snatched up a piece of paper and a stub of pencil. "You're here, right?" He drew a dot and labeled it with the current year. "You were born, when, fifty years ago?"

Ben cringed. "Jesus, *no.* Do I seem so old?" He plucked the pencil from Cob and made a dot near the first one, labeling it "2062."

Cob blinked. "Wow, okay." He looked Ben up and down. "I'm only a little younger, but you look *much* older."

Violet sighed. "Girls, girls, you're both pretty." She gestured at the paper. "Get on with it."

"Okay, so, you go back to 1935," Cob went on, drawing a dot far to the left of the paper and connecting it with an arc to the "2100" dot. "Where, very tragically, Claudio Florence murders you." He set the paper down on the desk and smudged out the arc and then smudged out the "2062" dot. "Ergo, you were never born, you never went back there, and we all forget you, because you never started this agency."

"What? No, no, that's not logical at all," Ben said. "*My* lifetime is still set. I didn't undo myself. I just died at my current age, only it's now in the past."

"I still think we would forget you," Cob said. He balled up the paper and tossed it over his shoulder. "Which is pretty fucking dangerous for this whole gig. So *that's* your imminent danger, buddy."

"Actually, I think it's more dangerous if Florence goes back to Roanoke again and snatches me before Ambrose does," Violet said. "What would happen? Would I fade out here, midsentence? What would happen to my dad?"

"See? Imminent threat," Cob said. "We don't know what he's doing or when he's doing it."

"I'm not a murderer," Ben said. "That's stooping to his level."

"There's murder and then there's war," Cob said. "There's killing because you're a sick fuck who enjoys it and there's…" He turned to Violet. "What did the good doc call it?"

"Strategic target elimination," Violet replied.

"Yeah, that. Which is totally different from being all, 'Woo, I like chopping people's heads off.'" Cob quieted for a moment and looked pensive. "You guys don't know. I saw him at it. He almost got me once. He *did* get somebody I cared about."

"I'm not doing this, not this minute," Ben said. "Look, let me get my bearings here. We can debate this when I'm cleaner and everyone's had some time to think." He finally made his way upstairs.

~

Cob watched Ben leave and shook his head. "He's gonna screw everything up, he's gonna wind up being the death of one of us, or himself."

"He's just being cautious," Violet said. "Besides, we didn't all agree 'take Florence out.' We agreed to *consider* it. If you'll recall, I asked about rehabilitation or maybe even snatching him out of his own timeline, the way he wanted to do with me."

"And do what, then? Raise him to be an awesome guy?" Cob asked. He laughed. "So you'll basically adopt this kid knowing he might have an evil streak?"

"What's your solution, then?"

Cob thought of the blood on the light bulb, the blood pooling around Elizabeth's body. "We find him as a kid, what's wrong with *killing* him as a kid?"

"*Mister Cob.*"

"Like you wouldn't do that to Hitler?" Cob felt a pounding in his head, an insistent throb over his left eye that blossomed across his whole forehead. He did his best to ignore it, but his voice grew louder the more the pain thrummed. "Like you wouldn't flip the switch on Ted Bundy or Bin Laden or, yeah, *Jack the Ripper*? Because, little lady, we have that chance." He flung his arms wide. "Hell, send me back and forth doing that over and over again, not just to Claudio Florence but to *all* those sick-o freaks. Use me as an assassin until I drop dead." He took a step toward Violet and jabbed a finger at her. "Because it'll be *soon*, so I might as well do something good with my sorry, shallow life, right?"

They were inches from each other, Cob's brown eyes boring into Violet's blue ones. He was dying, he knew that, and he knew he wasn't good enough for her, but he wished she would bridge the gap between them and—

"I'm not your little lady," she said. "And what you're advocating is pretty brutal, especially if you're talking about doing it to these guys in childhood."

I blew it.

Cob stepped back. "Not necessarily." His voice was quieter now, the pain in his head subsiding. "Look, I don't know. I'm not the most moral guy. I don't know what the right thing to do is."

"The right thing to do is maybe to learn from the past, but don't...I don't know, don't risk it. Don't mess it up." Violet gestured around the parlor. "This place, what they do is about observation. Learning. Not acting."

"That's boring."

"Yeah? Well, *not* boring is going to get somebody killed, and I don't mean Claudio Florence." She put a hand on his shoulder. "I mean you, or Ben, or hell, even me. Let's stop this guy, not prevent him from even existing."

"Why not?"

"Because." Violet clenched her hands into fists. "Because not everybody is all bad or all good. Because even somebody who worked with him had the capacity to change." She paced. "Because maybe Claudio has people who care about him— yes, even him—who might be messed up without him in their lives. I don't know. But it's not for us to play God." She grew more and more animated as she spoke, and Cob watched the play of light over her hair, her skin, the flash of her eyes.

"You're too good for somebody like me, aren't you?" he muttered.

Violet stopped pacing and turned to him. "What?"

Cob smirked. "Forget it." He nodded backward toward the staircase to the second floor. "He's the one who'd be good for you."

"Ben? Good for me like...what, like *that*?" Violet raised an eyebrow. "Instead of who, you?"

"I didn't—"

Vere's voice interrupted Cob. "Miss Moto." His head poked up from the lab stairs as he ascended. "Where the devil is that woman? I'm in desperate need of some dinner, and I'm all out of bread down here."

Violet stared at him silently.

"I didn't mean that," Cob said. He moved from Violet and pointed to the kitchen. "Think she marched off there after your partner made a mess of the rug, doc." Vere nodded and headed to the other room. Cob didn't look back, but he heard Violet flop down on the couch.

Kris was nowhere to be found in the kitchen. "I'll whip you up something," Cob offered. He poked his head into the icebox. "Salami?" He withdrew a small plastic container. "Or…" He shook it, then opened it and gave the meat inside a whiff. "Hoo, no. That stuff's been doing some time traveling of its own."

Vere took the container and deposited it into the trash. "There's a covered plate of watercress we didn't have with lunch," he said. "I'll fancy it up a bit." He pulled down a few canisters from the spice rack. "So did you youngsters discuss the removal of Mister Florence?"

"Ben didn't take it so good," Cob said. He found the plate of sandwiches and put it on the counter. "He thinks Florence can be rehabilitated or something."

"I don't know," Vere said. He crossed to the sink, primed the water pump, and washed his hands before peeling back the clear wrap on the sandwich plate. "People are complex, Mister Cob. How Florence is may simply be how he is. We may not be able to change or save him." Vere took another plate down from an upper cabinet and transferred the top bread of the sandwiches to the empty plate. "He could be a product of his identity plus the *zeitgeist* of his moment in time."

"So you're saying maybe if we did take him out of his timeline, he might *not* ever turn into the psycho killer he is now?" Cob asked.

Vere shook his head. "Mm, not necessarily." He sprinkled paprika on the open sandwiches. "Oh, how I wish we had deviled eggs. Doesn't that sound delicious?" He walked to the icebox and peered inside. "Blast. Oh, but jam, yes, that will do nicely."

"What do you mean, then?" Cob asked.

"Fetch me a packet of biscuits. Top shelf," Vere instructed. Cob opened the cabinet Vere indicated. "Those go so well with jam. No, Mister Cob, what I mean is that suppose we remove Claudio Florence and set him up with a nurturing family, expose him to all the things that would induce racial tolerance in others and then, yes, perhaps that saves him. But that *zeitgeist*, lad. That would still exist, as would the entire environment that created such a creature in the first place." He punctuated his words with little jabs of a teaspoon. "You see? We remove one monster," he explained, miming digging something out of the air with the spoon, "and yet one more—or even *two* more—spring up in its place." He chuckled. "Bit like gray hair that way."

Cob laughed. "Pluck one, you get two back." He slid the biscuit packet across the counter to Vere.

"And those two new gray hairs," Vere said, "who's to say they wouldn't be even worse than Mister Florence?"

"*Worse*?" Cob blinked. "How can you be worse than Jack the Ripper plus raging racist?"

Vere sprinkled rosemary on the sandwiches. "People never fail to find ways to be terrible to one another. I'm sure someone would find a way."

Cob cringed and felt another painful throb in his head. He rubbed his temple.

Vere spotted the gesture and eyed Cob. "It's getting worse, even just today."

"I can handle it."

Vere put the tops back on the sandwiches. "What's Miss Lessep's argument against this plan, hmm?"

"Why don't you ask her?"

Cob turned. Violet stood in the doorway. "Did you ever find Kris?" she asked.

"She probably went out through the back," Vere said. "I suspect she went home. Poor thing hasn't taken any time off since this whole fiasco began." He pulled a sleeve of biscuits from its packet and arranged them on the now-empty second plate. "So, fine, dear, what's your argument against removing Mister Florence's influence on history?"

"I don't know that I said I was against it," Violet replied. "After all, the science came along to lengthen life in the face of disease, to explore the stars, and now to time travel. Why *not* experiment and see what it's actually capable of?" She eyed the sandwiches. "May I?"

Vere nodded, and she took one.

"Thank you." She took a small bite of her sandwich. "So it's unnatural for me to exist in *this* time and place," she went on after she'd swallowed, "and yet if I'd lived and died when I was supposed to, I'd probably have gotten smallpox or died in childbirth much younger than I am now."

"But you said you felt robbed of your real life," Cob pointed out.

"Sure I do," Violet admitted. "But I'm also a little bit glad to be alive *now*, healthy and witnessing the most exciting invention of the century, you know?"

"So how does this explain your position on Florence, dear?" Vere asked. He spooned clots of jam on the biscuits.

"It means if we can take him out in the past, either his own or just during one of his murder sprees," Violet said, "then why not use this technology to its potential?"

159

"I have to admit to both of you, one worry does plague me," Vere said. He put the lid on the jam and returned it to the icebox. "A paradox. We might well be creating a paradox if we remove Florence at a very young age, either to protect or to…to *eliminate* him entirely. Such a thing could be catastrophic to all life as we know it. Time travel is a precarious thing, really."

"If it's so dangerous, why did you invent it in the first place, then?" Cob asked.

Vere smiled. "Selfish reasons. Reasons that, yes, would indeed cause a paradox." He waved a hand through the air. "I'd never try it for that purpose now, mind you. All right." He snapped his fingers. "Let's make this a proper meal, shall we? Grab some glasses, Mister Cob, and let's set the table."

~

The table set, Vere returned to his lab briefly to hang up his white coat. When he returned, he asked Cob if Ben was downstairs yet.

Cob gestured back toward the kitchen. "Think finally, yeah."

Vere rose from his chair and walked back to the adjoining room. Ben was indeed there, robe-clad and opening cabinets.

"We have a very meager supper out there," Vere said, pointing to the dining room. "You're welcome to join us."

"Thanks." Ben let the cabinet he'd been holding open fall shut.

"Tell me something, son," Vere said. "History has patterns, does it not?"

"Sure," Ben replied.

"In your professional opinion, do you believe that the war could be prevented without removing or killing Claudio Florence before it begins?"

Ben's cheeks puffed out as he exhaled a heavy breath. "Look, I said I don't like the idea of killing, and—"

"Hang about," Vere said, holding up his hands and patting the air between himself and Ben. "I'm not trying to convince you of the viability of that idea, I'm just asking a question."

"If we do that, there are other consequences based on things he's done, him and his people," Ben said. He nodded out to the dining room and lowered his voice. "Violet would have lived and died as Virginia Dare, if we do that, because Claudio would have never recruited Richards, who would have never kidnapped her."

Vere's eyes widened. "Ah, I see," he said, nodding. "But that's just it, Benoy. I think *we* kidnapped her. We kidnapped the whole colony and tucked them away somewhere safe until we could reach them again."

"What do you—*what*?"

"Benoy, the Lost Colony is lost because *we hid it*. Don't you see? At some point, we bring the entire colony to the future, and *that's* how we prevent Violet from dying hundreds of years ago." Vere almost wanted to hop up and down, but dreaded the risk to his bones.

"Eddy, that's crazy, there were over fifteen hundred people at Roanoke," Ben said. "We can only transport one, two people tops with your tech."

"You don't have to transport all of 'em." Cob was standing in the doorway. "Just one. Violet."

"Where do you suggest we put the rest of them, then?" Ben asked.

Cob grinned. "There's a gorgeous place across a kind of veil from this world," he said. "Only saw it once, but it looked really nice, and it's full of Mothmen." He laughed. "I don't *think* they're hostile, but maybe we should ask Violet if she wants her family living with a bunch of winged alien things."

Sunday, November 27, 1966, Point Pleasant, West Virginia, USA

It was no longer late at night. It was barely dusk. And this was an open field. Overhead, a dozen Mothmen sailed through the air.

Cob looked back behind him once again. Just before he stumbled into the field, memories of Elizabeth plagued him, and then there was the other man there, pale, cadaverous.

Familiar.

Now in the dazzling sunlight, away from the dark of the back country roads, he could think more clearly. The slender man wasn't just any man; he was Claudio Florence, the leader of the RAA.

But that's in my own present. How is he time traveling, too?

A Mothman soared down from the sky and landed, gently, on nearly human legs right in front of Cob. "Greetings," it said in a feminine voice. "It has been years since one of your kind ventured this way. You must have bent the laws of physics repeatedly in order to do so."

Cob's head throbbed. "I, um, guess?"

"This was an error on your part, crossing as you did?"

"Well, I was looking for one of you," Cob admitted. "Proof you existed and weren't, I don't know, an owl or something."

"No, we exist," the creature confirmed. She spread her wings wide, and the span was startling—nearly twice her height. The axillars were covered in a downy fur, like the rest of her body, but the inside linings were full of feathers, long and elegant and indistinguishable to Cob's eye from those of large birds. "I am called Phalène."

The word was familiar, but Cob couldn't quite place it. Before he could question her, she was emitting what sounded like faint giggles. "That is how you perceive my name, at least. It isn't quite exact in any of the languages we speak."

"I'm Rupert Cob, but most people just call me Cob," he told her, giving her a little bow. "Nice to meet you."

"I was wandering in your realm," Phalène went on, "also a bit by accident. We are able to cross freely but try to avoid it, as it causes your kind undue alarm, and we aren't able to communicate as well on that side." Phalène reached out a gray hand and touched Cob lightly on the shoulder. "Do you want to go back? It's very near, the place where you crossed."

"What are you?" Cob murmured.

Phalène's strange red eyes narrowed. "I am a walker on two legs, a flyer on two wings. I hold the title of historian in our tribe. I am the daughter of Agnetha, granddaughter of Zhiel, from the line of Gael, one who was killed by your kind many centuries past." Her wings fluttered. "Time is different here, and as historian, I often travel to the past to observe and record." She nodded at Cob. "But you ask what I am, not who I am. Perhaps I should ask the same of you. What are *you*?"

"A human. *Homo sapiens.*" Cob smiled. "I don't really get all the biology of it—"

"But a human homo sapiens is *who* you are?" Phalène pressed. "That is the sum of your identity?"

"No, of course not."

"You are a bender of the laws of physics," she continued.

"A time traveler," Cob said.

"And is *that* who you are?"

Cob considered this. Was it? Or did time travel allow him to satisfy his desire to know, understand, and maybe even to triumph, somehow?

I should have saved Elizabeth…

"No," Cob replied. "Time travel is a means to an end. My identity–who I am—is a…a seeker."

"A seeker? Of what?"

"Knowledge. Understanding." He saw the shadow of a knife falling across Elizabeth's dead body. "Justice."

"Justice." Phalène nodded. "Excellent. You can seek justice for the one who killed Gael. It was one like you, a time traveler."

"Do you know the person's name?" Cob asked.

"Gael's children met him. He called himself Braiden Welty, but that was an untruth." Phalène waved in the air next to her; an image hovered there, as if projected onto an invisible screen. It showed a room with low, white tables. A man took a small object from one of the tables.

"Brimley Wheaton," Cob murmured.

"You know him? You've traveled together through time?"

"Not together. We're friends. Neighbors."

Oh, God, Wheaton, what did you do? I was the one who referred you to the agency! Did you abuse your trip somehow?

"You can bring justice for my ancestor?" Her voice took on a plaintive note.

Cob's heart sank. He'd forget this interaction when they wiped his memory, but maybe he could explain this before it happened. "I'll try," he said.

"Thank you, seeker," Phalène replied. She steered him toward a spot a few feet behind, and suddenly night bore down again.

The slender man separated himself from the shadows. "Did you have a fruitful trip, Mister Cob?"

Before Cob could answer, Claudio was upon him, scrawny limbs wrestling him down to the ground with a surprising strength. Claudio shoved a sweet-smelling rag over Cob's mouth and nose. Once Cob felt a swimmy dimness fuzz at the edges of his vision, the rag was removed. Claudio forced a pill down Cob's throat, and then all ability to see and hear clearly was taken from Cob. His palm was hot, flashing, and Cob gagged and dissolved away, molecules whizzing through time and space.

Tuesday, August 31, 2100, Avon, Vermont, NBE

"There's a gorgeous place, just across a kind of veil from this world," Cob said. "Only saw it once, but it looked really nice, and it's full of Mothmen." He laughed. "I don't *think* they're hostile, but maybe we should ask Violet if she wants her family living with a bunch of winged alien things. I met one, talked to her, and I promised her I'd try to help her with something." His grin faded. "If I see her again, I can apologize that I couldn't do it."

Ben sank down on a stool and rubbed at his eyes. "You met a Mothman and talked to it?"

"Moth*woman*, I guess? It was one of the memories Eddy restored. All flooding back to me now," Cob said. "I'm the only one who can get people over there. You have to have time traveled a bunch to even access it. The only one who fits that bill is me."

"Maybe we should try it out," Violet said. "I can go back to Roanoke with Cob just after Ambrose took me and send everyone else to this other…what, dimension? Planet? What is it?"

Cob shrugged. "It's really nice, whatever it is. Gorgeous. Quiet. Probably safe."

"If we do this and I'm not erased from the present, then we'll know we can do things and not mess our own timelines up," Violet said. "It'll save my family, keep them away from Claudio. They'd have to live there though. Forever, I guess."

Ben got up and drifted away from the kitchen. "I need an aspirin," he muttered as he wandered out toward the front parlor.

Violet's gaze met Cob's. "He's just scared," she said. "Considering everything."

Cob shrugged. "I get it." He glanced in the direction Ben went. "He probably just feels like giving up, honestly. I would, too, if I were a little more like him."

"You don't feel like giving up?"

"I sort of do," Cob said. "I mean, it's gonna be hard and scary and people might get hurt."

And I might die trying this crazy thing.

"But it's gonna be hard and scary and people will get hurt if we don't try, too." He frowned. "Plus, you might just…" He let his voice trail off.

It doesn't matter if my head explodes while I'm trying to save her, so long as I save her.

Violet crossed the room and gave Cob a peck on the cheek. "Let me check on Ben. I'll try to convince him."

Once Violet was gone, Vere moved around Cob and put the unused dinner plates away. "You shouldn't encourage her," he said. "Not in your condition. If you keep going on like this, I can't begin to predict how things might accelerate for you, health-wise."

"I understand," Cob said. "But I can't say I don't feel something there."

"You'll put her through quite a bit if you make it seem as if it has a future," Vere said. He gave Cob a sad smile. "Perhaps you think all I know is science, that I don't know people."

"I never thought—"

"But *trust me*, Mister Cob," Vere said, shaking a finger at him, "I know loss. I know loneliness. I know *pain*." Vere paused. Cob noticed wrinkles in the other man's face that weren't apparent even moments earlier. "I dare say nobody wants that for such an important young lady."

"No, sir. Nobody does."

~

Ben stood in the upstairs sitting room, a place he usually spent time with a favorite book or poring over schoolwork, when it seemed his dissertation was still something worth writing. Now it wasn't his special study, but simply a place to get away from the incessant debating over the bad ideas Cob proposed. He looked at himself in the mirror above the fireplace. His eyes were hooded and tired.

The knock on the doorframe was so light at first Ben thought he'd imagined it. But there in the mirror he saw her, pale face and hair, lingering halfway between the room and the hall.

"May I come in?"

"Free country." Ben gave a bitter laugh. "Well, or sort of, anyway."

Violet took a step forward and looked around. "This is nice," she remarked. She approached a salmon velvet settee. "Lovely piece."

"Recent acquisition," Ben said. "Wilbur—" He stopped. "It's an antique," he said, "from a friend."

Violet settled herself on it, smoothing out the folds of her skirt on her lap. "I know you're worried about me, about everyone."

"I think you'll still disappear," he blurted out. "That's what I'm worried about." Ben turned to face her, not just lock eyes with her in the mirror. "I understand linear time," he continued, "not physics, not paradoxes, not that little diagram Cob tried to draw me. I understand how Event A relates to Event B, and I understand how they continue in a line moving forward." He became more animated. "I understand the depths of needing to know and understand facts, to have *answers*. That's what makes sense to me. Events. The details of those events. I don't understand the bigger science, and I don't think even Eddy understands that stuff as much as he'd like." He had a sudden longing to fall to his knees on the floor in front of her, to take her hands in his and kiss them.

I can't lose you.

But he didn't. He stopped pacing and kept his back to her. He stared straight ahead at a window overlooking the tree-lined boulevard. Carriages and stampers and hovercars kept up a steady stream of traffic. A man in a dark suit bowed to a woman passing with a clockwork dog. The dog emitted a tinny bark, and the man tipped his top hat to it.

"All of that out there, all that world," Ben said, gesturing at the window. "We change one major thing in the past—and it *is* a major thing—and maybe you don't disappear, but maybe someone out there isn't born, maybe a different one is, maybe my great-great-grandfather never emigrates to this continent." He whirled around to Violet. "We just can't *know*."

I can't lose you!

The thought became percussive in his mind, desperate and rhythmic and unrelenting.

Violet took a deep breath and squared her shoulders. She regarded Ben with an even, measured look that implied all business and logic. "Look, we can't know, okay? But the colony disappeared. I disappeared along with it. Those are the biggies, right? If all goes according to plan, those two things will still happen."

"But the prevailing theory of what happened to the colonists was that they were absorbed into the local tribes. Thousands and thousands of people born from unions between the groups might cease to exist." Ben went to a chair opposite Violet and sat down. "And even if we're somehow okay with that, what if you still stop existing in the present when we decide where to...remove Claudio from history?"

One edge of Violet's mouth quirked up. "Nice euphemism."

"Nothing's been decided," Ben snapped.

"Okay, if I disappear, you could still kidnap me from an earlier point in time," Violet said. "And if you object to taking the colony to the other dimension, who knows what might have been the real reason the colony disappeared, right? Claudio could have gone back alone and killed them all. We're testing a theory, and we're saving so many people's lives in the process."

"I don't like to test theories," Ben said. "I like to know facts and study them as static texts." He left the room and went back downstairs. Violet's footsteps echoed behind him.

Cob and Vere were still in the kitchen. "Guys, I think we've got some investigation to do before going off half-cocked," Ben called, gesturing at them to join him in the front parlor. Cob and Vere frowned at each other before entering. Vere sat down in front of the unlit fireplace.

"The last bit of reconnaissance didn't go well, Benoy," Vere said.

"That's because I was alone." Ben lifted his chin in a half-nod to Cob. "You and me, we're gonna get to the bottom of what really happened at Roanoke. The first time. The real fate of the colonists. *That's* what we need to know before I'll sign off on this crazy plan to send them to Mothman World or whatever we're calling that place." He strode to the bookshelves and scanned them before pulling down the volume he sought. "I'll create an exact timeline of when it's theorized the colonists all truly disappeared. We'll go back as close as Eddy can get us to that precise moment and stay far, far away from everyone."

"Aw, man," Cob whined. "I wanted to actually talk to people and stuff."

"Talking to people is what led to some unfortunate circumstances in that same time and place, Mister Cob," Vere said. His eyes grew wide. "Oh, dear me, that woman. That woman, Benoy. She was likely working with *him*, wasn't she?"

"Who do you mean, that client?" Ben considered this. "Yeah. Or else she was just another creepy Rénartian looking to live out her white supremacy fantasy." He glanced at Violet. "You're real popular with them, you know."

Violet looked away. "I hate that," she said, her voice low. "Of all the weirdness about finding out who I really am, that's definitely the worst part." She looked at Ben but her eyes didn't quite meet his. "I feel like it's my fault somehow."

This was a surprise. "I hope you know I don't think you're like them, these people who look to you as a symbol of their ideology."

Violet shook her head. "No, I know, but I still feel guilty somehow."

"You didn't do anything wrong, miss," Vere said. He waved a hand at Ben. "Come on, son, what's the rest of this idea of yours?"

"You want me to go with you?" Cob asked.

"Yeah, it didn't really go so well me trying on my own," Ben replied. "And I think you by yourself could be equally dangerous. Let's go together and keep each other out of trouble." He chuckled. "Well, I'll keep you from doing something brave but stupid, and you keep me from accidentally getting myself killed."

Cob barked out a laugh. "Sounds good."

Violet joined Vere on the sofa facing the fireplace. "I don't like this," she said. "What if you accidentally go when Ambrose did and cross some kind of timeline or something? What if he doesn't get me away safely?"

"Let's get him here," Ben said. "Find out specifically when he went and avoid him if we can."

Vere rose and went to Ben's desk. "I'll get in touch with him," he said.

"Wow, we're really finding out something huge here, you guys," Cob said. His eyes sparkled, though Ben noticed the other man's forehead took on a sheen of perspiration.

He isn't well, is he? This might be the last mystery he gets to solve.

Ben held out his right hand to Cob, inviting the other man to shake it. "You up for solving the biggest missing persons case in all of recorded history, buddy?"

Cob grinned. "Am I ever." He clasped Ben's hand in his and shook it. "And we're buddies now?"

"Watch it," Ben said.

Across the room, Vere spoke quietly into the phone before hanging it up. "He'll be here shortly, but in the meantime he gave me the date of his arrival at the colony." He handed Ben a small slip of paper. "Reference this against your target arrival before we begin to determine the coordinates."

"And clothes," Cob said. "We need to look…what, kind of Renaissance Faire-esque?"

Ben groaned. "Oh, God." He sat down and paged through his book. "We want to be as stealthy as possible anyway, so I'm thinking camouflage. Fatigues."

"Yeah, but if someone *does* see us, we're gonna look even weirder then," Cob said.

"Compromise," Violet suggested. "Greens and browns, but period appropriate." She grinned. "I bet none of us dreamed as kids about someday picking out camo-themed Pilgrim wear."

"This colony wasn't a Pilgrim group," Ben said. "The Pilgrims were a religious sect that—"

Cob groaned. "Stick to the books, man, and take care of that stuff yourself. I don't want to feel like I'm in school when we actually get there."

Friday, October 6, 1587, Roanoke Island, British colony

This was the pain of hot pokers, fire, and ripping, tearing, rending. This time, however, Cob didn't permit himself even a second of incapacitation—he fought through the pain, clenched every muscle in his body, and forced his eyes to open, his limbs to move.

I have to find Ben. Have to find him. Get to him. Now. Now. Now. Go.

Sure, Ben was grating on him; the two men couldn't be more different, and Cob knew what would happen between Violet and Ben after he was—

Dead. You'll be dead, man. Face it. This pain right now is nothing compared to what's in store for you down the line. Get it together.

He grit his teeth and scrambled to standing, looking around a wooded area. It was dusk, and the scraggly copse of trees in which he stood was on a small hill. Between branches, he could make out a lower-lying area with some form of civilization on it. A circular wooden fence surrounded buildings with crudely fashioned chimneys visible above the fence line. No one appeared to be around, but Cob still felt a need to keep his noise to a minimum.

He couldn't call out for Ben, but he could look, and yet their forest-colored clothing would make this search more difficult. He pushed aside bush limbs and picked his way over fallen logs. This was no modern hiking path, cleared of scrub and made hospitable for weekend campers. This was real, virgin forest, untouched and not designed for human navigation.

Trees rustled on Cob's left. He snapped to attention, and there was Ben clambering toward him, making his own feeble attempt to be quiet. Cob pressed a finger to his lips and pointed down on the flat land of the colony site below.

"We that close?" Ben whispered.

Cob nodded.

Ben smiled for an instant, but then pressed his lips together. "Sorry, this is kind of cool," he whispered. "I want to see it, just for a second."

"That's all we're doing, seeing," Cob whispered back. "Go see to your heart's content, man. Hell, we should probably get closer, even."

"But they can't see us."

"I got it, I know, we are as ghosts. Now go get your first look." Cob pointed behind him. "Good sightline a few feet that way."

Ben inched past Cob and then stopped, ramrod still. "Oh, my God," he murmured. "I can't believe it."

"You did time travel once already, you know," Cob said. "Does it really inspire that much awe?"

Ben turned back to him. "I saw a bridge and a corpse. It could've been anywhere, any time. This, though." He gestured at the colony buildings. "This is *history*, right here in front of me. Definitive. This couldn't be just any time or place." He looked at Cob intently. "It's what I think about all the time, wishing I could understand what this life was like, what the past all means. It's kind of a big deal for me."

"You could've seen this any time since you met the good doctor, you know," Cob said.

Ben studied the ground. "I could have."

"Why—" Cob shut his mouth. If Ben were braver, he might be in Cob's very predicament by now, brain being eaten away by these adventures. Maybe caution meant Ben would live long enough to see Vere develop a way around the physical damage time travel could cause.

"Why what?"

Cob shook his head. "Never mind."

Ben turned back to the view before them. "Dammit, that fence." He gestured at the land below. "I want to see more, and it's blocking so much."

"Yeah, but if somebody comes and carts people off, or if people start leaving," Cob said, "we'll see it, even from up here."

Ben's frown deepened.

"You want to go in, don't you?"

"We can't."

"Yeah, I know we can't," Cob said, "but that doesn't stop you *wanting* to."

"Of *course* I want to. But unlike some people, I have restraint and control."

"Restraint and control are way overrated, buddy."

"That attitude has served you really well, too," Ben said.

"I'll have you know that—"

Ben held up a hand to Cob as his attention was distracted by something below. He pointed at the colony site.

"What is it?" Cob whispered. He craned to get a better look. "I don't see anything."

"That's just it," Ben said. He was no longer whispering. "I don't see anything, either, except the buildings. I don't think anyone is actually down there."

Cob gaped at him. "Did we get here too late?"

"Only one way to find out." Ben moved past the tree line and descended the side of the hill.

"Whoa, whoa, hang on." Cob scrambled after him. "What happened to observe and be careful and reconnaissance and shit?"

"Honestly, I think we're too late, man. Look, it's getting dark, right? There should be candles in the windows, smoke in the chimneys. But there's *nothing*. There's no guard at the gate. There's a little post for 'em, see? But do you see guards?"

"No."

"No guards, no colonists," Ben said.

"You think the doc screwed up?"

"No, this is an imprecise science and even my estimates about when the colony disappeared could have been off." Ben walked forward again. "We can safely get in there and find some clues, though, clues that are probably fresher than what John White found when he got back here from England. That was three years past when they went missing. All kinds of stuff could've been damaged or destroyed in that time."

The gates loomed over them now, and Ben turned to Cob, who trailed him by a few feet.

"So we go inside and look for some clues," Ben said, "but we leave whatever we find untouched."

~

Thomas Warner heard the men before seeing them. He tried to speak but his words came out in a cough. It was enough to draw the strangers deeper into his house. He'd been curled onto his cot for months, barely moving, as his food supply dwindled down to nil.

The first man who entered was dark-haired, with round, friendly features and sunburned skin. He gestured back to the outer room before entering. "Oh, my God, I found somebody." He turned back to Warner. "Are you okay? You don't look so good."

Before Warner could reply, the second man entered. He was lean, with much darker skin and hair than the first man. Taller and more slender than his companion, he looked uncertain and nervous. Both of them were the pictures of robust, good health compared to Warner.

"Who are you?" he croaked.

"I'm Cob," the first man said, "and this is Ben," he said, nodding back to his companion. "We were trading with the natives nearby. Thought we would stop by your camp and meet you, but didn't find anybody."

"We're down from Nova Scotia," Ben added, casting an annoyed look at Cob. "From the colony there."

Warner nodded. "Aye, I met a woman from there once." He coughed again, and a spattering of blood dusted his hand. "I am not long for this world, gentlemen. Perhaps I could implore you to bury me, when the time comes." He struggled to sit up a little. "I'm Thomas Warner, soon to be the *late* Thomas Warner."

"Where is everyone else?" Ben asked. "This was Raleigh and White's settlement, wasn't it?"

"Aye." Warner's lungs rattled, but he kept the cough in and swallowed a mouthful of bloody saliva. "White's been gone for some time. The others...oh, my word, it was terrible."

He recounted a tale of an elderly man—bent-backed and silver-haired—entering the settlement on a pretense of trading one night months earlier. "I was standing sentry that eve," he said. Cob and Ben drew closer to him, leaning in to listen to his parched, thin voice. "You mightn't believe it to look at me now," Warner said, "but I was strong once, young and capable. Not as I am now."

Cob nodded. "Things can happen suddenly, man. I get that."

Warner frowned. The men's speech was odd, but perhaps it was his delirium.

"Who was this man?" Ben asked.

"He told us his name was Caleb French and that he was a fur trapper who'd become lost."

Cob described the man, in almost perfect detail. "Does that sound like him?"

"Yes, completely, though he was quite near the end of his years," Warner said.

Cob and Ben looked at one another. "Claudio," Ben said.

"Sounds like," Cob said. "Go on, Mister Warner. What did this guy do?"

"*Guy?*" Warner chuckled, but it became a hacking so great he sat up and pounded his chest with his fist. "My, you certainly speak strangely," he murmured when at last the coughing subsided. "This man—this French or whomsoever you recognize him to be—he was taken in by one of our founding families, the Dares." He shook his head. "Poor Ananias and Eleanor, they had their only child spirited away in the night, likely by a wild dog. They never found a scrap of the babe. At least they were able to baptize her before she went missing. So I'm certain they found the idea of a guest, someone to take care of, rather appealing, even if only for a night or two. An old man is a poor substitute for an infant daughter, though." Warner felt a tugging at the corner of his eyes, and he squeezed them shut tight. "They never came to services that Sunday, so I went looking for them. Dead, the both of them, pulled to pieces in the night. I discovered Goodman French hiding in a cupboard, forced him out, and called for support. My fellow sentryman, Goodman Cage, came at once, and in the struggle French was killed."

Ben gasped. "Wait, you *killed* him?" He looked at his friend. "Claudio dies *here*? *Now*?"

171

"Last spring, it were," Warner clarified. "Not *now*. I've been ill for some time. This didn't happen recently." He studied the men. "Who was this murderer? Was he from your colony?"

"We were sent to track him, bring him to justice," Cob said.

"You needn't worry on that," Warner said. "He's likely been dealt holy justice in the bowels of hell."

"So what happened to the other colonists?" Ben asked.

Warner couldn't stop the tears now. "Myself and Goodman Cage, we were sentenced to isolation here. The rest of our party were angered that we were unable to hold a trial for French. Since we were innocent of which of us dealt the deadly blow, they left both of us here while they joined the Croatan tribe, for better food and shelter." He coughed, weakly this time, and wiped his mouth with the back of his hand. "Cage wandered out into the wilderness, and I expect the wolves got him. I was about to strike out on my own when the illness struck. My hope was to last until White's return, but alas, I fear I shall not."

Panic seized Warner at a sudden thought, and he pulled at Cob's shirt, leaving a bloody handprint on the rough green cloth. "You must bury me, gentlemen. You must leave a sign for our governor so he can find the others amongst the natives."

"I think we can do that," Ben said. He looked on the verge of tears himself. "We'll leave a note carved into a tree directing the way."

Warner relaxed and fell back against his pillow. "Perfect, sir." He drifted to sleep and dreamt of this man taking a knife to bark.

Tuesday, August 31, 2100, Avon, Vermont, NBE

These people were strangers, arcane-looking woodcuts on a page in a dusty textbook. And yet the words "your parents were murdered" still caused Violet's blood to run cold.

"But they got him, these guards," Cob said, his words tumbling out in a rush of reassurance. "They got him. He died back there, stuck in the past."

"Not for years," Violet murmured. "You said he looked very old. How many others is he going to kill between now and somewhere in his future lifetime?"

"It's impossible to tell," Ben said. "No recording, no way of even totally proving it was him."

"Oh, come on, it was him," Cob said. "Who else would *do* that? To *them*, specifically? It was revenge for them letting Virginia slip through their fingers."

He let out a bitter laugh. "Plus he's just a psycho. I think we've established that."

"The others, they went off with the tribe?" Violet asked. "They got away safe?"

"They ran away, leaving two men to die," Cob replied. "That was *cold*, you guys. That was some messed up frontier justice right there."

"Technically, the frontier period is classified as being many centuries later and much farther west," Ben said. "The entire *zeitgeist* was different then, and lawlessness was necessary because—"

"Okay," Cob said, throwing up his hands. "Okay, that is *super interesting*, but now is not the time."

"I kind of sense it's *not* super interesting," Ben muttered. He sat down and stayed silent.

Violet gave him a sad smile. "It's hard staying quiet when someone's wrong, isn't it?"

Ben leaned forward and nodded. "You know, it really is. *So* hard."

"Well, try to be brave and see if you can manage to ignore it, man," Cob said. "Just until we get done saving the day, all right?"

"You're asking a lot of my bravery."

"You are," Violet said, her smile now a little less sad. "Look, okay, I think the best thing to do here is worry about saving my family, at the very least. If this is the timeline, they die, right? So we send them somewhere they won't die." She felt a fluttery nervous feeling in her chest. "I want to go this time. I want to see them."

"I'll have to go with you, if we're taking them to the Mothman dimension," Cob said.

Violet nodded. "Yeah, that's good."

"What about the others?" Ben asked. "They *probably* made it to the Croatan tribe, and if so they were *probably* okay, but if we change this one thing, save the Dare family, the rest of the colony won't necessarily feel the need to abandon it as punishment for Warner and Cage. They might try to make it through one more winter waiting for White to come back with supplies."

"Well, if it's life or death, we'll get 'em over to the other dimension, too," Cob said.

"Yeah, but that's gonna mess up a lot," Ben said. "I've explained this. People might never be born. Entire generations might not be born."

"We have to play this by ear," Violet said. "Ben, look, I know you're worried about ripple effects, but time travel means everyone we know of can be saved. *Everyone.* So if some people are going to die horrible deaths and we have a way to prevent that? Then, I'm sorry, I'm going to do that. I'm an officer of the law. I can't let people suffer."

I can't let my parents get murdered. To hell with everyone else.

Ben nodded. "Well, I guess this doesn't necessarily affect *me* too much. I'm not descended from anyone from that region, not even a little bit. But still. I have no idea if someone descended from them traveled to India, perhaps, met my ancestors, had some impact on their lives. How do you know *you're* not going to be similarly affected?" he asked, gesturing toward Cob.

Cob shrugged. "I don't."

"We agonized over what might happen if Violet ceased to exist," Ben said. "What if you do?"

"Guys, I'm not well," Cob admitted. "I think we can all let go of the illusion that I'm not in some massive pain a lot of the time, and I think there might not be much of me left no matter what. If I disappear from history…well, then, I do. I think if there's gonna be a paradox, though…" he paused, frowning. "Call me crazy, but I feel like the universe won't let that be, that if there's a paradox likely, it might self-correct." He looked from Ben to Violet. "Is that nuts? I feel like that's nuts."

"No," Ben said. "Eddy explained this to me once. There are logical theories behind that. Some MIT researchers applied a rule to the Novikov self-consistency principle that would support that. Basically, if there's gonna be a paradox, something happens to prevent it."

Cob held up his hands in surrender. "Whoa, whoa," he said, "watch it with the big words. Some of us only went to Harvard."

"I can't correct you, and I can't use multi-syllabic words," Ben said. "Got it."

"Last plea of a dying man," Cob said, clasping his hands together as if in prayer.

"You're *not* dying," Violet said. "I don't care what anybody else says, even you. We'll get this done and then we'll get you back to Doctor Vere's friend and get you all fixed up."

"We could do that now," Ben suggested. "There's no particular reason to do this immediately."

"Yeah, there is," Cob said. "What if that guy does fix me up but it makes it so I can't access that other dimension? Face it, Ben. We need me a little bit broken to make this plan work."

Ben threw up his hands. "Fine. Go." He looked at Violet, his eyes wide and worried. "Please be careful."

"You both forget I chase bad guys around as my job. You know, that, right?" Violet asked. "I get paid to be in danger, and I'm damn good at getting myself out of it."

Wednesday, September 1, 2100, Avon, Vermont, NBE

Cob sat on the bed in Ben's guest room as he waited for Violet to finish dressing and being briefed on the trip. He'd gone up here to rest, but no rest was available to him. His head pounded, and his vision grew dim around the edges.

It won't be long. You've got to prepare yourself.

Rupert Cob was thirty years old. He'd seen centuries pass, learned the depths of long-buried secrets and mysteries, and now he was about to die.

He took a long, deep breath through his nose and released it through his mouth, willing the pain to subside.

I don't care if I die, so long as it doesn't hurt much more than this.

Pain was no stranger to him. Hangovers, sprains, and the effects of his trips… they clung to him now, like invisible scars. Pain was manageable, if he understood its source. Drink a bottle of whiskey, and the next day will be full of dehydration and nausea. Uncomfortable, but understandable, and he'd known the odds when he took the first sip of the night. But this, this incomprehensible pulsing from inside his brain, even if he let the neuroscientist explain it all to him again, it was still confusing and without direct, obvious source. Why should time travel do this to him? Was he already susceptible? Was he already at risk somehow, something to do with genetics? What if Violet went too many times, would this happen to her as well?

I'm not coming back alive. I'm going to die back there, five hundred years ago. My body is even now probably buried in North Carolina, among the fields on the island. I'm probably deep beneath a national park on Rénartian soil.

That last thought gripped him with sadness. It wasn't the knowing he wasn't coming back. It was that he wouldn't be able to come back *here*, to Empire territory, to be laid to rest near family, however little they appeared to matter to him. It was his family's money and legacy that let him live this life of adventure. Didn't he owe it to them to end those adventures in the family plot, here in Vermont?

If the end starts to come, I won't make Violet bring me back, but maybe I'll make her leave me over there, with Phalène and her kind. Or, hell, who knows what should happen to me?

He smiled. The other side did seem a better place, a place of sunshine and imagination, where the Dares could bury him and he'd always be near the creatures who were the source of his last voluntary trip back in time. He'd paid Ben Jonson to let him find out whether Mothmen were real, and now he knew and could join them forever.

Cob winced as he rose from the bed, walking to the small writing desk on the other side of the room. The top of the desk was hinged, and he pulled it down to reveal several slots filled with different colors of stationery. Attached to one of the stationery compartments were two U-shaped iron fittings, carved with scrollwork, in which rested a fountain pen. He pulled a chair over and sat down, withdrawing a sheet of pale blue paper from its small shelf.

"I'm going to ask you to do something for me," Cob's pen scratched across the page. "I know, selfish to the very end, right? But, really, this is for you as much as it is for me."

He continued to write, pausing each time the pain in his head became too much for him. Breathing deeply was a help, as was closing his eyes.

Dammit, I don't want to be weak, not now.

They had to leave, and soon, while Cob was still strong enough. Above the writing desk was a window, overlooking the back garden and the roofs of the neighboring homes and businesses. Cob watched as a cardinal danced and fluttered on a branch, its bright red feathers standing out starkly against the pale blue of the midday sky.

A hundred birds, a thousand, a hundred thousand...they've all sat on that branch as the branch grew from a sapling to a tree to this ancient, centuries-old thing out there now. How many pairs of feet have walked the boards of these floors? Did the wood come from another tree, hacked down with an axe in the days of Poe and Polk, Waterhouse and Whitman?

Rupert Cob was shifting from life to history, and before the day was over, the transition would be complete.

He saw Thomas Warner's young, drawn face before him, the man's eyes shadowed, his cheeks hollowed, consumption or influenza raging through his gaunt frame. "The *late* Thomas Warner," he'd joked. Now Cob thought of himself that way, the relic, the vestige, the man whose last duty was to sacrifice and die. Where time was concerned, he was already gone.

From downstairs, he heard voices, doors opening and closing, and urgent footsteps. One voice lilted high and sharp above some of the others; it sounded like Miss Moto was back in the building.

"This isn't a time for strife," he wrote, "or mourning, either." He paused, resting the cap of the pen against his lips. He grinned and then continued to write. "God, that sounds trite," he wrote. "When somebody reaches this point, they start to sound really damn pretentious. Please remember me as I was, not as this sentimental idiot."

A gentle knock fell on the other side of the closed door. "Mister Cob? Are you awake?"

"Come in," Cob said. He hastily scratched a few last lines, folded the letter, and put it in an envelope. He wrote Violet's name on the front and turned around just as Vere opened the door. "Doc, can you hang onto something for me?"

~

Violet smoothed out her skirt, admiring the swaths of starched brown silk edged in crisp lace. "Where'd you get this?" she asked, turning to Ben.

He was looking at her face, not the outfit. The corner of his mouth formed a subtle half-smile.

His eyes are so brown.

She cleared her throat, her embarrassment immediate and distinct, as if she'd said the words aloud.

He can't tell what I was thinking.

But could she tell what he thought?

That smile was not the smile of someone content that all details of a business deal or an investigation were going well. That was the smile of a man gazing upon the object of his affection.

"Ben? The dress? Where'd it come from?" she tried again.

"Hmm?" He seemed to wake up from a trance or a dream. "Oh, well, you know, research. It's what I do. I think that one Kris helped me piece together from thrift store finds and then anything that wasn't perfect we made."

Violet drew back. "You *made* parts of this?"

Ben shrugged. "Kris can knit lace. I…" He laughed and hung his head. "I sew."

"*Wow.*" Violet's laughter joined Ben's. "Learning a lot about you today, Mister Jonson."

And about myself.

She finished pinning her hair according to the woodcut in Ben's book on the Roanoke colonists. The woman pictured had a sweet face, not quite round and not quite angular, with sad eyes and a gentle smile.

"Do you think she'll find me familiar?" Violet asked. She laughed again. "That's dumb, I know. I…well, did you ever meet someone who looked like they could be your relative, even though they weren't? I wonder if she'd see me and think something like that, that's all."

"I don't know," Ben replied. He straightened his cravat and tugged at the neck of his shirt. "God, how did people wear this stuff? I feel like I'm choking."

"Here, you've got the top button done wrong, I think." Violet crossed the room and peered at Ben's shirt. "You've got the second button in the top buttonhole. No wonder you're choking. Can you—"

"What, like this?" Ben fumbled at the button beneath his cravat.

"Here, just—" Violet reached out and slid the top of the cravat from its position. Her hand brushed Ben's, and a spark of electricity shocked them both. "Oh!" Startled, Violet stepped back again. "Sorry, it's the carpet, I suppose," she mumbled.

"No, those shoes have no rubber insulation," Ben said, gesturing at her feet.

She pointed at his neck. "Just, I think you know what to do, right?"

Ben nodded. "You'd better find Eddy and get started. I'll be along."

Violet scurried from the wardrobe room to the lab down the hall.

Stupid, stupid, stupid. Focus. Besides, what about Cob?

"Hey there," Cob greeted her as she entered. "You all set?"

He looked even more ill than he did earlier in the day, his skin pale except beneath his eyes and in the hollows of his cheeks, where it was bluish and ashy.

"Ben's still finishing," Violet said.

Vere emerged from the opposite door. "Benoy isn't going," he said. "We have to keep him healthy for a later trip in case there are complications."

"But I think he believes he's—"

"*No.*" Vere was firm. He and Cob exchanged a look. "Mister Cob can handle the barrier between the worlds, and you need to assist him. You haven't traveled so much that you're in any danger, and neither has Benoy."

"So it's repeated time travel that…" Violet gazed at Cob, her chest now aching. "I thought, I mean, I wasn't sure, but…really? That's what's wrong with you?"

"We don't know," Cob said. His voice was rough. He looked away. "I'll be fine, right, doc?"

"Son, I think it's time to be completely honest with everyone," Vere said. He put a hand on Violet's shoulder. "There's a chance Benoy or I may have to retrieve you alone."

"What? No!" Violet squirmed away from Vere. "Cob, no, you're going to be *fine*. Let's do this. Ben."

"No, no Ben," Cob said. "Just you and me against the world, kid." He took her hand in his. "Doc, can you give us like two seconds?"

"I have to get my backup battery regardless," Vere said, shuffling back outside.

"Violet, I…I'm no good at this stuff," Cob said. "But don't pin any hopes on me, even though I think you know I—"

Violet took his face her in her hands and silenced him with a kiss.

Thursday, May 11, 1587, Roanoke Island, British colony

It didn't look that different from places she was used to. Campgrounds, hiking trails, state parks… Violet took in the edges of the colony grounds and saw nothing remarkable, except for the knowledge that the woods ringing the walls and gates were, in her time, shopping centers and hotels. What she thought of as civilization was still unknown. And yet this was where and when she was born; this was where, if not for Claudio Florence's plans, she would have died.

But as a baby? Or could I have grown up?

She closed her eyes and inhaled deeply. The air held no scent of pollution, nothing chemical or artificial. She smelled the woods themselves, the mud and flowers and even a musky odor that suggested the presence of animals. There was a hint of wood smoke on the air, too, an autumnal smell that made her think of harvesting gourds and drying pumpkins. In her costume, she looked like a woman used to boiling root vegetables in a cauldron-like pot over an open flame.

Is that my imagination? Or a memory?

"Come on," Cob urged. "We have to find Warner and then your folks." He strode down the hill toward the front gate.

"Are we at the right time?" Violet asked as she followed.

"Yeah, I think so," Cob replied. "When Ben and I came back too late, it looked abandoned." He pointed to a plume of smoke rising from a chimney. "See that? There are still people here."

"Oh, good."

A young man stood at the gate. Cob's grin widened the closer they got to him. "Hey, my *man*."

"Beg pardon?" The young man narrowed his eyes and studied Cob and Violet. "Halt there, the both of you."

Something caught Cob's attention from the guard to a place a few feet into the woods. "Whoa. I haven't seen that one before." He wandered off. Violet couldn't tell what drew him away.

"I, uh, I must apologize for my companion, goodman," Violet said, trying to remember how she needed to speak in this time. "He is suffering from illness and we seek shelter."

"Who are you?" the guard asked.

"That fellow is my husband. My name is Virginia Lessep, and we—"

"*Violet!*"

Violet turned at the sound of Cob's voice. A giant winged creature stood in a clearing with him. Cob seemed ecstatic and waved his arms at her.

"By your leave, sir," Violet said. She curtsied as best she could and ran to Cob and the creature.

"Do you see the gateway?" Cob asked once she reached them. He pointed behind the creature, but when Violet looked all she saw were trees and grass.

179

"No, but as long as *you* see it, that's all that matters," Violet replied. "I take it this is a Mothman." She shrank back a bit from the thing, all mouse-colored fur and batwings.

Cob laughed. "You're pretty sharp."

"Yes, well, that kid back there probably doesn't think so. Let me see if I can get inside," Violet said. She nodded at the Mothman. "You and this one should probably stay here and guard the gateway in case it closes or something." She frowned. "Do they close?"

"I think so," Cob said. "I can't really communicate with him on this side, only over there." He looked up at the creature. "Can you understand me, man? Or lady? I can't, sorry, I can't really tell."

The Mothman cooed, bird-like.

"Yeah, no, that's not gonna work." Cob shrugged. "Sorry, Violet. I'll stick around here. You find your folks first, then we'll get everybody else over."

"This'll require a lot of convincing, I'm sure," Violet said. "Do you think there's time?"

The Mothman cooed again and sat down, folding its long legs under itself. It gave a little shudder of wings before hunkering down deeper into the tall grass and closing its eyes. It was invisible to anyone not looking for it, its coat blending into the colors of the pasture.

"I think it wants a nap," Cob said. "We're probably good for a while." He sat down beside it. "Don't panic, but don't dawdle, either," he urged her.

"I'll try." Violet trudged back toward the gate, where the guard was now holding his musket out, the barrel pointing straight at her.

"Goody Lessep, you did not identify your original location," the guard said. "Your husband behaves strangely. I must take you to speak to Governor Dare."

Dare?

Violet's heart sped up, but she fought to retain her composure. "Of course," she said. "It would be an honor to make his acquaintance."

~

"Sir, two unknown persons have breached the colony, and—"

Ananias heard no further words from the guard, though the young man kept speaking. Standing halfway across the room was a woman who could have been Eleanor's twin. She was slender, with white-blond hair pinned up in small curls around a heart-shaped face. Even from this distance, he could see her eyes were sea blue, just like his wife's.

But it was not Eleanor, for Eleanor was younger, her hair darker, her figure more buxom. Still, the resemblance was uncanny.

"You are a White, somehow," Ananias said. "John only had one other child besides my wife, and it was a boy."

"My name is Lessep," Violet said. "My husband and I come from the north and seek shelter. He is ill, and the rest of our group has returned to England."

"No, it hasn't," Ananias said. "You are not English, though indeed you resemble my own Eleanor. Your speech is odd." He stood up straighter. "There was a woman here once, a spy from the English or the Spanish who claimed she was from Nova Scotia. Some thought her a witch."

The young woman fidgeted. "Please, governor. I beg you. My husband is very ill. He rests in a field, having visions of invisible monsters. I believe it is a fever. If you have medicine, I can pay you."

Ananias studied the woman. "Pay me with what?" He spread his arms wide. "We have no one to trade with. Our supplies from England have dwindled. We eat what we grow. Our coats are animal hide. We have no use for money." Perhaps once they might have, if money could have stopped the shadowy figure who stole his daughter away. This woman was far too late for that. "Lest you think I am the lout my father-in-law believes, I have no use for anything *else*, either." His lip curled up into a sneer. "I am faithful to your cousin."

"My cousin?"

"That's who you are, is it not? Eleanor's cousin?"

The young woman eyed the guards lining the wall behind Ananias. "I suppose I should stop denying it," she said, her words measured. "Yes, I am."

"John sent you to see that I am governing well?" Ananias asked.

"Not in so many words," the woman said, "but I am beginning to suspect it."

"He sent you without supplies?"

"We were set upon by thieves," the woman replied.

Ananias shook his head. "The savages are unpredictable."

The woman flinched but said nothing.

"John and I do not always see eye to eye," Ananias said. He stroked his short beard as he paced. "Still, you are family to my wife and are in need. Take Eleanor and me to your husband. She will tend to him, and I will discuss what little we can provide for you. It pains me to say that we cannot bring you inside, however, lest his fever spread to others."

The woman relaxed and smiled. "Of course, sir."

~

"Cousin Virginia? But I didn't—oh!"

Eleanor Dare was more beautiful than the pictures in Ben's books. Violet blinked in astonishment. It was like looking in a cloudy mirror, seeing her mother. Ananias looked from one woman to the other. "The resemblance, I am certain, you can both appreciate," he said.

Eleanor smiled. "Perhaps my husband already told you. Our daughter is called

181

Virginia. How lovely that Aunt Cornelia had the same notion as I."

Violet nodded. "Lovely indeed."

Eleanor's smile disappeared. "Husband, this woman is an imposter." She stepped toward Violet. "I have no Aunt Cornelia, and I presume your mother is not accidentally called that as well."

Violet fought back an urge to run. "Please, ma'am. Sir. If I tell you the truth, you won't believe me. I'm here to save your lives."

"Who are you really?" Eleanor demanded.

The door to the public house banged open, and the room was filled with a loud voice, accompanied by a rustling of wings. "She's your daughter, Misses Dare, and I'm helping her prevent your murder."

Violet spun around. "Oh, my God, Cob, you brought that *here*?" The doorway was filled with the Mothman's giant form. As if in reply, it raised its head and screeched.

The Dares both dropped to the floor, and the guards raised their muskets. "A demon!" Ananias shouted. "Shoot it, Warner."

The guard from the gate trembled. The Mothman entered the room, stepped over the Dares, and stared at the guards. Warner raised his musket higher, but the Mothman batted it away as if it were a twig.

"Governor, I don't think I can," Warner said, his voice reduced to a whimper.

"We have to go now," Cob said. He withdrew a small pistol from his coat and aimed it at Ananias. "Sir, ma'am, we're leaving. Now." He nodded at Violet. "Take your mother. I'll bring your dad along here."

Ananias scrambled to his feet. "You will do no such thing."

Cob fired the pistol into the ceiling. A rain of wood chips and sawdust sprinkled down. "Won't I?" Cob asked. "Come on, *governor*. God, what is it with you people with that title that you gotta be raging dicks about everything? Sheesh. Less talking, more walking."

Violet held out her hand to Eleanor. "Ma'am, please come with us. I promise we won't hurt you."

"But the demon!" Eleanor shrieked. Tears streamed down her face. "And you, you can't be my daughter unless you're a ghost."

Violet grabbed Eleanor by the arm and pulled her out the door. "This isn't exactly how I hoped this meeting would go," she said. "I don't have any way to prove anything, but yes, I'm your daughter."

"My daughter is dead." Eleanor struggled a bit against Violet's grip as she walked behind her. "A man came in the night and stole her. We never saw his face."

"Yes, he stole me. He didn't kill me."

"That was mere months ago. How is it that you are so fast grown?"

They reached the outer gates of the colony. Here and there, a few residents stopped their activities to stare. "You there!" a man called. "Unhand the governor's wife."

"We have to hurry," Violet urged. She picked up her pace and looked over her shoulder. "Cob!"

Cob emerged from the building with Ananias in tow, the Mothman walking behind them. Shrieks rose up from the residents milling about. The Mothman spread its wings, took flight, and soared over the outer fence. It let out a high-pitched keening from the other side.

Silence fell. Both Eleanor and Ananias ceased resisting Violet and Cob and let themselves be led through the front gate and out to the clearing.

"There." Cob pointed to the same spot he'd indicated before. The Mothman was now nowhere to be seen.

"Where'd it go?" Violet asked.

"The other side," Cob replied. "I can see it, just a little." He nudged Ananias forward and released him. "You two, say your goodbyes to your daughter, and then you're coming with me." He strode across the clearing. "To *safety*," he added. "We're doing all this to *save you*."

"Is he telling the truth," Eleanor asked, "or are we being sent to hell?"

"It's true," Violet replied. "Look, it's very complicated, but I *am* Virginia. I grew up somewhere time moves more quickly. Because of that, I know that if I don't send you and everybody else here to safety, you'll be murdered by a very bad man."

"The man who stole you?" Ananias asked.

"The man who took me was rescuing me from the murderer," Violet replied. "Where I live, I'm safe. I'm happy. And I do things like save good people from harm." She tried to smile, but tears fell instead. "Will you let me save you?"

"We have to go *now*," Cob said. "The door is closing."

"Go with him," Violet said. "He also saves good people. You can trust him."

"But the demon!" Eleanor protested.

Violet shook her head. "It's not a demon."

Ananias took his wife's hand. "Eleanor, I think she speaks the truth," he said. "God help me if I am proven wrong, but I believe it isn't hell we're being sent to. I cannot distrust a woman who so clearly shares your face and soul, my love." He smiled at Violet. "Other things fly and travel through worlds. Things like angels." He took Violet's hand and kissed it. "Thank you, daughter, for sending us to heaven."

~

Cob staggered from the gateway alone. Violet rushed to catch him. He was light in her arms, his face even leaner than before. "I can't get anybody else over," he whispered. He coughed, and a thin spatter of blood shot through the air.

"Oh, God." Violet eased Cob to the ground. "You're gonna be okay. I'll activate the retrieval and—"

"No, I'm going to die here," Cob said. "I want to. I want to be here. Get the rest of the folks to trust the Croatan tribe and go with them so they can eat, make it through the winter, at least." He coughed again and clutched Violet's hand. "Promise me you'll write the message. You know the one. Bury me under the tree. *Promise me.*"

"I promise." Violet said through tears. "But please, let me try to get you some medicine. We can still get back home."

"No, I want to be part of it." Cob smiled and gazed up at the sky. "I want to be a part of history forever." He looked back at Violet, his grin blood-smeared. "Kids'll come here. People will make bad TV movies about this. And you'll know—*you'll know*—that I was here, that I got your folks to safety. When people talk about the word carved on the tree, you'll know it's my headstone." He winked at her. "Keep it our secret, Violet. Just that, keep that little bit our secret."

She clutched his hand hard and held it close to her heart. "That's a hell of an awesome secret to share with somebody," she said, laughter mingling with her tears.

His smile broadened. "It really is, isn't it?"

His grip on her hand loosened.

Thursday, September 2, 2100, Avon, Vermont, NBE

"Here, just…" Kris tried to take Violet's hand, but the gesture was met with a moan and a furtive dodge. Kris sighed. "Look, you're filthy, okay? Nobody wants to talk to you until you're feeling up to it. It's fine. Let me get you clean, get some food in you. Please?" She tried to see a spark of comprehension in Violet's eyes. Matted, sweaty locks of hair hung down in front of her face. Kris once again tried to reach out to touch her, and this time Violet didn't draw back.

Once Kris pushed Violet's hair back behind her ears, she could see most of the grime was dried tears—long, dirty streaks streamed down from her eyes to her chin. *She was crying, she's dirty, and Cob didn't come back with her.*

Kris imagined Violet lugging Cob's body into a hole. She wanted to ask, even if it meant having her fears confirmed, but she didn't. Instead, she coaxed Violet into taking her hand and letting herself be led to the basement utility shower.

"Soap, towels, everything's here. I washed your normal clothes. They're finishing up in the dryer. There's a robe." Kris pointed to a fluffy white garment hanging on the back of the door. "I'll check your clothes and bring them down when they're ready."

"He's dead," Violet said. Her voice was clear and smooth, her tone lucid. "You figured it out. Did everyone else?"

"I don't know," Kris replied. "They saw the state you were in and had me come down to help."

"I couldn't see them," Violet said. "Not yet."

"Do you want me to tell them?"

Violet nodded.

Crap. Okay. That's not how I wanted to spend my afternoon.

"Do you want me to tell them any…details? Anything specific?"

Please say no.

"No."

Thank God.

Kris patted the top of the stack of towels. "Get clean. Get feeling more like yourself. I'll get some tea for you, too." She took a step toward Violet. "You're safe. You're fine."

"For now." Violet smiled at Kris. "I'll be all right. Thank you."

Kris took the spiral staircase back up to the front office parlor. Ben hovered near his desk.

Did his hair always have that little sprinkling of gray in it? Has his forehead always been that lined?

"Is she okay?"

"She will be," Kris replied. "I gotta check on her laundry and get her something warm to drink." She jerked a thumb toward the kitchen. "So, um, I'm gonna—"

"He's dead, isn't he?"

Kris stopped and sighed. She looked at the floor, noting absently that her right boot needed polishing.

Let me think about that, my dumb old scuffed boot, please don't make me say it, please, Ben…

"Kris?"

She kept her eyes on her boot. "Yeah, he's dead."

"Shit."

She couldn't help but laugh. "Shit, yeah." She looked back up at Ben. "Understatement."

"Did she say anything specific?" He squeezed his eyes shut. "Never mind. No, don't. Not yet."

"She didn't," Kris said. "Let her tell us when she's ready. She's not doing so great, but she'll get there."

185

"But hey, she's alive, right?" Ben smiled.

God, you should be thrilled, shouldn't you? She's great, the other guy's worm food, and now you've got her all to yourself.

A kernel of rage grew in Kris's chest. Her heartbeat sped up. "I have to do the stuff with the things," she said before hurrying off to the kitchen. Once there, she leaned against the sink. Her eyes stung. She gripped the porcelain to keep her knees from buckling as she cried.

Part V: The Hero

The airplane stays up because it doesn't have the time to fall.
–Orville Wright

Thursday, September 2, 2100, Avon, Vermont, NBE

Violet wiped the steam off the mirror and looked at herself. She was clean now, but she looked older—her cheeks were drawn, her mouth seemed etched along either side, and her eyes were both bloodshot. She pulled on the robe and dragged a comb through her wet hair.

"Hey, here, I got stuff." There was a soft knock at the half-open door. Kris poked her head in and proffered a pile of clothing folded into a perfect square. She set a teacup down on the counter. "I'll let you get dressed."

"Wait."

"Yeah?"

Violet looked at her, willing her to understand what she wanted to ask without having to do so. "Did—"

"Ben asked," Kris said. "I told him." She shrugged. "He's glad you're okay. You probably want to talk to him." Her jaw clenched. "It's none of my business."

"No, what?" Violet put the bundle of clothes down.

"I don't know," Kris said. "I *like* Ben. He's my boss, but he's also my friend. This whole thing makes me feel awkward."

Violet chuckled. "It makes *you* feel awkward?" She stopped. "Oh, wait, no, are *you*—"

"Oh, my God, a thousand times no." Kris laughed. "No, I, ah, no. I am of the ladies-who-like-ladies persuasion." She held up a hand. "And before you go *there*, you're awesome, but you're not my type, either."

"You wound me." Violet allowed herself a little smile. "Okay, now that we got all *that* out of the way." She picked up her dress. "I'll be up in a few. I'm feeling better, but it's a hard day."

"For everybody," Kris said. She left, and Violet finished dressing. She wound her wet hair into a messy braid before making her way upstairs.

Ben was on the sofa, paging through a book she recognized as one of the Roanoke volumes. Bodhi was curled up beside him. His ears pricked up when Violet entered.

She cleared her throat. Ben dropped his book as he leapt to his feet, shaken. "Sorry, sorry. I, ah…"

"Look, I know Kris told you. I'll explain it all."

"If you don't want to, we have time. It's fine, I can—"

"No," Violet said. She sat down on the cushion Ben vacated. Bodhi walked over into her lap and curled up. His body felt comforting and warm, and she scratched him behind the ears, eliciting a low, rumbling purr. Ben sat down beside her. "Let me get through it so I don't have to say it again." She detailed the events at the colony site, all except for where she'd buried Cob. She rushed through the story fast and told Ben to stay quiet every time he tried to ask a question.

"All right, that's all of it," she said. "Now, yes, ask anything else you want."

Ben shook his head. His eyes were shiny and turned down at the edges. "I'm so sorry you had to see that."

"I've lost people, you know. I lost my first partner on a stakeout gone wrong."

"I'm still sorry." Ben put his hand on hers. "He was heroic. I'm proud of him."

Proud of him? When all you did was argue with him?

Violet cleared her throat again and slid her hand out from under Ben's. "I think I'm gonna go lie down, if that's okay. Is that okay?" She nudged Bodhi off her lap. The cat protested with a short, quack-like meow.

"Of course. Upstairs." Ben waved a hand at the staircase. "The room at the top—"

"I'll find it." She suddenly didn't want to see his face right now, hear his voice, any of it.

He doesn't deserve my anger. He didn't do anything. I have to get out of here. I have to sleep.

At the top of the stairs, Violet turned the corner and nearly ran into Vere. "Oh, I do beg your pardon," he said.

"It's okay." Violet took a step to the side to let him pass, but Vere held up a hand.

"Just a moment." He fumbled inside his jacket and produced an envelope. "Don't read it now, dear, I'm sure you're exhausted." He averted his gaze. "It's been a trying day for everyone." He held out the envelope to her. "When you feel up to it, Mister Cob left this with me. He wanted you to have it."

"What is it?" Violet took the envelope. Her name was written on it in black ink, the letters shaky and cramped.

"I shouldn't know." Vere scooted out of Violet's way. "Do take care. We'll sort everything else out when you've rested."

Violet nodded and proceeded to the guest room. She flipped the envelope over and slid her thumb beneath the seal.

The handwriting in the letter grew frenetic and harder to read toward the end. She wondered if it was already his brain beginning to fail him, or if he'd been in a rush.

When somebody reaches this point, they start to sound really damn pretentious. Please remember me as I was, not as this sentimental idiot.

She smiled and read on.

I can't say I don't think Ben is kind of a twat. But he sells himself short. He did this amazing thing by throwing in with the doc and all his craziness. He wants to know things, and that's something you guys have in common. Something I can understand, too. The need, it's like a fire in my gut, and I know that's how it is for Ben, too. Maybe you can help him make that fire burn a little brighter, huh? Give the poor guy a shot. I think he digs you. You'd be good for him. Help him be brave—I'm not brave, Violet, I'm stupid. Show him the difference.

Cob's signature blurred on the paper as Violet's tears hit the ink.

~

As Ben talked, Kris drew and made notes on a whiteboard on her lap. "We could wipe his mind, more than just a post-trip wipe would do," he said, "but we'd have to do it when he's younger, before he can, you know, turn into what he becomes later."

Kris's marker squeaked against the board's surface. "If he just basically has amnesia then, what's to stop him from still growing up with the same influences and still doing all the crap he ends up doing?" she asked. The marker's ink grew streaky. "Hang on, this is running out." She deposited the board onto the coffee table and went to Ben's desk. "You still got that pack I left for you a few days ago?"

"Center drawer," he said. "So what if we took him *away* from any potential negative influences?" He picked up a book from the table beside his chair and flipped through it. "Raised by his mom, who moved him around the country due to her job. Hmm." He turned back a few pages. "Father unknown. Do you think if he knew his father things might have been better?"

Kris found a new marker and returned to the whiteboard. "What if this, what if that," she said. "Maybe being exposed to *any* family made him all batshit? What if they were all huge jerks? Or maybe his mom was *less* jerky? Or, hell, what if none of them were and he was rebelling against them?" She made a few more notes. "Look, it's not up to me, but if I were you I'd think about taking him so far away that…" An idea struck her, and she looked up at Ben. "Whoa, wait, what if you get him as a kid and then take him to be raised over *there* by the Dares?" She laughed. "Nah, that's nuts. That's dangerous, too."

Ben's mouth narrowed into a thin line. "Cob died to rescue those people," he said. "If anything would go wrong, if he'd turn out even worse, they're in danger. He can't…ah, I—" His voice broke.

"No, I know." Kris nodded. "You want it to mean something, what he did. He saved Violet's parents' lives. What I'm suggesting puts them in danger again. I get that."

"Besides, he was the only one who could get over there," Ben said.

"Right." Kris made more notes. "But, hmm. What if that thing, the gun Mister Wheaton brought back, what if that can be a kind of, I don't know. If things are, like, the same, don't they react with each other, no matter where they are? Like a quantum thingamabob?"

"I don't think it works like that," Ben said. "I mean, sure, we can ask Eddy what he thinks, but that's a big leap, Kris."

"Yeah, maybe." She shrugged. "What do I know? My best subjects were all artsy. If you want me to draw the guy's picture, that's what I'd be good for."

"Oh, hey, now," Ben said. "No, it's a good idea, using an object as a kind of key." He smiled. "I don't hire stupid people, you know."

Kris smiled back. "Thanks."

Ben stood and walked behind Kris. "Um, so, what is all this, then?" he asked, pointing at the whiteboard.

A horizontal line divided the board into two stacked rectangles. Dashes split the line into small segments, and smudgy writing rose from half a dozen of the line segments.

"It's Florence's lifetime," she replied. "See, this is now," she said, pointing to the farthest line segment to the right, "and here's his childhood all through here." She indicated the leftmost line segments. "And then each of his time travel trips are up here, down here, and they're all labeled. At least the ones we know about."

"So we find the best time to get to him?"

"Yup. When he's the least protected, but also not, like, you know, a baby. Because that's kind of creepy, mindwiping a baby."

Ben chuckled. "Not terribly efficient at achieving our goal, either."

"Yeah." Kris circled a segment halfway between Claudio's childhood and adulthood. "Now, here, he's a teenager. That could be something." She handed the board to Ben. "Think about something in there, look up where he was during all that. Based on just the little bit I know, I think there could be some potential there."

"See? Brilliant." Ben took the board. "I'm going to talk to Eddy about this. Do you mind checking on Violet again?"

"I'm okay."

Kris looked across the room. Violet stood in the archway between the foyer and the front parlor.

"You look better," Kris said. She rose. "Do you want some more tea? I was just going to make a sandwich for myself, actually. Could make you one, too."

Violet shook her head. "I'm not hungry."

"You should try to eat," Ben said.

"Yeah, come on," Kris said. She made a beckoning gesture. "Give me a hand, at least."

"I'll be back, ladies," Ben said. He disappeared down the stairs to the lab.

"What's he up to?" Violet followed Kris to the kitchen.

Kris outlined her ideas as she took sandwich-making supplies out of the refrigerator. At the mention of sending Claudio to the same place as her parents, Violet made a low humming sound, bordering on a growl. Kris turned from her food preparations and held up her hands.

"Hey, hey, just brainstorming," she said. "Look, if someone can use that weapon to get over there, it could mean there's easy transport back and forth. You could see your folks again, right?"

"He doesn't deserve to be raised by them." Violet rubbed her temples and shut her eyes. "My head hurts."

"Do you need some aspirin or—wait, is this a normal headache or—"

"I'm fine," Violet said, her voice stern. "Sorry. Sorry. I don't mean to take this out on you. It's an interesting idea, but I don't know how I feel about it." She opened her eyes and took a plate down from a cabinet for Kris.

"Well, we might not even be able to do it at all, if somebody can't figure out what Claudio knows," Kris said. "Ben'll probably have to call in the folks who tried to take care of Mister Wheaton in the first place, have them help."

"Sure." Violet slumped against the counter. "Maybe…you know, maybe it would be good for Ben if he kind of took point on that, finding Wheaton and interrogating him some more. I'll help him. Investigation is my thing. I would be good for that. But he could stand to actually get out and do this."

Kris spread peanut butter on a slice of bread. She looked over at Violet. "He's done a trip now. And the man gets out of the house. It's not like we're talking about an agoraphobe here."

"No, I know, I just think it should be strongly encouraged, that's all," Violet said.

"Hell, *I* haven't done a trip yet," Kris said. She spooned out a glob of jam on top of the peanut butter. "If we're measuring people's investigative capacity based on their time travel experience, I have zero."

And I might like to change that, someday when we're not chasing a serial killer.

"I'm sorry, did I say something that—" Violet stopped when Vere and Ben's voices wafted in from the front parlor. A moment later, they both entered the kitchen.

"Miss Lessep, there you are." Without a comment, Vere plucked the sandwich from its plate. "Would you like to join me on a visit to a friend of mine?" He took a bite of the sandwich.

"Hey, that was mine," Kris protested.

"You know better than to expect to eat your own food when he's in the building," Ben said. "Is this your first day?"

Kris swatted Ben on the arm, and both of them laughed. It felt good to have a brief moment of normalcy, even if normalcy meant Kris made another sandwich.

"I guess," Violet said. She glanced at Ben.

Kris turned back to her food preparation.

None of my business.

"I'll come," Ben said.

None. Of. My. Business.

"So who're you guys going to see?" Kris asked. "The cleaners?"

"Yes," Vere said. "Miss Lessep, you've now met D.B. Cooper, members of the lost colony of Roanoke, and you're being targeted by Jack the Ripper. How would you like to meet one of the Wright brothers?"

Violet blinked. "Um, yes, please."

Kris took out two new slices of bread. "Don't get too excited," she told Violet. "He's a giant nerd."

Ben and Vere both gaped at her.

"That's a bit rude," Vere said.

"You say 'nerd' like it's a bad thing," Ben said.

Kris shook her head. "I'm sorry," she said, "I forgot we have the president and vice president of the nerd brigade right here."

~

"I don't want to go." Alison crossed her arms. "I don't want you to go, either."

"Isn't it my job?"

Alison studied her husband. Slender but tall, he took up the entire doorframe between the kitchen and dining room. From the living room, she could hear Violet and Ben speaking in hushed tones. She pushed herself away from the counter she'd been leaning against.

"It's your job, my job, only because we can't do anything else," she said. "Look, I care about stopping all this, but what happens if they stick this psycho off in some other universe?"

Wilbur frowned. "Psycho?"

Alison sighed. "Crazy person. Insane person? Come on. There were creepy crazy people in the nineteen hundreds. This is not a new concept. Psychopath?"

A light seemed to go on behind his eyes, and he nodded.

"You've read books and been on the internet since you've been in this time," Alison went on. "I've seen you. Your lips don't even move when you read."

"I'm an engineer, not a psychiatrist," Wilbur said. He walked toward Alison and planted a soft kiss on the top of her head as he rubbed her back. "I've yet to memorize every bit of slang and turn of phrase to gain popularity in the past two centuries." He let out a low rumble of a laugh. "Reminds me of going to Europe for the first time. Everything seems in a different language now and again. I'll be going along quite contentedly, thinking I've finally got the hang of this time. Then from nowhere you say something that sets me all to sixes and sevens."

"Sixes and sevens?" Alison leaned in to hug Wilbur. "I think the language barrier works both ways, dear."

He returned the hug. "I have to help, though," he said. "Come along with us. Please."

"I'm surprised you want to," Alison said. "What happened to that man Wheaton was truly sad."

"Perhaps I can help make it right," Wilbur said. "Won't you come?"

"No. Doctor Vere might need me." Alison stood up on tiptoe and kissed Wilbur. "Make them keep you safe, and then we're both retired. How's that?"

"How will we live?" Wilbur asked.

"You can become a mechanic," Alison said. "And I'll finish the degree I started."

"That was thirty years ago," Wilbur said. "Won't they be suspicious at your college how you stayed so young?"

Alison shrugged. "I'll tell them I'm a vampire." She pointed toward the living room. "Those two can't wait forever. Go on."

She watched him join the others in the front room.

~

"I promise you, we took Wheaton home," Wilbur said. "It's shocking his rooms should be empty."

Ben pulled the door shut. "I have to get this back to the landlord," he said, pocketing the key.

"What kind of condition was he in?" Violet asked. "You said it wasn't good, Mister Wright."

"It wasn't," Wilbur agreed.

"Ben, you and Kris had pretty much found the perfect point in Claudio's time—"

A door opened down the hall, and Violet quieted as an elderly woman came into view. The woman carried a small dog under her arm and smiled at the group as she passed.

"Excuse me, ma'am," Wilbur said. "Do you know Mister Wheaton here?" He pointed at Brimley's empty apartment.

"Oh, yes, terrible business," the woman said. "He was drunk in the alley outside. A disgrace."

"When was this?" Violet asked.

"Are you friends of his?" The woman clutched her dog tighter. "I don't think I'd like to expose Bucky to that sort of fellow, if you're also…well, I don't want to be indelicate, but—"

"FBI," Violet said, pulling out a wallet badge from inside her jacket.

"Oh!"

"Mister Wheaton is part of an ongoing inquiry, and you would be greatly helping your country if you assisted us, ma'am."

Wilbur noticed Ben nod at Violet, clearly impressed. He covered his own smile with his hand.

"Missy, I was born in the RAA before you were even a gleam in your father's eye," the woman said. "Only moved to this side of the great divide because of my late husband, the lazy bum. If Bucky and I could afford it, I'd be back home in a heartbeat." She shook a finger at Violet. "That fellow in there was a shiftless drunk, and if he's left for good, it'll only brighten this sad old place that much with his absence."

"Ma'am, if—"

"Arrest me," the woman barked. Bucky added a short editorial bark of his own to his mistress's voice. "I don't care. He was wandering around outside and some skinny fellow was following him. That's all I saw." She squeezed Bucky. "Come on, let's get some fresh air." She harrumphed her way past Violet and down the stairs.

"Hoo-kay," Ben said, clasping his hands together. "So, Mister Wright, crazy apparently runs rampant in this building."

"This entire century, it seems," Wilbur said. He turned to Violet. "What were you about to advise when we were all so rudely interrupted?"

"Just that maybe we should find Claudio—*young* Claudio—and get him to our present. We can either still pursue the gun angle or not," Violet said, "but at least we'd have pulled him out of his own time before he started his political career." She pointed in the direction the woman exited. "I think the 'skinny fellow' she mentioned was probably Claudio from *this* time, and I'd bet money on something bad happening to Wheaton."

"So we should stop him before it does," Wilbur said. "Find him at an earlier stage of his life?"

"It'll have a huge ripple effect, even that," Ben said. He climbed down the stairs, and Violet and Wilbur followed. "For better or worse. We should still be cautious."

"I think perhaps too much caution got your friend Mister Cob in a dire spot," Wilbur said. "I don't often recommend such a thing, but sometimes a bit of recklessness is warranted." He thought of sailing across the skies, screaming at the top of his lungs.

Without recklessness, Orville and I would have been failures. With too much caution, I might not be with Alison.

"Yes," Wilbur continued, closing the door of the apartment building as the group convened on the sidewalk, "recklessness. Just a bit." He held out his hand to Ben. "What do you say, Mister Jonson?"

Ben glanced from Wilbur to Violet and back again. He took a deep breath before clasping Wilbur's hand and shaking it firmly.

"Just a bit," said Ben.

Wilbur laughed and released Ben's hand. "That's the spirit." He tried to ignore how clammy Ben's hand had been.

Nerves, that's all. Perfectly normal to be this nervous.

Perfectly normal.

~

"*All* of you want to go?" Vere took off his reading glasses and pinched the bridge of his nose. "Benoy, this seems excessive."

"This is our one shot," Ben said. "I don't want to keep time traveling until we know how it might affect more of us physically. And if Violet, Wilbur, and I *all* go, we have a better chance of making this attempt count."

"I'm hesitant to try even this time, given the fate of the only recently departed Mister Cob." Vere glanced at Violet, whose cheeks colored pink. She wandered away from the others, pretending to study a paperweight on Vere's desk. "We don't want another tragedy, do we?"

"That's what we're trying to avoid," Ben said. He, too, looked toward Violet.

Oh, son, don't put her through it again.

"And you?" Vere took a step toward Wilbur. "Why do you want to go? We can't afford to lose you as well."

"Something terrible happened to that fellow you sent me after," Wilbur said. "If it was because of this tyrant, I have to help."

Vere threw up his hands. "Fine."

"Hey, you fought them, back in the war, right?" Violet asked. "Ben told me. Before you went to college, you were in the war. You saw what his people are capable of. You were around for the splitting of the country."

Vere nodded.

"And Cob saw him murder people," Ben said. "Look, I know I wasn't on board with this before, but he has to be stopped, one way or another. You have to send us all back so we can take care of it once and for all."

"By bringing him back here." Vere set up his equipment, despite his misgivings. "I hate that part of the plan, you know."

"We just need time to figure out how to deal with him," Ben said.

"For the record, I hate that part, too," Violet said, "but it's a little better than endangering my folks any further."

"Do you remember this?" Vere asked Wilbur as he cranked a dial on his control panel. "This, right here?" He pointed to a particular button.

"Of course," Wilbur said, joining him at the panel. "For me, it's only been a few months."

"I can't adequately prepare you for yet another time, Wilbur." Vere finished his preparations. "Are you all right with the uncertainty?"

"My whole life has been based on it," Wilbur replied. "What's a bit more?"

Monday, January 20, 2053, Reynard College, St. Louis, Missouri, USA

"You look the youngest."

"I...oh, good grief." Violet rolled her eyes and grabbed the black gown hanging on the hook in the vestibule. "Man, I am *so* glad Empiricist colleges didn't make you wear these stupid things all the time." She pulled the satiny material over her head and down, covering her sweater. "This is going to be uncomfortable with a capital 'un.'"

"We'll have to pretend to be professors," Wilbur told Ben.

Ben's smile faltered, the edges of his mouth pinching. "Sure. Sure. Fine." He muttered something under his breath.

"Hmm?" Violet pulled her hair out from under the collar of the gown. "What was that?"

"Nothing," Ben said. He exhaled and smiled again, this time more genuinely. "You look very—"

"Student?" A young man wandered by, a stack of flyers in his hand. "Are you an incoming first-year?"

"Um, yeah," Violet said. She drew her ears back, tensing her forehead and willing any telltale early-thirties wrinkles to smooth themselves out. "Yeah, hi, I'm, uh, Veronica." She held out her right hand. "Veronica Dare."

The young man blinked. "Whoa, like...like that's..." He thrust a flyer into Violet's hand instead of shaking it. "Some coincidence, Miss Dare. Some coincidence indeed. You *have* to come tonight." He stepped closer and put a hand on her shoulder. For the first time Violet noticed the strange, feverish light behind the young man's eyes, the extreme shortness of his hair, and the ominous curl of the tattoo snaking out from beneath the collar of his student robe. "My name's Davis. We're hosting the first talk of a very important new club tonight. If you're anything like your name suggests, I think you'll find it very enlightening." He grinned and squeezed her shoulder. "Promise me you'll come."

Violet glanced at the flyer. "Reynard Purification Society," it read, followed by a time and location. Beneath that, the words "DARE TO BE DIFFERENT" in all-caps. "DARE TO RESIST."

She felt a sinking in the pit of her stomach.

Davis canted his head to one side and smiled. "Do you know where your family's from, Veronica?"

"I'm not—maybe New Ham—"

"*Europe*," Davis cut in. "Just like me." He swept his hand in the air, indicating the hallway. "And just like him, and her, and—" His eyes fell upon Ben. "Well, not *him*, of course, but they were colonized by us, eh?" He laughed.

Violet looked at Ben, her heart racing.

God, I'm so sorry, please know how sorry I am. You shouldn't have to hear that.

"I guess," Violet said. "This is pretty interesting. Who's running the meeting?"

"Not sure," Davis said. "There's a bunch of us. Some new guy wanted to speak. Didn't catch his name."

Claudio Florence. That name won't stay a secret for too much longer.

"I'll see you tonight," Violet said. She tried to shrug off Davis's hand without appearing rude. "I'm sorry, I have to go to class," she said, pointing up the hallway.

"Right. See ya, Miss Dare of the most-honored Dare family." Davis gave her a little salute and jogged down the opposite side of the hall, pressing more flyers into more hands.

Spread that hate, buddy. What happened to you, after all this? Did you die defending this madman's ideas?

Violet returned to Wilbur and Ben. "So I guess I'm going to a white supremacist meeting?" she whimpered. "Jesus, I'm sorry," she said to Ben.

Ben shook his head. "It's all right." He looked away. "I can't even remember the last time I was in an RAA state, even if it hasn't started yet. It's weird to hear that stuff, that's all."

She wanted to turn his face toward her, but she resisted. "We have a lot to do before we get there."

"Before *you* guys get there," Ben said. He gave a bitter chuckle. "I think I'd stand out a little, as your new friend made abundantly clear." He nodded to Wilbur. "You go. The both of you. God knows I'm no good in a fight anyway."

Help him be brave.

Violet pictured Cob's letter, pictured his poor ravaged body coughing up blood in a forest centuries long gone.

I'm not brave, Violet, I'm stupid.

Cob's hand slipping from hers, the skin soaked with sweat...

Show him the difference.

"Listen, Ben," Violet said, a hitch in her voice, "I didn't—"

I didn't bury Cob in a grave marked with mystery just so you could slink off with your tail between your legs, dammit.

She cleared her throat and tried again. "I didn't think you'd run when things got tough." She looked at him, narrowed her eyes and stared him down. "I *need* you, Ben. I need your knowledge, and Wilbur and I both need backup, okay? So you are *coming*. Forget being out of place. Forget whatever weird little cover story we've concocted for all of five minutes, and just *step the hell up*."

Ben's eyes widened, but he remained silent.

"This is not some covert undercover thing, not for long," Violet continued. "This is get in, get the package, and get out."

"The package?" Wilbur asked, holding up an index finger. "Is that—"

"Claudio," Ben said.

"Right." Wilbur lowered his finger. "Er, how does 'package' imply—"

"It's cop speak," Violet said. "Look, don't worry about it, is basically what I'm saying, right, guys? We're going in, we'll take him out of the room, and then we'll get Eddy to retrieve us. One, two, three, easy as that."

"Not so easy," Ben said. "Nothing's ever that easy. Cob learned that."

"We're not Cob," Violet said.

I'm not brave, I'm stupid.

"It's good we're not Cob." Violet looked at Ben. "It's *good*." She paused, eyes scanning his face with its lean cheeks and bushy eyebrows. "It's *good* that you're you, Ben. It is." She felt herself drifting, leaning, then pulling back. It wasn't the time or place, not now.

"Right, so that's in an hour," Wilbur said. "I'm a bit keen to look around and learn, if I may." He nodded to Ben. "You care to join me? Were you born yet? Might be interesting."

"Sure," Ben pulled his gaze from Violet. "Sure, but let's meet back here well in time for the meeting."

"I need some air," Violet said. She wandered outside.

Thursday, September 2, 2100, Avon, Vermont, NBE

Claudio pulled the cloak around his face. He paid the stamper driver and read the placard on the house—Jonson's Exotic Travel, right where Jonson and Vere's assistant led him. Claudio knew the weapon would be here. Wright got it from Wheaton, and Wright was working with Vere all along. All Claudio had to do was follow the girl back here.

The building was dark, but it wouldn't be completely unattended. Claudio had studied the place, both close and afar, and for housing a lot of secret technology, it was remarkable in its unremarkableness. Three stories, slatted wood painted a reddish shade, somewhere between salmon and puce. Gingerbread scrollwork hung down from the soffit above the front porch, and the sign designating it as a business instead of a private house was carved into a modest stone placard screwed into the front face between two downstairs windows, both of which were heavily curtained.

If Claudio strolled right up to the front door and turned the key in the bell, what would happen? Would he be shot on sight? He grinned at the prospect.

Let them try. Let them try to kill me. I've killed so many in such a short time.

A strange thought occurred to him. All his time travel, all his murders and no consequence. His conquering of half the continent with barely a scratch during the entirety of the bloodiest conflict in the continent's history.

Can I even die?

Claudio dared to turn his face to the sky, where dusk gathered and the moon rose high and silvery and full. The hood of his cloak slid away from his face, moonlight falling cold and casting an eerie glow on his sharp cheekbones and the bridge of his long nose.

Has something blessed me? Is this my job now, to scrub the earth of lesser creatures, all the while living on and on?

It struck him, then, why and what he must do. A holy man such as himself needed a holy weapon, one not forged on this side of the divide between worlds. It was his right, and he ought to take it.

But what if he tested this theory first? What if to prove himself worthy of this holy weapon, he performed the perfect task, the perfect act of revenge? To reach where he would need to go for that would require another trip, and Ambrose's tech wasn't nearby. Perhaps he would have to access Vere's lab after all.

He walked to the porch, squared his shoulders, and reached for the bell.

Monday, January 20, 2053, Reynard College, St. Louis, Missouri, USA

"You made it." Davis beamed at Violet and shook her hand. "The speaker's about to begin. Come on in."

The room was full of young men, all white, many blond. Violet scanned the room, feeling sick and uncomfortable. Her cheeks burned.

I don't want to be these people's poster girl.

She glanced behind her, where Wilbur lingered in the doorway. Occasionally students regarded him with suspicion, while others gave him congenial nods. Ben was nowhere to be seen. Violet tried to catch Wilbur's eye, willing him to look at her, to somehow answer her silent question.

Where's Ben?

As if finally hearing her, Wilbur looked back into the hallway, scanning it up and down, before turning back to Violet and giving her a shrug, his eyes sad. He shook his head.

Violet allowed herself to be led to a seat in the second row.

We'll never get him if we're not together, all of us.

She looked down to the end of the row and was relieved when Wilbur sat down.

They exchanged a look. Violet understood it was all up to them now. Whether Ben arrived or not, they would somehow maneuver Claudio out by themselves. This Claudio, this young man, wherever he was, didn't know them. He could be persuaded.

"Thank you, thank you."

Applause thundered throughout the room. Violet turned her attention to the stage, and there beneath a shaky spotlight stood a scrawny young man with an unmistakable figure and face. The white spot gleamed on the angular planes of his face, throwing the hollows of his cheeks into stark shadow.

He looks like Death.

And it was true, his white face above a suit of black clothes hanging loosely from his slender body, young Claudio Florence looked a skeleton, a Grim Reaper. All he needed was a scythe in one bony hand to complete the image.

Wednesday, September 2, 2043, Rivierdorpe, Missouri, USA

This wasn't quite right.

Claudio thought he'd aimed for the old apartment, the strips of flypaper hanging in the windows, the sounds of unruly kids yelling at each other outside. But this was a shopping center, some parts enclosed mall-style and some parts storefronts open to a pothole-pitted parking lot. Half-lit signs buzzed above glass double-doors with wheezing pneumatic hinges. Shoes, coffee, electronic cigarettes, payday loans and check cashing. Torn red, white, and blue bunting from the vacated headquarters of a failed mayoral candidate.

A dingy car rattled into the lot, the front passenger door robin's egg blue but the rest of the vehicle a sickly pea green. An actual gas-and-electric hybrid that rumbled along the ground, even, not a hovercar or a stamper.

I know that car.

Claudio ducked behind a post in front of a five- and ten-dollar store and watched as a scrawny woman, barely out of her teens, dragged a child from the back seat.

"Charlie, come on."

An indistinct whine.

"Fine, stay there." The mother slammed the door and stalked up toward the front of the payday lender. Claudio kept his back to the post and slid around, staying out of sight but keeping a view of her.

Flickers of memories. Claudio stifled each one and instead stared at the mother as she tugged at the shop door. She cursed at finding it locked and pulled a short pipe from her jeans pocket.

"That shit'll kill ya." The man seemed to come from nowhere. His skin was pale, paler even than Claudio's own, and his head was shaved so close the skin almost glowed. A tattoo of a copperhead snake wound from one ear to the other.

The mother stepped back. "Stay away from me. I have a restraining order."

"I got parental rights."

"You do *not!*" She tucked the pipe between the index and middle fingers of her right hand and jabbed at the air between them. "You are a fucking *psycho* and a *rapist*, and you—"

The man interrupted her with a string of curses so vile even Claudio found himself shocked. He'd said—he'd thought—similar things about this woman, about *all* women, really, but to hear someone else scream them at her still surprised him.

I came here to kill her. Get out of my fucking way, snake-man.

Even then, Claudio knew. This wasn't some ex-boyfriend of hers, wasn't a fling gone wrong or even just someone stalking her.

This was Claudio Florence's father.

He could do it right now, could kill not just his good-for-nothing mother, while his still-small self fussed not twenty feet away. But he could also kill *him*, who'd apparently…what, exactly?

"It *was* rape, you cocksucker!" Claudio's mother screamed. "You see this?" Suddenly she tugged at something on her face, which she then held out to the man. "*This* is what you did. This and that psycho fucking kid of yours. He sets fires to the carpet. He *scares me*." She was still holding the thing out, and Claudio couldn't quite see it, but the man recoiled.

"What the hell?" The fight was all out of the snake-man. He cringed and backed up.

Claudio's mother closed her fist around the object. Her whole body shook. "You left me with a cracked cheekbone, a broken eye socket, and everything under there was all bleeding and meat and liquid."

Claudio clamped his hand over his mouth.

"This one ain't real no more." She shoved her hand against her face again. "You just took and took and took from me."

Kill them both.

Claudio looked across the lot at the car. He could almost make out a tiny dark head, likely bowed over a coloring book. He looked back to his parents, but now his mother was stalking off into the alley between two storefronts.

The man watched her go, hairy-knuckled fists balled tight at his sides.

Give me a reason, old man. Just one reason. I don't need you alive to become what I am now, this god, this indestructible force of change. I am perfection, and it's my job to destroy the imperfect in this world.

The man strode off to a waiting hovercar. Its sides were painted with flames and a tiny bumper sticker reading "YOU'RE ALWAYS FREE IN YOUR OWN DAMN MIND."

Claudio stared at the words as the car ascended and flew off. A dim memory told him the kid in the road car was staring at the bumper sticker, too.

He rapped on the window, and the child rolled it down.

"She isn't going to come back," Claudio told himself. "Not until she's slept off a bender and you've been two weeks in foster care with a woman who'll stick pins in you. Call the police, otherwise you'll get far too warm in here. Might as well wait as little time as possible."

"Who're you?" Charlie asked.

Claudio shrugged. "A self-made man, I suppose." He stared off into the direction his father took off. "Runs in the family."

He readied his knife before pressing the spot on his palm that returned him to the Jonson basement laboratory. Vere was tied to the chair as Claudio had left him.

"Maybe I'm not brave enough to kill some people," Claudio snarled, his head pounding, "but others leave me no trouble at all."

Vere squared his shoulders. "I am a soldier, Mister Florence, and I demand that you let me die on my feet."

Claudio canted his head from side to side. "Mm, that's a very brave request, Doctor," he said. He turned and slashed across Vere's throat. "But I'm going to have to say no."

Monday, January 20, 2053, Reynard College, St. Louis, Missouri, USA

Davis leaned over to Violet. "I heard really amazing things about this kid, after I left you earlier," he said. "He's gonna be big."

"He's gonna be something all right." Violet glanced at Wilbur. He was the only person in the row not applauding.

Gradually, others stopped applauding, too, gasps sprang up in different corners of the room. Violet turned to the center aisle, along which someone walked, loudly, in decisive, measured steps.

Ben stopped when he reached the front row. He alone applauded, but in exaggerated, slow claps.

"Brav-*o*!" he called up to Claudio.

Claudio put his hand along his brow line to shield his eyes from the spotlight. "Can I help you?" he asked. He nodded up to a spot above the lighting rig. "Hey, Jer, can you—" Claudio slid his hand along his throat, and the spotlight turned off. "Thanks." He hopped off the stage. "Usually I don't get a 'bravo' until I've actually said my piece." He looked up and down at Ben and laughed. "But, uh, something tells me you're not going to like what I have to say."

A smattering of nervous laughter from the audience.

"You know, whenever someone not of the *pure race* comes to hear me speak, to heckle me, they're committing the political sin of forgetting," Claudio said.

Ben blinked at him. "Excuse me? Forgetting? Have *you* forgotten the Holocaust? Slavery? Genocide in almost every nation in the world?"

"Slavery, see, that's a good example," Claudio said. "The Civil War wasn't a single-issue conflict. The Confederacy was interested in more than just preserving their noble way of life. They were concerned with the implications of a federally controlled government."

"That's a subject for debate among historians and social scientists," Ben said. "Not this little Nazi propaganda rally you got going on here."

Violet tensed in her seat and balled her hands into fists. If things got ugly, she knew some moves that would at least temporarily incapacitate Claudio, though how the audience would react to that was another matter. Maybe instead it would be better to get Ben out of there and hope Wilbur could blend in and sneak off on his own.

She gauged the numbers. Twenty on one side of the room, perhaps another three dozen on the other. All young and fit. She did more scanning of the room and realized there were only two other women in attendance.

These aren't good odds.

"I thought I remembered this."

Another voice, eerily similar to that of the young man standing in front of Ben. Violet couldn't get a good view, so she rose and squinted down the center aisle.

The same face and body, only now decades older. From inside his jacket pocket, the Claudio Florence whom Violet recognized from the newsfeeds withdrew something smooth, something gun-like and yet not.

Oh, my God. That's the weapon.

Why hadn't she brought a gun? She owned one, a little snub-nosed Taser- and laser-job the bureau issued her. She thought of it, in her dresser drawer at home, useless. Hell, they were in the past, weren't they? The damn thing probably hadn't even been built yet. Maybe hadn't even been *invented* yet.

"Mister Jonson, I don't know that we've technically had the pleasure, not officially, at least." Claudio stepped forward, the weapon still trained on Ben. "Ben, I'd like you to meet me." He patted his chest before gesturing across the aisle. "And me."

"Um, what?" Younger Claudio peered at his future self. "Are you—you look like my—"

"I'm not your father," Claudio snapped.

Ben wore a smile tinged with madness. "Shouldn't you be erasing each other by now?" he asked. "This—I'm sorry, I know I should be scared here or something, but this is all very split-screen-in-an-old-movie kind of cool."

"Ben," Violet couldn't help herself. As soon as she'd blurted out his name, she clamped her hands over her mouth.

"Veronica?" Davis's face fell. "You *know* this Pak—"

Violet didn't let Davis utter the full word before slapping him across the face. "You shut your racist mouth, you piece of shit. You hear me?" She scanned the crowd. "All of you. I don't even care anymore. You found me out. Do whatever you want, but at least let me die saying this—you're all *evil*." She looked at young Claudio. "And you're the worst of them. Getting them stirred up like this, starting this whole crap."

"You mean I'm not the worst of them?" the elder Claudio asked. "I'm hurt, miss."

"That's Miss *Dare* to you." Violet felt her adrenaline pump as Claudio's brow furrowed. "That's right. I am *Virginia Dare*, and your own little lackey *rescued me* because of the fucked up way you were going to use me for this." She spread her arms wide, indicating the room. "I am *not* going to be the mascot of what you're building here, not now or *ever*."

Claudio raised the weapon higher, aiming it over Ben's head and toward Violet. "I'm sorry to hear that," he said. Violet could almost imagine a gleam of tears in his eyes.

Almost.

"I'm afraid," he went on, "that I'll have to erase you." His confused scowl melted into a grin. "Much the way I erased Doctor Vere to procure this device."

Ben flew at Claudio without hesitation, knocking the weapon away from aiming at Violet. She fell to the ground and covered her head, intent on crawling to the fight and knocking Claudio off-balance, but the sound of screams made her shudder and stop.

Students rushed to the back of the room in a stampede, nearly trampling Violet under sneakers and sandals. Davis was no longer beside her. She struggled to her feet, searching for Ben—*oh, thank God, there!*—and Wilbur. She heard a strange sound, not quite a gunshot, not quite an explosion. The smell of ozone filled the air.

Wilbur?

Where Wilbur Wright stood a second earlier was nothing but a scorch mark marring the plaster of the wall.

"*No.*"

Ben leaped; the gun fired again—this time into the ceiling—and then gunshots rattled off, their irregularity familiar to Violet from her academy training. *Someone who doesn't shoot very often, or at all.*

The younger Claudio stood with a tiny pistol in his hand, the barrel smoking. He looked startled and scared, and for the first time Violet could see that given another direction in life, a kinder direction, he might have been handsome in a fragile sort of way. His hair fell over his forehead, making him seem less a college student and more a lost little boy.

"I don't know what I..." The young man's voice trailed off, and Violet followed his gaze.

The older Claudio was on the floor, clutching his abdomen. Blood seeped from between his fingers. Ben stood nearby but made no move to help him.

"I'm not your father," the older man gasped. "And I'm not supposed to die. I *can't* die." He laughed, but the laughter became a cough. Blood spattered across the hardwood planks. "Wanna see how much I can't die?" He raised his own weapon and fired it at his younger self.

Both men vanished.

Friday, September 3, 2100, Avon, Vermont, USA

"I think he's coming to. Do check out that woman, though, would you, Kris?" There was a murmur and a pause. "Ben? You all right, lad?"

The face staring down at Ben as he opened his eyes was fuzzy and backlit. The voice was wrong, but still he murmured Vere's name.

"What's that, then?" The face leaned in closer to his own. Ben's eyes focused on the features, the long, almost bulbous nose, and the sandy hair streaked with a few lines of gray along the temples. The voice was heavily accented but not with Vere's Mid-Atlantic rounded consonants and long vowels. Instead it was mushy and fast, a thick Cockney.

"Am...brose?"

Ambrose nodded. "You're all right, boy-o, ain't ya?"

No. Not even a little bit, not if what Claudio said was true.

"He killed Eddy, didn't he? Claudio, I mean." Ben tried to sit up, but his head pounded.

"Oof, watch it, there. Haven't given you the antidote yet."

Before Ben could protest or question, Ambrose stuck a long needle into Ben's arm and pushed down on the plunger. Whatever the syringe was filled with was thick and sent fire racing through Ben's veins. He shouted and squeezed his eyes shut.

"What the hell is that?"

"The antidote, you dolt," Ambrose said. He pulled the needle from Ben's arm and shoved a wad of cotton onto the injection site. "Blimey, did we not retrieve you fast enough this time? You've already forgotten? Prevents the clots, it does, so you don't risk a bloody aneurism every trip, right? Only been givin' you this shite for five years now, ever since we started the agency."

Ben's head cleared, and he finally struggled up to sitting. "Wait, wait, wait, *we* started the agency?"

"Course we did, lad. Us three." He canted his head to one side, where Kris stood holding a tray of instruments, both medical and electrical.

It was then Ben took the room in at last—*really* took it in—and saw that what Vere managed to rig up as a serviceable if Mary Shelley-esque cellar laboratory was transformed into something sleek and gleaming, an O.R. and a computing workroom combined. The walls were white, and flat-paneled screens decorated them every few feet. Some showed Ben's own vital signs, which he recognized due to their movements growing more fevered as he felt his heart speed up. Some showed a moving diagram of the time travel accelerator, and still others showed newscasters, muted, their words scrolling at the bottom of the screen in closed captioning.

It was the newscasters who then drew Ben's attention. One network showed a man and a woman, both of different ethnic groups, while a graphic in the top right of the screen indicated the feed originated in Missouri.

"Is that right?" Ben gaped at the screen, unable to pull his eyes away. The woman was Asian, perhaps in her early fifties, and the man, despite being white, spoke with her with what seemed congeniality and respect. "How are they allowed on the same show together if it's coming out of the RAA?"

"The what what what?" Kris asked. She looked at the screen. "Hey, Aunt Sybil's on. That's awesome. I only ever get to see her on TV, living this far away." She put the tray of instruments down. "There's always holidays, but still, that's only a few times a year."

"You travel between here and there a few times a *year*?" Ben asked. "*You*? They let you?"

"Um, if you mean you and Ambrose, being my bosses and letting me have time off, yeah, *they* do." Kris stared at Ben. "You're acting super weird, man. Oh, hey, I think this lady you brought back is waking up." She scurried off to another table.

Ben hopped off his own and followed Kris. "The lady?" There Violet was, just now coming around, too. Kris gave her an injection while she was still drowsy. "Violet, you mean?"

"Is that her name?" Kris asked.

A tall man rounded a corner.

"You brought somebody back?" he asked.

"Pop?" Violet was now awake and looked up at Michael. "What're you doing here?"

Michael laughed. "Pop? Hoo, that'd be funny, wouldn't it, babe?"

Ambrose came over and threaded his arm through Michael's. "The only kids we got walk on four legs."

"Hey, but maybe we should talk about that," Michael said. "Lotsa kids need good homes."

"You think ours is a good home?"

"What the hell?" Violet got down from her table. "Ben, what's going on?"

We did it. We stopped Claudio, or rather Claudio stopped himself.

He had to be sure, though. Vere would prove it. If Claudio killed him to get the weapon in the original timeline, then his demise undid Vere's murder.

"Guys, I'm sorry we're acting so strange. This is…" He turned to Violet, suddenly unsure of what all this meant for her identity. Was she Violet Lessep, adopted daughter of Michael, plucky FBI agent and time traveler? Or was she Virginia Dare, the first child of English parents born on NBE soil?

No. Not NBE. This was probably still America. Probably.

"Violet," she said, holding out her hand to the man who raised her but now didn't seem to know her. "Violet Dare."

"Pleased to meet you," Michael said, taking it in his own. Instead of shaking it, though, he turned it palm down, bent low, and planted a light kiss on her knuckles.

"Must you be so dramatic?" Ambrose asked.

"I must."

"Guys, where is Eddy? I want to ask him if we were successful."

"You said that name before," Kris said. She muted the TV. "Who are you talking about?"

Who am I talking about? If we changed things, who would Eddy be in this new reality?

"Our, ah, other partner. Doctor Edward Vere." Ben turned to Violet. "You remember Eddy, don't you?"

"Of course," she replied. She glanced at Michael. "I remember everybody."

It wasn't just Vere who was missing, of course. They should've been coming back a trio. Ben wondered what to tell Alison.

"Violet, would you like some tea?" Ben asked. He turned to Ambrose and Michael. "I need to debrief her on—"

"I bet you—"

"This *decade*," Ben said, cutting Kris off. She rolled her eyes.

"You are such a prude," she said.

He rushed at her and enveloped her small body into a bear hug. "I'm so glad some things never change."

"Ugh, get off me, weirdo," Kris grumped. She wriggled out of Ben's embrace. "Whatever. Go drink your stinky tea or something. Jesus."

Violet followed Ben upstairs. The first floor of the building was largely unchanged, but one row of bookcases was replaced by a computer system so advanced Ben doubted he'd even be able to find the on switch. As he passed it, its screen sprang to life. "Good evening, Mister Jonson," a crisp voice said. "How may I be of service?"

Violet drew back a step. "Whoa, what the hell is that?"

"I am the SmartWare sixty-five hundred," the voice replied. "Are you a guest user? Please state your name. If Mister Jonson provides me with permission, I will set up an internet account for you."

"Uh, Violet Dare."

"Very good, Violet Dare," the voice said. "Mister Jonson, may I set up an account for Ms. Dare?"

"Um, sure."

"Very good, sir. Ms. Dare, what would you like to research this evening?"

Violet looked at Ben. "Wilbur Wright," she said, her eyes never leaving his.

"Wilbur Wright, born Millville, Indiana, 1867, died Dayton, Ohio, 1912. Best known for his work with brother Orville Wright to invent practical air travel. Grew up in—"

"Thank you," Ben said. "That's enough."

"Died 1912, Ben," Violet said. "Did he die the same way he did originally? Or is that just what the official record says now?"

"I have a research question," Ben said.

"Yes, sir?"

"The Second Civil War of the United States. Started in the 2050s."

The computer was silent for a long moment. "I have no record of that," it finally said. "Would you like me to check my archive of fiction of the twenty-first century?"

Ben grinned. "We did it."

Violet didn't smile along with Ben. "*I* have a research question," she said.

"Yes, ma'am?"

"Edward Vere, Ph.D."

Another long pause.

Ben felt panic rise in him. Why would their work undo Vere? Vere was a scientist, Vere worked in a secret lab, Vere wasn't a target, Vere's death was only due to Claudio, and now Claudio didn't exist.

"I have no record of Edward Vere, Ph.D.," the computer said.

Maybe he didn't go to grad school in this timeline, for some reason. Maybe he got the science bug in the war—

The war that never happened. The war Vere survived.

"Edward Oxford Vere, born 2040 in New Hampshire," Ben said.

Another pause. "Edward Oxford Vere, born 2040 in Concord, New Hampshire. Died July 4, 2059 in Chicago, Illinois."

2059? 2059 meant Vere was just a teenager, before he finished college, before he and Wilbur invented time travel together, before *anything*.

But it would have been during the war. He wouldn't have been in Chicago, not if he'd been in the war, been a soldier, been elsewhere other than whatever happened in Chicago. But it couldn't be.

"No, I think that's the wrong one," Ben said. His voice quavered, and he sank against the back of the sofa.

This isn't the right sofa. This one's the one that was in here before Eddy bought the other one at a flea market, the nicer one. The one with the Victorian scrollwork on the arms. And where is Bodhi? Why isn't he curled up by the fireplace like he always is?

"That's the wrong one," Ben repeated. "Do you have another Edward Vere?"

"Edward de Vere, seventeenth Earl of Oxford, born 1550 in Essex, died 1604. Often speculated to have been the true author of the works attributed to William Shakespeare, though scholars—"

"*No.*"

The computer's voice ceased. Ben slid to the floor, burying his face in his hands. Violet touched his arm, but he didn't move.

And Eddy's the one who told me there was a cat sleeping under the bush in the backyard. Eddy told me about Bodhi, and I took him in.

"My cat's gone, too," Ben muttered. He tried to explain, but his throat felt tight.

Violet looked pained. "I have a research question," she said.

"Yes, Ms. Dare."

"Edward Vere, the one from New Hampshire. How did he die?"

"Hovercar accident. No fault cited. I have no other information, ma'am. It's a local police report without charges. Would you like me to read his obituary? It appears in the following Sunday's *Lake County News Sun*, page seventeen, column six."

"No, thank you."

Tears coursed down Ben's face.

"That's not okay," he said. He exhaled and pressed his thumbs against his eyelids, swiping away the moisture. "That's *so* not okay. The fucking war. The war we stopped? The war actually *saved* Eddy from dying in such a stupid way? That's, no. No." He looked up.

Violet pulled him close to her, resting his head on her shoulder. "No, it's not okay," she agreed.

"Your dad doesn't know you."

"That's not okay, too, but he's still here," she said. "I still have him, he just… it's different now. He's happy, though, right? He gets to be with someone who wasn't brave enough to be with him before." She drew back, moving so that her eyes were level with his. "But you, oh, my God, talk about *brave*."

"I couldn't let him do it anymore," Ben said. "He took so much from people. He was going to make it so I couldn't walk in a goddamned building just because I'm not white? No."

"You did it, you know," Violet said. "You. Not your research, not your books, not your worries, and not somebody looking for adventure."

No, not me. It's never me. I'm not that guy.

"You did it," Violet went on, "because it was enough. His crazy was enough. Who knows how many people you saved by just standing up to him?"

Out of the corner of his eye, Ben noticed a book on the coffee table. He picked it up. *A Short History of American Aeronautics.* Brown cover with a sepia-toned photograph. Two tall, lanky men in tweed strode along a sidewalk together, both of them in dark bowlers, one of them with a moustache.

The clean-shaven one in front was the only one of the two looking at the camera, a fringe of blond hair visible beneath the brim of his hat. Ben opened up the front cover and found an epigraph there.

"I wish to avail myself of all that is already known and then, if possible, add my mite to help on the future worker who will attain final success," it read. The attribution revealed it as a quote from Wilbur.

Eddy always said you were a show-off.

"This is a new world," Ben murmured, "but we can't ever forget."

Violet's grip tightened on his shoulder. "We won't. Everybody else may have, but we won't forget. We're in this together."

Epilogue:
The Dismantled Fortress

"...for hope is always born at the same time as love..." – Miguel de Cervantes Saavedra

Friday, May 13, 2101, Avon, Vermont, USA

Ben closed his grade book and tossed it across the room. It landed with a soft thud on the corner of Kris's desk. "I declare this term *done*."

"Hey," Kris protested.

"Send that to the records department to get final grades entered for me."

"I don't do clerical anymore," Kris said. "Remember?" She plucked the lab coat off the back of her chair. "Technician. *You* promoted me."

"I did?"

"You did."

"It's the brain fog, you know, from changing things." Ben stood and pushed his shoulders backward until he felt a satisfying crackle in the middle of his spine. "God, I hate sitting for that long."

"You used to love sitting."

"I used to love a lot of things."

Kris grinned. "I know what you love *no-ow*," she said, the last word coming out as taunting musical notes. "You love a certain blond woman who likes to dress like it's 1850, don'tcha?"

"Hey, in the original timeline, her fashion sense was what everybody was wearing," Ben protested. He looked down at his frayed jeans and bleached T-shirt. "I used to dress a lot better, too."

"Like how, velvet smoking jackets?" Kris giggled. "That's what you had on when you got back last time."

"That jacket was awesome," Ben muttered. "Jesus, you'd think the lack of a war would *improve* aesthetics, not cause them to devolve." A very small orange tabby kitten wandered up from the basement staircase. "There you are, Shanti." Ben rose and plucked the kitten from the floor. "Did you get lunch?"

The front door opened. "Hey, I brought coffee."

"Coffee? Seriously?" Ben crossed the room and greeted Violet with a quick peck on the cheek. "It used to be nothing but tea for you."

"Yes, well." Violet tapped the kitten on the nose. "There's a lot of stuff I'm getting used to. Trying to go with the flow and stuff." She handed Ben a cardboard holder with four paper coffee cups in it. "And that's not a real kiss, mister."

"Not now, there are children present," Ben said.

"I'm not a child, not a secretary, not a breeder, but I'm still leaving this den of iniquity," Kris announced. "You may grope freely, animals. Speaking of whom, let me get this baby her food." Kris took Shanti to the kitchen. The kitten squeaked and climbed up to perch on Kris's shoulder.

Violet giggled and pulled one of the coffees free of the holder. "You think Kris suspects what we're up to?" she asked once the other woman left the room.

"Nah. She thinks we're going on vacation now that my term is over."

"And now that I don't exist, have no job, and can just be a lazy layabout all the time?" Violet sipped her coffee. "That's part of this whole thing I thought I'd like, but the reality is a lot more dull."

"I know you hate not being an agent anymore." Ben took one of the coffees out and set the rest on Kris's desk. "But hey, when my government contract comes through, I can hire you to be part of the official historical investigation team. You'll have a paper trail, a Social Security card, the works."

"Sounds like nepotism," Violet said. "Won't they get suspicious when they find out we're a, you know."

"A thing? An item? A matched set of bookends? The only people on Earth who remember that this state used to belong to Great Britain not so very long ago?"

"Yes, yes, yes, and yes," Violet replied.

"Eh, screw 'em."

"Wow, the old you would probably not have said that."

"The old me would also not be going on a secret mission tonight."

"No, you'd just have sent a client and then demanded she tell you all about it, right?"

"That used to be all you were good for," Ben said. He walked to his own desk and pulled open a drawer. "I had this made for you, by the way. Figured you might want something a little more powerful than just your fists of fury, if we were going to do some kidnapping."

"I don't like calling it kidnapping," Violet said, "but I do like presents."

"Ta da." Ben set a small black cylinder into her hand.

"My Taser laser." Violet beamed. "It doesn't quite, well, it's not..." Her voice trailed off, and she laughed. "I can't expect it to be exact, can I?"

"Ambrose made it. I told him it was part of the grant, projecting future technology and then confirming it through travel into the future."

"You're the best." Violet leaned in and kissed Ben.

"Shall we get on with the kidnapping?" he asked.

"Again, not crazy about calling it that." Violet followed Ben downstairs to the laboratory.

"What would you call it if we're going forty-two years in the past, tracking down a kid, and then, you know, napping him?"

"I'd call it looking up an old friend, is what I'd call it," Violet replied. "I'd call it saving the world."

They were downstairs now. The lab was dark, Ambrose and Michael having gone home hours earlier. Ben flipped the switch that set the room aglow. "The world seems pretty good lately," Ben said. "How exactly are we saving it?"

"I didn't say we were saving the whole thing," Violet said. She wound her arms around Ben's neck. "But this will definitely save our little corner of it."

"They're waiting, back there, in their pasts," Ben said. "Eddy, Wilbur…"

Violet nodded. "We'll get them back where they belong," she said. She gave him a long kiss, then pressed the retrieval device into his palm. "Ready?"

About the Author

K.W. Taylor is the author of the urban fantasy Sam Brody series, about a dragonslaying disc jockey (*The Red Eye* and *The House on Concordia Drive*, both 2014 from Alliteration Ink). She has an MFA from Seton Hill University. Taylor lives in a restored Victorian home in Ohio with her tech writer husband and—unlike every other novelist in the world—an insanely photogenic kitten. She teaches college English and Women's Studies and blogs at kwtaylorwriter.com. *The Curiosity Killers* is her first science fiction novel.

CPSIA information can be obtained at www.ICGtesting.com
Printed in the USA
BVOW08s0931310516

450129BV00001B/4/P